D0437458

THE
ISLAND

ALSO BY BEN COES

THE DEWEY ANDREAS NOVELS
Power Down
Coup d'Etat
The Last Refuge
Eye for an Eye
Independence Day
First Strike
Trap the Devil
Bloody Sunday

THE ROB TACOMA NOVELS
The Russian

THE ISLAND

BEN COES

ST. MARTIN'S PRESS
NEW YORK

THE ISLAND. Copyright © 2021 by Ben Coes. All rights reserved. Printed in the United States of America. For information, address St. Martin's Publishing Group, 120 Broadway, New York, NY 10271.

www.stmartins.com

Library of Congress Cataloging-in-Publication Data

Names: Coes, Ben, author.
Title: The island / Ben Coes.
Description: First edition. | New York : St. Martin's Press, 2021.
Identifiers: LCCN 2021016161 | ISBN 9781250140821 (hardcover) |
    ISBN 9781250140845 (ebook)
Subjects: GSAFD: Adventure fiction. | Suspense fiction.
Classification: LCC PS3603.O2996 I85 2021 | DDC 813/.6—dc23
LC record available at https://lccn.loc.gov/2021016161

Our books may be purchased in bulk for promotional, educational, or business use. Please contact your local bookseller or the Macmillan Corporate and Premium Sales Department at 1-800-221-7945, extension 5442, or by email at MacmillanSpecialMarkets@macmillan.com.

First Edition: 2021

10 9 8 7 6 5 4 3 2 1

To Mabel

A soldier surrounded by enemies, if he is to cut his way out, needs to combine a strong desire for living with a strange carelessness about dying. He must not merely cling to life, for then he will be a coward, and will not escape. He must not merely wait for death, for then he will be a suicide, and will not escape. He must seek his life in a spirit of furious indifference to it; he must desire life like water and yet drink death like wine.

—G. K. Chesterton, *Orthodoxy*

THE
ISLAND

I

It was seven o'clock in the evening in Iran. The sky was a smoky gray as sunset approached. Yet inside the office of Major General Muhammed Shakib, Iran's top military, national security, and intelligence officer, whether it was day or night was irrelevant.

On this day, this was especially true. For on this day, Shakib would make a decision that had the potential to turn all Iranian days into darkness—or perhaps strike so deeply into the Republic's greatest enemy so as to ensure daylight for centuries.

Today was what Shakib had been born, raised, trained, and groomed for. A simple "yes" or "no" was all that was required. One small word, yes or no. He chuckled grimly as he contemplated the fact that one word could change the future in such a dramatic and permanent way.

Attack America? Yes or no, Muhammed?

It was what he alone was chosen to decide, and yet he had grave misgivings. The proposed attack was audacious, and had the potential to bring the United States of America to its knees. *But what if it failed?* he kept asking himself. *If we fail, the United States will turn*

Iran into a glass parking lot. Even if Mansour and his Hezbollah army succeed, in all likelihood they would still turn Iran into a radioactive crater.

So why do it?

But then he remembered his calling—and his fealty.

Shakib's office was vast. It occupied the Tehran-facing corner of the top floor of the headquarters of QUDS Force, in the beautiful southern-Iran city of Ahvaz. The office had fourteen-foot ceilings decorated in ornate woodwork and windows that looked out upon the base.

Shakib had responsibility for two other Iranian entities in addition to QUDS. VEVAK, the Republic of Iran's secretive international clandestine agency, and Hezbollah, the foremost terror entity in the world. While Al Qaeda and ISIS often garnered greater attention, it was Hezbollah that, in the background, undergirded almost all lethal, illegal actions against the West. Hezbollah was where Shakib put his best men from both QUDS and VEVAK. Hezbollah was Iran's bomb builder, assassination factory, and terror machine, the front edge of a war Iran believed it was in.

Yes or no . . . that was the question before Shakib. His mind replayed the operating briefing.

Shakib had barely slept—and on the black leather sofa in his office at that. What the Supreme Leader wanted was what should happen, and Suleiman wanted the attack, whatever the consequences. Shakib realized that Suleiman was senile, and before that insane, and yet to say or do anything to oppose him would be suicide. Even voicing his misgivings might result in Shakib being relieved of his duties . . . or imprisoned . . . or hauled in front of a firing squad and shot. Of course he would approve Mansour's design—but something bothered him on a level that was beyond official duty. Shakib was angry, for Mansour had lied to him and only him, and now Shakib was cornered.

Mansour's lie had occurred that afternoon. Following prayers, General Shakib, along with Iran's top military, intelligence, security, and religious leadership, had met inside the office of Iran's Supreme Leader, Ali Suleiman.

The briefing had lasted less than thirty minutes. It was about a proposed Hezbollah action against the United States of America, on American soil.

The briefing had been led by Zakaria Mansour, the commander general of Hezbollah. Mansour had been handpicked by Shakib himself after time in QUDS and VEVAK.

Mansour had designed the entire operation. He chose an Arabic word. He called it Aljazira.

The Island.

Aljazira was about turning Manhattan into an island, literally.

Mansour was tall and thin. He was muscular, but there was something else about him that made him more powerful than men much bigger and stronger. He had a dashing look and way about him, his black hair parted in the middle and long, feathered back. His face was chiseled and handsome; sharp features, aquiline nose—and yet an overall sense of the potential for violence, a scar beneath his right eye clearly visible—and eyes that had a savage, calculating quality. He wore a blue button-down beneath a smart-looking Canali suit. He was the only one standing, amid large, long leather sofas, beneath twenty-foot ceilings and the ornate woodwork of the Supreme Leader's office.

A large screen displayed Mansour's presentation for all to see. Mansour began by nodding respectfully to Suleiman and saluting Shakib. He held a small black remote.

The first slide showed all New York City from above. A crystal-clear photo taken by drone over the city and its five boroughs. Suddenly, a red digital line illuminated the border of the island of Manhattan.

"Your Excellency, what I present today is an operation designed to inflict great damage on the Great Satan," said Mansour.

"I look forward to hearing about it, Zakaria," said Suleiman.

"The pieces are all in place, Imam," said Mansour thoughtfully. He counted out with his fingers. "Manpower, weapons, and most important, opportunity."

"Will you be there?" said Suleiman.

"Yes," said Mansour. "I leave tomorrow."

Several heads turned, and glances were exchanged.

"I'm glad to hear that," said Suleiman. "Please, go on," he said, waving his long, spindly fingers through the air.

"Time requires, if it is all right, I summarize," said Mansour.

He held a remote with a red laser pointer, pointed it at Manhattan, and detailed his plan.

It took Mansour less than five minutes to outline the operation. A low chorus of mumbling and exchanged glances—most indicating disbelief—cut through the room, but Mansour continued. His voice throughout remained calm, patient, and above all respectful.

After he was finished, there was a long hush. All eyes went to Suleiman, who stared at Mansour. Slowly, Suleiman's head began to move up and down, nodding his approval, nodding to Mansour to continue.

One of Shakib's deputies, his chief of staff, Brigadier General Ghaani, spoke up.

"Surely trying to kill the president, even just an attempt on his life, will provoke a response that could prove catastrophic?" said Ghaani.

"I disagree," said Mansour. "The Americans are weak. Their military is spread thin and has been devastated by decades of war. With Dellenbaugh dead, there will be pandemonium. A power vacuum. They don't have a vice president. Under their constitution, the Speaker of the House will become president. This man, Congressman Healey, is a pacifist and can be bought off. Besides, killing Dellenbaugh is just one part of the plan. A distraction. While they focus all their efforts on stopping us, we will execute the second half of the operation, which will devastate the entire country. They will be so ruined that they will be unable to respond."

For his part, Mansour had kept his boss, Shakib, apprised of his work over the four months it took to design and prepare the attack on the U.S. president. Shakib knew the details, yet now, hearing it out loud before the uninitiated at the highest levels of the Republic was astonishing. Everyone in Suleiman's office understood that, if executed properly, it would be the greatest terror attack ever, larger than 9/11 by a long shot—and would inflict unimaginable devastation on America.

"You have my blessing," said Suleiman. "Now, is there anything else?"

"Thank you, Imam, *Commander in Chief*," said Mansour, referring to the Supreme Leader's title in times of combat, a subtle but dramatic display of honor. Mansour glanced at Shakib as he spoke. "There is one other aspect to the operation I would like approval for," he continued.

He hit the remote and a photo appeared of a man. It was a grainy black-and-white image showing an American, rugged-looking and tough, with thick, dark hair cut short, and his face had a layer of stubble across it. Beneath the man's eyes were thick stripes of eye black. He had on a military uniform and clutched an M4, aimed up at the sky. The man had a faraway look, past the photographer, a cold look. In the original photo, he was one of six men. But the technologists had the face of this man isolated and blown up.

Suleiman visibly sat up, and his demeanor turned sharply, his nostrils flaring in barely concealed anger.

Every man in the room knew who he was. This was the number one enemy of the Republic.

An American soldier named Dewey Andreas.

They all knew who he was and what he'd done, entering Iran two years before and stealing the Republic's first nuclear device in an operation that was disavowed by the CIA. A year later, Andreas killed the chief of all Iranian intelligence and military activities, Abu Paria, Shakib's predecessor and mentor, a beast of a man who built QUDS Force from its very beginnings. Andreas had killed Paria—a 280-pound man of mostly muscle—in a brutal, bloody fistfight in the restroom of a Macau casino, stabbing a ballpoint pen into Paria's carotid artery then leaving Paria to bleed to death on a linoleum floor.

Andreas was a menace to Iran.

"And what is it you would like, Zakaria?" said Suleiman, his obvious admiration for Mansour visible to all in the room.

"An insurance policy," said Mansour. "I would like to eliminate Iran's top enemy, today, near his home."

"And if you don't succeed?" said the cleric.

"I would never bet against a great adversary," said Mansour, "and if we fail at killing Dewey Andreas, the operation will still succeed. Anarchy will reign. He will be irrelevant."

"Son, why not simply surprise the Americans?" said Suleiman, waving his fingers.

"It is just an instinct, Imam," said Mansour. "I am not scared, if that is what you are asking. He is a worthy adversary and thus I choose to kill him. That is not fear. That is strategy."

Suleiman cleared his throat. He looked at Mansour, then signaled for him to come and sit in an empty chair next to him. Suleiman placed his hand on Mansour's.

"Allah will be with you," whispered Suleiman, gripping Mansour's wrist and speaking quietly so that only the two of them could hear what was being said. "Take your vision to its future, my blessed one. I trust that you will spill only as much blood as necessary."

"So I have your blessing?" said Mansour.

"Yes," said Suleiman, nodding. "Kill them."

2

Dewey Andreas was a proficient swimmer. He grew up near the ocean and learned how to swim in the bitter-cold water of Penobscot Bay, off a small Maine town called Castine, where currents ripped across the headlands of the remote, pine-crossed peninsula with fury and might.

At ten years old, Dewey and his older brother, Hobey, were out sailing and got caught up in a sudden summer squall. It turned into a microburst, on what had seemed like a perfect, sunny July afternoon. Winds from a rapidly approaching steel-black sky cut overhead and moved in an attack pattern toward Castine, like a tornado. The 420 the Andreas brothers were sailing was like a leaf in a hurricane, thrown about as they attempted to tack back to shore. But the boat capsized and threw both boys into a bitter-cold, swirling, purple-blue, current-crossed, ferocious ocean. Hobey managed to hold on to a line attached to the sailboat but Dewey was thrown under the roiling sea. They were only a few hundred yards offshore, but the sudden winds, the overwhelming waves, the frigid temperatures, and the chaos of the swirling whitecaps soon had the ten-year-old struggling simply to get back to the surface each time a wave took him under.

All Dewey could remember was struggling to get enough air—to get kicked under and then swim back up to the surface for one more breath, thinking in those last moments only about his favorite horse, a black mare named April. Then he blacked out under the violent water.

Mr. Gilliam, a lobsterman from Stonington, had seen the Andreas boys get flipped into the water by the storm's first gale winds. Gilliam's lobster boat came out of nowhere alongside where he knew Hobey and Dewey had gone down. Gilliam's stepson, Matt, leaned down off the side of the boat with a long wooden pole usually used to retrieve lobster pots, and grabbed Dewey from the unforgiving waters with a hook at the end of the pole, catching Dewey's life preserver at the back of his neck as Dewey lay facedown in the crest of a deep wave, before rescuing Hobey, who was still clutching to the small sailboat.

Dewey was a competent swimmer, but ever since that July day he preferred to feel the ground beneath his feet.

After graduating from Boston College, Dewey joined the U.S. Army Rangers, despite the fact that a recruiter from the Navy SEALs tried to get him to head out to Coronado. The recruiter was an alumnus who'd watched Dewey run the football for BC for four years, during which time Dewey broke several BC rushing records including the most important one, most touchdowns during a single season. But as much as Dewey respected the Navy SEALs, and even longed to be one, he knew he would have a hard time with the water. At the very least, he knew it would bring back memories, memories of nearly drowning, and he didn't want to earn a living doing something he wouldn't enjoy. He had a deep-seated fear of the ocean that he couldn't shake, though he'd spent plenty of time on the water, near the water, in the water, and underwater.

So, he joined the U.S. Army Rangers. Dewey learned how to operate on land, to jump from airplanes and helicopters, to use all manner of weapons, to climb with rope and without, but mostly how to distance himself from all distractions and all competition in virtually every challenge placed in front of him and his fellow class of Rangers by the hard-driving trainers at Fort Benning.

Which was why it seemed unusual that, at this very moment, Dewey was in a building at the Washington Navy Yard in southeast Washington, in a windowless building that housed a large swimming pool. The pool was designed for training purposes only. It was twenty feet deep, and surrounded by equipment used to test and train individuals in various forms of water survival.

Dewey was here because Polk ordered it. Bill Polk, the head of the CIA's National Clandestine Service, which included Special Operations Group, believed Dewey needed to understand how to survive in water.

At this particular moment, Dewey wasn't showing a lot of progress. He was in the water, submerged deep. His hands were tied together—bound tight behind his back—and his ankles were bound as well. In addition, a blindfold was tied tight across his eyes. He appeared lost, halfway to the bottom of the pool, already having made a fatal mistake in the calibration between air inside the lungs, body weight, and gravity. The goal was to learn how—while shackled and blindfolded—to survive by bobbing to the surface for a breath of air then sinking so as to be able to kick the bottom and reach the surface for another breath of air. Dewey was trying to exhale so that he could sink all the way down and kick his feet against the concrete pool bottom in order to push himself back to the surface for a breath of air, but he was horizontal, several feet above the bottom of the pool, and had lost his equilibrium and therefore where he was in the pool, and he was out of air. He stopped struggling and drifted listlessly toward the bottom.

A tall man in a mid-thigh red-and-white tactical wet suit was watching from the side of the pool. Rob Tacoma's hair was wet. His only accouterment was a fixed-blade combat knife, sheathed to his outer thigh. Tacoma had had to jump into the water twice already in order to help get Dewey back to the surface.

Tacoma was an ex–Navy SEAL. He was also Dewey's closest friend. After Polk spoke to Dewey, Dewey asked Tacoma to help him learn how to survive in water. Tacoma could never teach Dewey even half of what he knew, but he'd been trying to teach him the basics. This exercise was about understanding the relationship between water and the human body, specifically about oxygen and its impact on body weight, as well as determining one's position in the water relative to the surface in simulated nighttime or hostile conditions. Another goal of the exercise had to do with managing emotion and controlling panic, which the blindfold only exacerbated. Ideally, Dewey should have by now fallen into a steady pattern of up and down, getting air from the surface then slowly exhaling, thus decreasing the amount of oxygen in the lungs and rendering his body less buoyant.

Of course, some believed there was an even deeper meaning to the exercise.

Dewey was nearly sideways near the bottom of the pool. His legs made one last attempt at a kick then went still. He was clearly struggling. Tacoma shook his head as he realized he would have to jump in again.

"Wow," Tacoma muttered aloud.

He dived into the pool, descending quickly. He grabbed Dewey's arm, shaking Dewey. Dewey's arms were like tree trunks, and Tacoma shook, then pinched Dewey near his elbow, trying to open up another level. When Dewey still didn't respond, Tacoma went to remove the blindfold. But as he did, he saw Dewey's hands lurch to his thigh and grab the blade. Before Tacoma could react, Dewey had the knife out of the sheath. He slashed the blade to his feet, cutting the thin rope around his ankles, then twisted his hands and severed the ties around his wrists. Before Tacoma knew what was happening, Dewey had his arm around Tacoma's neck, where he shoved the blade, locking Tacoma down.

Tacoma didn't bother fighting back. He showed a two-fingered peace sign, indicating that he'd given up. Dewey dropped the blade and kicked off the bottom of the pool, swimming back to the surface.

By the time Tacoma picked up his knife and swam back up, Dewey was already out of the pool, on all fours, coughing up water and trying to catch his breath.

Dewey looked at Tacoma as Tacoma climbed slowly and calmly out of the pool.

"*Fuckhead*," said Tacoma with a hint of anger in his voice. "That's not the point of the goddam exercise!"

"I thought you said it was about survival," coughed Dewey, still on all fours, struggling to get air.

"It is."

"Well, I survived. Theoretically, you didn't."

"You asked me to fucking train you, asshole!" yelled Tacoma, standing up. He resheathed the SEAL Pup.

Dewey sat down, looking up at Tacoma. He started to catch his breath, though he was still breathing heavily. He couldn't help looking up at Tacoma with a shit-eating grin.

"I guess that settles it," said Dewey, breathing heavily and grinning.

"Settles what?" said Tacoma.

"The age-old debate: who's tougher, Delta or SEALs."

"The only debate that settled is who's a bigger asshole," said Tacoma.

Dewey laughed. He put his hand out and Tacoma pulled him up.

"So, what's next?" said Dewey.

"What's next?" said Tacoma. "Glad you asked. I'm going to teach you about waterboarding."

Dewey and Tacoma lifted weights for an hour and showered in the locker rooms. Dewey got dressed before Tacoma and went out to the parking lot. He had on a pair of khaki shorts that had hems that were fraying. He wore worn-down L.L.Bean boots and a white short-sleeved button-down. He stood and waited next to a motorcycle—a black Suzuki Hayabusa. It was parked next to a bright red Ferrari 488 Pista with black racing stripes.

When Tacoma came out of the building, he looked stylish. He

had on light gray pants, a blue button-down, and a pair of white suede loafers. It was an outfit most human beings could not come close to pulling off, but Tacoma looked as if he was stepping off a Hollywood set. His hair was short, thick, and neat-looking. He was still buttoning his shirt as he approached Dewey.

Dewey squinted as Tacoma approached.

"What time is the croquet tournament?" said Dewey.

"I'm meeting someone," said Tacoma. "Someone female. I realize you don't know too many of them, but I do."

Dewey nodded, smiling, though it was obvious—at least to Tacoma—that he'd struck a nerve. He hadn't meant to.

"Cool. What's her name?" said Dewey.

"I didn't mean it that way."

Dewey looked at Tacoma.

"Don't worry about it," said Dewey.

"Yeah, well, I do worry about it. When was the last time you went on a date? It's been over a year. You're thirty-nine years old."

"Forty," said Dewey.

"Oh, Jesus," said Tacoma. "Really? I'm not even thirty yet."

Dewey laughed.

"So, what's her name?" said Dewey.

"Something. I can't remember. She's Canadian. I met her in Miami."

"Weight Watchers?" said Dewey, climbing onto the motorcycle.

"On the beach," said Tacoma, winking. "She needed help removing her bikini."

"What's the plan?" said Dewey.

"I'm flying up to New York," said Tacoma.

"Nice," said Dewey as he turned on the Hayabusa and revved the engine, then hit the kickstand as he pulled on a helmet.

"She probably has a friend," said Tacoma. "You can fly up with me. My place has like four or five bedrooms. Seriously, why don't you come up? Double date. I'm telling you, she's seriously smoking hot and I'll tell her to bring a friend just as hot. We'll go out dancing and then spend some time showing them Manhattan, in particular the bedrooms of my condo. It has an indoor pool."

Dewey smiled.

"Sounds fun," said Dewey, "but unfortunately I'm getting fitted for orthopedic shoes in the morning."

"Fine, be a lame ass," said Tacoma. "I'll be back in a few days and we'll continue our lessons. Next up is what to do when one of your floaties pops."

3

As Shakib thought about Mansour's briefing, he stared at the one-page graphic of Manhattan given out by Mansour. But his mind was elsewhere. Something gnawed at Shakib. A strange feeling. All along, Mansour—his handpicked leader of Hezbollah—had inserted an extracurricular action into the overall design without telling him.

By introducing it in front of the Supreme Leader, Mansour had received approval for a part of the overall attack on America that he'd never discussed with Shakib. It was not only in violation of the chain of command, it was treasonous.

Now, for the first time, Shakib studied the underlying extracurricular part of the operation. It was a targeted assassination on an American citizen, two hundred miles away. An irrelevancy, and yet Mansour hadn't told him of it.

His chosen lieutenant had betrayed him and left him no out.

If Shakib stepped in and attempted to call off the operation, he would incur the wrath of Suleiman. If he said yes, he would be handing over supremacy to Mansour—if he survived—because the most stunning aspect of all in the operation was Mansour's participation. He would be the one to lead the assault. He—or one of his gunmen—would be the one to kill J. P. Dellenbaugh—or die trying.

What he didn't understand was why part of the operation involved a mouse-chase beforehand, and why hide it? Shakib put his feelings about Mansour's treachery behind him. He realized that was less important than the overall advancement of Iran's objectives. Shakib studied the document as objectively as he could as a military commander.

Why now?

The larger situation was remarkably opportunistic. U.S. President J. P. Dellenbaugh would be at the United Nations.

But that was in Manhattan. Andreas was living a peaceful life in Washington, D.C., and though VEVAK had primary knowledge of where Andreas would be, why was this necessary?

He read through the proposed operation anyway. The concept was simple: eliminate Andreas. They had a pattern marked and would strike him near his home in Georgetown, at a restaurant he had made the mistake of frequenting.

It was an operation born of overthinking—and fear.

For the second time, Shakib read the file on Andreas.

ANDREAS, DEWEY [File #133-465]
USA
ENEMY OF THE REPUBLIC
RATING PER QIDT 9 JANE: #s
INTERPOL "Non-exigent"
KNOWN DATA—
CURRENT OCCUPATION:
TIER 1 LANGLEY NO/SEC
CIA OPERATIVE, "NON-OFFICIAL COVER"
Ex-DELTA Force—NARCO and Counter-intel

- Assassination of Rumallah Khomeini, brother of Ayatollah Khomeini: Bali
- Extraction/abduction of Russian intelligence chemist ?????
- All-American collegiate football player/elected to enter the military vs professional

U.S. Army Ranger: Rank #1 (of 188), Winter School
FIELD RATED 4.98
JSOC 4.99 PRD
DELTA FORCE—recruitment date unknown
Advanced Field Group, aka Vanguard
- One of six in his class, believed to be the only one alive

KEY OPERATING STATISTICS:
- China—assassination of MSS chief Fao Bhang, Beijing
- Russia—exfiltration of Vibohr
  - Vibohr later assassinated by Andreas in Montreal
- Iran—theft of Republic's first nuclear device
- Macau—murder of MG Abu Paria, head of all Republic intelligence, security, and military forces
- North Korea—sighting per ANSKAR of Andreas near Pyongyang day of Kim Jong-un "heart attack"

COMMENTARY:
Andreas is classified as a Tier 1 by his own government. He is one of only four individuals to achieve the rating since its inception in 1992.

Andreas has inflicted great damage on the Republic.

He has been sighted by a tertiary near his home in Georgetown, Washington, D.C., over the past several weeks.

An opportunity to remove an enemy of the Republic such as Andreas now exists. A pattern has been observed in terms of his behavior.

Andreas is armed at all times—and is ruthless. But his knowledge of cold arms and face-to-face combat is stronger. Detailed files of Andreas's background, discovered by MSS, reveal a brutal trail of broken necks, his signature.

Andreas trains during the morning and then goes back to his town house in Georgetown. Andreas then walks to a small neighborhood restaurant for lunch. There is remarkably little if any perimeter security.

It is my opinion, we should remove Andreas despite the

fact that he, at last report, will not be in New York City and far from the planned attack, the greater attack. Removing him is straightforward and thus why not do it?

OBSERVED STRENGTHS:

As much damage as he has done, Andreas is most of all elusive

There are no physical weaknesses

Andreas is comfortable with all manner of cold weapons and improvisation

Andreas is responsible for theft of the Republic's first nuclear device

Andreas killed General Abu Paria in Macau

Andreas should be considered extremely dangerous

If armed, proximity to Andreas should be considered an Active Kill Zone

Andreas has high-level backing and is known to be close to DCIA Calibrisi and POTUS Dellenbaugh

PSYCHOLOGICAL WEAKNESSES:

More than a decade ago, Andreas was disavowed by the U.S. government and falsely accused of murdering his wife. Though innocent, events surrounding his wife's death forced Andreas into exile. By this time, Andreas lived outside the U.S. for an extended period during which he was "inactive" and little is known about the time. He reemerged when the oil platform he was working on was targeted coincidentally by Alexander Fortuna. Andreas survived the attack and ultimately killed Fortuna, and, one year later, his father, Aswan.

Andreas was targeted for assassination by China MSS—during the operation, a Chinese sniper accidentally killed Andreas's fiancée, Jessica Tanzer, leading Andreas to seek revenge upon and ultimately kill Fao Bhang, head of MSS, who'd ordered Andreas's murder and was responsible for his fiancée's death.

Both incidents point to a possible weakness involving exploitation or use of people close to him or female who . . .

The door to Shakib's office opened and Mansour stepped into the room. After he closed the door behind him he walked toward Shakib's desk.

Mansour, twenty-eight, was six feet tall and wiry, even a little gaunt for a soldier. His face had a layer of stubble on it since the briefing. Mansour smiled as he approached Shakib's desk. He stopped and saluted, staring at Shakib.

"Good morning, General," said Mansour.

"Good morning, Zakaria," said Shakib.

"I'm leaving for New York," said Mansour. "You said you wanted to see me before I left?"

"You look a little tired. How did you sleep?"

"Actually, I didn't, sir. I've been cleaning up a few loose ends. I plan on sleeping on the flight over."

Mansour wore a tan-and-green sweatshirt, and jeans. Mansour was a soldier—a product, over a rugged nine-year period—of Imam Ali Officers University, Iranian Defense Forces, Revolutionary Guard, QUDS, VEVAK, and, ultimately, Hezbollah, where he now served as overall commander, the link between the Iranian government and the terrorist group widely considered to be the most ruthless, evil, and capable in the world.

He looked more like a graduate student than a soldier, but appearances could be deceiving and indeed, Mansour's smiling, intelligent, happy demeanor was unusually ironic when considering the damage he'd inflicted on various enemies of the Republic, both internal and external, over a violent career. Mansour ran all strategy and operations for Hezbollah, dictating moves through a tight-knit group of four deputies, who then managed the day-to-day tactics across a diaspora of lieutenants spread across the Middle East, Central and South America, and even the United States. Though in charge of a wide spectrum of activity, Mansour still insisted on leading all high-leverage scenarios from the ground, in theater. He knew men at each echelon of the structure and had carefully handpicked the men who would be there beneath his command for the assault on New York City.

In each step along Mansour's climb within the military and intelligence hierarchy, he had exhibited overwhelming skill, not simply as a killer of men—something he was without peer among Iranian agents—but as a leader of men.

It had been Mansour who saved Bashar al-Assad just minutes before assassination. Mansour had flown by night chopper into Damascus as the al-Assad government was falling. At the outskirts of the Presidential Palace atop Mount Mezzeh, Mansour was in a Mil Mi-24 chopper shot down thirty feet in the air by a surface-to-air missile, triggered by an Israeli commando from Sayeret Matkal. The chopper dropped from the sky like a rock. Mansour crash-landed with two other fighters, both of whom were killed on impact along with the pilots as they slammed into a courtyard in front of the palace, where al-Assad—a key Iranian ally and puppet—was locked down in an office suite on the fourth floor, minutes away from sure death at the hands of Israeli Special Forces. Mansour had emerged from the flaming chopper and—over the course of the next half hour—singlehandedly taken out four Israelis that night, protecting al-Assad until backup came in.

But Mansour didn't ever talk about Damascus because he didn't give a damn about Damascus or al-Assad or the past. The only thing Mansour cared about was the present.

Mansour looked at Shakib, then his eyes went to the desk. A photo of Andreas was visible to both men.

"I'm disappointed in you, Zakaria," said Shakib calmly.

"I know, General Shakib. I expected this."

"You could not have told me?" said Shakib.

"You would've said no," said Mansour.

"Andreas is not our concern, certainly not right now. You slipped in the authorization behind my back."

"I apologize, General," said Mansour. "I did what I thought was best for Iran."

"You went over my head," Shakib said sharply.

19

"I was asked to design the attack on the United States," said Mansour. "As the overall commander, I was willing to suffer the consequences of disobeying a direct order, sir. I did it because I believe it's prudent to remove Iran's greatest enemy."

"*You went around me!*" Shakib bellowed.

"I took a calculated risk," said Mansour, "because as irrational as it might seem, I actually care about avenging Abu Paria's death, just as I would yours, sir."

Shakib paused.

"I'm calling off not only the attack on Andreas, but also New York City," said Shakib.

Mansour nodded, looking into Shakib's eyes, but saying nothing.

"In addition, while you will not be court-martialed, Zakaria, I am demoting you. I want you back at QUDS. You'll be an instructor based in Kerman."

Kerman, to the south, was a backwater, away from borders with other countries, devoid of even the potential for the kind of conflict Mansour was used to. Both men understood the severity of the punishment—but also the fact that Shakib could've had Mansour shot for treason for what he'd done.

Mansour nodded calmly. "Yes, sir," he said. "I spent time there. It's nice country."

"I will review your status in a year," said Shakib. "You are an exemplary soldier."

"Thank you, General," said Mansour. He saluted firmly, with a stoic look on his face, then placed his hand at his side, feeling along his belt. He turned and started to walk across the large office, then stopped.

"May I ask a question, General Shakib?" said Mansour politely.

"What?" said Shakib.

"Did not the Supreme Leader approve of eliminating Andreas?" said Mansour.

"How dare you! What you did was treason! You're lucky to still be alive! *Get out!*" barked Shakib angrily, pointing.

Mansour rotated—his left arm whipped sideways, and a knife shot from his hand. It was a fixed-blade double-edged ROSarms hunting blade. It somersaulted through the air, flashes of silver and a high hum—then the knife stabbed Shakib in the left eye, slicing straight through the eyeball and puncturing through the membrane protecting Shakib's brain—all before Shakib could even react.

Shakib dropped to the floor, groaning. Blood burped from his eye socket as he writhed in agony, reaching for it. Soon his face was covered in blood, and the carpet beneath became stained in a fast-growing pool of crimson.

Mansour approached and went around the desk. Without emotion, he reached down and grabbed the hilt of the blade, yanking up and wiping blood and veins onto Shakib's shirt.

Mansour stared calmly down at his former mentor. Shakib was still conscious, but moments from death. His left eye was wet, raw, and gutty.

"You were wrong, General," said Mansour as Shakib took his last breath. "It was you who was the traitor."

4

President J. P. Dellenbaugh stood with a visiting family of con-stituents in front of a large cherry desk inside the Oval Office. The family was from South Dakota, a young couple and three small children, all dressed up. Dellenbaugh grinned widely as he stood beside the couple, behind the three children, his arms somehow enveloping them all. She was the cousin of a professional hockey referee Dellenbaugh had gotten to know during his time in the NHL. A favor to a long-forgotten colleague, a man who'd sent Dellenbaugh to the penalty box many a time, usually after yet another of Dellenbaugh's infamous fights.

In fact, when memories of his former career in the NHL came back, on days like this, it always put the president in a good mood. White House staffers always liked it when events had some sort of hockey tie-in, because it seemed to give Dellenbaugh an extra step or two. It was easy to forget the past, a pair of Stanley Cups, an MVP trophy, too many fights to count . . . when one's job was now president of the United States of America.

The Oval Office was warmly lit. The ceiling was a cut-out space and lights were hidden along the inside edges, casting light up, ac-centuating the oval itself, its detailed, precision woodwork, and shining a honey-yellow light through the room. The sky outside was a shadowy gray as evening encroached. The French doors to the private slate terrace outside the Oval Office were open. The Rose Garden. A faint scent of roses and drying leaves came in through the doors. Though it was chilly in the office, the lightly gusting wind created a sense of invigoration. The coming fall.

Three bronze statues were displayed on a mantel above the fireplace, where a fire now roared, stoked by the winds from outside. One was Abraham Lincoln. Another, Ronald Reagan. The third was Gordie Howe.

At age sixty-four, Dellenbaugh still appeared ten years younger, despite a professional career most people would describe as high stress and physically punishing. He spent more than a decade as a professional ice hockey player, a top-line right-winger for the Detroit Red Wings, before retiring from the NHL and running for United States Senate at the age of thirty-six. Dellenbaugh had been elected to the U.S. Senate on his first try, becoming the state of Michigan's junior senator by defeating the four-term incumbent, Jake Smith, who, at the time, was widely considered to be the most formidable Democrat in the country and was mulling a run for the White House. The RNC, who had recruited Dellenbaugh to run, had expected Dellenbaugh to do well on his first run for office based almost purely on his popularity as a pro hockey player in a state that loved its Red Wings. But they had not expected him to win, and when he beat Smith he became a national politician. What the RNC didn't know, what even Dellenbaugh himself didn't understand, is that when put around people, especially large crowds of people, J. P. Dellenbaugh had a commanding speaking style, filled with fire, a hint of anger at times; a loud, booming voice; and he was able to take crowds large and small into a state of near delirium, when he chose to do so, which was pretty much every time he faced a large crowd of people.

After a few photos were taken, the family was ushered out of the Oval Office. The White House photographer departed as well, and soon Dellenbaugh was alone; well, as alone as you can be when you're president. He removed his suit coat and his tie and threw them down on one of the large leather sofas in the middle of the room. Already seated on one of the sofas was a large man with a mop of black hair. This was Hector Calibrisi, the director of the Central Intelligence Agency. He was reading papers from a file as the president conducted political business.

A side door opened and Dellenbaugh's chief of staff, Adrian King, stepped into the Oval Office. He was dressed in a gray pin-striped suit.

"Mr. President," said King.

Another door opened and two more staff members stepped in. One was dark haired, slightly overweight, in a natty tweed suit. This was John Schmidt, the White House communications director. The other person was tall, thin, bald, and wore thick Coke-bottle glasses. He had taken off his suit coat and had his sleeves rolled up but was still wearing a tie. Cory Tilley, the head of White House speechwriting.

"Where are we on the speech?" said Dellenbaugh as he went to the coffee service and poured himself a cup.

"I've submitted two drafts, Mr. President," said Tilley.

"I read the first. You haven't nailed it yet, Cory," said Dellenbaugh, sipping from the coffee cup. "I want to say, fuck you to all you countries trying to help Hezbollah, Hamas, Al Qaeda. I'm sick and tired of hosting countries on our soil that give money and support to terrorists trying to hurt us."

"Sir, I think both drafts get that message across," said Schmidt. "The first one is polite, the second one is fairly direct."

"I don't think either draft hits hard enough."

"Mr. President," said Tilley, "I thought about actually putting a 'fuck you' in there, as well as a 'fuck off' and a 'go fuck yourself' and a 'screw yourself, bitch,' but then John reminded me it might not be in the overall image we're trying to project this close to the election."

Dellenbaugh and everyone else started laughing.

"The second draft is vicious, Mr. President," said Tilley. "Sir, you are basically threatening to evict the United Nations from New York City."

"Mr. President," said Schmidt, "this is the last United Nations speech before reelection. We're, or I should say, *you* are up for re-election. Now is not the time to start driving wedges or scaring people. I have a mortgage, sir."

Again, Dellenbaugh and everyone else chuckled.

"We're up by twenty points," said Dellenbaugh.

"There's no need to create an international firestorm less than three weeks from the election."

"I disagree," said Dellenbaugh. "This speech isn't about glossing over differences."

"Mr. President, don't pull the trigger until you know the gun's not aimed at your own head," said Schmidt.

"Don't give me that Harvard bullshit," said Dellenbaugh.

"I went to Washington and Lee, sir."

"Whatever. We're poking the goddam bear. Set the second draft into the teleprompter."

Dellenbaugh walked behind his desk. He took another sip of coffee then put the cup down. He glanced at his chief of staff, Adrian King, who was seated in one of two floral-patterned end chairs.

King looked at Tilley and Schmidt. With the faintest of a nod, King shooed them out of the Oval Office.

After they left, Dellenbaugh went to the center of the Oval Office, a seating area with matching eight-foot-long custom-made white leather George Smith chesterfield couches, facing each other across a glass coffee table. Dellenbaugh took a seat across from Calibrisi. King sat down next to Calibrisi, legs crossed.

Dellenbaugh looked at Calibrisi.

"Why are you here, Chief?" said Dellenbaugh.

"GID was closing in on a Hezbollah accountant," said Calibrisi, referring to Jordanian intelligence. "They found a computer in the basement of a home outside Amman. GID found a file. It was a fresh email stream, just a few days old, indicating there's some sort of operation under way to attempt to assassinate you, Mr. President."

"Isn't there always?" said Dellenbaugh.

"Yes and no," said Calibrisi. "This time it's yes."

"What are the details?" said King.

"I know you're not going to like this," said Calibrisi, "but all it shows is fund flows. Payments. There's no detail on the parameters."

"I'm flying to New York City in the morning," said Dellenbaugh. "I'm speaking at the United Nations."

"I don't think the UN speech is a good idea," said Calibrisi. "Postpone and let me sic some alligators on this."

King stood up, shaking his head, but Dellenbaugh raised his hand to shut him up.

"Do you have any hard intelligence, Hector?" said King.

"Yes. Eight hundred thousand dollars has been paid over the last two months by Iran, into Hezbollah, through an accountant, in order to do whatever it is they're going to do. No, I don't know if it's going to happen tomorrow or in a week, or ever. But I'd rather be safe than sorry."

"Did they find the accountant?" said King.

"Yes," said Calibrisi. "Jordanian intelligence over-toxicologized him before we knew about anything. They told us about the emails after they'd already killed him and before we could get there."

King's frustration was visible. Both Dellenbaugh and Calibrisi knew the signs. The White House chief of staff was about to blow his stack.

"You tell that fuck, what's his name, *Sadir*, the head of GID, that he's no longer welcome inside the United States, that miserable fuck!" said King, referring to head of Jordan intel.

He walked in between Dellenbaugh and Calibrisi.

"There's no *fucking* way the goddam president of the United States is *not* traveling to one of his own *goddam* cities to deliver a *fucking* speech!" said King, pointing at Calibrisi. "Is that crystal clear, Chief? Bolster up your fucking security! Lock the UN down, but President J. P. Dellenbaugh is not scared to go anywhere in his own country, got it?"

Calibrisi looked at King with a serene stare. He turned to Dellenbaugh.

"Someone is moving in for an attempt on your life," said Calibrisi calmly. "Well funded. Sophisticated. We're behind. Domestic security is FBI and local police."

King threw up his hands.

"Are you seriously suggesting we postpone?" said King. "*The speech is tomorrow fucking morning!*"

"Yes, that's exactly what I'm suggesting," said Calibrisi. "Give us time to figure out what's going on."

Dellenbaugh put his coffee cup down, spilling a little on the table.

"I agree with Adrian," said Dellenbaugh. "I'm speaking tomorrow, threat or no threat, so clamp down. Keep it secure."

Calibrisi nodded silently.

"I'll reach out to Dave McNaughton," said King, referring to the newly appointed head of the FBI. "I'll make sure he tees up NYPD. Have Bill Polk put some frogmen offshore," added King.

"Good defense beats any offense," said Calibrisi facetiously.

"I'm not going to avoid some so-called terror threat in my own goddam country," said the president. "If they get to me, maybe they deserved to."

Calibrisi stood up.

"Fine," said Calibrisi. "I'm outvoted. I'm putting this on the *emergency priority* tac list," he said, looking at Dellenbaugh. "I want legal authority to deploy assets on domestic soil. I want sign-off now."

"You got it," said Dellenbaugh.

"I'll paper it," said King. "Get moving."

5

Dewey took the Hayabusa through downtown D.C., along the Potomac, then cut up Rock Creek Parkway near the Kennedy Center. He flexed his wrist and was soon gone in a wake of burning rubber.

He could handle any motorcycle and he loved Ducati—but the Hayabusa was pure fury and might, and he pushed the bike to the outer reaches of what the machine was capable of.

It was early afternoon and the two northbound lanes were practically empty.

Once clear of the marble apron near the Kennedy Center, Dewey unleashed the motorcycle. He hit sixty in 3.2 seconds and a hundred at 5.6, pulsing the throttle and reading the wind breaks through a tree-lined canyon in order to hit the clear roadway at maximum speed.

Dewey liked cars. He'd driven his share of Ferraris, Lamborghinis, and Hellcats. He loved horses, and by age ten had spent more time traveling on the back of a horse than most equestrians do in a lifetime. He grew up on a farm, and horseback was how they reached the outer fields, costing nothing in fuel, running the stallions and mares because they needed to be run.

But as much as he liked either one, Dewey only met his match when tucked against the danger and heat of a motorcycle.

He didn't like motorcycles, he didn't love them—it was beyond that. Somehow, when he was on one, the machine was like an extension of his own body.

He roared the six-hundred-pound monster up the black tar of Rock Creek Parkway, feeling the wind, and at a sharp turn near the Connecticut Avenue exit, he slammed to the left, feeling the faintest scratch of the roadway against his bare elbow. He knew the corner, the motorcycle, and himself so well that even at a hundred and fifteen miles an hour Dewey knew exactly how far he could take it. He straightened, fluttered the gas, and shot fast out of the turn. He looked down, where the digital read "134" in green numbers.

Dewey's mind went calm as nearby trees became like a green patina and the oncoming air slashed across his face. Then the old familiar sadness washed over him like a slow, powerful wave coming in before a storm.

Dewey's mind—as he weaved up Rock Creek Parkway—was on a windswept, open field at the edge of a cemetery on the coast of Maine. Brilliant blue sky framed the dark ocean down the hill. Dark pines stood atop ice-crossed rock. Whitecaps framed in bluish black crested, in the distance, under fierce Atlantic winds. An old cemetery on a hill just above Penobscot Bay, a resting place for the dead set aside more than two hundred years ago to honor Castine's sons and daughters, farmers, sailors, soldiers, and their families, a resting place for a proud American town. Like every town in America, but this was the town Dewey had grown up in, had married his high school sweetheart in, had baptized his only son in—and now he stood at the edge of the cemetery and he was back there, and he revved the Hayabusa, kicking it to 160 and feeling a terrible but very real sense that he was intentionally putting himself in danger, and yet he flexed his hand and watched as the digital in green digits indicated 169 mph. It was the only way he could still find his memories now. He could never explain to anyone, but he needed to find that cliff in order to look out and see the images and memories from his past—memories of his wife and son, of being a father and husband. It had been so long ago, but as he moved at a scary speed, his mind drifted into that long-forgotten period of his life.

One memory flashed in his mind at that moment. It was the cemetery. Stone and marble so old the names couldn't be read, covered in lichen. He came to two blocks of granite, one a large slab of pink rock, the other a small, silvery gray square with specks of black.

HOLLY ANDREAS
FAIR DAUGHTER, COME HOME NOW

On the other grave:

ROBERTSON ANDREAS
DEATH BE NOT PROUD

It had been so long ago. He fought to find the memory. More than a decade now, and memories grew old and blurred. Dewey could only find it now at the edge of a chasm—at the place he found only when tearing up a two-lane road at speeds most professional motorcycle racers wouldn't dare. Wind chopping at the visor, but at this speed his helmet was irrelevant. All that mattered was Dewey's skill atop a motorcycle, which was elite.

His son, Robbie, had died of leukemia at age six, and, stricken by grief, Holly had killed herself six months later, but now all he remembered was the feeling after her funeral that autumn day. . . .

How he knelt in front of the graves of what was once his family.

"We used to go sledding over there," he said out loud in the cemetery that lonesome day when he visited the graves of Holly and Robbie, looking at a steep hill in the distance. "It's the stuff I never did with you that I miss the most. Like sledding. I'm sorry."

It was his first time in the United States in almost ten years. He'd been kicked out of Delta, falsely accused of murdering Holly, who had shot herself with one of his pistols at their small house near Fort Bragg. After being acquitted, in thirty-one minutes, Dewey representing himself, he'd left the U.S. for the hard world of off-shore oil drilling. During a decade of moving country to country, a nomad with no friends or connections, he worked his way to a top job in the oil industry. Gang chief on the largest oil platform in the world, off the western coast of South America. Capitana—now but an asterisk—the target of an attack by Alexander Fortuna and his well-funded jihad. Destroy the largest American energy company, and Fortuna had done just that. But Fortuna knew not the man who ran Capitana, who ran it like a battlefield commander ran brigades of men. Dewey had escaped before the massive $20 billion oil field was destroyed. He'd hunted Fortuna down and killed him.

Dewey pushed the Hayabusa even harder now, registering 177 on the digital box near his left hand, as thoughts of Jessica entered his mind. He felt water on his cheeks, tears washing down, and they mixed with the wind. He tasted the salty water as he forced himself to remember.

Jessica had guided Dewey from afar, from FBI Headquarters, like a compass, as Dewey hunted and killed the greatest terrorist since Bin Laden.

Jessica Tanzer, the head of the FBI's office of counterterrorism, came to Castine out of respect, knowing what Dewey had been through, and understanding his sorrow and closure as he finally saw the graves of his lost family.

Dewey pushed the motorcycle harder now, passing a delivery truck at 180 mph, moving north on the Rock Creek Parkway as, in his eyes, he saw not road but rather the vision of Jessica just a year after the funeral, in Argentina, on a perfect summer evening, after a day of riding horses along a cold, beautiful stream.

They were in their suite, with temperatures in the low eighties and the Andes in the distance. They were to be married in less than a month. Jessica was dressed only in his white button-down, too large, down to her thighs, and she was naked beneath, and the shirt wasn't buttoned, and he could see her breasts, for she wanted Dewey to see them. Watching as she walked toward him for the completion of the most perfect day ever, and then as she was shot through the back by bullets intended for him . . .

The sudden circle of red . . . Jessica's eyes, in pain, communicating to him.

I'm sorry.

The events all coursed through his mind in moments and seconds. He had to relive it because it was the only way to see the look on Jessica's face just before she was killed. The look of longing and utter and total love. Dewey had to go back in order to see the moment, even though the pain was too much, but he saw her eyes. . . . Dewey saw her arms reaching out to him, her beautiful frame through the white fabric . . . and he suddenly remembered her turning and smiling, and then the bullet hit her from behind, and in a fraction of a second they both realized what had happened, and despite her pain, Jessica's mouth had moved and called out to him one final time, "I love you," as she dropped to the ground and died.

A war that has no end.

As he reached the exit ramp off the Rock Creek Parkway, Dewey cooled the Hayabusa down, slowing, downshifting in a throaty, bearlike growl. He stopped thinking about it. He knew he could never get it back, not Jessica, Holly, or Robbie. All he had now were the moments, moments only accessed when he forced himself to challenge death.

He didn't like to think about his past. He'd long ago put his past behind him. But the harder he worked to separate himself, to numb himself, the more he understood that his past was inextricably linked to his present and future. That he could never escape the ramifications of what he had done first as a Ranger, then Delta, and now as an operative for the Central Intelligence Agency. If he could forget his past, perhaps then he could come to believe that he could meet someone and fall in love and have the child he so desperately wanted. He could never replace Robbie but maybe they would have loved each other? If he could forget his past, he could make himself believe that he wouldn't be responsible for the death of another woman, of two women.

But he could not forget the past; Dewey vowed to never again put a woman he loved in harm's way. The guilt he felt, the shame that haunted him, was already too much to bear. So he would never love again.

Yet, he recognized Rob was right. A little social interaction might not be such a bad idea. Maybe he *should* go out on a date with someone once in a while? He didn't want to be a hermit, after all. The problem was, every time he did that, he fell in love. Holly and Jessica were the only women he'd ever been with. He hated how naïve he was, and how simple. He needed to put his past behind him.

Dewey's solution was always to keep on going without thinking too much. To put aside the past and the future and occupy the present. Forget it all for a precious few moments and enjoy the thought of something as simple as a trained, highly technical motorcycle ride on the most powerful production bike in the world. Or a good meal. He was hungry. He'd worked up an appetite. He would get a big lunch then go home and take a shower, maybe go for a run later, seven or eight miles, and he would try to keep each mile under six minutes.

Dewey cut across M Street then took a right on Thirty-fourth Street. He stopped in front of the pretty brick façade of his town house and parked the bike. He climbed off and left his helmet on the Hayabusa. He walked to the corner and opened the door to a restaurant called Alta Strada. It was his neighborhood restaurant, the place he went to for pizza and pasta, both of which were delicious. He knew most of the people by name. Sometimes he would come in at night and sit at the bar alone, drinking a Peroni or three and eating a bowl of Bolognese.

Dewey stepped inside. It was a small restaurant and normally it was filled with customers and waitstaff, bustling with activity, but Dewey could see no one, not for a moment or two. Alta Strada kept its lights low, and his eyes had to adjust. Then he saw the carnage.

Blood pooled on the linoleum floor, tables overturned.

He lurched back for the door, trying to get out, but then all he could hear was the low staccato *thwack thwack thwack thwack thwack* of suppressed automatic gunfire—and he pivoted, diving down to the ground just as slugs pulverized the door, barely missing above him, shattering the glass.

Two gunmen flanked the inside of the restaurant from left and right, standing a few feet from the door. They were pumping bullets at Dewey. But Dewey was on his stomach, beneath the fusillade, screened by tables and chairs.

He recognized the sound of an Uzi—that gunman was to his right. The other weapon—which Dewey was more fearful of—was an AR-15. He felt the brute thuds of slugs as they pounded the wall to his left, just a few feet away.

The gunmen, whoever they were, had him locked in. He knew he didn't want to take a bullet from either weapon.

Dewey scrambled along the floor, shielded by tables and chairs, crawling. He swept his eyes horizontally at ground level as the assassins moved in, trapping him in a storm cloud of bullets. He registered at least a dozen corpses, lying in contorted positions, drenched in crimson, including one of the waitresses he knew by name, Jan. Dewey reached for his left ankle and removed a combat blade—Gerber eight-inch fixed steel with a serrated upper edge. With his other hand he reached to a holster beneath his left armpit. He took out a pistol: Colt M1911A1 .45 caliber, semiautomatic, chambered and ready to go.

From the floor, in between chairs and tables and corpses, he made out the legs of the killer to his right. Dewey trained the pistol on one of the terrorist's legs as the killer to his other side kicked aside tables and chairs. Dewey fired twice, pumping two bullets across the thicket of bodies, tables, and chairs, hunting for him. The first bullet hit the killer's right knee, the second struck his ankle, and the man fell down, crumpling, screaming in agony.

The other killer was to Dewey's left, beyond the tables that now shielded him. The gunman continued firing at Dewey, moving concentrically closer.

Mixed in with the furious drumbeat of automatic-weapon fire was a throaty, deep groan of miserable pain, coming from the man Dewey had shot. He lay contorted on the restaurant floor, squirming like a caught fish, but still alive.

The other killer dropped to one knee, gunning beneath the tables at Dewey. Bullets twanged as they struck the metal of chairs and tables. Dewey lay dormant in a protected nook, just inches from being in range. If he tried to reposition he feared he would expose the upper part of his body as well as his head. But the killer was getting closer—and the man he'd already shot had stopped groaning and was now trying to get to the submachine gun that had fallen from his hands when Dewey's bullets struck.

A slug hit the wall less than a foot from Dewey's head. The killer was adjusting his angle; he knew where Dewey was hiding.

From somewhere outside, there was the high-pitched sound of sirens in the distance.

Dewey tried to count the rounds between the brief pauses when the killer with the AR-15 changed out mags. As the bullets came closer, he anticipated the end of the mag. Dewey saw a pattern in the killer and felt his best odds were his Gerber. He tucked the .45 back in the holster, and found the heart of the upper steel of the Gerber. When he heard the mag click empty, Dewey abruptly stood, throwing aside a table with his left arm as with his right he swung the blade through the air, hurling the knife in the direction of the assassin. The blade somersaulted across the dimly lit restaurant. The gunman finished changing out the mag and fired one more time, one more burst at Dewey, then pivoted, but Dewey had guessed correctly. The blade hit the killer at the nape of the neck, slicing deep. The sound of gunfire stopped as the man was kicked backward, tumbling to the floor, dropping the weapon, and reaching to his neck, his hands searching for the hilt of the knife as dark red blood spilled like oil from the gaping hole in his neck.

Dewey's eyes shot right. The other man crawled to the abandoned Uzi despite his shattered legs and the blood now coursing like water on the restaurant floor. He was on his stomach. His hands clawed the ground as he went for the gun. Dewey watched as the killer reached the Uzi and turned the muzzle toward him. He charged at the injured terrorist . . . but as he started to dive at the gunman, Dewey caught a glint of silver. It came from his left, near the bar.

Another person. Someone else was there.

As the wounded killer found the trigger, Dewey realized that if he went for the man with the Uzi, he would die.

Dewey lunged toward the shadow at the alcove next to the bar. He dived at the cap end of a silencer he'd seen as if in a dream, a flash of moment, an instinct. In that collection of milliseconds he was in the air, he could see nothing but the empty space at the opening to the alcove. Then he saw the suppressor moving in his direction and a killer emerged from the alcove.

Dewey's right hand grabbed the suppressor just as the assassin acquired him in the crosshairs. The man pumped the trigger. The bullets spat from the gun, just inches from Dewey's skull. But Dewey held tight to the silencer as he tackled the killer and took him hard to the ground, slamming the man down with all his weight.

From behind him, he heard movement and then words in a language he didn't understand.

The sirens grew louder—there were multiple police cruisers closing in.

Dewey forced him onto his back, clutching the suppressor as the gunman continued to fire at him, barely missing. He struggled and wrestled with the killer. Each man gripped a part of the gun, pulling and yanking. The killer was big, and had strength. He was young. He kneed at Dewey, punching Dewey in the torso with his left hand. He hit him again, and a third time; he had established a weakness and Dewey felt the punches—trained and brutal. Holding the muzzle of the killer's gun in his right hand, Dewey reared up and slammed his left fist into the assassin's chin, snapping his head back. He punched him again, in the nose, shattering it, but the killer still fought, trying to get Dewey in the aim of the suppressed Walther. Dewey reared up and punched again, then again, splattering blood everywhere as the assassin moaned and started to drown in his own blood. He felt the man ease his grip on the gun. Dewey ripped it from his hands and stood. He fired a hollow-tipped

230-grain HST into the assassin's shoulder, lowered the suppressor, and shot again—into the man's ankle, shattering it—and the thug screamed in pain.

As if by instinct, Dewey pivoted and ducked, just as the killer with the Uzi acquired him from the blood-soaked floor. A burst of slugs sailed above Dewey's head as Dewey fired the pistol. The silenced bullet spat from the gun and tore a dime-sized hole in the center of the man's forehead.

Dewey looked the other way as his arm, clutching the gun, reflexively followed the trajectory of his eyes. There, he found the man with the knife in his throat. He'd removed the blade and was sitting up, blood spilling from his neck, his white T-shirt stained dark purple. He was trying to lift his weapon to shoot at Dewey but he couldn't, he was too weak. He was barely moving. He would soon die. Dewey trained the pistol on him from across the restaurant and pumped the trigger. There was a metallic *thwack* as the bullet hit the man in the right eye, splattering the wall behind him in brains, bone, and blood.

Dewey turned the gun on the man he'd just taken it from, below him now, just feet away from him.

He knew he shouldn't kill him. It was a highly coordinated, thought-out attack. It was obviously a designed operation. An assassination. They had come for him.

Dewey knew he had enemies, but this one had come all too close.

This was about revenge. It was a targeted hit.

That he was known by hostile intelligence agencies across the world was no secret. But the boldness of the attempted kill—near his home, on American soil—meant that someone was watching him. Nebuchar Fortuna or Chinese MSS, or perhaps VEVAK, even GRU. Dewey knew they all wanted him dead. He knew each group had active termination orders on him, and he'd exposed himself.

After returning from a mission two weeks ago, all Dewey wanted was a few weeks off, or a few months, but he was wrong. He could never let up.

He stared down at the assassin, bleeding profusely from his shoulder and ankle. He stopped screaming. He was drifting into shock and could no longer feel it, though he was still alive. Dewey knew that was important.

All three men were Middle Eastern, but that no longer mattered. China's most talented assassin was an Egyptian. One's nationality didn't matter in this world, at least not as much as it used to.

A world he wished he wasn't part of now as he trained the tip of the suppressed PPK on the lone remaining killer, even as sirens pealed in a rising decibel, coming closer and closer. . . .

Dewey knew he should keep the man alive.

Under a CIA pharmaceutical protocol, the badly bleeding Arab would likely spill the beans. Yes, he shouldn't kill him, he should show restraint. But Dewey didn't believe in restraint, especially as he noticed Gary, one of the bartenders, who'd served in the Navy, as he always told Dewey, splayed out facedown in a shiny pool of wet red behind the bar.

Dewey stood above the killer. The man was bleeding badly and suffering. His shoulder was a riot of wet, shiny red.

"May I take your order?" said Dewey politely as he trained the muzzle on the killer's forehead. "The chicken is excellent today. Freshly killed."

The assassin's mouth flared for a brief moment into a grin, though he said nothing. The pain was taking over. He was drifting into shock.

Dewey knew it was a valuable time in the interrogation, a human being going into shock because of pain. In some cases, the passage into shock was instantaneous and the potential harvest of information impossible, for once in shock the individual became incoherent. But he was fighting it and Dewey recognized it.

It was a window—and Dewey had placed his bullets surgically. The pain from the bullets was intense, but neither deadly nor nerve driven. But make no mistake, the man on the ground was suffering a pain most people would never know.

Dewey also understood pain and had long ago learned its many stages. Falling into shock was the first step in a prisoner's ability to be mined for information by the interrogator.

Dewey had the killer right where he wanted him.

"Who do you work for?" said Dewey calmly, staring into the assassin's eyes. He kept the pistol trained on the man's forehead.

Dewey heard a police officer yelling from the street.

The sirens were loud and incessant, and he understood the police were now just outside.

He wasn't worried about killing the two other men. He was worried he might not get to kill the man bleeding out at his feet.

"Who sent you?" repeated Dewey, this time with a harder edge.

The man was in his late twenties. He had short-cropped black hair and was good-looking. He stared at Dewey with a detached glare, despite the pain, refusing to answer. Then he spoke.

"I'm dead already. Do you think I want my last act on earth to be that I became a coward?"

"Iran," said Dewey. "You have the same way of talking as someone I knew."

The man grinned and nodded, yes.

"Abu," he said as he coughed and wheezed.

"So I was the target?" said Dewey.

The man said nothing.

Dewey looked to the shattered door. He heard shouts from police officers, barking from outside. He pumped a silenced bullet into the man's stomach. The Iranian groaned, coughing blood.

"Fuck you," he spat out.

"I'll tell you what," said Dewey, eyes casting between the killer and the door. "Your injuries are salvageable. Tell me if I was the target and I'll let you live."

The first SWAT officers stormed in. They kicked in the door, through the hanging shards of glass, yelling at Dewey.

The man coughed as crimson trickled from his mouth.

Behind him, Dewey heard shouting from one of the SWAT commandos. He had a deep, military voice and was slightly panicked. He was shouting at Dewey—

"Drop the gun!"

The Iranian looked at Dewey and spoke as SWAT took over the restaurant:

"If I know you, that was a lie, Dewey Andreas."

As the killer stared up at him, Dewey pumped the trigger, blowing a dime-sized hole through his heart.

Dewey turned, letting the handgun fall to the floor, then raised his arms just as muzzles—at the end of rifles held by numerous SWAT—acquired him in near perfect unison.

"Don't shoot," said Dewey in a commanding voice, holding his hands up and spreading his fingers as bright white halogen lights suddenly illuminated him amid the carnage. "I'm U.S. government. *Don't fucking shoot!"*

6

In a small glass-walled office three doors down from the director of the Central Intelligence Agency sat a young woman with eye-catching wheat-blond hair. It was one of her most distinctive features even though she rarely gave it a thought, and kept it in the simplest of styles because she didn't care. It was straight, cut so that it just touched her shoulders, and in front were bangs in a neat, perfect line above her blue eyes. Her face was soft and chiseled, with smooth skin and reddish cheeks, and beautiful lips perhaps a size too big. Not glamorous but a rather old-fashioned, elegant, timeless beauty. She had a reserved manner and style, a bit standoffish, to most even a little cold. Her looks, demeanor, and most of all her accent were quintessentially British. Her name was Jenna Hartford.

Jenna was focused on two large LCD screens on the desk in front of her. Jenna had once been British intelligence's top operations architect, responsible for the design of black operations across the globe, including the assassination of Fao Bhang, the head of MSS, China's intelligence agency.

When her husband, Charles, was killed by a car bomb in London intended for her, she had attempted to quit MI6. Instead, Derek Chalmers, her mentor and the head of MI6, convinced her to move to the United States and work for Hector Calibrisi at the CIA. In the four months since arriving at Langley, Jenna had been a cipher. She worked incredibly long hours and spoke to almost no one, with the obvious exception of Calibrisi, and Bill Polk, who ran the National Clandestine Service.

The job of an architect was a mixture of an understanding of a situation on the ground, in extremely personal terms, in order to pinpoint possible actions, with an almost preternatural instinct for mapping operators into the ground-level picture. There were only four really good architects in the Western coalition of CIA, MI6, and Mossad. But everyone acknowledged that the five-foot-five, thirty-two-year-old Jenna was far and away the best.

That she'd turned down more invitations to drinks, dinner, bike rides, or coffee was well known already inside Langley's hallways. For the most part, she didn't give the time of day to anyone.

Jenna's door was three down from the office of Hector Calibrisi, the director of the CIA. Her office was glass-walled on the interior and exterior, but bookshelves occupied the walls adjacent to other offices. It was part of a larger suite of offices, the CIA director's suite, behind a wall of steel, flanked by gunmen. The director's suite constituted the southeast penthouse corner of the building.

She was currently designing an action for her former employer, MI6, tracking down a former British intelligence agent who had been believed dead, but who'd been seen in Novosibirsk, the largest city in Siberia, by a French DGSE field agent. After analyzing bank records, various signals intelligence, and the agent's detailed biographical file, Jenna had been able to pinpoint the rogue with the help of MI6 hackers, by focusing in on the man's known thoracic issues. He had a bad heart, and had been born with it. After a thorough, and quite illegal, scan of health facilities across Russia, then pushing the data against financial activities, Jenna had found the traitorous man in a town forty miles outside Kiev. She didn't care how or why the agent, a man named Perkins, had gone to the dark side. Instead, her focus was on designing a mission to eliminate him.

Her cell phone vibrated. It was a "44" phone code, which meant the call had come from Britain, her homeland. It was her mother. She didn't answer it, and reached to turn it off, clicking a button on the side.

Her attention moved to her computer. An icon on her second screen caught her eyes. She opened the application. It was a so-called green flash, indicating a real-time situation involving one of Langley's NOCs, or non-official cover agents. NOCs were Jenna's primary architectural building blocks.

In this case, it was one of the few agents she knew well—and her eyes shot to the screen:

DCPD GEORGETOWN 9144. BLKG 3 A S 881
ASC 6, REPRO 42
3:08:31 PM EST
GPS: ALTA STRADA 36/H
: GUNFIRE
: MULTIPLE CASUALTIES
: DC METRO PO SWAT ON SCENE
: EST 17–22 FATALITIES CIV 14

FLASH
: POSSIBLE TARGET NOC 2495-6
: ANDREAS, DEWEY

NEED FOR IMMEDIATE DCIA ATTENTION

FLASH
DCPD AT SCENE/FBI QUANTICO, CASE TEAM 4 (VA BEACH #1)
6.R [DOMESTIC ECA]

PER STATUTE 44.B.2: POSSIBLE CONTRAVENTION OF LO-CAL/STATE LAW ENFORCEMENT WITH CIA NON-OFFICIAL COVER AGENT

FLASH FLASH FLASH FLASH FLASH
: IMMEDIATE EXFILTRATION REQUIRED
: IMMEDIATE EXFILTRATION REQUIRED
: IMMEDIATE EXFILTRATION REQUIRED

Jenna looked at her watch. It was 3:09. Whatever had just happened had literally *just* happened.

Suddenly, a red alert—another icon—appeared on the screen. It was a garbled text from Bill Polk through some sort of encryption engine.

> We have Dewey. Run a quick analysis on this with
> preliminary op response, also ref approx 800k wired through
> GID tertiary to HEZB forget file no, yesterday. Back in 10

Polk, the head of NCS, the deputy director of the agency, wanted to know what, or rather, why what just happened to Dewey happened, and what to do about it.

She smiled ear to ear. It was the first real challenge since coming to Langley. That it involved Dewey Andreas crossed her mind. Jenna had already exposed Dewey to life-threatening operating parameters, in China and North Korea. She was used to exposing agents to danger in an operation and had no emotion whatsoever about it. It was one of the reasons she was a good architect. But there was also something about him. Jenna remembered meeting him for the first time and feeling a tingle when he looked at her. He was rugged but he had something else about him still. She scanned the spec sheet again and realized there had been a firefight and a team had been sent to kill Dewey, but that he'd survived.

Again, Jenna's cell phone vibrated and again the number "44" appeared on the screen. Her mother again.

"Oh for fuck's sake," she said.

She placed an earbud in her ear and hit the phone screen.

"What is it, Mother?" she asked impatiently. "I'm in the middle of something."

"It's your father's birthday," said Jenna's mother in a lilting aristocratic British accent. "The entire family will be there," she added, "including your aunt Winifred."

"I know, Mother, I just don't think I can get away," she said, reading the screen.

"Jenna, it is your father's seventieth birthday," said her mother in a patrician tone. "Bring a friend. You've been in the United States for six months. Surely you have made some friends, perhaps a . . . boyfriend?"

Jenna was silent.

"You know how much your father and I want grandchildren," her mother intoned.

In six months, Jenna had been on a grand total of zero dates, despite being asked many, many times.

"You have a way with words, Mother," said Jenna.

"I'm sorry. I just. . . . well, can you try, Jenna dear?"

Bachelor SOG agents as well as rising single officers in the CIA hierarchy all knew of the arrival of Jenna Hartford. She was on loan from MI6, beautiful, mysterious, talented, and elegant, and sat three doors down from Hector Calibrisi. So many had asked her for a drink or dinner she'd lost count, her answer invariably being "No, thank you."

Calibrisi and Polk protected her as best they could, though really it wasn't necessary. She was fully prepared to take care of herself.

"I have a very active social calendar," said Jenna to her mother, lying.

"The Austin boy from Yale told your father he's attempted to call you on several occasions. He's a successful hedge fund man and I don't need to tell you he went to Eton and was president of his form. He said he attempted to reach you more than once."

Jenna typed, looking for more information on the situation in Georgetown.

"Well, Mummy, maybe that's the problem now, isn't it?" said Jenna.

"I have only the best of intentions for you, my love," said her mother.

"I know, Mummy," said Jenna softly. "I'll try and make it."

• • •

Jenna heard the sound of activity. The footsteps grew louder but there was no discussion. She saw Bill Polk pass quickly by her door, followed by Calibrisi. Several moments later, Jenna saw Dewey walking behind them. He moved across the front of her doorway. He was bleeding; his shirt was torn.

"Dewey?" she said, calling out from behind her desk. "Dewey?"

Nothing happened and then a moment later, Dewey turned. He stepped into the frame of the door.

"Jenna?" he said. "Hey."

"Hi," she said. "Are you okay?" she asked with a concerned look on her face.

Suddenly, in her ear comm, she heard her mother's voice.

"Of course I'm okay," said her mother. "I was just—"

Jenna tapped her ear, cutting off her mother.

"Yeah," said Dewey.

"I read the scans," she said with a concerned look. "They knew you were coming."

Dewey pretended he didn't hear, and changed subjects.

"So, how's it going so far?" Dewey asked politely, looking around her office in curiosity. "Do you like working here?"

"Sure."

"What's it like?" he said. "Don't you get tired of being in an office all the time?"

"Not really," she said.

Dewey smiled.

"Do you like living in Washington?" he asked. "I meant to check in on you after we got back. I apologize."

They both knew he was talking about North Korea.

"It's great," she said.

"Where do you live?"

"Kalorama."

"*Schmancy*," said Dewey. "I hear even the homeless people wear Gucci."

Jenna smiled. "How about you?"

"What about me?" said Dewey.

"Where do you live? Do you like it?"

"Georgetown," said Dewey, "but you already knew that."

"Because of the attack earlier? That doesn't mean you live in Georgetown."

"You know the profile of every person in this building," said Dewey, grinning.

Jenna giggled.

"I do not," she stammered with a pretty English accent.

Dewey nodded toward Calibrisi's office.

"I have to go," he said.

"What is it?"

"I assume it's about what just happened," said Dewey.

"Well, your meeting won't officially start until I arrive," said Jenna. "Bill asked me to run analysis on it."

Dewey felt blood dribbling from his elbow. He looked down. There was a small pool of red on Jenna's carpet. Her eyes followed his.

"I'm sorry," he said. "I'll clean it up."

"Don't worry about it."

He glanced around, then stepped outside her office, walked into the central cubicles, which were mostly empty, and returned with a newspaper someone had been reading. He threw it down over the pool of red, even as he then dripped on top of the newspaper. "That should soak it up," he said. He attempted to wipe up the blood, though it only made his shoulder bleed more. Jenna watched as he turned the small pool of blood into a larger one. Finally, he stood back up. "Sorry about that."

"It's fine, Dewey."

Dewey was several inches taller than Jenna. She was close to him now, less than a foot away, looking up at his shoulder, then into his eyes. She wanted to hold the shirt tighter, to take care of him, though she didn't do that; in fact she didn't move.

"So what you're saying is, you have to do analysis for those guys?" said Dewey.

"Yes."

"Do I have time to get some stitches?"

"Yes, of course," she said. She put her hand on his wrist. She walked him to the door.

"Go get sewn up," she said. "I won't start until you get there, promise."

7

Mansour flew from Tehran to Algeria, refueling in the swelter-ing heat of Algiers.

He was in a silver-and-red Bombardier Global 7500, owned by a French-Arab businessman, an importer of wine and cigars, and occasionally other things, like missiles, who Hezbollah had lent $30 million to a few years before, and as with anyone doing business with Hezbollah was now paying Hezbollah back, in the form of a ride on his jet—and use of the luggage hold. Mansour was the only passenger aboard other than the crew. Because of Voges, Mansour's entry into the U.S. would be a "clean insertion."

A pretty black-haired flight attendant was there to wait on Man-sour, prepare his dinner, cater to his every need, but he barely ac-knowledged her existence. He tried to sleep but he couldn't even close his eyes. He kept staring at a video on his phone. It was from the camera on the weapon of one of the men in Georgetown. It showed Andreas walking into the restaurant and diving down out of the fusillade from the man filming. Mansour saw the mistake im-mediately. All three men should have converged on him. By remain-ing back, they'd given Andreas a precious few seconds to escape.

Then he reread a text. It was from eight minutes later. A hacked live-transcribed voice scan from Washington police. Three men were dead at the scene—and an American was still alive.

Mansour wanted to believe he'd anticipated Andreas's behavior but he knew he hadn't, and that the beginning gambit had failed miserably. Andreas was still alive. In addition, not only would the U.S. government begin poking around, Andreas would be wakened. It was why Mansour had risked everything to try for a shot at him. It irritated him. But Mansour knew that the plan was still impervious to Andreas.

After touching down in Algiers, he saw that General Ghaani—Shakib's chief of staff and the third most powerful man in Iran—had called him three times.

It was dark when Mansour stepped down onto the tarmac. He dialed.

"Hello?" came the steely voice of Ghaani.

"General Ghaani, it is Commander Mansour. I saw that you called. I was on a plane."

"I'll cut to the point, Zakaria," said Ghaani. "General Shakib was found dead in his office earlier this evening. You were the only one to visit him."

"I killed him," said Mansour bluntly.

Ghaani was silent.

Mansour said nothing.

"Did I just hear what you said?" asked Ghaani.

"That depends on what you think I said."

"You . . . killed . . . *General Shakib*?" said Ghaani, finally.

"I was in the same meeting you were in," said Mansour. "The Supreme Leader approved the mission. Shakib was a traitor. If you disagree I suggest you speak to the Supreme Leader."

Mansour hung up. He had to make one more call. He steeled himself for a few seconds. Technically, the man worked for Mansour. But he was not a soldier. Rather, Rokan was a computer hacker. He was delicate and prone to flights of fancy and fear. Yet his role in the coming maelstrom was perhaps even more important than his own. Mansour hit speed dial. After a short pause, a voice came on.

"Commander," said Rokan. "What can I do for you?"

"I'm in Algeria," said Mansour. "Things are about to begin. We execute our plan tomorrow and you need to be ready to do your part."

"I'm not nearly prepared!" said Rokan. "Do you understand the amount of encryption I need to move through? If I don't have the proper algorithms, it's all pointless!"

"There's no need to yell," said Mansour.

"But I need another few days."

"You don't have another few days," said Mansour. "Whether you like it or not, it's happening tomorrow."

"Then leave me alone," said Rokan, his voice agitated. "I need to . . . to—"

"Don't be nervous, Rokan," said Mansour. "I know you and I know you're ready. We will be providing all the distraction you need. All you need to do is meet the messengers at the hotel."

"Jesus, Zakaria, you think that's all I have to do?" shouted Rokan.

Mansour held the phone away from his ear.

"That is by far the easy part!" he yelled. "We're talking about the Federal Reserve. If I don't get killed getting in, I have to hack into an iodine sheet field."

"You'll do fine," said Mansour reassuringly. "Just do your best."

In a private hangar of Houari Boumediene Airport, the Bombardier took on more fuel. While the jet was refueling, Mansour met a man on the tarmac. Mansour approached under darkness, with fragments of light from the fuel truck illuminating the two men. The other man was pale skinned, and spoke with a German accent.

Mansour towered over the short, rotund man, an international arms dealer originally from the United States, named Kyle Schnabel. Schnabel stood at five-foot-four and weighed three hundred pounds. He was a billionaire several times over.

"Mr. Schnabel," said Mansour.

"Hello, Mr. Mansour," said Schnabel. "Where is the money?"

"Where are the Strelas?" said Mansour.

"Where's the money?" said Schnabel.

"I have nothing to do with the money," said Mansour.

"Well, I suggest you consider having something to do with it," said Schnabel, "that is, if you want your Strelas."

Both Schnabel and Mansour glanced around the tarmac. They were alone.

"Are they sanitized?" said Mansour.

Schnabel looked offended.

"Of course," he said. "Clean as it is possible to achieve. All Thales circuits and AESA tracking capabilities have been either disabled or removed," said Schnabel. "I employ only the top SIGINT experts in the world."

"Thales is interwoven with the firing sequence," said Mansour.

"Correct," said Schnabel. "Which is why for twenty Strela missiles that will cross Interpol borders without attention, the price is what it is. By the way, where do you intend to take these?"

"None of your business. Your terms are outrageous," said Mansour angrily. "I can purchase a single Strela for less than a hundred thousand dollars."

"You might be able to buy a Strela or two for that, and you will be picked up as soon as you cross into a monitoring country, and I'm talking about Echelon," said Schnabel tartly. "That's Canada, Australia, Europe, and of course, the United States. Let's face it, Mr. Mansour, if the missiles were intended for Iran you wouldn't need me. The price was explained. I have gone through great trouble to have the missiles here and to have them bleached. There are twenty in all. Technically they don't exist. All metadata and crystal code has been erased. But unless the money is wired immediately, I'm perfectly happy to not transact with you. The fact is, I shouldn't be doing this."

Mansour stared at Schnabel an extra few moments.

"Fine," said Mansour, putting his phone to his ear. "What is the price?"

"One hundred million dollars, as agreed," said Schnabel. "I pay my expenses in terms of flying here to meet you, et cetera."

Mansour's nostrils flared as he spoke into the phone yet stared at Schnabel across the dark runway. He wanted to put a bullet in him, and yet he couldn't, and the truth was, a hundred million was neither here nor there, for Mansour would've paid even more for the sanitized surface-to-air missiles.

Schnabel looked at his phone, opened to the Swiss bank account where he'd instructed Mansour to wire the money. When he saw the digits suddenly change, and "$100,000,000" appear, he nodded to a man at the perimeter of the airport.

Fifteen minutes later, a shiny white, clean-looking delivery truck rumbled toward the jet. The back of the truck opened and men in business suits started moving missiles to the jet. It took less than five minutes to stow them onto the plane.

As the luggage door of the Bombardier was closing, Schnabel approached Mansour.

"Now that you have them, what will you do with them?" said Schnabel.

Mansour said nothing, but he removed a pistol from a holster at his waist and trained it on Schnabel's head, then stepped closer. It was a Caracal .9mm semiautomatic handgun, with a silencer screwed into the muzzle.

"You will regret this," said Schnabel.

Mansour stepped closer and put the tip of the suppressor against Schnabel's forehead.

"I know I shouldn't kill you," said Mansour, "and your services are very valuable, but there can be no traces."

Schnabel was perspiring, and had a nervous look, but then he looked up at Mansour:

"I installed a control mechanism in one of the missiles," Schnabel said. "Think of it as an insurance policy. A ticking time bomb. Once it reaches a certain time, the missile is programmed to explode. I simply need to type in a six-digit number to disable it."

Mansour pushed the gun harder against Schnabel's forehead, though he didn't budge.

"Do it right now," said Mansour.

"Now why would I do that?" said Schnabel.

Mansour paused and stared at Schnabel. He realized he couldn't kill him. He put the gun back in the holster.

"How do I know you'll enter the code?"

"You don't," said Schnabel in a crisp German accent. "But unlike you, I live up to my agreements. If I didn't you wouldn't have your missiles, you miserable towelhead."

"Fine," said Mansour.

Mansour turned and started to walk back to the jet.

"I want another ten million," said Schnabel to Mansour's back, as he walked away. "Mental aggravation."

"I'm warning you."

Mansour turned, raising the pistol.

"Do you think you're the first madman I've ever dealt with?" said Schnabel, smiling. "I trust Iranians as far as I can throw them."

Mansour grinned. Slowly, he nodded yes as he took out his cell. "I deserved that, Mr. Schnabel," he said as he typed into the phone.

After more than a minute, Schnabel looked down, registering the payment.

"It's been a pleasure doing business with you," said Schnabel.

"You as well," said Mansour, across the dark tarmac. "I learned a valuable lesson tonight."

"What do you mean?" said Schnabel with a quizzical stare.

"Insurance," said Mansour. "In addition to ordering someone to pay you, I also directed one of my deputies. If my plane does not land without interference, you are to be hunted down and killed."

"Mutually assured destruction," said Schnabel, nodding matter-of-factly. "The foundation of any healthy relationship."

8

Rokan, thirty-three, was short—only five-foot-two—and wire thin. He wore thick square glasses. His hair was curly and brown, his skin was olive colored. Rokan was Iran's top computer scientist.

He was in a hotel suite in New York City. He was seated at a desk, with his laptop open. He was typing furiously into the laptop as, from the outside, the honking of horns and sound of traffic along Forty-second Street created a low din.

A bag of ice was in his lap.

Rokan had been a code developer and QC tester inside Iranian Cyber Defense Command when Stuxnet hit. The year was 2009. The computer virus, developed by the U.S. and Israel, targeted Iranian nuclear centrifuges at Natanz, penetrating a closed-loop system, disconnected from the outside world. Someone had brought the virus in on a thumb drive, by accident, but as intended by the designers of the virus. Stuxnet destroyed more than one thousand centrifuges. At the time, the centrifuges were processing HEU for Iran's "nonexistent" nuclear weapons program. Rokan was the one who identified the cyberattack, a novel zero-day attack on appliances that governed the behavior of the centrifuges, manufactured by Siemens, whose software the U.S. and Israel had attacked, unbeknownst to the German conglomerate who sold the appliances to Iran in violation of various international laws. When the Stuxnet virus hit, it caused the centrifuges to speed up to maximum velocity as, at the same time, it made the engineers overseeing the process believe exactly the opposite, that the centrifuges were spinning along as normal. A thousand centrifuges burned themselves into useless carapace shells of their former selves. It was too late to save the first thousand centrifuges—but Rokan was able to isolate the virus and kill it before it infected the other nineteen thousand centrifuges at Natanz. He was also able to pinpoint the Natanz employee who'd unwittingly brought the Stuxnet virus into what was supposed to be a digital network completely separated from the world outside the facility. The nuclear engineer who'd brought it in was taken outside and executed by gunfire less than ten minutes after Rokan had found the entry point for the virus. Rokan was immediately elevated within ICDC.

Seated inside the hotel suite, Rokan felt nausea and heaviness on his left side, and burning in his stomach. He picked up the bag of ice and held it to his torso. Rokan wasn't an ideologue. He wasn't even religious. But he was Iranian. He had pancreatic cancer. He had volunteered for this job. He'd approached Mansour about it.

Rokan knew that a vulnerability existed in the U.S. Federal Reserve, in particular within the digital security infrastructure, specifically in the software underlying the Fed's interrelationships with banks and countries around the world, a system called Fedwire. Rokan wrote a white paper on it as a student, highlighting the almost unbelievable fact that fully *95 percent* of the Fed's assets were digital. It was code. Zeros and ones. Only 5 percent was in cash. But Rokan's largely unread white paper at Tehran University was a cryptographic exercise in "zero-day theory." In essence, he posited a way to hack into the U.S. Federal Reserve system architecture and wipe out most of America's wealth, or at least screw things up for a long, long time.

Now, as he sat with ice against his torso, Rokan studied the schedule yet again. He had only to meet the four men in the lobby, then go to the Fed. But could he do it?

Suddenly, his cell vibrated. It was Mansour.

"I'm calling one last time. You will do fine," said Mansour calmly before Rokan had even said hello. "I forgot to ask, how is your pain, brother?"

"It's okay," said Rokan.

"I don't believe you," said Mansour. "I know it must be very hard. Rokan. But we have only a few hours left. I put my faith in you, my brother. This is the last time we will speak on earth, my great friend and fellow soldier. You have a mission to accomplish, and I know you will succeed. I will meet you in heaven."

9

Jenna tapped her ear. The call she'd been on with her mother redialed.

"You hung up on me," said Jenna's mother.

"Bad connection, Mother."

"As I was saying, it's your father's seventieth birthday. He would be—"

She cut her off.

"May I bring a friend?" said Jenna.

"Of course. Whom, may I ask? And does this individual work with you?" said Jenna's mom.

"You know I can't answer that question. He's just a friend, that's all," Jenna said. "Daddy will like him, so will you. His name is Dewey."

"Jenna, my dear," said her mother, "you may bring whomever you would like. The only thing that matters is that your daddy's precious girl, and my beautiful child, is there."

"Thanks, Mom," said Jenna. "He doesn't speak much, by the way."

"You'll be in your bedroom at the quarterdeck. You can put him wherever you choose."

"Can't hear you," said Jenna. "Must be the connection. See you tomorrow."

After Jenna hung up with her mother, she hit a button on her phone.

"Call Igor."

Dewey took an elevator several floors belowground. He went into NCS, a massive set of rooms like a private health club, reserved for only CIA operators. It was a large labyrinthine array of pools, saunas, sparring rings, weight racks, a firing range, track, basketball court, and a few other things. He found a surgeon, who cleaned up the wound, shot Dewey's arm up with a local anesthetic, and sewed up the gash. It required seventeen stitches in all.

Dewey took a shower and changed in the Special Operations Group locker room. It was a quiet place, and the lockers were spacious; each locker was thirty inches wide, and was done in dark mahogany. He found his locker. It didn't matter how he left it, the inside was invariably neatly taken care of by someone on the SOG staff. Inside was a line of hanging shirts, and a stack of pants, neatly folded. Dewey reached for a pair of blue khakis, pulled them on, then found a white button-down. He looked at the bandage on his shoulder. Blood was starting to soak through. He looked on the top shelf of his locker. Behind a toothbrush, toothpaste, deodorant, and a few other things, Dewey pulled out a roll of duct tape. He wrapped tape around the bandage, over his shoulder, a tight wrap, ripped the tape with his teeth, then put it back on the shelf.

As he pulled on the white shirt and buttoned it, his eyes went unconsciously back to the shelf. He saw a glimmer of glass. Dewey reached to the back and pulled out a bottle of Jack Daniel's. It was half gone. He unscrewed the cap and put the bottle to his lips, then took several gulps. He rescrewed the cap and put it back on the shelf, then headed for the meeting.

IO

In a beautiful, high-ceilinged co-op thirty-five stories above Madison Avenue on the Upper East Side of Manhattan, a thirty-one-year-old man with sharp Eastern Bloc features was staring at a large concave-shaped LCD screen. This was Igor. He had shaggy blond hair. He was watching a video, hacked off the restaurant's security cameras. He was isolating the figures in the video other than Dewey and running their faces against a variety of applications based on facial recognition. Like watching dominoes fall, he watched as the computer pushed the faces of the men sent to kill Dewey against a wide, multilevel, non-jurisdictional layer of metadata cued off millions of unique identifiers aggregated into a single person. Within half a minute one of the men popped a grid. Then, a few seconds later, the others did as well.

HUSSAIN, Assaf
MOHAMMED, Pierre
NUSSUF, Jean

Igor heard a low beep and tapped his ear.
"Hello?" said Igor.
"Igor, it's Jenna Hartford from Langley."

"Hello, Jenna."

"Hi," she said. "Where are you?"

"That seems rather forward of you," said Igor in a thick Russian accent, "but I must admit I find your curiosity intriguing and quite sexy."

"Oh for God's sake. I need you to run some analysis, Igor. I'm sending you access to some tight-access stuff, very recent."

"Alta Strada?" said Igor.

Jenna paused.

"How did you know already?" said Jenna. "No one has access to it."

"Apparently someone does. While you were flirting with me, I did some research," said Igor. "I ran the three Iranians against various databases. All three were Hezbollah. All three were members of Black Regiment, the main feeder into Hezbollah."

"I wasn't flirting with you," said Jenna. "What does it mean?"

"Well, it would seem Dewey has spent time in Iran but I didn't think he pissed someone off so much they'd risk sending Hezbollah into the U.S. Then again, he did steal a nuclear bomb? Actually, now that I think about it, that would certainly piss me off."

"Obviously, that's what the logical conclusion is, but what if they want to sideline him because they're planning something bigger?"

"That seems highly unlikely."

"I agree," said Jenna, "but even if the likelihood is under one percent, it's worth running down."

"I love it when you show off your mesmerizing intelligence, Jennifer."

"It's Jenna, not Jennifer. Can you run the numbers?"

"Yes, let me dig deeper into the three killers," said Igor. "If what you're saying is true, it would mean a level of planning that should be discernable in the metadata. If they're planning on something bigger I think it will show. I assume this is covered from a legal perspective."

"Yes, this is under an Agency NO/SEC Protocol now; do whatever you need to do. Time is of the essence. Financial information, travel information, what they bought at the small shop at some airport, how they paid for it. If there's a live operation going on, not only will Dewey's survival represent a blow to the planners of this operation but more importantly it might cause whatever plan they have to be initiated sooner."

"I agree. I'm on it," said Igor.

"I'm going into a debrief with Dewey, Hector, and Bill. I need anything real-time."

"I love it when you order me around with that accent," said Igor, a hint of frustration in his voice. "I'm going to go put on my leather pants before I start doing the analysis."

"I just threw up in my mouth," said Jenna. "Please, just get me whatever you have."

II

Dewey hit speed dial and the phone started ringing.

"Hey," said Tacoma. A din of music was in the background. "You gotta talk loud, I'm at a bar."

"Move someplace quieter."

"Okay, give me a sec."

After nearly a minute, Tacoma came back on the line.

"Yeah?" said Tacoma.

"Someone tried to take me out at that little Italian place near my house."

"The place with the good pizza?" said Tacoma.

"Yes, Rob."

"Seriously? Jesus. What, you try and cut in line or something?"

Dewey didn't answer.

"It sounds like you survived though?" said Tacoma. "That's something. Think positive!"

"Great analysis, dickhead," said Dewey.

"Who was it?" said Tacoma, taking on a serious tone.

"Iran," said Dewey.

"Well, you did sort of steal a nuclear bomb from them," said Tacoma. "I mean, not trying to criticize you or anything but what do you expect? I'd be pissed off too, you selfish bastard. Oh, and you stabbed that dude Paria in the neck. That must've hurt."

"Thanks, Rob," said Dewey. "Very helpful."

Tacoma laughed.

"Listen, the reason I'm calling is because you need to be aware of it," said Dewey. "Head on a fucking swivel, Rob."

"Got it. Thanks, brother."

12

In minutes, Igor had built a landscape of transactions spread across a geographic area.

He sat in one of the less spacious rooms in his twenty-million-dollar duplex condominium at the Carlyle. A curved screen was on top of a glass table. To the side, against the wall, a stack of data servers undulated with different colored lights.

Using a MATLAB algorithm he'd written years before—highly customized and designed to access data in various forms and through various channels he did not necessarily have permission to access—Igor was able to map out the signals activity of the three Iranians going back a month: travel patterns, purchases, meals.

The algorithm scanned every existing terabyte of security footage for a month against a facial recognition application. At the same time, by matching Interpol historical data and identifying points of intersection into the Interpol grid, Igor was then able to, in effect, create a storyboard of the movements and activities of the three Iranians.

They'd been in Washington only two days. Before that, they were in and around New York City for at least a month, moving constantly.

He reached for his cell phone.

13

Calibrisi's office was large and spacious. From the outside, the glass showed black mirror. But from the inside, the view was a forest of trees.

Interior walls, facing a rectangle of workstations, support staff for the highest level of the CIA, the inside part of the director's suite, were also glass though they were not mirrored.

Calibrisi's desk was on one side, directly as one entered. It was large—a blade of Ipe wood atop steel stanchions, with piles of paper and odd artifacts, such as a misshapen bullet and a cracked hand-held mirror, and several framed photos. Bookshelves were filled with books; on one side was the nonfiction side, filled with arcane volumes about particular phases in war and diplomacy. The other side was fiction, and was lined with first editions from writers Calibrisi admired.

The other side of the office was a spacious seating area: two matching ten-foot velvet sofas in tan, facing each other, and comfortable chairs at each end, all surrounding a rectilinear glass coffee table. By the time Dewey entered, there were several people there in addition to Calibrisi, Polk, and Jenna.

He made eye contact with Jenna, who was seated on one of the two sofas, a laptop in front of her, on her knees. She smiled at Dewey, then went back to typing.

He didn't recognize any of the other staffers, five in all, two male, three female.

Dewey looked at Calibrisi, who was behind his desk. Dewey walked behind the desk, out of earshot of the others.

"You look good," said Calibrisi, scanning Dewey.

Dewey's arm had a long, thin bandage on it. He didn't respond.

"How many stitches?" said Calibrisi, attempting to make conversation.

Dewey looked at Calibrisi with a blank expression. He thought it would be him, Calibrisi, Polk, and Jenna.

"How you doing?" said Calibrisi, taking a step closer.

"Is this really necessary?" said Dewey quietly.

Calibrisi stared at Dewey, saying nothing. Low conversation permeated the other side of the office. No one could hear them.

"Even if they were after me, so fucking what?" said Dewey, barely above a whisper. "It's no secret that my files are out there."

"What's your point?" said Calibrisi.

"Is all this necessary?" said Dewey, nodding toward the gathered CIA hierarchy. "Isn't it pretty goddam obvious what the hell happened?"

"You have no idea what just happened," said Calibrisi. "We need to know if this was simply a revenge hit on you—or the exploitation of a vulnerability in our last-line infrastructure."

Calibrisi nodded to his assistant, Lindsay, outside the office.

"What the hell does that mean?" said Dewey.

"This most likely was a revenge hit by Iran, but we don't know yet."

Dewey turned just as Lindsay entered with a bottle of Poland Spring water and three Advil, handing them to Dewey.

"Thanks," said Dewey. He unscrewed the cap and took a gulp, then threw down the Advil. He drank the rest of the bottle. Lindsay took it from him.

"You need to go on vacation," said Calibrisi. "We'll pay for it. Do whatever the hell you want. Everest. Tahiti. Maybe not Iran though. I want you to disappear for a few months."

Dewey walked to the big window, which showed a massive sweep of trees, leaves of red, orange, and yellow.

Calibrisi stepped into the middle of the office and sat down.

"Hit it," he said, nodding to Jenna.

The lights dimmed and a large LCD screen descended from the ceiling just in front of the windows. The screen was blank for a moment, and then, as Jenna typed, three photos dominoed across the screen. All three were male, Arab, and young. One showed a man in a military uniform, the next man was caught from afar in a surveillance photo, and the third man was cut from a black-and-white photo from *The New York Times*, where he was in the background— part of a security team—for Ali Suleiman, the Supreme Leader of Iran.

Names appeared beneath each photo.

HUSSAIN, Assaf
MOHAMMED, Pierre
NUSSUF, Jean

"Assaf Hussein, Pierre Mohammed, Jean Nussuf," said Jenna. "Three Hezbollah operators."

She paused. Several people looked at Dewey—who was standing near the door.

"Their target was Dewey," continued Jenna. "Alta Strada in Georgetown, which I'm guessing you frequent?"

"Yeah," said Dewey.

A photo of the outside of the establishment flashed, then a photo of the carnage after the attack.

"Well, in any event, you settled into a pattern and Iran locked it in," said Polk. "They sent in a kill team."

"Hussein is a Vienna Level Seven weapons expert, Mohammed has been in Gaza since the age of sixteen," said Jenna. "Nussuf is well known inside QUDS, a respected operative." Jenna paused. "The question is, why?" she said. "Why send in this level of firepower?"

"Revenge," said Mack Perry, the deputy director of SOG, in charge of running teams of CIA paramilitary, and spies, across the globe. Perry pointed at Dewey. "Dewey humiliated them. Stole a nuclear weapon. Their first nuclear weapon. They're pissed off."

"I would also mention the fact that Dewey killed Abu Paria," said Thorndike, one of Perry's deputies. "That's equally significant."

Jenna nodded. She looked around the room.

"I agree," said Angie Poole, another high-ranking CIA deputy director. She was in charge of the Middle East inside Special Activities Division. "It would be just like Suleiman or VEVAK to strike back."

"Why the timing?" said Calibrisi.

"Maybe it was the first time they were able to infiltrate all three men simultaneously," said Perry.

"Or the first time they had solid informatics on Dewey," said Jenna.

"Why the overwhelming force?" asked Calibrisi.

The room went silent.

Dewey was now sitting on the front of Calibrisi's large desk. He had a blank expression on his face.

"Obviously, they knew who they were dealing with," said Polk. "What's your opinion, Jenna?"

There was a long pause. Everyone looked at Jenna.

"Jenna?" said Calibrisi.

Jenna felt her phone vibrating. It was a text from Igor.

You may be right

Jenna quickly typed back:

$800k *missing* re GID HZBOLAH ?

"I don't know enough yet," Jenna said, putting her phone down. "Obviously it looks like revenge, but the foundation of a successful operation is subterfuge. The Iranians have developed innovative approaches to field work."

"What are you suggesting?" said Polk.

"Imagine that this is not about revenge," said Jenna. "That they moved on a priority target just before embarking on a larger attack. Perhaps this was an insurance policy, removing an important American agent. Dewey's papers are all over dark zones and he is considered a Tier One target. It might not be revenge. It could be a tactical move. This could be the first rung on a ladder."

All eyes were on her.

"That's absurd," said Angie Poole. "The Iranians don't have the capability to develop a matrix-pattern architecture like the one you're suggesting. The thought that they would try to sideline Dewey as part of a larger op is ridiculous. They were trying to kill him because they don't like him, period. If they're attacking the U.S. sovereign, they're not going to focus in on one individual. Iran came here to kill Dewey; it's a discrete operation. This was what it looks like: a kill hit on Dewey, a revenge hit."

"I agree with Angie," said Perry.

"Me, too," said Polk. "This was a revenge hit."

Calibrisi looked at Jenna.

"What are the odds that you're wrong?" said Calibrisi.

"Well, in my opinion, close to nil," said Jenna confidently, looking around the room. "But there is a first for everything."

As the office emptied out, Calibrisi got Dewey's attention and indicated he wanted him to remain behind the group. When everyone was gone Calibrisi closed the door.

He turned to Dewey.

"I want you to go away for a few weeks or maybe a few months," said Calibrisi. "Regardless of whether Jenna is right or wrong, the bottom line is you need to lie low. Go somewhere."

"No, thanks, Chief," said Dewey.

"It wasn't a suggestion."

Dewey shot Calibrisi a hard stare.

"It's an order?" Dewey said, half-grinning in disbelief.

"Yes," said Calibrisi.

"What if Jenna *is* right?" said Dewey. "What if an attack *is* under way?"

"She might be, but there are plenty of people who aren't being targeted by Hezbollah who can handle it," said Calibrisi. "They studied you and sent a team in once they found you. This is not the first time. It's just like Australia and . . . Argentina. I want you to leave town, right now, and get out of the country. That's outside the U.S., and also no UK or Europe. I need you dark for a few months. I already sent a NET team to your house. They're locking it down and I want you to go there, pack a bag, and buy a one-way ticket somewhere. Stay in the most expensive hotels in the world, charter a sailboat in Pago Pago, sit on a fucking beach, I don't care. Just get the hell out while we figure this one out."

"I'll take it under advisement," said Dewey.

Calibrisi caught Dewey's sarcasm.

"I'm not suggesting it," seethed Calibrisi, leaning in.

"Sounded like a suggestion," said Dewey, looking down at his shoulder, then meeting Calibrisi's glare.

"Go home, pack a bag, and disappear. That's an order."

Dewey looked at Calibrisi without emotion.

"I'm not leaving," said Dewey. He reached for the door and looked back at Calibrisi. "Get the NET team out of my house, or I'll get 'em out for you. I don't need a bunch of fucking baby-sitters."

Dewey walked down the hallway, ticked off, even a little irate, though he didn't show it. He was pissed off Hector would send an agency security squad to protect him, but also because of the pain in his arm. It ached.

He knew he shouldn't be pissed off at Hector but he nevertheless was. Sometimes he felt trapped inside the CIA's web of tentacles. He didn't want this life, not anymore. But as hard as he tried to get out of it, the more he felt himself being drawn back in.

As he walked by Jenna's office, he slowed, then stopped and looked in. Jenna's office was empty.

He leaned in and looked around. There wasn't much there, just a long, sleek crystal glass rectangle atop bronze stanchions—her desk—with a laptop on it, and a small green leather love seat in front of the desk. The love seat looked old and comfortable, light green leather with creases and dark spots, worn soft over decades, and was shaped in sloping curves. Dewey stared at it for a moment and then could smell the scent of perfume, a very faint wisp. Dewey's mind flashed to a grassy field—a sunny day in Argentina, beneath an ancient overhanging branch of a tree in the middle of nowhere. Just above the bend of a slow-moving, teal blue stream. The day Jessica Tanzer was killed by a bullet intended for him.

Don't let anyone in.

Dewey turned for the elevators, embarrassed that he'd even stopped—but then he felt a hand on his back.

"Dewey?"

He heard Jenna's soft British accent.

"Is everything all right?"

Jenna stepped past him into her office. She was half a foot shorter than him. She looked up at Dewey with a quizzical expression.

Dewey stood just inside the door as people from the meeting shuffled by.

"Yeah."

Jenna, leaning closer, asked, "Are you okay? You've been through what I imagine was a very traumatic experience." She placed a hand on Dewey's hand. "Will you sit down?" She pulled his hand, tugging him gently in.

Dewey stepped into Jenna's office and sat down on the leather sofa. It was as comfortable as he imagined. Jenna shut the door to her office.

She moved to the chair behind the desk and then stopped. She paused for a brief moment and then turned. She walked back and sat down on the love seat next to Dewey. There were several inches between them but they were close.

People walked by and could see in.

Dewey looked at Jenna.

"Oh, who bloody well cares what anyone thinks?" she said in a crisp English accent. "You asked me how I like living in the U.S.? I have no friends whatsoever, Dewey."

"You're working," said Dewey. "Hector said you're on loan from London. It's probably not the best time to make friends."

"Yes, but everyone is human."

"Not in this world," said Dewey.

"Yes, even in this world," said Jenna.

Dewey averted his eyes. He didn't say anything, but he glanced in her direction. Her bangs were cut in a straight line above her face. His eyes met hers for a brief moment.

"So where should I go?" said Dewey.

"Is that what Hector was saying?" said Jenna. "Leave the country?"

"Yeah."

"He cares about you," said Jenna. "Obviously someone is trying to kill you. He's just trying to save your life."

"You said this wasn't about revenge," said Dewey. "You think there's something else going on?"

Jenna looked at him. A frustrated look appeared on her face.

"What do I know?" she said. "I'm an architect. Everyone else thinks they were after you. An isolated incident."

"But you think there's something else coming?"

"Yes."

"So why would you want me to run away? If we're—"

"You're simply one individual," said Jenna. "Just because I'm right or might be right—and we *are* under attack—doesn't mean you, Dewey, have some sort of overarching responsibility! Revenge or attack, it doesn't matter: they're trying to kill you! Do you honestly not see that? They *tried* to bloody well kill you!"

Dewey sat in silence.

"Do you want a drink?" said Jenna.

Dewey said nothing.

"I happen to have a bottle of one-hundred-and-twenty-two-year-old Jameson," Jenna said, pointing to a shelf. "It was a gift. I don't really drink."

"Well," said Dewey, standing up. "Lucky for both of us, I do."

Dewey went to the bottle and uncorked it, then poured some into a glass. He took a large gulp. "Definitely good stuff."

"Jesus," she said, laughing out loud. She shook her head in a slightly shocked manner. "Oh my God," she said. A small grin appeared on her face.

Dewey refilled his own glass, then poured a second glass with just a little. He handed the second glass to Jenna. She took it and, as she looked at Dewey, took a small sip.

They were seated next to each other, and Jenna looked down and realized her leg was touching his.

"I know that this was a designed operation," said Jenna, "and while it may not have worked out for them, they had you. I know enough to recognize a very good architect. He or she will have a secondary team waiting in the wings. Hector knows it because he would do the same."

"I'm not running away," said Dewey.

"Why not?" said Jenna, taking a swig of Jameson. "You've run away in the past."

"What's that supposed to mean?"

"I'm sorry, but the first time, to the North Sea? An offshore oil platform? The Exxon project off the coast of Africa? Capitana? Australia? Castine? Argentina?"

"I didn't run away."

Jenna nodded to Dewey. "Even though I don't know you I see patterns. I know it's hard for you, but today was just another chapter in an ongoing architecture," said Jenna, her face becoming abruptly sad. "An architecture of those who want to kill you."

Dewey downed the glass and leaned forward, then poured himself another glass.

"So you agree with Hector?" he said.

"No," said Jenna, taking another small sip of whiskey.

"I thought you just said that I should leave?" said Dewey.

"No. I mean, oh, I don't know," said Jenna.

Dewey stared at her. She had a slightly dazed look on her face. Her eyes were a hazy, almost pure green. They were sitting together on the leather George Smith love seat, in Jenna's office. The back of Jenna's hand was on his knee, as if by accident. She was already a little tipsy after two or three sips of whiskey.

She smiled. Her hand, the back of which had been on his knee, reflexively moved and her hand found his knee and held it.

Jenna stared at Dewey and took a small sip. Her eyes shifted and looked at the ground, as if she was calculating something. She looked back at Dewey, shaking her head no, or more accurately, *What am I even doing?*

"I have an invitation," said Jenna. Her hand went from his knee to his hand. "From me, and I don't want you to assume I think anything, or am inviting you other than because I think, tactically, it's your best option. But how would you like to go to my father's seventieth birthday party tomorrow? It's on a boat, off Long Island. You'll have your own bedroom."

Dewey exhaled.

"A boat? Like a Boston Whaler?"

Jenna giggled.

"No, it's slightly bigger."

"How big?"

"Big."

"I know your family is from aristocracy," said Dewey.

"No control over that," said Jenna. She took her hand from Dewey and shot it to her bangs and swooped them to the side.

Don't let anyone in.

Dewey had read Jenna's file. Jenna had designed two separate operations that Dewey worked. In both operations he'd come a hair's width from death. Both operations were massively complex. Both had succeeded. Dewey's eyes went emotionless and cold. He didn't say anything.

Finally, Jenna broke the silence:

"Is that a no?"

"I appreciate the offer," said Dewey. "I think I'd probably just end up embarrassing you."

Involuntarily, Jenna frowned.

"Have I ever said anything that would in any way make you think that I would or could possibly think that?" she asked.

There was a long silence.

"No, you haven't," said Dewey.

"Have I in any way indicated that I have anything, wealth or whatever?" she asked in a sharp, cutting, elegant British accent. "Have I ever done that? Do you think that I'm like that?"

"Well," said Dewey. "You did say something about firing your chauffeur for not having any crumpets."

Jenna's face went from offended to a smile.

"The truth is, my parents think I have friends, that I'm social, and popular, and am attending 'glamorous diplomatic parties,' and, well, Dewey, the truth is, I don't have even one friend. Not one. In six months I haven't even been on one date," she said, her voice confident, not apologetic, though quiet. "It might seem incredible, but outside Bill and Hector, you're the only person I even know, and I work for them. As pathetic as it sounds, you're my best friend."

Dewey's cold eyes softened, if ever so slightly.

"You're mine too," he said.

Jenna burst into laughter.

Dewey laughed with her for a moment, looking into her green eyes, and then he heard the voice:

Don't let anyone in.

Dewey pretended to be looking at the floor in front of him, yet he found her in his peripheral vision. She was looking at him.

Dewey knew he couldn't accept Jenna's invitation. If she was right, and Iran was striking the country, he wasn't going to go hang out on some British royal yacht; after all, America had kicked Britain's ass, and it was just something he instinctively didn't want to do.

Hang out with British people, especially royals. It was an invitation to her yacht. He just couldn't sacrifice his morals like that.

Then again, he worked with her. Maybe she was really serious and it was a good idea to get away? No doubt it would be a sweet setup. He'd been on many yachts like this, but always in a tactical wet suit, packing guns. This would be the first time he was actually invited.

But no, Dewey couldn't allow himself to care about another person. Even now, he still found Jessica's voice in his head at night.

But his eyes kept getting drawn back to Jenna, her eyes, and how her hair feathered above her ears. He fought to keep from looking at her, but he was only partially successful. Her face was intelligent, warm, and she was showing Dewey a part of it she'd never shown anyone, despite the fact that she barely knew him.

When he looked at her, he felt lost for a moment.

Again came the voice, more insistent this time:

You killed her. You killed Jessica.

"I can't," Dewey said, standing up. Jenna remained seated.

He downed the remaining whiskey in his glass and put it down on the desk. He walked to the door.

Dewey turned and looked at Jenna. She was still seated on the couch.

She had on a sleeveless tan, red, and blue plaid Burberry blouse. Her arms were thin but not too much so, lithe, sculpted, smooth, all the way up to her shoulders. Beneath her linen slacks her feet were clad in white penny loafers. Dewey was at the door and she looked back at him with a relaxed, lackadaisical expression.

"I understand," said Jenna.

She took another sip of Jameson, and showed Dewey a mischievous smile.

Dewey said nothing else. As he pulled the door open, he looked back and watched as she swept her hand across her forehead, pushing her bangs aside. Her face went into a sultry blankness. Jenna stared Dewey down from the couch, holding his gaze with a smoldering energy, daring him to look away. Finally, he did, casting his eyes to the floor, even as his mouth formed into a smile.

She waited a moment, until he glanced back at her, unable to wipe the shit-eating grin off his face.

"So, does that mean you'll go, Dewey Andreas?" she said softly.

"Sure," said Dewey.

"Pick you up in a couple hours," said Jenna.

14

A half hour after Dewey left, Jenna picked up her keys and walked out. She needed to get home and change, and pack, and maybe take a shower, before she picked up Dewey.

Her head went warm when she thought about picking him up, going to the boat with him, having dinner, seeing him in the morning. It went from her head to her chest up and back through her head, like a wave. She felt it, and then remembered she couldn't.

"Stop it," she said aloud to herself angrily. "This is about work."

Well, sort of, I suppose, she thought.

She dialed Igor back as she walked to the elevators.

Igor began speaking, not saying hello:

"I ran down the eight hundred thousand, that was actually quite helpful," said Igor in his sharp Russian accent. "These three have been in the United States for at least a month."

"Where?" said Jenna.

"They're all in New York City," said Igor. "They move around a lot, these three. Who even knows if there are others? They sleep in shitty motels, always moving. There's no way anything but the raw signals metadata could catch them. Police, FBI, there would be no way even a great detective would find them. Only the metadata shows the trail."

"What's the trail?"

"A lot of movement. A lot of cash. That's where I am. These guys are highly trained. I'm working on it but they were stealthy."

"Why Dewey?" said Jenna.

"They spent two days in Washington. The rest of it in and around New York. I think Iran developed intel on Dewey and someone told them to go kill him. Revenge for Paria."

"What were they doing the other twenty-eight days?" Jenna said.

"They would spend entire days taking cash out of ATMs all over the city, even in New Jersey and Connecticut. Then they disappear. Off the grid for a day or two. They spent eight hundred thousand dollars in cash. On what? I don't know," said Igor.

"Can you find out?" said Jenna.

"Perhaps."

"Perhaps isn't good enough."

"Jenna, I kid. Figuring things out is my middle name."

15

Mansour climbed back aboard the Bombardier, now topped off with fuel and loaded with Russian-made shoulder-fired surface-to-air missiles and several shoulder-fired launchers.

But the interaction with Schnabel had not gone as smoothly as he hoped, and now he worried about the German arms merchant. It was no secret that Schnabel sold weapons and weapons systems to anyone with the money. A potential buyer had to be able to afford his prices, which were exorbitant. But Schnabel was also a buyer and paid in cash for virtually anything, from a box of bullets to a kilo of prerefined Siberian uranium, and everything in between. Mansour felt a vague electric paranoia, a cold feeling in his spine. Perhaps Schnabel would blow up the plane anyway? Or perhaps he hadn't even put a bomb in one of the missiles? The doubt was what created the paranoia, and it had all been self-inflicted. The last thing he needed right now was to worry.

He sat in a wide black leather seat and reclined. He ultimately realized that it didn't matter, it was not worth worrying about, because if Schnabel blew up the plane he'd be dead, and if he didn't it was all back to the original plan, and he'd probably be dead in a few hours anyway. Mansour was tired and his eyes became droopy as he stared down at the North African coast—dotted in lights—then saw black just as the jet soared out above the Mediterranean. He finally fell asleep, drifting into a deep slumber. It was his first sleep in almost two days.

Then he heard loud, insistent beeping coming from his cell. He picked it up and looked at the text. It was a video. It was a short clip, in dark tones, but with enough light to show what was occurring. The video was taken from the ground, on the floor, a sideways angle, in a shaky hand. The focus of the video showed a large man with thick, dark hair, holding a submachine gun, then firing, first to the left, then to the person taking the video, and then it abruptly cut out. They'd retrieved the video from Nussuf's phone.

He recognized the man. It was Andreas. It was Mansour's first time seeing video of the man Nussuf and his team had been sent to kill in Washington.

The idea to kill Andreas had come from Mansour—it was his design, and it had failed. This was the American thug who killed Abu Paria in Macau. He replayed the video again, and again.

Andreas was large, as advertised, and he towered over the screen in the short clip. He swept the submachine gun at Nussuf with calm and, clearly, precision—before the clip ended.

Mansour felt a warm spike of adrenaline run up his back. He felt fury as he watched Andreas kill his own men.

Mansour had put his best three lieutenants on it, but the mission had failed—and three men he had trained from when they were young recruits, teenagers, were now dead, all killed by the man they'd been sent to eliminate.

Mansour felt guilt, though not because he didn't go. Rather, he felt guilt because he should've gone. He should've been the one to confront Andreas. He should have known. Now Nussuf, Hussein, and Mohammed were dead.

He shut off his phone and closed his eyes. He asked aloud for help to fall back asleep, talking to his God in a whisper, yet all he could see now was Ward 6.

It was at Ward 6 when Mansour had caught the eye of Abu Paria, the head of all Iranian military and intelligence activities. That was when Paria first caught wind of Mansour and plucked him out of a life of crime and thrust him into a life of terrorism.

A juvenile detention facility in Moscow, one of sixteen such prisons, Ward 6 was a hard place, long concrete buildings with bunks and fluorescent lights, then darkness, and guards patrolling along the bunks with rifles and dogs, even at night, always they were there. There were no weekends at Ward 6.

Mansour hadn't done anything to deserve it, other than be the son of a teacher during a time when anyone could be accused of anything and killed for it by a thirty-year-old self-appointed judge, jury, and executioner. One of them shot Mansour's father in their living room, for no reason, in front of Mansour, his brother, and his mother.

When Mansour was fourteen, a year after they shot his father, his mother died of cancer. He was sent to Ward 6 by a neighbor on the local volunteer committee, a man who thought Mansour needed the state's attention and watch. On his second day at Ward 6, he was punched in the face by an older boy. On the morning of his third day, he awoke shivering on his bottom bunk, his blanket missing.

Most of the teenagers at Ward 6 were the children of hardened Iranian criminals, tough boys who grew up in the slums of Danesh, Baghestan, Mellat Park, Qods, or one of the districts, or one of the many other slums surrounding Tehran like a noose.

He learned to get along. To survive. By fifteen, Mansour had a knife of his own, a *skin*, a piece of metal he'd ripped quietly from the meal room, which he sharpened at night against the concrete floor, and kept nearby, tied with string beneath his left forearm. For some reason, the others at Ward 6 had never taken to Mansour. It was rumored his mother had been French. In April of that year, Mansour was attacked in his sleep, even as armed guards were inside the dormitory. Two older boys, one with a wire. They were going to scare him—or choke him to death. But Mansour had seen them coming. A stitch of undulating shadow in the light from the yard. He heard them approach.

In silence, he stabbed the first one in the chest, straight through his heart, then garroted the second one, dragging the blade across his neck. He dragged them back to their bunks and placed them on their beds, all in silence, in the secrecy of the night, without being seen by the guards. The other boys alerted the guards and Mansour spent a year in solitary confinement. When he came out he was sixteen years old. After a year of doing nothing but push-ups and sit-ups, angry that he'd been punished for defending himself, Mansour now stalked Ward 6 like a predator.

A year in solitary confinement had hardened him, and he grew into his frame despite the lack of food. He reemerged into the general population of the juvenile facility as if coming in from the jungle.

A week after being let out into the general population at Ward 6, at the beginning of mandatory exercise, Mansour stepped into the prison yard and registered someone to his right. It was a glint of metal. A boy with a weapon in his hand was watching Mansour. It was the younger brother of one of the prisoners he'd killed.

Mansour's eyes swept left. There were two others whispering to each other conspiratorially, one of them eyeing Mansour. He turned and ran, charging toward the entrance, but it slid suddenly shut. He could see the eyes of the guards watching the coming violence from behind the gate.

What Mansour did next was why Paria came to recruit him.

Mansour turned and entered the yard as several of the juvenile delinquents converged on him. They were shouting, like a mob.

Mansour charged at the brother of the boy he'd stabbed. He was coming at Mansour at a jog, with a hateful look on his face. In his hand, he clutched a knife.

The others were coming as well, at least a dozen, from every direction.

As Mansour freed the metal skin tied to his forearm, the boy swung first, slashing at Mansour, but Mansour ducked and stabbed his blade into the boy's stomach. He pulled it quickly out, then swung blindly behind him, hitting another one of the attackers in the face, cutting through his jaw and mouth. Blood spilled down to the concrete. The younger brother was on the ground now, bleeding out, and Mansour grabbed the knife from his hand. He slashed both of his arms wildly, striking at whoever was closest, ducking and moving when he sensed someone on him, constantly swinging the blades and stabbing as deeply as the blade and his strength would allow.

The sirens in the yard finally went off, followed by rifle fire, into the air, and yelling from the guards. When the situation calmed, Mansour was standing in the middle of bodies. His hands and arms were coated in blood. Mansour killed nine people that day.

By dinnertime, Mansour had been picked up at Ward 6 in a white van and taken to a facility south of Tehran, a training facility for Hezbollah.

As the luxurious jet began its initial descent toward the coastline of America, cutting miles high above Manhattan, Mansour stared out the window at the country, at the city, at the island, he was about to attack.

They would first destroy the tunnels into Manhattan. The vehicle tunnels. There were four: Holland, Lincoln, Queens-Midtown, and Brooklyn-Battery. It was by far the easiest part of the mission. The explosives were in vans, already set to be delivered.

Active shooters would come next. By Mansour's count, more than five hundred embedded Iranians as well as Lebanese on borrow from Hamas, and several Tunisians, Moroccans, and Egyptians, heeding a call they'd long ago agreed to in order to be allowed to come to the U.S. This was the unknown. Would they sacrifice their lives for a higher purpose? Mansour believed they would.

The bridges. There were so many. The bridges. Mansour's simple insight: that the bridges would take care of themselves as people fled the island. A simple notion but powerful: the bridges would quickly be jammed with abandoned cars and screaming people, as his embedded soldiers moved on foot with submachine guns, mowing down anything that moved.

Within the chaos, Mansour had designed a mushroom cloud of random violence atop which could be placed a sleek geometric pattern of precise and ultimate harm to the U.S.

The attack could only happen after the president of the United States arrived at the UN. Then and only then would the plot be instigated. If executed properly, President J. P. Dellenbaugh would be trapped inside the UN. Any efforts to rescue him would be met with lethal violence. The PZR Strelas stowed in the luggage compartment of the Bombardier would be delivered to a construction site—a field—next door to the UN. The terrorist was a famed Hamas shooter named Hamash. He'd been in New York City for a week now, sleeping in the shadows.

Mansour himself would lead the team into the UN: two buses filled with elite Hezbollah gunmen. They would smash the security at the UN in the mouth. Mansour believed that half his men would die upon the initial takeover of the first floor of the tower. But by sheer numbers they would overwhelm a UN security set they'd studied for months, along with various members of the Secret Service, FBI, and NYPD, and take the entrances with a combination of surprise, overwhelming numbers, and superior firepower—at least in the first two to three minutes, when it mattered.

What occurred next was on Mansour and Mansour alone. The timing would need to be perfect.

Maybe that was why he couldn't sleep.

Mansour needed to create a distraction just as the buses arrived, in the minutes following the destruction of the tunnels. Mansour needed to distract them as Hezbollah gunmen swarmed the facility.

Mansour knew they would have to kill hundreds in order to kill one. A team would move to a floor above Dellenbaugh, then work its way down as Mansour worked his way up. Trapping the president and killing him.

Mansour couldn't sleep as the jet moved west across the sky, above the Atlantic Ocean. It was because he also saw the flaws in the design of the attack. If Hamash was unable to shoot down the helicopters as they approached the UN, Dellenbaugh would soon be rescued.

In addition, Dellenbaugh was not a typical target. He was an athlete, a fighter, who just happened to be a politician. An excellent politician. But he was a fighter first.

16

After returning from Langley, Dewey had gone for a run up Rock Creek Parkway into Maryland, then returned via the streets of upper Georgetown. He took it at a fast pace, more as a way to clear his mind and collect his thoughts, letting the pain cut to the core, though by the time he was five miles away he felt his body reacting in a way he knew wasn't good. He was out of shape. Not dramatically so, but he hadn't run in weeks and with each step he felt the beer, Jack Daniel's, cheeseburgers, steaks, and occasional cigarette with which he'd fueled his body.

Dewey was standing in his kitchen, shirtless, dressed in a pair of running shorts, leaning into the sink, his head beneath the faucet. He was drenched in perspiration, still breathing heavily fifteen minutes later. The duct tape was holding. He hadn't seen a trickle of blood the entire time.

Dewey knew the cobwebs could either be kicked off gradually, with less effort and less pain, or suddenly, and he always chose the latter. Dewey didn't enjoy pain but he understood it and he'd long ago discovered his body's capacity for enduring it, compartmentalizing it, isolating it in a part of his mind and divorcing it from his actions. In Delta training so many years ago, Dewey had twice run himself into unconsciousness. Compared to that pain, a hard run in an out-of-shape body, with the occasional dry heave into the bushes, was nothing.

He had his head beneath the faucet and was chugging cold water from the tap. After more than a minute of gulps, he felt something rubbing against the back of his legs. It was large, soft, and furry. He looked down and saw Wrigley. Wrigley was Dewey's dog, a massive Saint Bernard, covered in brown, white, and black fur. A dog Dewey had rescued, a big dog with a square head and a perennial smile. Dewey shut off the water and turned, giving Wrigley a scratch on his block of a head as the dog licked Dewey's sweat-covered leg.

"Wrigley, that's gross, dude," said Dewey, though Wrigley kept right on trying to help dry off Dewey's leg. Dewey knelt and let Wrigley slather his tongue across his face, shutting his eyes, enduring it.

"Okay, Wrigley, good boy," he said, standing back up and reaching for a paper towel. He wiped slobber from his face. "You want a snack?"

Dewey opened the refrigerator and looked for something to eat. The refrigerator held little except for a few six-packs of beer and some random items he'd aggregated on those rare occasions when he was in town and had thought about making himself a meal. There wasn't much—some cheddar cheese, eggs, ground beef, milk—and as he discovered, it was all several months past expiration.

Dewey took out two cans of beer, opened both, chugged one, then took a sip from the other.

He shut the refrigerator door.

"I guess maybe we won't have a snack," said Dewey. "We could both probably skip a few meals anyway."

Wrigley looked up at him, his huge tongue dangling down as he panted.

Dewey put the beer down. He leaned down and wrapped his hands beneath the large dog and lifted him up into the air, holding him. It looked awkward, but no one was around and Dewey didn't care, and Wrigley didn't seem to mind.

Dewey nuzzled his sweaty face next to Wrigley's snout. Wrigley's warm, gooey tongue slapped across Dewey's forehead, eyes, and nose. Dewey just shut his eyes and endured it, laughing.

When the doorbell chimed, Wrigley started barking. Dewey put him back down. He glanced at his watch. It was eight thirty.

"Uh-oh," he said to Wrigley.

Dewey walked to the door and opened it. Jenna was standing on the brick doorstep. She was dressed in a pink dress suit, the bottom part shorts that went to the middle of her thighs, with a wide leather belt across her torso. He looked at her for a few seconds, trying not to check her out but not being successful at it.

"Hi, Jenna," said Dewey.

"Hi," said Jenna. "Is this your place?"

The front entrance foyer of the town house was high-ceilinged, with coffered woodwork, ornate, old-fashioned wallpaper of a hunting scene, and gorgeous furniture. Yet whatever interior design awards the stunning town house perhaps might've won before Jessica died and left the town house to Dewey were long since obliterated by the current occupant. Dewey's eyes followed Jenna's as she registered large piles of mail, weapons, ammo, dog toys, a dog bed, and what appeared to be dirty clothing. A half dozen submachine guns lay on the ground to the left, along with a cache of knives and a stack of cardboard boxes filled with ammunition. At the far wall was a rolltop desk, opened, yet stacked with handguns and boxes of bullets.

"Yeah. Come on in. My, ah, house cleaner quit a few weeks ago."

Dewey's eyes involuntarily glanced down. Jenna's legs were smooth and defined. She had on open-toed high-heeled sandals with white leather straps that weaved up her calves to her knees. Her hair was neatly braided atop her head, a honeycomb of blond hair that revealed Jenna's face, though her bangs remained dangling across her forehead.

At the same time he looked at her, Jenna took Dewey in.

He had on only a pair of shorts.

He was half a foot taller than her and she looked up at his face, then her eyes scanned his thick chest. There was little subtlety to him. Dewey was a wall, layered in muscle, and he towered over Jenna, but not intentionally; if anything it was calming and safe having him there, and yet Jenna noticed evidence of conflict, scars both large and small; from bullets and knife blades alike.

"I guess you're not ready?" Jenna said.

"I lost track of time."

"If you've had second thoughts, I understand."

"No, not at all," said Dewey. "I went for a run but apparently I'm not as fast as I used to be. Can you give me a few minutes?"

"Yes, of course."

Suddenly, Wrigley inserted his large black and brown head between them. He came up to Jenna's torso. She smiled and reached out for him.

"That's Wrigley," said Dewey. "Wrigley, this is Jenna."

Jenna clutched Wrigley's head as he sniffed her. She was smiling, then she looked at Dewey.

"Should you maybe put a shirt on? Maybe even take a shower?"

Dewey laughed.

"Oh, yeah, of course. I'll be right down. Make yourself at home."

Jenna watched Dewey walk upstairs, trailed by Wrigley.

She looked around the first floor of the town house. There was a large round table in the middle of the entrance foyer. A white vase sat in the middle of the table, with stems of flowers now brown and dead, hanging listlessly. She walked to the table. Around the vase were magazines, covered in dust. A pile of newspapers. On top, a yellowed *Wall Street Journal*.

Jenna roamed around the downstairs. She felt a lump in her throat. The kitchen looked as if it had never been used. She opened cabinets and found plates, pots and pans, and, in other cabinets, a spice rack and then boxes of pasta and cans of tomatoes. They, too, looked as if they'd been there a long time.

A small, intimate room off the kitchen had walls of deep, soothing yellow, a large flat-screen television, shelves filled with books, a luxurious sofa and club chairs facing the screen. Beneath the screen, on the ground, was a flannel shirt, crumpled up, and an empty Jack Daniel's bottle. Jenna knelt and picked it up.

Her eyes were drawn to a shelf behind one of the sofas. There were photos and she walked slowly to them. The first she picked up had a silver frame. Inside the frame was a picture of a woman, a head shot of a stunning woman with auburn hair, green eyes, and a chiseled, elegant, dignified look.

The next frame was also silver and showed Dewey with the former president of the United States, Rob Allaire, inside the Oval Office, as he wrapped a medal around Dewey's neck and Jessica looked on from the side, smiling. A medal awarded for stopping the infamous Lebanese terrorist Alexander Fortuna.

A third photo made Jenna fight back emotion. Unlike the others, it was in a wooden frame. It was a picture from a dinner somewhere, and there were plates and wineglasses, candles, and, in the background, a sweeping lawn, lit by lanterns around the edges of an outdoor terrace. She recognized Hector, of course, and Rob, and Katie Foxx—and then there was Jessica in Dewey's lap, folded into his arms, her head tucked against his neck.

She didn't like to think about all the cruelty in the world, the randomness of events that were so final, so unfair, so brutal, but she'd watched as her husband was killed by a car bomb meant for her, and for whatever reason the photo made her swallow hard.

Dewey took a quick shower, dried off, and stepped into the bedroom. Wrigley was watching him from a dog bed in the corner of the room.

The bedroom was massive, with ceilings of antique brown beams, and four large windows that looked down on a cozy, cobblestone Georgetown street, across from other town houses of historic brick, flower boxes filled with blooms, brass lanterns burning natural gas and flickering inside glass-and-gold sconces.

Jessica had bequeathed the home to him. It's where they would've lived. Now it was his, but it was like a sarcophagus to him. It was only Wrigley that made him able to stay in the town house.

Still, despite the hard memories, no one could walk through the historic, perfectly decorated, eight-bedroom town house and think it was anything but gorgeous, including the Chippendale dresser Dewey now approached, set before red Farrow & Ball wallpaper.

He tried not to think about it, willing thoughts of the past from his mind. Then a drop of blood dripped from his arm to the carpet—and he remembered the attack. He stared at himself in the mirror.

War that has no end.

Dewey went to the dresser and removed a few items—pants, shorts, T-shirts, button-downs, a toothbrush and tube of toothpaste—and packed them into a small leather weekend bag. He opened the top drawer and removed a bottle of Jack Daniel's and tucked it in. He pulled on a pair of khakis and a short-sleeved white button-down. He put his watch on—a green beveled Rolex with a gold band, a gift from Tacoma—and stepped into a pair of Bean boots. Dewey turned around and looked at Wrigley. He had moved and was now on the rug next to Dewey's bed. Wrigley was looking up at Dewey with a sad look. He knew Dewey was about to leave again.

An Agency-approved and -hired dog walker came every day, whether Dewey was there or not. He knew Wrigley was taken care of. Sometimes he was gone at a moment's notice. That's why he had the dog walker. Dewey knelt next to the huge Saint Bernard and scratched him with two hands, then leaned closer and kissed Wrigley on the head.

"You're a good boy," said Dewey.

Wrigley leaned up and gave Dewey a big lick across his face.

"Thanks," said Dewey, standing.

From a bedside table, Dewey removed a worn leather sheath and strapped it around his ankle. He found a shoulder holster and strapped it beneath his armpit. He counted four mags, took three, and put them in the duffel. He took the last mag in his left hand and closed the drawer. He opened the drawer beneath and took out a handgun—pistol, .45 caliber, semiautomatic, with a patina of scratches and sheen from oil. Colt M1911 A1. He slammed in the mag and tucked it into the holster. He found a blue blazer in the closet and pulled it on. Finally, he went back to the dresser and opened the top drawer. He took out a long cylindrical object made of black alloy, a custom-made suppressor, and pocketed it.

From under his pillow, Dewey took a knife: it was a fixed-blade, double-serrated, eight-inch Gerber combat blade. He ran his thumb across the ornate script carved into one side of the blade.

Gauntlet

A gift from his classmates in Ranger School.

On the other side of the blade, his initials, etched in block letters:

D.A.

He tucked the knife into the sheath at his ankle and walked to the door.

Jenna was looking at the photo of Dewey and Jessica when she heard Dewey enter. She turned and saw him.

"I'm sorry," she said, putting the photo back on the shelf.

"For what?" said Dewey.

"Prying? Snooping?"

"You already know everything about me."

"No, I don't," she said. "She was so beautiful."

Dewey smiled. "Yes, she was very pretty and smart, like you."

Jenna blushed. There was an awkward moment of silence.

"Shall we get going?" Jenna said.

"We shalleth," said Dewey, in a very inaccurate and exaggerated British accent. "Forthwith, milady! Call my footman and get my trusty steed!"

Jenna shook her head, laughing. "You really apparently think you're funny?" she said.

"You seem to be laughing," said Dewey.

• • •

Jenna slammed the gas and shot the white Porsche 911 C4S Targa down the block, then left, and was soon moving across Washington at a fast clip.

"So, is there anything I should know?" said Dewey.

"This isn't an operation, Dewey," said Jenna, "and by the way, thank you for coming."

"You don't have to thank me, Jenna," said Dewey. "I'm glad you invited me. I'm just saying, I wouldn't mind some basic information."

"Like what?"

"Like, what are your parents' names? How many people will be there? Who are they? How long is the boat? How many people are there in China and what are their names? What's the meaning of existence? When a tree falls in a forest and no one is there to hear it, does it make a sound? Basic stuff."

Jenna giggled as she drove.

"I can answer some of those questions," she said. "The boat is two hundred and forty-three feet long. I don't know how many people will be there. There are twenty-eight staterooms but my mother doesn't like it when it's overcrowded, so I'm guessing six or seven couples. And yes, a tree makes a sound."

"Who are they?"

"Friends from England, maybe some New York society friends of theirs. My father and mother cruise the American coast every summer,' Jenna added. "Tomorrow is his seventieth birthday. I promised my mother I would be there."

"Where's the boat?"

"Off the coast of Long Island."

"And what should I call them?" said Dewey.

"Just call them Bobby and Jemima," said Jenna. "That's all. My father is the kindest person I know. My mother can be a bitch but it's only because she loves me."

"Jemima?" said Dewey. "Did you just say Jemima?"

"Yes, why?"

"Nothing, just seems like an unusual name."

"It's been in our family since the Reformation."

"Does she make good pancakes?" said Dewey.

Jenna glanced at him with a confused look.

"Um, I don't know, I suppose, yes, but forgive me but that seems like a slightly random question," said Jenna.

"Will Mrs. Butterworth be there?" said Dewey.

"Who? What are you even talking about?"

Dewey started uproariously laughing at his own joke.

"I see you really do find yourself quite amusing." Jenna said, holding back a smile.

"That was funny," said Dewey defensively.

"I don't understand but maybe you can explain it to me someday? Now stop laughing at yourself. Whatever it was, it was not that funny," she said as she abruptly started giggling, not at the joke, but at how Dewey was still laughing at something so silly and stupid.

They both laughed for nearly a minute, not exactly understanding why; it was more about the sound of each other's laughter and the knowledge that they weren't laughing at the same thing but just laughing.

They were on the highway for a while longer, speeding toward Andrews, and Dewey looked absentmindedly out the window as Jenna drove.

"I'm so glad you came," Jenna said politely.

Dewey looked out the front of the car, not responding.

There was a long stop in the conversation, several minutes, as Jenna drove and Dewey sat quietly in the passenger seat. It was hard to comprehend the fact that he was about to go somewhere and it would have nothing to do with work. To just escape for a few days and get away from everything.

"I'm glad, too," said Dewey. "Thank you for inviting me."

Dewey remembered what Tacoma said. He put his past thoughts behind him and just thought about the moment where he was. Jenna had on a very faint trace of perfume, or something that smelled good.

It was Dewey who finally broke the silence.

"So, do your parents know I'm coming?" Dewey said.

"Yes, of course," said Jenna. "I told my mother I was bringing a friend."

Dewey nodded.

"Just so you know, my mother is a nut and thinks I should've been married a week after my husband died," she said. "She already has us married with three children. That has nothing to do with you, as she doesn't even know your name yet. She's just a crazy but lovable old loon and I adore her. My father, however, is sane and will immediately love you . . . ummm . . . I mean like you."

"He won't love me?" said Dewey with a sad face.

"Oh my God," Jenna giggled. "I'm trying to bloody drive, don't make me laugh again!"

"So she's going to think we're a couple?" Dewey said.

"Yes," said Jenna, "but before you start inflating your already overinflated ego she would think that if I brought a cadaver."

"Got it," said Dewey. "So I'm basically a notch above a cadaver? I'm honored."

Jenna burst out laughing. "Stop."

"Shouldn't we stay in the same room?" said Dewey.

Jenna shook her head as she weaved in and out of traffic, smiling.

"I'm just saying, if your parents think I'm your date, we need to own it."

Jenna swerved to the side of the highway and slammed the car to a sharp halt. They were in the breakdown lane along the highway. It was dark outside. Cars and trucks sped by at a furious clip. She looked at Dewey.

"I know you're kidding," she said.

Dewey leaned toward her and his lips met Jenna's, as his hand found her thigh. Her eyes shut. Her lips were soft, and there was a cool, light taste, and her thigh was smooth and bare, and she shut her eyes and met him. Both of Jenna's hands went to Dewey's stubble-covered cheeks as her eyes closed, and the kiss lasted a minute or two.

17

Taimur sat in the driver's seat of his Cadillac Escalade. The SUV was black on the outside, with a black leather interior, spotlessly clean. The engine was idling. Taimur had just dropped off a couple who'd flown into JFK.

He prided himself on the fact that he was an Uber Black driver and could afford the expensive Cadillac. He cleaned the vehicle constantly.

He'd saved more than $50,000 in the past two years from driving for Uber. Yet now, he knew, his plans to bring his sister and mother to the United States were irrelevant. All that mattered now was his part of an epic struggle against the Great Satan. He would spend the night in his car, waiting all night for the signal.

"Finally," he whispered to himself, as a young man approached and knocked on his window, though Taimur waved him off. He watched as the bald man in a tuxedo flipped him off.

He looked to his right, on the seat, where a pair of Uzis lay, thinking about how satisfying it would be to shoot the fat, entitled asshole, but he did nothing.

Taimur used his fingerprint to enter his Chase banking account.

In minutes, he arranged to wire everything to his sister in Parand, a section of Tehran south of the center of the Iranian capital.

He'd been waiting for this moment and now it was here. He couldn't believe it. Finally, he would be put to use.

Taimur reread the text:

When the ground itself shakes it is time

The time was now here, the one he'd been waiting for. All of them had been waiting. The attack was here. He felt elation and disbelief, even though he would likely die in a matter of hours. He would be a part of a revolution against a country he'd lived in for ten years now, a country he loved on one level—but Iran was his blood. Taimur turned on music, Farhad Mehrad, whose songs he knew by heart. He reclined the seat and listened as he placed his right hand on one of the Uzis, softly rubbing the magazine as he sought a few hours of sleep before it all began.

18

10:00 P.M.
SS DORSET
NEW YORK HARBOR

Dewey and Jenna arrived at Andrews and climbed from the car just as a sleek black EchoStar helicopter descended from the sky. The chopper's only decoration was a dashing family crest on each side of the fuselage; yellow, green, and red, with lions and swords, crossed inside of a shield.

The pilot was young, late twenties, and had a thick mustache. He smiled.

"Hello, Barnes," said Jenna. "This is Dewey."

"Hi, Jenna," said the pilot. "Nice to meet you, Dewey."

Jenna climbed in first, followed by Dewey. The cabin was intimate and luxurious, seats in honey-brown leather.

The chopper coursed north along the Eastern Seaboard, running at eight hundred feet above the jagged, light-filled expanse below—Baltimore, Wilmington, Philadelphia, and then, in a spectral distance, the conic halo glow of light that came from New York City.

The helicopter cut across the south edge of New York City. Dozens of other choppers moved in the sky.

As the chopper slowed in a slow arc lower, it flew east, away from the central Manhattan island, then was eliding at a hundred feet above a harbor dotted with all forms of boats, sailboats, trawlers, oil and LNG tankers, container ships, large and small motorboats, ferries, and then the sight line opened up toward the bright eastern sky, and Long Island glistened in a dazzling carpet of lights. A few minutes later, the chopper moved even lower as, in the distance, a large yellow, green, and red yacht came into view, illuminated against the evening. It was a castle on water, a sprawling vessel with hundreds of windows, different floors, decks, all glowing in light from the ship. The stern of the yacht read DORSET.

Jenna saw two individuals standing at the fringe of the helipad, smiling. They were older now. She hadn't seen them in more than a year. Her mother looked beautiful. She had long brown curly hair and a sharp, angular face. Her father loomed with his big frame, holding her mother's hand and shielding her from the wind, even as they laughed and smiled. He retained a thick mane of dark blond hair, too long, swept to the side but always being blown around in the wind. Her father had a rugged, handsome face, and a mustache.

The yacht was massive and Dewey ran his eyes over the length of it.

"Those are my parents," said Jenna.

Dewey looked through a different window, spotting Jenna's mother and father, but he said nothing.

"Please don't treat them other than you would anyone, even though there are servants and other people running around. They're not like that. I'm sorry if you feel I'm 'taking you to meet my parents.'"

"I've been on yachts like this before," said Dewey as he unlatched the chopper door.

"Really?" whispered Jenna.

"Yeah, but this is the first time I was invited."

They crossed the windswept helipad to meet her parents. Jenna ran the last few feet, burying herself in her father and mother's arms as they reached down and cradled her.

Dewey was dressed in a white button-down that was tight to his chiseled frame. His thick brown hair was blown back from his face, which was covered in a layer of brown stubble. The traces of a small bruise sat beneath his eye, still healing, a wound suffered on a recent mission.

"Oh Mummy, Dad," said Jenna. "I've missed you so much!"

She pulled away, gathering herself. "Mother, Father, this is Dewey Andreas, a friend of mine."

"Dewey?" said Sir Bobby Farragut, reaching his hand out. His voice was British, but it had a hard country edge, a hint of Scotland. "Welcome aboard. It's a pleasure to have you, and thank you for delivering our beloved daughter."

Dewey shook his hand. Farragut was a large man, as tall as Dewey.

"Thank you for having me, Bobby."

"Of course."

"And this is my mother," said Jenna, smiling.

"Jemima, am I right?" said Dewey, taking her hand politely.

Jenna started giggling.

"Such an ass," she said, shaking her head and looking at Dewey.

"What's so funny?" said her mother, laughing. Farragut was also laughing. None of them, except perhaps Jenna, knew why.

"I don't know," said Dewey. "Your daughter is a mystery, Jemima."

"Oh, you don't even know," said Jenna's mother, still smiling. "But we love her so. It's so nice to meet you, Dewey."

"It's nice to meet you too," said Dewey.

Then there was a moment of awkward silence.

"Dewey, welcome aboard," said Farragut. "Your belongings will be taken to your room."

"It does have a connecting door to Jenna's suite," Jenna's mother piped in.

"*Mummy!*" snapped Jenna.

"Jem! For *God's* sake," said Farragut, chuckling.

"We're friends, Mum," stuttered Jenna.

"I'm sorry," Jemima said with a naughty smile, lifting her half-filled highball glass and sipping. "I was merely pointing out one of the benefits of where our guest will be staying."

Dewey grinned without saying anything as Farragut silently castigated his wife and Jenna's cheeks turned red from embarrassment.

"As long as there's a shower big enough to fit Jenna and me, everything should be fine," said Dewey nonchalantly.

A moment of silence was followed by a second of shock—and then they broke into laughter.

"*Dewey!*" shouted Jenna.

Jemima roared.

"I think I like your friend!" said Farragut, putting his arm on Dewey's shoulder, while he still continued to laugh. "Come on, you two, let's get you a cocktail. The party has already begun. It's the usual cast from London, along with a few Manhattan folk."

Farragut looked at Dewey.

"I was about to give you advice," Farragut said conspiratorially, "as you're about to meet a few dozen people, royalty, the prime minister and his wife, some billionaires, and such, but then I realized, I don't exactly need to give you advice, now, do I?" Farragut was guarded but warm. "I can tell someone quickly. Yes," he said, patting Dewey one last time on the shoulder. "I don't think I need to give you any advice."

Dewey followed Jenna down the stairs from the helipad. At the bottom of the stairs was the main deck, filled with people. Lights cast a golden glow over a crowd of approximately fifty men and women, all dressed nattily but casually: on the men white linen pants or khakis or madras shorts, button-downs and blazers, and on the women elegant skirts and casual summer dresses, mid-thigh. There was a cacophony of voices, conversation, the scent of cigar and cigarette smoke, music, and a general sense of festivity. When Jenna entered, all eyes went to her, for everyone knew who she was, and most she'd known since childhood.

A young woman in a tan-and-white uniform—a staff member—came rushing over with a tray topped with half-filled crystal champagne glasses.

"Kelsey," said Jenna.

"So nice to see you, Jenna," she said as Jenna lifted a glass from the tray.

"I've missed you," said Jenna, giving her a hug.

"Is that my Jenna?" said a slightly inebriated man in a pink blazer, with brownish gray hair, in his seventies.

The crowd laughed and everyone watched as Jenna took a sip from her champagne flute, then walked out into the middle of the crowd toward the man.

"Uncle William," said Jenna, reaching out to hug him. "Everyone, it's nice to see you all."

Dewey watched from the edge of the deck, then, as one of the staff members walked by, followed him. He went down another set of stairs, belowdecks, where a small army of similarly attired staffers—tan pants and white shirts for the men, tan skirts and white blouses for the women—were frenetically trying to manage the smooth operation of the party above deck: food grilling on stoves, liquor being poured, a hustle and bustle that to the untrained eye looked like chaos.

Dewey cut off from behind the female staff member and found a large cabinet filled with liquor bottles. He scanned the rows. He didn't see any Jack Daniel's, but there was a large handle of Jim Beam. He picked it up and unscrewed the cap and took a hearty gulp, then another. He paused and then took another large glug, then found a glass and filled it with whiskey.

A staff member approached.

"May I help you, sir?" said a male staffer, a young, tall, brown-haired servant with a precise British accent, clearly not expecting a stranger in the staff area belowdecks.

"Yes," said Dewey, placing the large bottle of whiskey down. "Would you have any Grey Poupon?"

"Let me check immediately, sir," said the staffer.

"Merci beaucoup," said Dewey.

He walked past him and climbed the stairs back to the main deck. He found a railing and stood alone, scanning the water and, in the distance, Manhattan's skyscrapers, dotted and glowing in light. Dewey turned and watched from afar as Jenna moved through the crowd, saying hi to old friends of her parents. When, finally, she caught his eye, she smiled and made her apologies to whomever she was talking to, then made a beeline for him.

"I was looking for you," she said. When she stopped in front of him she leaned forward and kissed him.

Dewey reached down behind Jenna and put his hands on her hips. Gently, he picked her up and held her so that her face was close to his. Their lips met again and then neither let go, and her arms reflexively wrapped around Dewey's neck and moved into his thick brown hair as they kissed.

"Well, I, umm," said Jenna, pulling away yet letting Dewey keep her elevated there, in the air. She was blushing. "I'm so glad you came," she said.

Dewey didn't say anything.

"I think my father likes you," she said.

She leaned toward him and their lips met again.

"Are you hungry?" she asked. "They saved dinner for us, cutie."

"Did you just say 'cutie'?" Dewey said.

She kissed him again and then her lips went to his ear, and kissed it gently.

"Yes, I might have. What of it?"

"How about something a little less . . . cute."

"Okay, tough guy," said Jenna, kissing his ear. "But you didn't answer me," Jenna whispered into his ear as she delivered tiny kisses to his ear. "Are you hungry?"

"Yes," said Dewey.

The long dining table spread across the main deck of the large yacht, and on each side of the table were fifty chairs. The table was packed with people, most of whom had already eaten but lingered over after-dinner drinks and dessert. Candles ran in a yellow line down the middle, from one end to the other, as music played, and a loud chorus of conversation enveloped the deck.

Dewey was seated at one of the corners of the table, next to Jenna, both of them next to Jenna's parents.

Toast after toast was made, all saying, in one way or another, happy birthday to Farragut, who tolerated it, and it involved a great deal of ribbing.

Several friends told stories of hunting trips with Farragut, and implied that he was not a very good shot.

The meal was filet mignon with green beans and potatoes. Dewey ate two steaks as, at the same time, he had a few glasses of wine. For most of the meal, as Dewey listened to the toasts, and laughed, and looked at Jenna, he kept looking across the elegant crowd, and across the deck to Manhattan. As much fun as he was having, he couldn't help feeling a sense of unease. When they went below to their rooms, Dewey looked at Jenna.

"Goodnight," he said, "and thanks again."

"Goodnight," she said as Dewey opened his door.

"Night, Jenna."

Dewey's room was a simple, small room, big enough for a single bed, with round porthole windows. The ceiling was coffered in brown wood. His bag was on his bed. A thin interior door led to a bathroom. It had a small bathtub and marble everywhere. There was another door which led into Jenna's bedroom. Dewey brushed his teeth and then went back into his bedroom and took off his clothing. He climbed into bed.

A little while later, he heard Jenna inside the bathroom. When he heard a knock at the door, he opened his eyes and saw Jenna's outline in the darkness. She was naked. He waited as she walked toward him and reached for the blanket, then climbed into the bed and suddenly their bodies were intertwined. Dewey's arms wrapped around her like a cocoon.

"I hope I'm not being too forward," said Jenna. "The heat in my room isn't working."

"Mine is," said Dewey as he felt her hand touch his stomach, and felt her leg lift up and wrap around his back, pulling his body closer.

19

The Bombardier Global 7500's provenance was cloaked within a UAE shell corporation, which in turn was owned by a German shell corporation, with numbers bought from a corrupt member of the German Bundesrat, enabling the plane to enter the U.S. without complication. It was almost four in the morning in America when the jet touched down at Westchester County Airport just north of New York City. The jet taxied to the Signature private terminal. A midsized delivery truck pulled up to the rear of the jet just moments after it stopped moving. The truck had a colorful logo on its side, a food service truck. The four men who climbed out of the truck were young and Iranian.

One of the men approached Mansour as the other went to the cargo hold of the Bombardier.

The man who approached was short and thin, no more than twenty-five years old.

"Commander," he said, saluting Mansour.

"Hello, Kouros," said Mansour. "Are you and your men ready?"

"Yes, sir."

Mansour stared at Kouros, but said nothing more.

Kouros and three others carried the large boxes from the jet to the back of the delivery truck. When they were done, the truck drove away.

Soon after, on the tarmac outside the dark private terminal, a silver Dodge minivan moved in and stopped beneath the stairs of the Bombardier. Mansour emerged from the cabin and climbed down the stairs. He climbed into the back of the minivan. Two men were already seated. The minivan sped away from the Bombardier just as the Bombardier's engines grew loud and the jet started moving, taxiing for takeoff.

They moved south from Westchester, cutting down the Hutchinson River Parkway, which was mostly empty. Half an hour later, they arrived at a nondescript office building in Yonkers, just north of Manhattan. They parked beneath an anonymous-looking five-story building filled with offices where insurance agents, dentists, tax firms, and divorce attorneys plied their trade.

Mansour and the two other Iranians took the elevator to the third floor. They walked down a brightly lit hallway to a door and entered a small office suite. Mansour flipped on the lights. The office suite was, for the most part, vacant. Lifeless, empty, and covered in a film of dust. A pile of take-out menus was on the floor behind the door. Inside the ratchet office suite there was nothing on the walls, and only a few desks and chairs. It was a sublet taken out a year before, by a local attorney, a second-generation Iranian, whose nephew was freed from Evin Prison by the Iranian government in exchange for the lawyer's "volunteer work" on behalf of the Republic.

Mansour walked to a conference table near the wall. One of Mansour's lieutenants put his backpack on the table and removed a laptop. He opened it and soon the screen displayed a map of Manhattan. On the map were hundreds of small red X marks. These were the active shooters. More than five hundred men had been embedded in or around New York City over many years, in New Jersey, southern Connecticut, in disparate parts of New York's five boroughs, and in small blue-collar towns within a fifty-mile radius of Manhattan. The map showed the ones who were now operational— the men who'd signed in and were being tracked. The purpose was twofold. Make sure everyone was accounted for, and second, make sure all of Manhattan was covered, especially Midtown and the East Side.

Mansour knew not every man sent to the U.S. would answer the call. Some would inevitably get cold feet. Each man who responded knew he would probably die. But even Mansour was surprised by the sheer volume of red *X*s. The map was colored in red *X*s. A digital readout at the bottom of the screen displayed a hard count. There were 514 active shooters now in Manhattan, armed soldiers, most driving Uber or Lyft or a taxi; others were Amazon delivery drivers, several seemingly homeless men, or dish cleaners at restaurants. All highly trained soldiers in the employ of the Republic of Iran. Waiting for the explosions.

Mansour felt a small spike of warmth as he looked at the numbers. Only three men had fled. The rest had answered the call, just as he would have. Just as he was.

The wheels were in motion. The questions had already been asked and answered.

Move when you feel the explosions.

Mansour stared at the map, lost in thought. Then he opened up a blueprint of the United Nations. Four *X* marks represented where men were already prepositioned, armed with MANPADs, shoulder-fired missiles. Two soldiers were in buildings on the western side of First Avenue with a direct firing line at the UN.

"Excuse me, Commander," said one of the men.

"What is it?" said Mansour.

"The Federal Reserve," he said. "It is imperative you get the men moving now."

Mansour nodded.

He picked up his cell and dialed. After a few rings, a voice came on. "Yes."

"It has begun," said Mansour. "Call the others. The operation is now live. You're now operational. Remember about being subtle. Yours is the only part that must be subtle. It is why you were chosen."

"Yes, sir, Commander," came a young voice. "We will do what we've been trained for, we will do it quietly, and then we will meet Rokan with the fruits of our victorious efforts."

20

A silver BMW M5 pulled into the parking lot of a suburban train station, outside New York City. The lot was already crowded, even now, at just before six on a Wednesday morning. Men and women taking the early train to get to the city and their jobs at large financial institutions, hedge funds, PR firms, publishers, media conglomerates, and a thousand other high-paying professions which kept the train crowded on a Wednesday morning. Everyone trying to get ahead—or stay ahead. Of course, the ones who were already ahead, far ahead, could show up whenever they wanted to.

Phil Lawrence was already far, far ahead, though he didn't show it, at least not ostentatiously. He first retired at age thirty-four, though now, at forty-eight, that year of retirement was hard to remember. He and his wife had traveled the world, staying in the finest hotels and resorts, visiting the South Pole and Tibet, and more than twenty other countries in between. His fraternity brothers at Saint Anthony Hall had not anticipated Lawrence's success. After all, he'd graduated from Columbia, where his academic record had been mediocre at best. At St. A's, he was known for his pool-shooting skills and his ability to attract women. After graduation, Lawrence had asked his father for a $100,000 loan, all of which he'd invested in a cross section of oil companies at every part of the supply chain, along with a mirror-image investment across the emerging biotech industry. By the time he was twenty-five, he'd paid his father back and had almost $70 million under management, most of it his own. When his father and a few friends were allowed to invest, Lawrence—by thirty—was running $8 billion, $6 billion of which was based on capital appreciation, rather than new investors. Lawrence made approximately 20 percent of all capital appreciation.

Lawrence had been approached by a multitude of hedge funds, mutual funds, insurance companies, and family offices. All wanted to acquire his fund. He contemplated a few offers to come aboard, with total investment freedom, and autonomy over a much bigger piece of capital. But Lawrence knew that if he worked for someone he would have to explain how he saw the patterns in the numbers, how he could look at tens of thousands of documents quickly, not really reading them—raw financials—and somehow process the blur of numbers and see patterns which told him something.

He sold his company to Black Rock when he turned thirty-four. He was already a billionaire and this just added to it. After his year of travel, he couldn't take it anymore. He hated being retired. Lawrence couldn't handle not putting himself in the middle of the complex, massively simultaneous data flow of the economy. He realized during that year that it wasn't about the money.

He repeated what he'd done as a younger man—starting with $100,000, which he again, for symbolic reasons, borrowed from his father. Again, he repaid the money and within a calendar year had turned that initial investment into $220 million.

It was the chairman of the Federal Reserve, Richard Baum, who called Lawrence and recruited him.

"Have you ever heard of the governors of the Federal Reserve?" said Baum.

"No," said Lawrence.

"The four Fed governors manage the actual day-to-day, minute-by-minute trading platform for U.S. Treasury securities," said Baum. "It's called Fedwire. Basically, the financial transactions of the United States government run through the four governors. During any single day, that amounts to almost three hundred billion, in a year over one hundred trillion dollars of activity. I'm calling you, Phillip, because I'd like to ask you to be one of the governors."

On the radio was sports talk, a NYC station. Mike Francesa was both praising and excoriating Bill Belichick, the coach of the New England Patriots, for something. Lawrence was laughing as he parked his car and hit a button on the console, turning it off.

It was his usual space, the corner of the lot nearest the train tracks, the spot he parked in every day.

He did notice a shadow as he turned off the car but didn't think anything of it. Had he been watching, he would have seen a dark figure move to the left rear of the M5 as he parked.

Lawrence opened the door but before he could begin to step out of the car, a long black suppressor appeared in the opening of the door. Behind it was a man in a ski mask. The man pumped the trigger. There was a low metallic *thwack*. A suppressed, hollow-tipped bullet ripped through Lawrence's throat. Another *thwack* and this time the metal tore dead center into Lawrence's chest, shooting blood across the far window.

The man tossed the pistol onto the ground. He lifted Lawrence and threw him to the passenger seat and climbed in, shutting the car door behind him. He pulled off the ski mask and took a plastic bag out of his pocket. He grabbed Lawrence's right arm, finding his hand, then his thumb. He removed a set of steel wire clippers, quickly grabbing the base of Lawrence's thumb. He squeezed as hard as he could, twisting the clippers so the blades dug in. Blood poured all over the center console of the car. The killer cut the thumb off at the joint.

He tossed the wire cutters to the floor and pulled a small blade from his coat. He inserted the tip of the blade next to the dead man's eye, along the edge of the orbital socket. Like plumbing an oyster, he scooped the eyeball out, cutting veins, then stuck both the finger and the eye into the plastic bag, which he put in his coat pocket. He looked around the parking lot and climbed out and shut the door to the BMW, then moved to the train platform, just as the 6:06 to Grand Central Station came rolling into Mt. Kisco.

21

David Fenner stepped down the front steps of a brick town house just as his wife, Natalie, was coming back from a run.

Fenner had short, tight-cropped brown hair and a laid-back demeanor. He had on a tan corduroy suit, a white button-down, and no tie.

A black sedan—Fenner's Uber—was waiting at the curb.

"How far did you go?" he said to Natalie.

Natalie stopped and leaned forward.

"Seven," she said.

"Good for you."

"What did you do?" she said.

"Five," said Fenner, walking closer and reaching for her, despite her sweatiness. He embraced her. "I love you, honey. I'll see you tonight."

"I love you, too. Seven o'clock," said Natalie, standing up. "Please don't be late."

"I won't."

Fenner walked toward the black sedan.

He glanced back at his wife as she ascended the wide steps of their brownstone. The home had cost him $6 million, followed by a $4 million restoration. There was no doubt it was one of the most beautiful brownstones in Park Slope. The money didn't matter, though. The Fenners were wealthy.

As a student at Babson College, he'd written a computer program that could be used to be the back end of any online gambling site. By the time he was a junior, it was the back end of most online gambling sites, and he sold the code for $120 million the fall of his senior year. In graduate school at MIT, Fenner wrote two computer programs, both of which he sold for a lot of money.

Fenner, like the other three governors of the Fed, was already wealthy before he agreed to help manage the very system upon which their wealth had been created, a system on which America's money moved in a complex paradigm of black boxes, wires, and air. Fenner, and the other governors, each earned $289,500 a year.

As Fenner looked at his wife stepping up the stairs, he thought about how much he'd accomplished, and a feeling of pride and happiness filled him for a brief moment as he opened the back door of the black Cadillac sedan. He climbed in just as a dark figure, looming inside, turned from the front seat. Fenner saw the gun just as the stranger turned. It was a silencer, he understood that. The man was wearing a black ski mask. Before Fenner's momentum had even carried him to the leather back seat, the man fired. There was a low thud. A bullet hit him in the chest and splattered blood across the seat and door.

The killer pulled the door shut and started driving. He went for several blocks and parked near a subway station. He took out a small plastic bag, then a pair of wire cutters, and cut off Fenner's thumb. He put it in the bag, then stuck the tip of a knife into Fenner's eye socket. He pried out the eyeball, taking it gently into his hand as his other hand slashed the blade through what was left of the veins connecting Fenner's eyeball to his skull. He put the eyeball in the plastic bag.

The killer climbed out of the car and walked to the subway station, falling in line with the swarm of human beings on their daily commute to Manhattan.

22

Ali awoke at 6 A.M. without the need for his alarm clock. He found the text and read it again:

Sale of Victory 8:25 am when clouds appear

For Ali, his time in the United States had been brief, less than a year. He'd come in through California, on a student visa, to study at the University of California at Santa Barbara. His application had been a lie. Ali was twenty-four years old and had stopped going to school at fifteen after volunteering for Hezbollah.

Ali's role—like hundreds of other volunteers—was straightforward. Upon the signal, he was to do his duty.

Any soldier selected was to be forever commemorated by Suleiman. Just to be selected was a great honor. Active shooter. All were from Hezbollah, Hamas, Palestinian Islamic Jihad, Houthi, and Canadian Jihad.

Ali carried a large duffel bag to his Toyota Highlander, which was parked in a belowground garage a few blocks away from his apartment building. The Highlander was black and shiny. Ali kept it spotless. He had to. It was part of the agreement with Uber. In a strange way, he was proud of his time driving for Uber. He had a rating from his customers of 4.97. He'd saved most of his money.

Ali knew he might not survive today. He had already arranged to wire his remaining money to his father. He opened the rear and felt for the automatic rifle hidden near a spare tire. He shut the back, climbed in the driver's seat, and headed for Manhattan.

23

6:18 A.M.
AIR FORCE ONE
ABOVE THE ATLANTIC OCEAN

Air Force One took off from Joint Base Andrews at just after six o'clock in the morning. A similar-looking plane took off six minutes later. Only one of the identical jets held the president, J. P. Dellenbaugh.

The back of Air Force One was filled with members of the White House press corps. The front of the plane, separated from the press by a secured doorway, was only half full. The cabin was luxurious, though its purpose was purely business. In addition to several rows of large, comfortable leather captain's chairs were four conference tables, each table having two chairs on either side. President J. P. Dellenbaugh sat at a table nearest to the front of the plane, alone. Seated in the back were six Secret Service agents and a small phalanx of presidential aides. At another conference table sat Secretary of State Bailey Miller and National Security Advisor Josh Brubaker. Another table was occupied by White House Director of Communications John Schmidt, and head speechwriter Cory Tilley.

Each big Boeing was flanked by a pair of F-18/As, each of which, on approach, curled in a trained, tight arc above the miles and acreage surrounding the airports, searching—with eyes and technology—for the telltale flash of enemy fire. It never came, at least not yet, but these pilots were trained to stop the one time when someone did try to take down the president of the United States while flying on Air Force One.

"This speech is going to piss off the Iranians, piss off our allies, piss off the Chinese, piss off the Russians, and pretty much piss off everyone else," said Dellenbaugh.

"You asked me to write a speech that reflects your worldview, sir," said Tilley. "Did I get anything wrong?"

The occasion was the president's annual address to the United Nations General Assembly. Dellenbaugh was to deliver the speech at 11 A.M., in front of government officials, delegates, and diplomats from across the world.

It was Dellenbaugh's and the CIA's belief, and the belief at the highest levels of the Pentagon and National Security Directorate, that the UN had become a vessel for terror; not a direct funder but a helpful piece of architecture through which terrorists could infiltrate the U.S. In addition, it galled Dellenbaugh that some young family in Nebraska had to help foot the bill for something that enabled America's enemies to enter the country and conduct business against the U.S. on U.S. soil.

Dellenbaugh smiled at Tilley.

"That's precisely what you did, Cory," said the president. "You know you're doing something right when you make everyone mad at you. At least everyone who's not a resident of the United States. We have bridges that are falling down in towns that are filled with teenagers addicted to opioids. Schools that are unsafe, forty thousand homeless veterans. It's time to put the world on notice: we need to take care of our own."

John Schmidt cleared his voice and looked at the president.

"They're going to call you an isolationist," said Schmidt. "America first, fuck the world."

"And your job, our job," said Dellenbaugh, "is to explain that what others see as isolationism, or selfishness, disengagement from the world, is simply a country that needs to take care of its own."

"Mr. President, you know I agree with every statement in that speech," said Schmidt, "but what I don't understand is why we need to announce that we're pulling back now. Why not wait until after the election? You're leading in every poll, so why introduce an external factor which could have unintended consequences?"

"I know how you feel about this, John," said the president. "I agree, the timing isn't ideal. But when will it be?"

24

Adam Jaklitsch was up by 5 A.M., as usual. Nevertheless, he had a few hours until he needed to be at the office. He sat in front of a computer, studying what was happening in Asia and Europe. Jaklitsch was not looking at publicly available information. In fact, few human beings on earth would be able to comprehend what he was looking at. It was a black screen with four quadrants, and in each one a series of numbers and letters moved slowly up the screen. This wasn't information about some company's stock price, nor even the current price of a country's currency. Jaklitsch was watching, in real time, the digital flow of funds from the largest banks, companies, and governments in the world in interaction with the United States Federal Reserve, moving along patterns he himself had executed. He was looking at the movement of money in its basest and most elemental format. He wasn't trying to make money. Jaklitsch was one of four people making sure money was even there in the first place.

Liquidity was a measure of readily accessible wealth. It could be in the form of cash, or savings, or assets that could be sold within a few hours.

For an individual, liquidity would include savings and checking accounts, stocks that could be easily sold, but it would not include other assets, such as a home or an IRA.

Liquidity was not a measure of overall wealth; in fact it was somewhat unrelated. An individual might have $50,000 in cash in a suitcase, but owe $200,000. This individual's liquidity would be $50,000, but net worth would be *negative* $150,000. Liquidity was important, however; oftentimes more important than net worth. Cash was king, and Jaklitsch and his three coworkers managed the actual financial transactions—mostly loans—that fueled the world economy.

America's liquidity was estimated to be—at any one time—$4.5 to $5 trillion. Of that amount, less than 5 percent existed in physical cash and gold. Almost all of it—more than $4 trillion—was kept in a foundational, highly complex infrastructure built upon a massively secure, single-purpose digital framework, which enabled the transmission and protection of America's sovereign wealth itself, in its basic form. A system of credits written in a computer language that was agnostic. This was the digital bank account by which America served as the foundation of the international economy. It was called Fedwire.

Immediately, Jaklitsch saw that there was a need for an injection of $10 billion to Bank of America, and he also saw that it would be repaid in less than an hour. This was one of but fifty such interactions the Fed would take this coming day, in essence allowing Bank of America to borrow from the digital foundation of America's currency and pay it back, all without the need for cash and other physical representations of such, such as gold.

Jaklitsch shut down the computer and looked around his apartment. He lived on Riverside Drive and 108th Street, in a two-bedroom apartment on the eighth floor of a beautiful old limestone building just down the street from Columbia University. He had a view of the Hudson River. He watched early-morning joggers moving in both directions through Riverside Park.

He walked to the door, shutting it, locking it, and went right, to the elevator, but as he turned the corner, he encountered a man—and the spheroid cap of an alloy noise suppressor, at the muzzle of a weapon. Jaklitsch's mind registered a black turtleneck and ski mask, then he felt the bullet as he was about to say something, to protest, but it was too late, and he felt it in the same moment he heard the *spit* of the gun. The bullet hit his chest but he didn't feel it other than a dull thud, like getting a tooth drilled under Novocaine.

The killer felt in Jaklitsch's pocket for his keys and dragged him back to the apartment, unlocking the door. He pulled him inside and shut the door. He removed a plastic bag, cut off Jaklitsch's thumb, then jammed the blade into the side of his eyeball and ripped it quickly out. He stuffed both in the plastic bag and left the apartment, then took the elevator to the ground floor. The stranger exited the building and disappeared into the crowd on its way to the subway station, most on their way to work.

25

Dewey was awakened at 6:40 in the morning by an insistent knock at the door. He climbed out of bed and went to the door, opening it. Outside, a valet was standing.

"Sir," he said in English accent. "The shoot begins in ten minutes, sir."

Dewey took a quick shower, brushed his teeth, pulled on a pair of khakis and a long-sleeved polo shirt in black and yellow stripes. He pulled on his boots. He felt himself swaying slightly as the boat moved with the sea.

There were several people already on deck when he got there. He saw Jenna's father, Sir Farragut, standing amid a small group of men, all similarly attired: canvas or wool pants, tweed shooting shirts with leather patches protecting the shoulder. Each man held the same shotgun, barrels open and empty over the elbow, and Dewey recognized the model: Beretta DT11 Black PRO, over-and-under .12-gauge competition gun.

Near the men, a butler held a silver service, on top of which sat coffee.

The sky had turned to a light blue, infused with orange.

Dewey looked over his shoulder. Manhattan was visible in clear light.

To the left, the deck faced away from the city. The yacht was so large that it held enough area for a competition skeet range. A semicircle of shooting stations faced the ocean. There were six stations in all. To the left and right, near the edge of the deck, were two trap-throwing houses, hidden by shingles, where the clays were fired into the air out over the ocean—while the gunmen on deck took turns trying to shoot the small disks from the sky as they flew in a blur.

Dewey felt a burst of adrenaline as he studied the two throwing houses, then the arc of the stations. He'd shot clays before, on a few occasions.

The butler approached and Dewey took a cup of coffee.

"Thank you."

Farragut saw Dewey and moved toward him.

"How did you sleep, Dewey?" he said.

"Fine, Mr. Farragut," said Dewey, taking an awkward sip from his coffee cup.

Farragut laughed.

"My name is Bobby," said Farragut. "Don't call me anything but that."

"Sorry, forgot, sir."

"Don't call me sir either," he grinned. "Now let's get you a shotgun."

Dewey followed him to a door at the side of the deck. Inside was a changing room, dark wood everywhere, lockers, and, along the back wall, shotguns in a neat-looking rack. On the left side of the rack were lined at least a dozen shotguns of all varieties; these were custom-made, fancy guns. But to the right were competition guns. There were empty slots but still at least a half dozen Berettas.

Farragut showed Dewey the last section of the gun room. It was a line of older shotguns of all varieties, along with a few modern waterfowl guns, for different purposes; not the ideal gun to be shooting skeet. Dewey studied the line of shotguns and then his eyes went to one gun in particular, a long, black, single-barrel, pump-action .12-gauge Benelli Nova Pump. He lifted it from the rack and looked at it. In seconds, he disassembled the gun, inspecting each part of it. Then he slammed it back together, pumped it, and hit the trigger. There was a click. Dewey looked up at Farragut.

"I'll take this one," said Dewey.

Farragut stared at the choice of weapon with a slightly confused look.

"You sure?" said Farragut. "Your shoulder might get a little sore."

"Yes," said Dewey politely, though his demeanor communicated that he knew full well what the firearm was and that it was the gun he wanted. Dewey pulled a belt on, lined with .12-gauge shotgun shells. "It's perfect," said Dewey.

"At least let me get you a proper shirt," said Farragut. "Your shoulder is going to get beat to shit."

"Thank you, Bobby, I'll be fine."

Dewey took one last glance around the gun room. He saw a steel door with a large lock on it and he registered it an extra moment. Farragut noticed Dewey's look.

"You're wondering what's behind the door?"

"Yes," said Dewey.

Farragut went over and slid the bolt aside, then pressed a button. The door moved in. It was a weapons cache.

Several shelves of handguns, beneath other shelves with various accouterments for the handguns—suppressors, lights, thermal and radiographic sights.

Another wall was nothing but ammunition.

Still another was a spread of serious-looking automatic rifles.

The last wall was more ammo and submachine guns.

"I was SAS," said Farragut. "Seven years. I enjoy firearms. Beyond protection, they are a wonder. Where do you work, if you don't mind my asking, Dewey?"

"I'm in between jobs," said Dewey, looking down at the Benelli and studying it with his eyes and hands.

"What is it you do, when you're not in between jobs, if I might ask?"

"I'm not sure, sir," said Dewey politely.

Farragut started laughing.

"Fine, that's none of my business. Let's go shoot some clays."

26

Samantha Stout, the top analyst in the Signals Intelligence Directorate, or SID, saw a flashing red icon on one of the two large computer screens in front of her. Stout hit a few keys and the screen shot to a live feed of a satellite grid looking down on Manhattan. The relief was black. The screen was black with a digitally imposed red border around the island of Manhattan. Above the city, from the view of the satellite grid, was a growing crosshatch of red lines, like a spider's web.

Across the top of the screen was bright yellow block print:

ALERT: LEVEL 2 TERTIARY

"Update," said Stout as she adjusted in her seat, speaking to her computer.

"Affirmative," came an automated female voice, in simplified terms the NSA's version of Alexa.

"Time of event," she said.

"One thirty-two A.M. eastern standard time."

"Duration."

"Ninety-seven seconds," came the robotic female voice.

"Post-action frame and follow," said Stout to the computer as she typed into the keyboard and brought the second screen into the dataset.

The first screen showed a black background with the world imposed on it in a map of yellow digital lines. The screen homed in on the U.S. and Europe, illuminated in thin lines like an air traffic controller's screen. Then, the map relayed the metadata from an event that had just occurred. The screen scrolled the event in real time, as if in fast-forward motion. Suddenly, there appeared a rapid cross section of red lines between Europe and the U.S., until the agglomeration of red was a blur. At exactly one minute thirty seconds, the miasma of criss-crossing red lines indicating signals activity disappeared.

Stout refocused the grid and followed one of the lines. It was the only line that went away from New York.

"Up two, over three, then tighten in," she said.

The view became of a larger area.

"Control east target," she ordered the computer.

She saw where the cluster of activity had arisen from.

"Berlin?" she said aloud, to no one. "Why Berlin?"

Stout typed and was soon inside the signals metadata. She cut down into layers of encrypted data like a butcher sawing through a cow.

A green splash of numbers, frozen in motion:

8579980002

It had been a phone call. That was all she could tell. From an old burner, a cell phone—not a SIM card. It was a number NSA had locked into more than two years before.

The alert—the flashing icon—was an automated response from an algorithm Stout had herself built. The number was active again.

ALERT: LEVEL 2 TERTIARY

One phone call followed by ninety-seven seconds of mad activity, then silence.

Stout saw a second occurrence before the signal trail went dead—a call, text, or email from the same device. She typed quickly, decrypting the second signal. It was a phone call to another burner. The duration of the call: fourteen seconds. She ran the signal against a GPS. The location appeared on a map, which she zoomed in on, a cold chill arising in her spine: the map settled down on a building in Yonkers, New York.

"Holy shit."

Stout stood and swept her blond hair over her shoulders. She walked fast down the hall and entered the office of her boss, Jim Bruckheimer, the head of SID, without knocking.

Bruckheimer was standing behind his desk. He was on the phone. Stout gave him an icy glare.

"Call you back," said Bruckheimer, hanging up. "What's up?" he said to Stout.

"I'm seeing an attack pattern," said Stout. "ThinThread. It came from a Level Two Tertiary, a phone call from Berlin. A call to a phone north of New York City then a classic attack cloud. In the hundreds, then it stopped. Minute and a half in duration."

Bruckheimer knew what it meant: Level 1 meant a terrorist. Level 2 was a signal, such as a phone call or e-mail, from a close associate to a Level 1. It meant a signal had been tracked to someone— or more specifically, something—SID was watching, such as a SIM card, a credit card, a laptop, a phone. It could be meaningless. A Level 2 could potentially be a noninvolved private citizen, such as a gardener who some Level 1 had called to get his lawn mowed. But America could not afford to be wrong. Most of all, Stout was worried about the cluster of SIGINT immediately following the first phone call.

"Who?" said Bruckheimer.

"We don't know the owner," said Stout. "All we know is this cell at one point in time was used in communication with a Level One."

"Does it scan?" he said.

"Right now I'm running against usual suspects," said Samantha. "Al Qaeda, Islamic Jihad, Lashkar-e-Taiba, HASM. Hezbollah, Houthis, Hamas, Haqqani Network, ISIS, along with all their various splinters."

"So tell me again, what's the attack pattern?" said Bruckheimer, picking up his phone and hitting speed dial.

"The first phone call initiated at least three hundred other calls in and around Manhattan, followed by thousands more. It was a mushroom cloud, then it disappeared."

Bruckheimer looked at his watch. It was 6:55 A.M. He put the phone to his ear.

"Who are you calling?" said Stout.

"The president is going to New York City this morning," said Bruckheimer. "He's speaking at the UN."

Stout looked at Bruckheimer. "I haven't run any of this down, Jim."

"Better safe than sorry," said Bruckheimer.

Bruckheimer heard a voice on the console, even as he stared into Samantha's eyes, both sharing a moment of silent recognition of the fact that the U.S. was potentially under attack—and they were behind.

"Yeah, Jim?" came a male voice. It was the deep, smooth baritone of Hector Calibrisi. "To what do I owe the pleasure?"

"We have something going on," said Bruckheimer. "This is real time. We're seeing an attack pattern in and around New York City. Signals-level data that started in Germany with a phone call, followed by hundreds of calls in and around New York City. We back-pulled the metadata. I know Dellenbaugh is going there this morning. It looks like a classic mushroom cloud."

"Got it," said Calibrisi. "I'm going to send a car over. We're going to the White House. I want to brief Adrian King," he added, referring to the White House chief of staff. "Tell your people to start running hard at this."

27

Kara Winikoff stepped into the kitchen. She went to the toaster oven and opened it, took out a toasted bagel, put it on a plate, buttered it, put apricot jam on it, and handed it to her daughter, Chloe.

Winikoff was dressed in a tight-fitting dark green wool and cashmere Chanel suit, with subtle pinstripes in yellow, red, and blue. Winikoff had bought the stylish suit at Bergdorf Goodman with part of her bonus her first year at Goldman Sachs. There were classmates of hers from HBS who made more, but not many. Her expertise was sought-after. In addition to understanding the basic financial underpinnings of the world economy, Winikoff, when she made managing director at Goldman at age twenty-seven, also understood the complex electronic grid that connected the global economy, the digital checks and balances of the world's wealth. Winikoff's knowledge plumbed the depths of the basic system underpinning the world economy; understood the electro-digital plumbing that connected banks and governments with the Federal Reserve, as well as the languages that connected it all into a securitized central framework with other countries, all of it undergirded by credit, represented digitally.

"I have to go, sweetie," said Winikoff, leaning down and kissing

Chloe on the forehead. "I love you. Good luck with your piano today. Daddy will be there."

"Why can't you come to my recital, Mom?"

"You know why," said Winikoff. "I'll see you tonight."

At thirty-one, Winikoff had been approached by the chairman of Goldman Sachs, John Hunt. She had met Hunt only twice before, even though he was technically her boss. Hunt asked her to come to his office suite on the penthouse floor of the Goldman skyscraper.

Hunt pointed to a pair of long white leather sofas facing each other in the corner.

"Thanks for coming, Kara."

"Am I in trouble?" she said. "Are you firing me?"

Hunt grinned, shaking his head no.

"In a way, yes," said Hunt.

"What do you mean, in a way, yes?"

"You're leaving Goldman Sachs," said Hunt.

"I love it here."

"I received a call today from Matt Labretton, the secretary of the Treasury. They would like you to be one of the four governors of the Federal Reserve."

Winikoff sat back with a blank, slightly shocked expression on her face.

The governors were the individuals who managed Fedwire, the electronic financial grid of the United States. She didn't know how they did it, but she'd built a career on spotting their moves just after the moves were made. Now, she was being asked—in a way, ordered—to take on a job she knew was more important than most jobs, even in the upper echelons of government, perhaps second only to the president if importance was measured in power.

"You've made more than a hundred million dollars in the last six years," said Hunt. "I don't have to do this but you deserve it: you'll receive severance of another hundred million. I'm very proud of you, Kara. We all are. You're the first governor I've ever met. There are things more important than Goldman Sachs."

. . .

After saying good-bye to Chloe, Kara walked outside to a waiting sedan. When she climbed in, a figure in a black ski mask was seated in the back seat. A handgun, in hands covered by black gloves, was trained at her arrival and before she could react she heard the low *thwap* of the bullet. She knew it hit her chest, her heart, but didn't feel any pain. She just knew she was being killed.

The man yanked her into the sedan and pushed her corpse to the floor. He removed his ski mask and gloves. He climbed out of the other door in the back seat and then climbed into the driver's seat. He drove down Park Avenue until he was at Fifty-sixth Street, then took a right and drove until he saw a parking garage within a few blocks of his destination.

He descended a floor then parked in the first space he could find. He climbed over the seat and removed a plastic bag. He took a pair of wire cutters from his pocket and cut off her left thumb at the knuckle and put it in the plastic bag. He reached for her head and carefully inserted the tip of the blade into the side of her right eye and popped the eyeball out. He cut the tendrils, nerves, muscles, and veins connecting the eyeball to her head and dropped it into the bag.

The back seat, his hands, her face, all of it was covered in blood.

He took a roll of paper towels and wiped his face of any blood spatters, checked his weapons, pulled off the gloves, and opened the door.

He took the stairs to the ground floor of the parking garage and went right, falling into a human mass of people on their way to work. As he walked with the swarms of people through Midtown Manhattan, he looked for the building itself, anonymous-looking but tall, looming in steel and glass:

The United States Federal Reserve.

135

28

Air Force One began its initial approach to JFK in Queens. At the same time the blue-and-white jet touched down, an identical plane landed at La Guardia Airport, twelve miles away. The doppelganger was a distraction, empty except for the two pilots.

Upon landing at JFK, the president climbed down from Air Force One under a bright early-morning sky. He crossed the tarmac, walking alone, as a line of photographers took photos. He was trailed by a small team of Secret Service agents. Dellenbaugh climbed onto Marine One and the chopper's rotors accelerated into a feverish whirr, slashing the air.

In seconds, Marine One was airborne, en route to Manhattan.

Once high in the sky, the president stared through the windows at Manhattan in the distance. The city's skyscrapers refracted bluish steel, silver, and orange. Dellenbaugh flew in silence, looking at the city from above, a privilege to be sure, and yet he could not enjoy it, for today Dellenbaugh was entering the lion's den.

Dellenbaugh had dark brown hair, parted on the right side. It was combed neatly when he left the White House, but by now his hair was slightly tousled. Dellenbaugh stepped out of the helicopter at a private helipad on the roof of a skyscraper above Wall Street. He was led to an elevator where he descended to street level, then climbed into the presidential limousine.

A man was already seated inside the vehicle. He had shaggy blond hair and was heavyset, with round, gold-rimmed glasses, and a handsome face despite the dishevelment of his wardrobe—jeans and an untucked, wrinkled button-down, worn cowboy boots, and a green sweater with a bright yellow stripe across the chest.

This was Mike Murphy, the president's top political advisor.

The motorcade cut up the East River, onto the FDR.

The motorcade was twenty-two vehicles in total, as well as several NYPD motorcycles. A dozen freshly washed NYPD cruisers, several sedans filled with VIPs—the governor of New York, the mayor, a few large donors with an interest in foreign policy—then, concentrically closer to the center of the motorcade, white vans carrying reporters and White House advance staff, and, still closer, a hardline security cordon of four black Chevy Suburbans loaded to the teeth with weapons, Secret Service agents, and Special Forces soldiers.

The motorcade took the FDR for a few miles then cut off into Manhattan and moved along shut-off avenues and boulevards toward the UN. As the president came close to the UN, the sidewalks were lined with a frenzy of Dellenbaugh supporters, along with news cameramen and police. Dellenbaugh waved as the motorcade sped quickly toward the United Nations. Then he looked at Murphy.

Murphy was a wunderkind in the world of politics. He'd run his first presidential campaign at the age of twenty-three, and won his first at thirty. He was also waving at the passing crowds of people, more enthusiastically, though with a hint of sarcasm. He'd been there so many times now he was cynical.

"You like me!" said Murphy, waving to the crowds there to see Dellenbaugh. "You really like me!"

Dellenbaugh laughed.

"I guess they can't see your sweater," said Dellenbaugh.

Murphy ignored the taunt.

"This is the only way to visit New York, Mr. President," said Murphy. "By motorcade with a bunch of armed guards."

"You don't like New York?" said the president.

"Are you kidding?" said Murphy. "I hate it. I've won eleven statewide elections here, but every time it's like sleeping with your sister."

Dellenbaugh took a sip of coffee. It was too early for Murphy's opinions, yet he wouldn't see him for a week. He took the bait.

"How so?" said Dellenbaugh.

"It feels good but then afterwards you're like, what did I just do?" said Murphy as he waved at the crowds.

Dellenbaugh momentarily gagged, then coughed.

"Why are we having this meeting, Mike?" said President Dellenbaugh, taking another sip of coffee.

"I wanted to see you tell these assholes off," said Murphy. "Cory sent me the speech. I love it."

"Is that the only reason?" said Dellenbaugh.

"No," said Murphy.

"We're winning by twenty points," said the president. "Frankly, this whole election cycle is a little disappointing. I was looking forward to a real election."

"Mr. President, this isn't about the election," said Murphy, becoming serious, "and I didn't come to see your speech. Danny Donato was killed almost five months ago."

As both men knew, Donato—the former vice president—had been killed off the coast of Hawaii, his jet shot from the sky.

Murphy's voice took a sharp edge. He leaned forward and pointed at Dellenbaugh with his index, middle, and ring fingers extended, like a blade. "By law, you need to nominate a new vice president. You should've nominated someone five months ago, the day after Danny Donato went down in a plane."

"Show me someone I could see being president, Mike," said Dellenbaugh, staring daggers.

"If you die, the Speaker of the House becomes president."

Murphy didn't have to say his name. Cam Healey, the U.S. Speaker of the House, was a bare-knuckles Irish Democrat from

Boston. Dellenbaugh knew what Murphy was saying. Were anything to happen to Dellenbaugh, Healey would become president.

Dellenbaugh leaned back.

"I've put four viable candidates in front of you. Two governors, including the governor of New York, and two solid Republican senators. Fine, you passed. But it's not academic anymore, sir. You need to nominate someone so we can get both houses of Congress to approve, before the election. You have majorities in both houses, but we're about to take a fucking bloodbath. You'll win reelection easily but the Senate and House are both lost. You'll have to cut a deal after reelection. Your vice president will be someone you don't want. That's the political situation. The real-world situation? You're tremendously exposed due to the lack of a vice president. The country is exposed. Mathematically, you can't lose. Although actually, you can. You know how? There's one way: you die."

"Are you saying what I think you're saying?" said the president.

"That depends on what you think I'm saying," said Murphy.

"Are you saying Healey might do something?"

"No," said Murphy. "I'm saying, before he thinks of it—or God forbid, before some nutjob or foreign country assassinates you—nominate someone to be vice president, sir."

29

The gas station wasn't very busy. It was hard to compete with the twenty-four-hour Exxon/Mobil station a few miles away, on the highway. But maximizing profit was far from the minds of the men now lurking inside the unlit garage. The owner of the station didn't necessarily care whether or not they sold gas at this hour.

The garage had four bays and, in a separate building attached to the garage, a brightly lit room at the front where the cash register was, along with cigarettes and various other nicotine products, and refrigerators filled with beverages for sale.

A middle-aged Hispanic woman sat behind the register, in the store, alone. She was watching something on an iPad, the sound of canned laughter from the show the only sound in the store.

In the garage, behind a locked steel door, four white vans were illuminated under dim lights cast by head lanterns on the men. There were four men in all—Shahin, the man in charge, who'd rented the place a few months before, and three others, Farhad, Mohsen, and Dariush. They were all Iranian. All were soldiers in QUDS Force, though each man was disgraced, for whatever reason.

All four had overstepped the boundaries, but Mansour saw their inherent fealty to Iran. These were talented, decorated soldiers—operators, who'd crossed lines and now they would give their lives as recompense to Suleiman and the Republic, who would use them, in turn, in an endless war, whose next chapter was about to be written. It was the way the Iranian government harvested its people, ammunition in a war of retribution against America.

The four men lugged blocks of heavy gray wrapped in plastic, almost as heavy as a similar-sized piece of concrete. These were blocks of an advanced explosive polymer called octanitrocubane. Originally developed for Czechoslovak military use and export, octanitrocubane eventually became popular with paramilitary groups, guerrilla fighters, and terrorists, due to the difficulty of detecting it. It had no smell and was undetectable by existing airport technology. Octanitrocubane was used to take down Pan Am Flight 103 over Lockerbie, Scotland, resulting in the deaths of 270 people.

The composite was a distilled version of the basic explosive entity; there was little filler, just pure chemical. The vans were packed up to the rafters. Each van had more than a ton of octanitrocubane inside, enough to destroy a city block, an airport, a government building.

But none of the above were the target this day.

As the sun awoke in the early sky, the four Iranians drank coffee together.

A Dodge minivan pulled up in front of the bays. A man emerged from the driver's seat, as well as another man from the passenger seat.

Shahin, Farhad, Mohsen, and Dariush stood between two of the vans. Each man was perspiring profusely.

All eyes turned to the windows of the garage bays. The two men who had just arrived were stocky, and clad in black tactical clothing.

All the men knew the man on the right. His name was Mansour. He was an infamous warrior inside QUDS, then Hezbollah.

None of the men in the garage recognized the other man, but his size and demeanor spoke volumes. He was tall, six-foot-three, and walked with a swagger. He held a silenced Glock .45 in his right hand.

When Mansour entered the garage the light was dim, but their eyes had adjusted, and refractions of the sunlight illuminated the garage. Mansour stepped forward and examined the four men in the gray light. He looked into their eyes as he walked close to each man, a stony look in his eyes, and no words.

Mansour removed a small, powerful flashlight and went to the farthest van. Over a silent few minutes, Mansour inspected each van.

When he was done, he stepped toward the bombers—Shahin, Farhad, Mohsen, and Dariush—without emotion.

"The preparations are not flawless, but they are good, and I thank you on behalf of the Supreme Leader and the Republic," said Mansour, in Persian, in a gravelly voice. "You each are making payment for errors of the past, and I too have made mistakes, but I want you to know, Shahin, Farhad, Mohsen, and Dariush, that, rest assured, when we are successful, your families will be rewarded with the gratitude of the Republic. I have personally seen to it. If I die today, which I expect I will, like you, I have arranged for your families to be taken care of."

Mansour paused and looked each man in the eyes.

"If you believe this will be easy you're wrong," Mansour said, looking at the tall twenty-five-year-old, Shahin. "Shahin, what is your tunnel and best route?"

"I'm going to the Queens-Midtown Tunnel," said Shahin. "Over the Tappan Zee and down."

Mansour stared at Shahin. Mansour knew that each tunnel was important, but the Queens-Midtown Tunnel was the most important. It emptied into Manhattan just below the United Nations complex. It was critical that Shahin succeed. Yet, Mansour didn't say anything; he knew that any of the men could get pulled over on their way to the tunnels, or, God forbid, get cold feet, and he didn't want any possibility of one of them saying something. By compartmentalizing the operation into three silos—tunnels, UN, and active shooters—Mansour was ensuring that each attack could stand on its own.

"Dariush?" said Mansour, looking at another man.

"The Battery Tunnel, sir," said Dariush. "I'm going down through New Jersey and will come from the west through Staten Island."

"Very good," said Mansour. "Mohsen?"

"I have the Holland Tunnel," said Mohsen. "I'll take a similar route as Dariush, then cut over near MetLife Stadium and down through Jersey City."

"What about you, Farhad?" said Mansour.

"I will be destroying the Lincoln Tunnel, sir, on behalf of the Republic," said Farhad. "Same route as Mohsen, just a few exits earlier."

"Very good," said Mansour. "Dariush, you need to get moving and drive as fast as you can without getting arrested."

"Yes, sir."

"It is imperative that each of you get as far into the tunnels as you can by nine o'clock. Then detonate the bombs at the same time," continued Mansour. "Do you understand how important it is in the overall mission that you detonate the bombs together? *It is the difference between success and failure!* Drive slowly if you are ahead of schedule. If you're early, get to the end of the tunnel and pull over and pretend you're having car trouble. But be in the tunnel, hopefully far into it, by nine A.M. or everything will be lost. Everything we have worked for."

The four men nodded in acknowledgment.

"This is the last time we will speak," said Mansour. "Thank you for your sacrifice. May we meet again in the afterlife, my brothers."

Mansour turned and walked toward the door.

The four Iranians climbed into the vans. The engines went on just as Shahin pressed a remote and the bay doors lifted up into the air. They all watched as Mansour tore away from the garage, heading south, toward Manhattan.

30

Breakfast after the clays was casual, a buffet of pancakes (blueberry, raspberry, and plain), bacon and sausage, kippers, lox, and fried eggs. Dewey took a plate and piled up a few eggs and blueberry pancakes, along with a pile of bacon, sausage, and some toast. He was surrounded by competitors from the shooting party, each congratulating him. Several servants also congratulated him.

He sat on a deck chair with Jenna's father and mother, along with a few other people.

"So, Dewey, where are you from?" asked Jemima, Jenna's mother.

"Maine," said Dewey.

"Where in Maine?" she said. "I absolutely love Maine. I went to summer camp there . . . a few years ago."

"Years?" said Farragut. "At this point it's decades, dear."

"Oh, do be quiet," Jemima said as everyone laughed.

"Castine," said Dewey.

"Castine?" said one of the individuals seated in the loose semicircle, in a refined British accent. "I believe that was the site of a great naval battle between England and the Colonies?"

Dewey nodded. "Yes, I believe you're right, though it was no longer a colony."

"Yes, thank you," the man said. "Your Paul Revere was in charge of the military operation. The Penobscot Expedition. Until Pearl Harbor, America's greatest naval defeat. Of course, soon after that I believe you routed the bloody hell out of us!"

Dewey smiled. He was drinking a Bloody Mary. After finishing a sip, he looked around, and at the man, but he said nothing.

"I've actually been to Castine," said Farragut, breaking the silence. "It's a beautiful town practically surrounded by water."

For some time, they grilled Dewey on Castine, on BC, where he'd gone to college, and then tried to probe into his military background, with Dewey admitting to little more than the fact that, yes, he'd been in the military.

The boat was crowded with other similar groups of guests of the Farraguts, gathered at tables, or some even sitting right down on the deck, talking and laughing. He saw Jenna seated with another group, one floor above, toward the back of the boat.

Meanwhile, a servant kept his Bloody Mary fresh, and he soon found himself enjoying the conversation with Jenna's parents. Jenna's mother looked like Jenna, except that her hair was auburn. Farragut didn't look like her at all, though he saw Jenna in her father's sharp intelligence.

The yacht was like a castle on the water, and every detail was attended to, down to the green aging of the copper patina on the balustrade closest to Dewey.

The massive harbor in the direction of New York City was dotted with boats, and a helicopter flew occasionally by, a news chopper or someone commuting to the city from Long Island.

Dewey stood up and thanked the Farraguts. He retrieved another Bloody Mary and found his way back to his room belowdecks. He wanted to take a shower. The shooting had been a workout. He took off his clothing and opened the door to the bathroom between his room and Jenna's.

31

Mansour sped the minivan down the Henry Hudson Parkway, moving down the eastern side of the island. When the highway split, in the Washington Heights section of upper Manhattan, he stayed right, following the Harlem River Drive into Washington Heights, and exited almost immediately into a large complex of brick tenements, finding the parking lot at the southern end of the massive apartment complex. There, five vans were parked in a line. They were different colors. All of them were used and even a little beat-up. Mansour and Ali climbed from the minivan. Mansour turned the vehicle off but left the keys in it and crossed the parking lot, and climbed into the front passenger seat of the closest van.

The vans left the lot even as the city was drowning in the traffic of the morning commute.

Mansour looked back, eyeing six men in the van. Each was cloaked in black with close-fitting communications-wired shock helmets and sunglasses, and was dressed in tactical gear from the waist up. Each soldier had on a black weapons jacket with the letters FBI in bright neon yellow across the front and back. The attire was based as closely as possible on what Federal agents would be wearing. If even one sniper paused first because he believed one of the Iranians was a Federal agent, it could be the difference between success and failure.

Mansour said nothing as he reached beneath the seat and pulled out a weapons jacket, stacked with mags, then reached to the ceiling and pulled down a rifle. It was a Steyr AUG A3 M1.

Mansour looked at the driver. He spoke quietly.

"What of the bus?" said Mansour.

"The bus is on its way," said the driver.

"How many?" said Mansour.

"Thirty," said the driver, Ali.

Mansour removed his phone and hit a number from his contacts. He was about to dial, but didn't. He decided not to. Everything was planned and in motion. He didn't want to disturb the equilibrium he'd built. Tactical weaknesses had yet to be exposed. Meddling was unnecessary. In fact, it was counterproductive. Instead, Mansour opened his Instagram. He found the page of his wife, Shaara, who he had not seen in over a year. Her long black hair looked like silk. Her face was like a painting by the greatest artist he'd ever seen.

If all went well Mansour might actually survive. He would be a hero in Iran, and in the Middle East. All he cared about at this moment was that he might see Shaara again.

"What happened in Washington?" said Ali from the driver's seat.

"That was yesterday," Mansour said. He pocketed his phone and stared out the window as the van sped toward the United Nations.

"What about the American?" said Ali.

"Andreas will be taken to some safe place because they realize his security perimeter was penetrated," said Mansour. "Thus, Andreas is irrelevant. It cost us three lives, but if he is out of the picture, in this way, the operation was successful."

Ali nodded.

Mansour's mind went to the video of Andreas killing his men. It didn't matter now. Even if the Americans were tipped off, he was too far away to matter, and besides, what was one man?

32

The presidential motorcade rolled up in front of the United Nations along First Avenue. Behind steel barricades, crowds were packed tight, thousands of citizens.

Dellenbaugh emerged from the back of the presidential limousine and crossed a wide and empty concrete courtyard. The area was surrounded at its perimeter by throngs of people and journalists, as news cameras from all over the world filmed the scene live, and both supporters and detractors of the president gathered to see him.

Mostly, there were supporters in the thousands, waving signs and yelling.

A flank of Secret Service agents collapsed around Dellenbaugh as he moved to a red velvet rope along the line of people. The president shook hands, and signed various objects, like books, photos, and several old Detroit Red Wings hockey jerseys with the name DELLENBAUGH across the shoulders. The president posed for photos, and even ventured into the gathered people.

"*Hey!*" called Dellenbaugh as he approached the boisterous crowd. "Thanks for coming out! My New York contingent!"

The crowd roared with cheers.

A woman approached, putting her sign to the side. She was standing next to a young girl, her daughter.

"Hello, Mr. President," the young girl said, reaching her hand out.

"What's your name, cutie pie?" said the president, crouching so he could see her face-to-face.

"Annie."

"Nice to meet you, Annie," said Dellenbaugh as he shook her hand.

"It's an honor to meet you, sir," she said. "Good luck today."

"Thanks, I'll give it my best."

President Dellenbaugh moved along the line, in front of the mass of people, shaking hands and saying hello. After handshakes, polite hugs, and waves to the crowd, the president and his security envelope turned and headed for the entrance to the UN building. Waiting at the center of the UN Plaza were António Guterres, the UN secretary general; the U.S. ambassador to the UN, Brad Wasik; and ambassadors from Israel, England, Germany, Canada, South Korea, New Zealand, Austria, Norway, France, Finland, Ireland, and Australia.

They chatted as they walked to the entrance to the UN building, posing before the cameras. While they didn't all agree on everything, it was a photo op, and, despite multitudes of challenges on the world stage, projecting solidarity was critically important. Yet, Dellenbaugh knew that today's visit was going to be explosive. He glanced up at the UN building as Guterres gently nodded and pointed, leading the American president to the UN building entrance just a hundred feet away.

33

The White House chief of staff's office was connected to the Oval Office by an elegant, windowless hallway with walls of reddish-brown bird's-eye maple, and illuminated by two silver sconces.

The Oval Office was a well-known setting, the subject and site of many photos in history books, newspapers, and magazines across the globe. But few had ever seen the chief of staff's office. It was a long, palatial spread of a room, if slightly thin. Walls of bookshelves, a large seating area of leather sofas, a big desk, all atop a gorgeous, striking oriental carpet in tan, red, green, and black, a gift to Adrian King from the king of Saudi Arabia.

Adrian King's office was a well-organized mess—stacks of books, files, and folders scattered across the office, but in piles whose contents he knew cold. His desk was spare, however. Just a pair of high-tech phone consoles and a photo of his daughters and wife. On the wall was a large framed photo of King standing over a bear he'd just shot on a hunting trip in Montana. The message was clear: I killed this bear. If you think you can out-tough me, go ahead and try.

King stood behind his desk, loosening his tie. He had short-cropped brown hair, speckled with gray, and a hard-nosed, Irish demeanor. His eyebrows were conspicuous, two shaggy, massive caterpillars he refused to trim.

Before the desk were two chairs. Two individuals were seated in them: Hector Calibrisi, the director of the CIA, and Jim Bruckheimer, the head of Signals Intelligence Directorate, who ran all high-level SIGINT at Fort Meade.

"Get to it," said King.

"You need to cancel the UN speech, Adrian," said Calibrisi.

"*What?*" said King. "Are you out of your fucking mind? I'm not in the mood for this, Hector."

Bruckheimer had a laptop screen up and pivoted it toward King. It was a digital map. At the center of the map was New York City; specifically, Manhattan.

"Manhattan," said Bruckheimer, pointing at the screen. "Signals data is why we're here."

Bruckheimer punched a key and the map of New York City was suddenly and abruptly lit up by bright yellow digital lines, a crosshatch of real-time data caught by SID appliances and software.

"What is it?" said King.

"SIGINT from seven hours ago," said Bruckheimer. "These are electronic, encrypted, cryptographic microwave and other assorted forms of electrical signals that we track, because sometimes they reveal something. In this case, there is a classic attack pattern. It all started after a text was sent from Berlin on a phone that Thin-Thread correlated to a Level Two Tertiary."

"What do the lines represent, Jim?" said King, leaning in and staring curiously.

"Anything electronic. Phone calls, mostly on burners, ghost email accounts, dark web, credit card transactions, social media. We don't know the content, we just know it happened, and that it started with a single text from a Level Two Tertiary."

"Got it," said King. "So you lock in the Level Two and this is everything that basically spins off of him."

"Precisely," said Bruckheimer.

"Just so I know we're talking the same language, what do you mean by 'Level Two Tertiary'?" said King.

"Level One is a terrorist," said Bruckheimer. "Al-Zawahiri, Jehad Mostafa, Yasin, Mansour, Bierscht. Architects like al-Rashid. Level Two is someone electronically, digitally, connected to a Level One. Someone who participates in a signal from a Level One, a phone call, text, e-mail, whatever. It means a signal was tracked to someone—or more specifically, *from* someone whose device we catalogued at some point because it intersected with a Level One."

"So someone who interacted with Al Qaeda?" said King, shaking his head. His face took on a concerned edge, which, for King, meant a hint of his Irish anger. He looked at Calibrisi. "Well?"

"Or Taliban, Hezbollah, Mujahideen, Hamas, ISIS, Antifa, al-Shabbab, and various other splinters. A Level Two could be someone who has nothing to do with terror," said Calibrisi. "A housepainter or whatever, who the Level One called."

"*So fucking what!*" yelled King. "How many times has this happened in the last week?"

"Has what happened?" said Bruckheimer.

"How many Level Twos have we detected in the last week?" said King. He took his suit coat off and tossed it to the floor next to his desk.

"I get your point," said Bruckheimer. "Are we making a mountain out of a molehill?"

"Exactly," said King.

"There were no Level Twos last week. The week before, there were three. Level Twos happen," said Bruckheimer, "but the signals activity in and around New York City following the only text this device has ever sent to the United States is astonishing. I've never seen it before. In our world, this is called an 'attack pattern' or 'mushroom cloud.'"

"Got it," said King, nodding, thinking. He looked at Bruckheimer. "Who made the call?"

"We don't know," said Bruckheimer. "Remember, these are signals. Electronic signals."

"What about human intelligence?" said King, looking at Calibrisi.

"Nothing. We're scanning everything, but again this is happen-

152

ing as we speak," said Calibrisi. "But one of our personnel was targeted on U.S. soil yesterday near his home in D.C."

"Who?"

"Dewey. It was Hezbollah. Fortunately, he killed all three of the attackers. Theoretically, it might be related," said Calibrisi. "You're learning about this in real time. Something is about to happen in New York City."

"So what are you saying?" said King, urgency in his voice, glaring at Calibrisi. "The president is flying up to New York City to deliver a goddam speech to the United Nations and there could be some sort of terror attack? Are you suggesting we call it off?"

"Yes, call it off," said Calibrisi.

King looked at Bruckheimer.

"I agree," said Bruckheimer.

King glanced at Calibrisi. He took a deep breath, then exhaled. He brushed his hand back through his hair. King took an empty coffee cup from his desk. It was white and ceramic, and had the colors of the logo of King's high school alma mater on the side, crimson and gray. King paused, then hurled the mug at the wall, just above the grizzly photo, where it shattered into a hundred pieces down on top of a pile of files. He looked at Calibrisi with a look of disbelief.

"The president left ahead of schedule," said King, picking up his phone. "He's already landed and is at the UN."

34

Samantha Stout stood in front of an oval-shaped, waist-high table. Four other individuals were with her.

The table Stout stood in front of was six feet in length and three feet across. The surface of the table was a digital screen composed of several smaller screens displaying various information—charts, live media feed, streaming live views from satellites, real-time on-the-ground video, and a dozen other sources of electronic content, all focused on the mushroom cloud of SIGINT. Stout and her analysts were poring through signals data, reaching forward, tapping the digital screen. It was a satellite map of Manhattan. She'd been able to back-trace some of the signals data and pinpoint individuals in the city who'd been part of the earlier attack pattern. It took ThinThread time to parse data, and the agglomeration of hard evidence came in waves. But it was growing. Moving red dots highlighted what she assumed were terrorists. It was growing into a red-dotted panoply as ThinThread identified, then catalogued and interfaced against the digital map. She couldn't count the number; it was in the hundreds—all moving, on separate routes. A large cluster was around the UN.

She put her cell to her ear and called Bruckheimer.

"Yeah?"

"I did a back-pull on the metadata. They have at least four or five hundred people in New York, mostly in Manhattan," said Stout. "Maybe more."

Bruckheimer held his hand up, interrupting King:

"We did a back-pull on the signals, mapped it against current activity," said Bruckheimer. "There are hundreds of what we have to assume are terrorists in Manhattan. A bunch are around the UN."

King hit the triangular phone console on his desk, a speed dial.

The phone rang twice, then a gravelly voice came on the line:

"Adrian," said Anna Lungren, the head of NYPD.

"Anna, you have a situation on your hands," said King. "I need you to also notify FBI."

"What's the situation?" said Lungren.

"I don't know," said King. "I just know it's about to happen. The president is at the UN. It's Hezbollah."

"Understood," said Lungren. "Thanks for the heads-up. I'll loop in McNaughton."

Dave McNaughton ran the FBI.

King hung up the phone and pointed at Calibrisi.

"Get an exfiltration team in the air," said King.

"Got it," said Calibrisi.

"I'll call the president," said King. "He's not going to be happy."

Calibrisi walked two doors down. It was his West Wing office, when he needed one, small but with a view of the South Lawn. He picked up his phone.

Calibrisi hit speed dial for Bill Polk. Polk was deputy director of the CIA, and ran the National Clandestine Service, which included Special Operations Group, the CIA's paramilitary and preemptive action team, and Special Activities Division, who recruited foreign agents, manipulated currency and elections, and constituted the intellectual side of operations against foreign actors and enemies.

"Hey," said Polk. "What do you need?"

"We need an exfiltration team at the UN," said Calibrisi.

"The president?" said Polk.

"Yeah," said Calibrisi.

"I'm assuming by air, otherwise he'd be in a car by now, right?" said Polk.

"That's right," said Calibrisi.

"Got it," said Polk. "The *Eisenhower* is up the coast. I think SEAL 4 is there right now. Where's the pickup, or should they go in?"

"Roof of the UN building," said Calibrisi.

"I'll get to work. You can fill me in later. They should be airborne in three or four minutes," said Polk. "What floor is he on, just in case?"

"Eighteen," said Calibrisi.

"Do we have any Tier Ones in Manhattan?" said Calibrisi.

"Let me run a scan," said Polk. "Back to you in five."

35

Traffic was heavy all over the city, vehicles scurrying down crowded streets and avenues at rush hour. Sidewalks were packed with people walking to work. Traffic became especially dense near the UN. Outer blocks, two or three streets away, were practically not moving. The block surrounding the UN complex was shut off to traffic behind lines of pylons and cordons, behind it dozens of SWAT and various other uniformed policemen, all clutching rifles and scanning the traffic as it diverted away from the UN.

Horns were blaring. A din of engine noise and traffic permeated the air.

Mansour was seated in the front passenger seat of the van. They were at Fiftieth Street, moving slowly in a line of traffic on Second Avenue. Taxis, Ubers, a bus; they were crawling south. At some point, as they came closer, he could see the UN building to his left, a block away, above other buildings.

"Closer," said Mansour. *"Drive!"*

36

Admiral J. J. Quinn, commanding officer of the USS *Eisenhower*, was in his office aboard the aircraft carrier when the call came in.

They were fifty miles offshore from Connecticut, there for a three-week visit purportedly for maintenance and training, though in reality they were running various speed and diagnostic tests on a new submarine fresh off the line at Groton Shipyard in New London.

The Navy SEALs had arrived unannounced two days before. As always, Quinn and his crew were expected to find them beds and make them feel at home. But Quinn and several of his top men had been SEALs in a prior life—and he welcomed the visit.

Now he understood why someone had dropped the team in.

His phone console beeped and the speaker came on.

"Admiral, you have a call."

"Who is it?"

"Bill Polk."

Quinn picked up the phone.

"Bill, how are you?" said Quinn.

"Fine, Joey," said Polk. "We need to exfiltrate the president from the UN. This is Emergency Priority. I'll call you when we get through this, just get them in the air."

"I'm on it," said Quinn, standing up and lurching for the door. "Thank you, Joey."

Quinn charged down the stairs and across a secure corridor to where he knew he'd find the brigade from SEAL Team 4. In a large, windowless room with bunk beds, computers, a pool table, a Ping-Pong table, a bare-bones utilitarian kitchen, TVs, and several dilapidated chairs and sofas, he found most if not all of SEAL Team 4. Quinn looked around as conversation stopped.

One of the SEALs, Minelli, stood up from a chair.

"Admiral Quinn?" said Minelli. "What do you need, sir?"

"There is an Emergency Priority situation," said Quinn. "You guys are flying to the UN and extracting the president. In-theater command control. I want you in the air in three."

37

Two bright yellow school buses came inching up First Avenue, one in front of the other, moving slowly in the massive traffic jam on First Avenue, most acute in the area surrounding the United Nations. The buses were in the easternmost lane, nearest to the UN, slowly approaching the cordoned-off building. From the outside, the buses looked empty, except for the drivers, perhaps on their way to pick up schoolchildren they'd dropped off earlier at the UN on a field trip?

At Forty-second Street, a block below the UN, all vehicles were asked to divert left, into a slow-moving traffic jam away from the highly secure UN complex, where President J. P. Dellenbaugh had just entered.

News trucks and a line of reporters occupied a roped-off section of sidewalk between Forty-second and Forty-third. The camera shot was ideal, an early-morning clear sky surrounding the gorgeous geometric glass-and-concrete edifice of the UN building, whose dark, reflective glass on this morning, with the powder-blue sky above, looked like the ocean.

An FBI officer stood at the corner of Forty-second Street and First Avenue, waving cars and trucks left. When the driver of the first bus waved, the agent allowed the buses to go straight into the cordoned-off area near the reporters, close to the perimeter. The agent held an MP7A1 aimed at the ground. He stopped the first bus. The driver opened the door.

"Yeah."

"P.S. One Twenty-two."

"You here to pick up some kids?" said the FBI agent.

The FBI agent looked at the driver, a bald, olive-skinned man with dark eyes, and he suddenly became still as he watched the driver looking at his watch, then to the horizon, as if waiting for something.

A dull *thwack*—then a bullet from a gunman crouched near the bus door blew a dime-sized hole to the agent's cheek, a kill shot. It blew out the back of his skull across the sidewalk and he tumbled awkwardly to the ground.

The driver and another man climbed quickly down and lifted the dead agent up, dragging him back onto the bus, even as the driver registered a police officer, who suddenly glanced in the direction of the bus and started walking toward it.

The driver turned to his men.

"Get ready," he said, looking down the aisle of the bus at a swarm of Hezbollah, all tucked down behind seats and near the ground, out of sight. "It's about to begin."

38

8:54 A.M.
SPECIAL OPERATIONS GROUP
BASEMENT LEVEL TWO
OPERATIONS ROOM
CIA HEADQUARTERS
LANGLEY, VIRGINIA

Polk entered the Special Operations Group ops room. It looked like the control room at NASA. Large digital screens covered the walls in every direction. A large bullpen filled with workstations occupied the area between the four walls.

All the screens were focused on areas outside the U.S. Two operations were under way, one in Surrey, near London, and the other in Hong Kong.

Polk walked to the nearest bullpen. He looked at an analyst.

"Give me any Tier Ones we have in or around Manhattan, Bobby," said Polk.

"I'm not authorized, sir."

"Go in through Turbulence," said Polk. "Six-six-one."

The analyst, a young black man with glasses, started typing furiously.

The screen went dark. Then a red flashing alert read: NO/SEC.

Polk leaned forward and put his hand on a glass print screen. Suddenly, three photographs spread out like playing cards across the screen. The first photo was a man with thick brown hair, a beard and mustache, and a sharp nose. Though only a head shot, the face and the neck showed a large man, muscular. Across the photo: NOC 2495–6.

Then below:

ANDREAS, DEWEY

The second photo showed a pale man with glasses and dirty blond hair. He had a large nose and a long face. Above all, he looked intelligent. A scar beneath his left eye gave him a somewhat dangerous look. Across the photo: NOC 3390 AB2.

SINGERMAN, AARON

A third photo showed a young man with blond hair and chiseled features, cleanly shaven. He was handsome and his look was casual, and it was hard to imagine that he could be a danger to anyone. NOC 887–01.

TACOMA, ROBERT

A flashing red box pulsated over a part of the map.

The analyst typed, zeroing in on the signal.

A satellite camera moved in, focusing down from the sky, and soon homed in on an object.

It was a large yacht.

The analyst tapped the keyboard. Suddenly, a series of photos appeared, imposed above the live video feed, as well as a bio.

>>GPSH SIG CAPTURE PER TF 0739 R CARNAVALE ADD/SAD >>

LOCATION TRACKER ZEBRA ALPHA [DOMESTIC] >> FILE#G520094462210 <<

>>AFFIRM NO/SEC
TIER 1———
>> S S D O R S E T

X. K. C. C. 0 9 0 5 5
>>GHS RING: NEW YORK CITY MSA3
ANDREAS, DEWEY
-ACTIVE-
TIER 1 NO/SEC[9]
NOC 2495–6
US ARMY RANGER
1ST SPECIAL FORCES OPERATIONAL DETACHMENT
SPANISH FLUENCY
FILES:
TBT8773 [AGENCY MEDAL OF VALOR]
TBN8919 [AGENCY MEDAL OF VALOR]
AS4–467
XC77–02 [MEDAL OF HONOR][AGENCY MEDAL OF VALOR]
KI-U664 [AGENCY MEDAL OF VALOR]
IU8002
PPL3450
RR9P7 [MEDAL OF HONOR][AGENCY MEDAL OF VALOR]
FR4189
JG6-77-BB
TAI-449B [AGENCY MEDAL OF VALOR]
ACTIVE TYPE 1 "PHANTOM"
COLD WEAPONS EXPERTISE ALPHA 1 [RANK 1 CIA DDS]
FIREARMS TIER 6 MASTER GUNMAN

Suddenly, the second screen focused down on Columbia University. It homed in on a building.

AFFIRM NO/SEC
TIER 1———
>> C O L U M B I A S I A
X. K. C. C. 4 5 4 3
>>GHS RING: NEW YORK CITY MSA3
SCHOOL OF INTL AFFAIRS/COLUMBIA
>SINGERMAN, AARON

-INACTIVE W/NOTICE PRECLUSION [RET F]-
TIER 1 NO/SEC [SPECIAL UNIT "RED DELTA" FINTECH]
NOC 3390 AB2
YALE UNIVERSITY, [CIA] PROGRESSIVE "Q" PROGRAM
[SUBH]
LONDON SCHOOL OF ECONOMICS, CURRENCY [8A RANKING]
WHARTON SCHOOL OF BUSINESS, [JACOB TURNER AD-
VANCED MATHEMATICS FELLOW]
FRENCH, GERMAN, HEBREW, RUSSIAN FLUENCY
RECRUITMENT VIA ATHANASIA, D., EX-SFO [NFLHCMR]
US MARINES
GOLDMAN SACHS
MATHWORKS >
CIA NCS
>SPECIAL ACTIVITIES DIVISION [CURRENCY STRATEGY
AND ADVANCED DIGITAL |OFFENSIVE| OPERATIONS]
DIRECTOR NON PROGRAM 22 [FEDERAL RESERVE]
FILES:
6-Y6650 [AGENCY MEDAL OF VALOR]
TBSD24
US677W
78X8T
HH133
ACTIVE TYPE 5 "COBRA"
COLD WEAPONS EXPERTISE GAMMA 6
FIREARMS TIER 2 EXPERIENCED

A third computer screen zeroed in on the Mandarin Hotel.

AFFIRM NO/SEC
TIER 1———
>> M A N D A R I N H O T E L N Y C 5 9 S T
X. K. C. C. B 1 1 2 1 G
>>GHS RING: NEW YORK CITY MSA3
>TACOMA, ROBERT

165

-INACTIVE PER PRESIDENTIAL ORDER "PROJECT BLACK-OCEAN"
466-B8-7531U866*
TIER 1 NO/SEC[5]
NOC 887-01
US NAVY SEAL BXUDT STAGE 4
TIER 1 ALPHA LEVEL ASSASSIN
CIA SPECIAL OPERATIONS GROUP
PRIVATE CITIZEN: RISCON LLC W/EXDDNCS FOXX, K EX
DDNCS NCS SPECIAL OPERATIONS GROUP (W:4910)
RUSSIAN FLUENCY
FILES:
TY56892
G677.3
TBN8919 [MEDAL OF HONOR] [AGENCY MEDAL OF VALOR]
077651
FFU795
FR4189 [AGENCY MEDAL OF VALOR]
ACTIVE TYPE 1 "LION"
COLD WEAPONS EXPERTISE ALPHA 2
FIREARMS TIER 11 GRANDMASTER GUNMAN [RANK 1 CIA DDS]

>>>>> F I N A L >>>>> F I N A L >>>>> F I N A L
[3] <<<<

There were three Tier 1s in New York City; two were inactive, and one, Andreas, was active.

Polk, of course, knew all three. He knew them well.

The numbers were linked to various after-action reports from various operations Singerman, Andreas, and Tacoma had been involved with, and Polk didn't need to reread them. Andreas and Tacoma were pure operators. Singerman was one of Langley's top currency experts and political masterminds.

Though Tacoma and Singerman were technically inactive, in times of emergency any NOC—non-official cover—could be activated.

He looked at the analyst.

"Let's initiate contact with all three, Bobby," said Polk. "Send a tracer. Have everything come in to me, then bleach the records under Emergency Priority, section four."

39

8:55 A.M.
FLOOR 18
UNITED NATIONS SECRETARIAT BUILDING
OFFICE OF THE UN SECRETARY GENERAL
FIRST AVENUE AND FORTY-SECOND STREET
NEW YORK CITY

In the lobby, Dellenbaugh separated from the group and walked with Ambassador Brad Wasik to a waiting elevator. They climbed aboard, alone.

Dellenbaugh looked at Wasik.

"I hear you're thinking about going back to Arizona and running for governor," said Dellenbaugh.

"Yes," said Wasik. "I apologize for not telling you first, sir."

"Don't apologize," said the president. "But I have another job I want to talk to you about."

The elevator doors opened on the eighteenth floor. As Ambassador Wasik and the president stepped off the elevator, Dellenbaugh was met by the head of the Secret Service, Gene Callanan. Callanan took Dellenbaugh's forearm sternly. He pushed Dellenbaugh away from the gathered crowd. Callanan handed the president his cell phone.

"Mr. President, it's Adrian King," said Callanan.

"Thanks," said Dellenbaugh, taking the phone. "What's up?"

Dellenbaugh was suddenly surrounded by a crowd, including employees of the U.S. Mission to the UN, as well as VIPs from other countries and from the secretary general's staff. He put the cell to his ear.

"We have a serious situation, sir," said King on the phone.

Dellenbaugh smiled as he moved through the crowd, stopping and saying hello even as he spoke to his chief of staff. Many of the faces were familiar, individuals who'd worked to get him elected president, who now worked for the administration—and he stopped to say hello to each one, even as he knew he needed to hear what his chief of staff had to say.

"Excuse me," said the president to one of the UN staff members, as he found Ambassador Wasik and gave him a look. Wasik saw the urgency of the call and situation. He led Dellenbaugh away from the throng.

The president stepped to the window and looked back at the gathered crowd, all there to meet him.

"A situation?" said the president.

"It looks like there could be an imminent terror attack about to take place on the United States," said King.

"*Where?*" said Dellenbaugh.

"New York City. If I had to guess, *you*, sir," said King.

"What the hell are you saying?" said Dellenbaugh, barely above a whisper.

"I think you should make an Irish exit," said King. "Get back on the elevator and we can reschedule the speech."

"No way," said President Dellenbaugh. "I'm surrounded by people and I'm about to give a speech I've wanted to give for a year now."

"Yeah, I don't think so, sir," said King.

"Who is it?" said Dellenbaugh.

"Hezbollah."

"I'm not backing down from giving a speech in my own country, Adrian."

"There isn't going to be any speech, sir," said King.

40

Farhad reached the entrance to the Lincoln Tunnel earlier than anticipated. He'd driven the speed limit from Sloatsburg, and there was traffic the entire way, yet still he was there already. He was too early, he realized—as the multitude of lanes funneled into four as they crawled toward the tunnels. He could not enter yet. He would get through to the other side before nine o'clock.

There was still an exit ahead, but he also feared that if he got off at the final exit before the tunnel, he might not be able to navigate back and reenter the tunnel in time.

There were two entrances ahead, each with two lanes of traffic. Just before the tunnel was an empty space, strewn with garbage, an embankment no bigger than a car or two. Farhad moved into the right lane and cut before another car. Horns blared. He pulled onto the small embankment and stopped. He was perspiring. People were yelling, horns continued to blare, but soon the noise died off and he just sat there, in park, waiting. It was all he had to do. Just a few minutes.

Dariush drove as fast as he could, down Route 23, west of the city, then Route 46, then Route 3 through New Jersey, picking up 95 just across from Manhattan and heading south. Traffic was terrible. Dariush crossed into other lanes haphazardly, weaving dangerously. He knew he had less than ninety minutes to make a trip that—at rush hour—should've taken at least two hours.

He rode up on trucks and cruised down the breakdown lane when things became jammed near Secaucus.

He got onto 278 and headed across Staten Island. When he came to the entrance of the tunnel, he breathed a sigh of relief, and then he remembered he was about to die.

As the lanes converged near the entrance to the tunnel, the van was next to a yellow school bus. A group of young girls in white-and-blue uniforms waved at Dariush.

At first, he didn't acknowledge them, but then he couldn't help thinking that one of the schoolchildren reminded him of his younger sister, Hannah.

"Hello there!" shouted one of the girls as they all waved, giggling and laughing.

"Hello," said Dariush, smiling as he waved back. He told himself he did it so as not to raise suspicion, but the truth was, he thought of his sister and how much he would miss her. He let the bus cut in front of him, and then swerved into the line of traffic. He was inside the Battery Tunnel a minute later. He slowed down and let others pass him.

In those moments, Dariush wanted time to slow down. He hoped the school bus would be out of the tunnel by the time the clock struck nine.

"Drive faster, little ones," he said aloud, to no one.

Mohsen had the rearview mirror aimed at himself as he drove. He smiled at himself in the mirror, and pushed his hand back through his thick locks, admiring himself in the mirror.

If he looked behind himself, Mohsen could see the wall of oc-tanitrocubane.

He was in the tunnel now, in the long queue of cars and trucks, and he smiled at himself again in the mirror.

In mere moments, he would be dead, and so at this moment, along his final drive, and last bit of time here on earth, he tried to distract himself by looking at himself in the mirror.

He saw a BMW in the other lane and it reminded him of his uncle.

Mohsen knew he was in his final moments. . . .

Shahin was the most important of the four. The Queens-Midtown Tunnel emptied into Manhattan just beneath the United Na-tions. The success of Shahin's attack was crucial to the plan and would create in-theater environmental chaos that would help to obscure the street-level attack by Mansour and a brigade of Hezbollah soldiers, all loyal to Mansour and to the Republic.

He was stuck in a line of traffic. Some sort of accident up ahead. By 8:15 Shahin was still in Queens, aboveground, in a line of vehicles inching along toward the entrance to the Queens-Midtown Tunnel.

By 8:55 Shahin was inside the tunnel. Ahead, he saw the lights of police cruisers. Every lane was shut except for one.

At 8:57, he was just a few cars away. Two cars looked dented and partially crushed. Two ambulances were on the scene.

A car suddenly stopped in front of him. Someone in the car was screaming. It was a woman. She recognized one of the cars in the accident.

He looked at his phone:

08:59:31

The woman was older, in her sixties, and overweight. She climbed out of the car crying the name of a woman, her daughter, whose car she recognized, crushed in from the side.

Shahin abruptly swerved out from behind the line and accelerated, just as a policeman ran to meet the hysterical woman. Shahin floored it, honking his horn as he went from 30 to 40 to 50 mph, but the noise just blended into the confusion and disarray. He hit the policeman first, slamming him with the right front of the van before he even was aware. He struck the woman dead center and she went tumbling under the van, her screams soon muted as Shahin bounced the tire of the van over her skull, crushing it like an egg.

As bullets clanged into the van, Shahin kept his foot to the pedal, weaving in and out of cars past the accident.

08:59:48

He saw digital signs demarcating the end of the tunnel just ahead, and as he swerved the last few hundred feet in between cars, he checked his watch. As the seconds ticked toward their ineluctable fate, he glanced one more time.

08:59:59

09:00:00

09:00:01

For a moment, Shahin thought perhaps something was wrong, and he felt, in that split second, a sense of relief, reprieve, as if somehow he might escape. . . .

Then Shahin suddenly saw white energy everywhere, and, for a fraction of a moment, felt warmth that grew hot, and suddenly there came the sound—and he felt the concussion as it blew out his ears, as he lost his vision, he felt pain, and saw the final moment and then it was all gone—it went black—as he was vaporized by the explosion. It all blurred into nothingness and one, a continuum, as suddenly he was immolated in heat and fire, as the octanitrocubane exploded out, sucking up oxygen, incinerating everything, including steel, and the end of the Queens-Midtown Tunnel suddenly fell down from above in white heat, unfathomable destruction that shot back into the tunnel and cascaded out the other end in massive chutes of chemical-laden flames.

The explosions occurred toward the end of each of the tunnels. The four vans had all made it into the last hundred feet of each respective tunnel. There were only four vehicle tunnels into Manhattan. For decades, this vulnerability had been studied by law enforcement and by those in charge of America's national security. Now, it was done.

In each tunnel, the concussive blast moving back into the tunnel melted every vehicle for fifty feet. The larger destruction occurred at the ends of the tunnels. Blue and orange flames blew out from the site of the actual detonations into a fearsome tornado of heat, fire, and seismic trauma. Within seconds, the blocks surrounding the end of the tunnels, where they fed up into Manhattan, were caught up in bluish-orange fire. Anyone or anything nearby was pulverized, melted, killed, by the first flash from the octanitrocubane.

Soon smoke, fire, and heat overwhelmed the surrounding areas, and buildings went alight in fiery winds as automatic heat-sensored alarms screamed from buildings all around.

The cataclysm was all fire and wind. The heat was beyond intense, shooting in every direction, scorching anything nearby the tunnel entrances.

The terrorists now had time to conduct an even broader attack on America. On the president. On the Federal Reserve.

Manhattan was cut off. It was an island.

41

Dellenbaugh felt his legs get kicked back by a powerful, invisible force, like a wind—and then he fell down onto his stomach—abruptly—and was thrown back like a toothpick in a hurricane.

The UN building shook violently—glass shattered along the west wall of the eighteenth floor as a concussive pressure slammed it invisibly, then came the sound of a distant explosion, and then others. The building was rocked, and screams mixed with the sound of shattering glass.

Emergency alarms wailed. . . .

Dellenbaugh caught himself by grabbing onto the wall.

The air was filled with screams as people were thrown through the air, across the room, down to the floor. When the percussion faded, the president got up and ran to the broken windows, as winds cut sharply across the wide-open suite of offices.

In the distance, he saw billowing silver-and-red smoke from explosions ripping high into the morning sky. He looked left and saw another plume of fire and chaos. Sirens roared from inside the building, and fires raged in the vicinity of the explosions. Dellenbaugh looked in shock at the storm clouds. He was disoriented, but he realized it was the tunnels leading into Manhattan.

He still had his phone—he listened for Adrian King, but couldn't hear anything except the faint echo of his name. He looked at the phone. It was red with wet blood. He reached for his ear and wiped his hand across it, then looked at it. It was covered in blood. He put the phone to his other ear. All he heard was sharp ringing—and the faint voice of his chief of staff.

"Mr. President!" said King. *"Mr. President!"*

"We're under attack," said Dellenbaugh.

"I know. We're on our way, sir. But you need to get to the roof."

"What about the explosions?"

"Don't worry about that," said King. "NYPD, FBI, everyone is on it. You need to think about one thing. *Get to the goddam roof!*"

"It's easier to get to the airport in a car," said Dellenbaugh.

"No longer an option, sir," said King. "They're coming after *you*. Do you *fucking* understand? They're coming from below. *Do you understand?*"

Dellenbaugh felt nauseous. Vomit started pouring from his mouth. After several violent retches, he spoke again.

"Yeah," said Dellenbaugh.

He looked at the people around him. Everyone had been dropped by the blast. Several people were moaning, and he saw a few unconscious after the shock wave.

"You okay?" said King.

"Yeah," said Dellenbaugh.

Dellenbaugh looked down and saw thick wisps of blood in his throw-up.

"You can get to the roof?" said King.

"Yeah," said Dellenbaugh, feeling a sense of stupor, even numbness. He absentmindedly put his hand to his ear, feeling the blood he knew was trickling out. "I got it."

42

The driver of the school bus stood up and took the lead position at the bus door. He held up his hand.

"For the Republic," he said.

Then the ground shook like a small earthquake, kicking the bus sideways though it didn't turn over.

The driver waved the first man through and then others, as they'd been assigned. There were thirty-four on each bus, and each man had long since made his deal with Allah.

The first gunman stepped to the sidewalk, stepping over the dead FBI agent. He was followed by other gunmen from the bus, all clutching rifles or submachine guns (SMGs). He started firing at the gathered media, pumping slugs into on-air reporters.

The other gunmen spread around the bus, shooting at anything and everything that moved. Right behind the first bus, the second yellow school bus also poured out.

Dozens of shooters remained on each bus—firing from windows to the west, away from the UN, pumping lead into people and cars, focusing in on any NYPD cruisers or official-looking vehicles, though it didn't matter; they shot at everything they could see moving.

Gunmen on each bus faced the UN and were there to provide

cover. Each gunman had on thermal optics. These soldiers were in place to soften up the interior layer of the security perimeter, the men closest to the president.

As the buses emptied out, several brigades of Hezbollah soldiers—dressed in street clothes—moved toward the UN complex, shooting in front of them as they charged forward, running at the UN building. Inside the buses remained highly trained Hezbollah snipers, who watched as the frontline gunmen moved toward the UN building.

Suddenly, glass shattered and bullets started flying from the UN back at the Iranians. A low *boom*, then another, and soon the Iranians charging at the tower started to drop, like dominoes.

The snipers knew how to work; there was no need for coordination. They started pounding the area behind the broken glass with slugs, even as bullets continued to fire in the direction of the men in front of them, running forward, also shooting.

A window on a higher floor in the tower shattered at the same instant one of the bus snipers was slammed in the forehead by a cartridge that opened upon impact and ripped out the back half of the man's skull, blowing it out across the side window in a bloody mess.

43

Dewey felt the first explosion and turned.

He was on the deck of the *Dorset*, on a wooden sheet of deck in the lee of a massive sail, along with dozens of people, all being served breakfast after the morning shoot. The *Dorset* was just south of Manhattan, in the harbor, treading water on a crystal-clear morning. Dewey was sipping his third beer even though it was 9 A.M., but shooting skeet often involves alcohol, and the truth was he'd had less than most. That's when he felt it—like thunder—and turned.

He saw fire.

Inside his ear, he heard a low beep.

Dewey saw the fiery plumes of smoke and flames, then felt a second and a third shock wave, as in other spots in the skyline, across the distance of the island, smoke suddenly appeared in the sky, rising above distant buildings. Dewey stared at the balls of smoke pirouetting into the blue sky from Manhattan.

He tapped his earbud:

"Identify."

"NOC 2495–6."

"Hold."

Dewey glanced around the deck. Silence and a sense of fear took over the yacht. He looked around for Jenna. She was standing at the far side of the deck.

"Dewey, it's Bill," said Polk. "Bringing you in. The president is at the UN and he's being extracted from the roof."

"I'm not sure that's a good idea," said Dewey.

"Why?" said Polk.

"They're ready for that," said Dewey.

"Too late and I disagree," said Polk. "They have an army of shooters running around the city. Active shooters. Bridges are cut off so the only NYPD available is Manhattan and it's not enough. Busloads of Hezbollah are cutting off the UN from the ground. The president departing by land is not an option any longer."

"Jesus Christ," said Dewey. "Wow. What do you need from me?"

"I need you to get over there," said Polk, "in case the roof extraction goes sideways."

"Is there a fastboat?" said Dewey.

"Yes," said Polk, "ex-UDT who are backup on the Black Hawks. But let's just assume the worst. We need you in there."

"Got it," said Dewey. "Rob's here too."

"Yes," said Polk. "He's my next call. I'll coordinate from above but in-theater I want you guys focusing on mission, got it?"

"Yeah."

"You have open-territory protocol. The president is trapped. I'm looking at his RPS and he's not moving. This is EP recon, Dewey."

"What about Quantico or NYPD?" said Dewey.

"They're fighting guerrilla wars all over the city," said Polk. "Iran embedded hundreds of active shooters; NYPD needs to deal with them. NYPD also needs to deal with the tunnels," added Polk. "The bridges into Manhattan are also blocked. As for FBI, you have a limited number on the island. Iran has strategic advantage. Get moving and focus on the target."

"Roger that," said Dewey, tapping out.

The entire party of guests aboard the *Dorset* stood in awe and shock, staring across the water at Manhattan and the smoky skyline.

Jenna said something to her mother and then walked over to Dewey. As she approached, so too did her father.

"They've blown up the tunnels into the city," said Jenna. "Not to mention what happened to you in Georgetown. Highly choreographed, tightly executed."

Dewey looked at her with a blank expression as Farragut came close.

"Would it be all right if I had access to the weapons room, Bobby?" said Dewey. "I need to borrow a few guns."

"Of course," said Farragut.

"Also, I need your tender," Dewey said, referring to the twenty-nine-foot speedboat used for quick trips to shore.

"Take whatever you want, though the helicopter would be faster," said Farragut.

"Thank you," said Dewey, "but whoever it is has probably already thought about that."

"I get it," said Farragut. "Do you need a wingman? I was First Battalion Alpha SAS."

Jenna grabbed her father. "Dad?"

Dewey nodded. "Sure, I could use you," he said, "but I think you need to calm down the people on this boat, and I would lift anchor immediately and head for open water."

"Good advice," said Farragut. "But we're staying right here. If you need us to do something, we will."

"Thank you for your hospitality," Dewey said, shaking Farragut's hand. "Please thank Jemima for me."

"I will. Look forward to seeing you again, Dewey."

Jenna led Dewey down a circular stairwell and unlocked the door. Inside was the weapons cache he'd seen earlier that day, military grade, neatly arrayed in racks.

"Take the tender up the East River and abandon it on Roosevelt Island, then swim in. You'll need to kill your way in. They'll already have taken the ground floor, but there's no other way. Then get up and find the president."

Dewey took a black MP7A1 and found a suppressor, screwing it into the muzzle. A Colt M1911A1 was already holstered beneath his armpit. He found a vest with a large watertight compartment in back and put it on, then loaded it with mags. He saw a pair of flippers and grabbed them. Then he saw Jenna watching him and the whole last day ran through his head.

He looked down at the ground.

"I'm sorry this ended, I was really having fun," said Dewey, without looking at Jenna. "I'll play it by ear once I get closer. Can you show me where the boat is?"

"Come on," she said.

She stepped into his path and put a hand against his chest. He finally looked her in the eyes.

"Please come back alive," said Jenna.

Dewey smiled.

"I will. Promise."

44

Mansour clutched the door of the van, Ali, the steering wheel, each holding tight. Just as someone behind them honked, the ground seemed to shake, and then glass shattered—it was the bus, to the right. The minivan bounced as if made of rubber. Then came the sound of an explosion. To the left, above the East River, a cloud of black-and-gray smoke erupted into the sky, then there were flames. The flames tunneled up within the smoke as the heat soared into the sky.

Another rumble, from a different direction, to the right, more diffuse, nevertheless made the ground shake for a second time.

Mansour registered two yellow buses then heard automatic gunfire coming in a cloud of noise from in and around the buses.

A white van was just a few cars away from the line of policemen, trapped in a bumper-to-bumper turn, where traffic was being diverted, when suddenly the van's back doors opened. Two men clutching AR-15s, clad in street clothes, leapt out, flanked the van, and looked to the line of officers, then trained their weapons and started firing at them, trying to hold the perimeter of the UN. The raw staccato of the AR-15s arose above the noise. Screams were next, as SWAT and police tried to lurch out of the way of incoming fire-power. . . .

The scene erupted in chaos. . . .

Mansour and Ali opened the doors of the van in unison, stepping out onto the street.

In the distance, in front of them, Mansour assayed the scene. He registered pedestrians—on the ground—blown by the explosion. Some of them were injured. Second Avenue was clogged with cars and buses, all of the occupants no doubt in a state of shock.

Then Mansour registered the layer: soldiers. Dozens of men, climbing from cars, clutching firearms.

Just as he and Ali stepped out of the sedan clutching weapons, so too did a small army of others. Mansour could see many. Stepping out of various vehicles: cab, Uber, and Lyft drivers; delivery people. But those were aliases. All were QUDS. Mansour checked behind him, too, and saw yet more men.

Twenty men in all; they'd been handpicked by Mansour. They were sent to the United States, many through Canada, a few under manufactured identities, all of them immigrants, from various countries. But all of them were Iranian, and all were QUDS. The top tier: Hezbollah.

The UN was on the banks of the East River. The apron ran from the side of the river a block north from the UN in an arc that spread in a half-moon to Second Avenue, then curved back into the East River below the UN. A cordon.

The area inside the arc was the UN, and the objective was straightforward: kill every person inside the arc, particularly the president of the United States.

The security would be vulnerable. Despite the fact that it was the president, the inner tiers of last-line security were rusty, even atrophied. It didn't matter if they were Secret Service, FBI, or NYPD—they weren't Delta or SEALs. The ones assigned here today were there as a gift to them, a prestigious and exciting opportunity to see the president. The protective unit, the envelope, was a chink in the armor.

Mansour kicked the door shut just as, a few cars away, a bearded Italian man in a black Suburban opened the door. He was dressed in a sweatshirt. He held a pistol. It was just a citizen. He was not one of them. He looked around, then saw Mansour. Mansour trained the AR-15 on the man and pulled back on the trigger. A spray of bullets pounded the Italian in the chest, throwing him back against the Suburban, splattering blood across the vehicle.

Suddenly, the sound of automatic gunfire erupted as Mansour started firing at other vehicles, and then the sound was amplified as every Hezbollah gunman also started firing. They shot pedestrians prone on the sidewalks, killing them like they were whacking weeds, then moved into the vehicles. They sprayed bullets into every vehicle in the vicinity of where they were, in the semicircle around the UN—and then, led by Mansour, they all turned and moved in toward the UN complex.

The gunmen shredded the line, firing indiscriminately both behind the line of gunmen and forward, at the UN, beginning the process of clawing their way in.

A few officers in the immediate area—not caught in the initial killing arc of Iranian bullets—returned fire and soon it was an all-out firefight, even as screams and smoke and ash from the explosion at the tunnel started to choke the air.

Mansour climbed into the back of the van. He grabbed a shoulder-fired missile launcher; a Russian-made 9K32 Strela-2. He strapped it over his shoulder, sights extended, launch tube balanced perfectly, gripstock in his hand—and a long, thin missile already loaded and ready to fly. The missile itself was a "directed-energy" blast fragmentation warhead, with detonation immediate and grazing fuses that had a fifteen-second built-in delay before automatic self-destruction, once fired.

One of the men in back opened the rear door. Two gunmen leapt out. Men and women in surrounding vehicles screamed, ducking or leaping from cars, trying to get away. But the gunmen positioned without firing, taking up position at each corner of the back of the van, covering the area. Mansour climbed out of the back, moved around the corner of the van, and knelt behind a gunman on the driver's side, then locked in the optic. He trained the MANPAD on the UN, counting out floors until he came to eighteen.

He waited, even as bullets ricocheted and clanked against the van.

There were more screams, then sirens.

Mansour looked at his watch, then put his eye to the optic. Then he fired the MANPAD.

The Strela made a loud boom and then it hissed and screeched as it soared toward the UN, trailing smoke, drowning out all other noise.

The missile screeched above the live weapon fire around the UN, tearing up at the tower as people screamed. The missile punctured the building approximately halfway up, shattering a large hole in the glass. A half second later, the explosion blew out a large wall of the windows on that floor, as well as the floors above and below. A cascade of glass dropped through the sky in front of the building, shattering in sheets and shards on the plaza directly beneath.

45

Professor Aaron Singerman, age forty-nine, stood in front of a massive chalkboard that spanned the front of the lecture hall. In front of him was a theater filled with students from the university, but not just undergraduates. There were students studying for MBAs, doctoral students at the School for International Affairs, from the law school, and even a few students from Columbia's School of Journalism.

It was a hard class to gain entry to. There were 102 students in the class, but more than 800 had applied for admittance.

Singerman was tall and thin, and his dirty blond hair was a tad messed up, behind a cowlick at the front of his head and a handsome face. He was a legend at Columbia. Theoretically, Singerman's seminar was about the history of numbers from the first recorded use of a number to demarcate value up to the present. Singerman taught his students that numbers were, in their own way, a form of artificial intelligence in and of themselves, and that the world was run by individuals who were able to manipulate and control numbers.

Singerman's lecture hall was on the top floor of the School of International Affairs, the eighth floor, and behind the students spread a wall of glass that showed the Columbia campus and beyond, to the Hudson River and New Jersey.

On the chalkboard, Singerman wrote down six numbers.

000000

"Tell me why these numbers are significant," said Singerman to the class. "Six zeros."

He looked out at the class. No one said a thing.

"Want a hint?" said Singerman.

Several people laughed and a bunch yelled out, "Yes."

"Those six digits, in that order and number, are the most important six digits that have ever existed, and they are critical to human life."

A black-haired female student raised her hand.

"It's 'Crystal Code,'" the student said.

Another student piped in.

"It has to do with the correlations between language and time," said the student.

Singerman kept a blank look on his face.

"It's a DNA sequence."

"Everyone knows, it was the first line typed by Gates when he wrote DOS."

There were several more guesses, each of which caused little to no reaction from Singerman.

The guesses at some point stopped coming and there was a palpable silence in the amphitheater.

Singerman went to the chalkboard. He started a line and drew one large zero around the line of zeros. With every sixth of the circle, he erased one of the zeros from the line. When he was done, he had a complete circle and no zeros leftover.

"Six zeros is the minimum mechanism for the control of metadata, that is, electronic signals," said Singerman. "It is the basis for anything nonorganic in our world today, from blockchain to spaceships, bitcoin, cars, weapons systems, whatever, and to control it is to have the ability to build or destroy. Do you understand?"

"But why?" said a student.

"How, Professor Singerman?"

Suddenly, someone at the back of the class screamed.

In the distance, at the lower part of Manhattan, billowing smoke and fire was taking over the sky.

Singerman suddenly heard a high-pitched beep in his ear. He pressed his earbud as he listened to the questions.

"Go," he whispered.

A digitized female voice spoke:

"You're active under NO/SEC forty-four. Identify NOC."

"NOC 3390 AB2," he said under his breath.

Singerman raised a hand to his class, trying to calm them down as others yelled, although he was now active and nothing else mattered.

He heard another beep, then a voice.

"Aaron, it's Bill," came the voice of Bill Polk, the head of the National Clandestine Service. "We have an attack about to take place on Manhattan by Hezbollah. I know you're teaching a class so just listen."

"It just happened," Singerman whispered.

He looked at the class. Students were moving to the back of the lecture hall, looking out the window. A sense of fear and pandemonium had taken over.

"Hold on," said Singerman, tapping his ear.

He looked at the classroom.

"Everyone, back in your seats," he said.

Singerman waited, and soon the students were back in their chairs.

He stepped out in front of the long lecture dais. Singerman crossed his arms and looked out at his students, many of whom were still preoccupied by the smoke in the sky, and others by texts they were receiving.

All Singerman cared about was getting out of there. "You guys need to stay here. Do not go outside for any reason. Text or call your friends and family in the city, and tell them to stay inside."

He looked around the classroom, which was quiet. Singerman lifted his briefcase and was soon outside the lecture hall and jogging toward the elevator, then the building's exit. Soon, he was cutting in front of Low Library and across the Columbia campus.

Another ear tap.

"Clear," said Singerman.

"The president is at the UN," said Polk. "We're extracting him now."

"So what do you want from me, Bill? I'm a financial asset," said Singerman, jogging down the steps in front of Low Library, moving across campus toward his town house on Riverside Drive.

"Get your equipment," said Polk. "Emphasis ammo. You still remember how to fire a gun, don't you?"

46

Dellenbaugh stood at the outer wall of the tower. Several large sections of glass had completely shattered. He stared out at a sky spanned in sharp clouds of smoke and fire, as if volcanoes had erupted.

Alarms wailed from inside the tower—and from outside the building. There was a constant *rat-a-tat-tat* of automatic gunfire from the streets below.

Dellenbaugh's eyes made first contact with Callanan, the lead Secret Service agent. Callanan was on his chest, on the floor, trying to stand up and move to Dellenbaugh, but his ears and nose were oozing blood.

There were loud groans coming from all over the floor.

But then one noise arose above all the other din. Dellenbaugh heard the explosive shriek as his eyes found Callanan. The shrill of a missile. From outside the building—and growing louder. The eerie, screaming whistle of the incoming missile was followed immediately by a deafening blast as an object came flying into the building, into the floor itself, and everything disappeared in a maelstrom of noise, heat, and destruction.

Dellenbaugh dived down just as the Strela ripped horizontally through the glass wall that had not already shattered from the concussion from the explosions. A sharp, powerful heat-filled outer stroke of steel, fire, and air came flying through the U.S. Mission on floor eighteen.

Dellenbaugh hit the ground just before a steel desk tore above his head, as if swept up in a tornado. He watched as a wall of crumbling glass slammed into Callanan's head, pulverizing him. Dellenbaugh grabbed a section of wall and tucked his head down, trying to avoid the overwhelming wave of projectiles caused by the missile that had just struck the building.

Dellenbaugh watched as people he knew, staff members, Ambassador Wasik, all of them, were suddenly eviscerated in an awkward, horrible sequence, too ugly, too many moments of death, to fathom and he shut his eyes. Then, even as he tucked low, trying to survive, Dellenbaugh felt a sudden, hard object stab into his torso. He lost his grip and tumbled until the wave of energy from the explosion dissipated. He looked down and saw a piece of thick glass embedded in his stomach.

"*Jesus,*" he moaned as he clutched reflexively at his abdomen, unable to catch his breath. Then he coughed out a mouthful of blood.

Dellenbaugh tried to breathe but the wind was knocked out of him, and every breath was clotted with blood. He looked down and saw a foot-long section of window in the shape of a triangle jutting out from his stomach.

"Oh, fuck," he whispered aloud, to himself. He looked around, from the floor, bleeding badly. He couldn't see any signs of life.

He spat blood.

"If you're alive, say something," he said as loud as he could, wheezing, coughing blood.

The pain was just starting. It was intense and he fought to remain lucid.

He called out again.

"*Say something!*" he shouted.

But there were no responses.

Both of Dellenbaugh's hands went to the shard of glass. It was thick, and he studied where it entered him next to his navel. Blood chugged from the seams, in spurts, and ebbs, and yet as he held it he couldn't do anything, as if all of his strength was gone. He started to try to slip it out, but it was stuck hard. But he knew he needed to stop the bleeding.

He saw smoke out through the broken glass window, a distant part of Manhattan, and felt helpless and desperate.

Dellenbaugh was on his back. Slowly, and in a considerable amount of pain, he worked his way out of his blazer and removed his tie. His shirt was ripped across the torso by the shard of glass. His hands were coated in blood. He tried to dial, but then dropped the phone as he felt his head drop to the floor.

He felt pain and watched as fog seemed to clog his eyes, and he felt tired. As hard as he fought, he couldn't escape the feeling of total fatigue. It was in every inch, every molecule, of his body. Dellenbaugh shut his eyes as blood pooled beneath him. He slipped into unconsciousness.

47

Glass poured down from above following the missile strike. Bullets slammed into the windows in the lobby, shattering them.

The security design for that day was complicated and somewhat political. Five security groups had worked to reconcile and negotiate various rights and rules regarding how the president's visit to the UN was to be handled. It was UN Security, Secret Service, NYPD, FBI, and DSS. Each had men at the UN. There had been twice-daily meetings for a week leading up to Dellenbaugh's visit. It was the first time, however, that anything had disrupted what had been a cool but smooth interagency security protocol. Now that chaos had ensued, whatever existed before went out the window, especially in the lobby, where each agency had multiple gunmen.

It was UN Security who were supposed to take the lead in a hostile situation. But the head of UN Security was on the eighteenth floor, with the president and the secretary general.

It soon became about survival, and not who was in charge.

Steve Koch—a senior-level Secret Service agent—was dressed in a navy suit. He stepped behind a steel beam as he watched chaos descending. It may not have been protocol, but Koch decided to start giving orders.

"We need to hold the perimeter of the UN complex," barked Koch. "Moriarty," he said to the deputy director of UN Security, "tell your men to hold the line! Jack," he pointed at one of the NYPD officers, "get men over here attacking the outer wall of gunmen from behind. Watch your field of fire."

Meanwhile, bullets continued to shatter glass. Several men were caught in the fusillade. Koch removed his .45 and turned from behind the steel stanchion. He pumped bullets through the broken glass at gunmen attacking and now in the courtyard, like wolves.

Koch looked at a man holding a rifle. He was black, and wore a sharp-looking uniform. He was one of the NYPD officers detailed to the president's trip. He clutched a rifle.

"Ricky, right?" said Koch.

"Yes."

"Get up to the third floor," said Koch. "Get a strategic advantage point. Shoot as many of them as you can. We're buying time here. They're trying to kill the president." Koch pointed to a dead security man. "Grab his mags. We need to hold them off. Kill as many of these motherfuckers as you can. Got it?"

"Yeah."

"Go."

48

Rob Tacoma stood naked in a large, marble-tiled shower, in one of several bathrooms in the penthouse condominium. The warm water was perfect.

Tacoma had spent $40 million and bought into the Mandarin at the development stage. Today, the condo was worth at least one hundred million dollars. But Tacoma didn't think about that, and he didn't care. It was simply where he stayed when he was in New York. The penthouse suite of rooms was dimly lit, with interior walls of wood and exterior walls of glass in every direction. The most amazing view was, without question, the front: a sheer wall of glass that looked out on Central Park and the crowded streets below, and people; distant, though, like objects seen from an eagle's aerie on a high mountain.

Then, he felt it. It was a sharp quiver to the very foundation of the building.

The massive apartment took up half the penthouse floor of the Mandarin Hotel. It also had come with a stunning, large, rectangular terrace that faced Central Park. The views were astounding. The most cutting-edge engineering firms had been hired. Glass was everywhere, clad upon a steel chassis as laid out by Skidmore, Owings & Merrill.

Yet, whatever had just exploded outside made the Mandarin tremor and bend.

Suddenly, he heard the sound of breaking glass.

Tacoma lurched for the shower door and sprinted naked into the living room, running to the windows that looked out at the city. He was soaking wet and tracked water even as he charged to the window and looked out as a pair of mushroom clouds filled with smoke and fire ballooned over the skyline. Then a third vibration shivered through the skyscraper and—a second later—two more explosions echoed from somewhere to the south, and then the telltale mushroom clouds of orange fire spiraled into the sky from there too.

Alarms inside the Mandarin began wailing from the hallways—and emergency government sirens on buildings all over the city started a frenetic medley of rising high-pitched chaotic distress signals.

The air was soon covered in a layer of haze as smoke was blown from each of the tunnels across the darkening sky.

Tacoma stood on the terrace. His eyes were drawn to the streets below, Central Park South, Columbus Circle, and he saw dozens of people running in every direction as guns were fired. He searched and then registered two, then three, then three more gunmen. They were different from the others, the pedestrians just fleeing. Each man was armed with an automatic rifle. Another low boom from one of the rifles went off, and he saw the flash. He tracked the sound, then saw a woman falling to the ground, shot in the head at close range.

Tacoma watched calmly as three gunmen moved randomly, looking for prey, pumping slugs. They shot anyone they could find, gunning people down in cold blood on the streets, people in cars, even gunning up at buildings, trying to sow terror and chaos.

Clouds of smoke clotted the air even as the gunmen moved, indiscriminately killing people.

Tacoma stood, staring out at the growing carnage. He plotted the explosions against a map in his head. He quickly realized the four tunnels into Manhattan had been bombed. He went back inside his condo. He picked up the house phone.

"Yes, Mr. Tacoma?"

"I need a suite in the hotel immediately. The most luxurious you have."

"I understand, of course, Mr. Tacoma."

"I also need you to send someone up. There's a woman who will be staying there and I'd appreciate it if you brought her there. Also, you need to tell your manager, initiate any emergency security protocols you have, immediately. *Lock down the hotel.*"

"Yes, sir."

Tacoma put the phone down and went back to the bathroom and nodded at the woman.

"I apologize, but you need to leave," said Tacoma. "It has nothing to do with you."

"What happened?" She stood, naked, under the massive showerhead. "This is too wonderful," she said. "Come back under the water."

Tacoma reached in and turned off the water. He looked at her.

"I'm sorry, but you need to leave," said Tacoma gently, taking her by the wrist and pulling her from the shower. "The city is under attack. You're being taken to a suite in the hotel." He pointed at the window. "I don't want you to leave the building. The streets are very dangerous."

"Why can't I stay here?" she said.

"You just can't, that's all."

"We finish the shower when this all dies down?" she said in a soft Danish accent.

"Yes," he said. "When you get to your suite, I want you to text your family, your friends, colleagues, anyone you know in New York City."

"Why?"

"Tell them to get inside, or stay inside if they're already there," said Tacoma. "It's for their own safety."

"I will," she said. She stepped forward and leaned in to Tacoma. They were both still naked. Her white hair cascaded down her back. They kissed for a brief moment. "I knew you were cute," she said, touching her hand to his bare, muscled torso, "but I didn't know you were such a gentleman," as she kissed him again.

If you knew what I was about to do, you wouldn't think I'm such a gentleman, he thought.

The doorbell chimed. The door opened and a refined-looking Asian woman stepped in.

"It will be my pleasure to take you to your suite, miss."

49

The NYPD officer, Ricky, ran for a stairwell at the back of the UN building, following orders from Koch. He climbed as alarms roared inside the stairwell. He entered the third floor of the tower and moved down the hallway. He lock-picked a door and entered an empty office suite, some sort of ceremonial room, which appeared as if it hadn't been used in a long time. An inner door near where he wanted to be was locked and he shot out the area around the steel door handle. He kicked in the door.

Ricky skulked to the window. He registered two school buses with men pouring out carrying automatic weapons. Ricky walked back, staggering a little, grabbed a satchel full of mags, went back to the shattered window, set the fire selector on a custom-rigged AR-15 to full auto, and started firing at the men swarming from the school buses—pumping bullets at the Iranians now attacking from street level.

Then he saw a man to his right and started targeting him.

50

Dellenbaugh opened his eyes. His face was matted to the carpet in a pool of sticky blood. He tried to breathe. He needed air, and he began to inhale. A sharp, stabbing pain slashed across him. He looked down. It looked otherworldly, like a scene from a horror movie.

He was on a thinly carpeted floor in an office suite. He had no idea how long he'd been out.

The piece of glass was large and thick, at least a foot long and an inch wide. It was embedded in his stomach but most of the glass was not inside him. Only the front tip of the shard had penetrated him, perhaps one or two inches—yet it was the worst pain he'd ever felt, or ever even imagined. His button-down was stuffed into the edges, but it was drenched in blood. He stared at the thick shard of glass jutting from his body, crimson flooding the surface. It looked surreal. He put his hand on it and just the faintest touch made sharp pain soar through his body. He let go, then grabbed it again and pulled. But it was lodged inside.

Dellenbaugh glanced around the suite. It was a picture of pure carnage.

Moments before, staff members from the U.S. Mission were gathered, along with several other UN countries' consulate delegations, including delegations from England, Ireland, Israel, Canada, most of Europe, South Korea, Japan, Mexico, and other countries. A hundred or so. Now, they were dead.

Next to him, Dellenbaugh saw one of his Secret Service protectors, Gene Callanan, lying on his stomach, dead on the floor, part of his torso missing.

Gene Callanan had been on Dellenbaugh's protective detail starting the day Rob Allaire had asked Dellenbaugh to be his vice president three years ago. Callanan's head was turned toward him. His face looked calm, his eyes were open; dull eyes staring into oblivion. His torso was severed by some sort of metal, a desk or cabinet, ripped apart by the missiles, sent into his body like a steak knife through butter.

At that moment, beyond any pain, Dellenbaugh could think only about what had happened in the moments before it had all come crashing down. He had to think about that—as much as he hurt. He alone was president. He had to register what had occurred.

Explosions in different parts of the island. Uptown and east, downtown, bursts of thick black smoke chuting into the morning sky.

The tunnels.

Dellenbaugh put his hand on the end of the glass shard. He looked around. No one was moving.

"Is anyone alive?" he said again.

But Dellenbaugh heard nothing.

He felt the glass in his gut. He knew he was alive. As long as he was alive he needed to fight.

"Is anyone there?" he shouted, tasting blood somehow coming up from his body.

He shut his eyes, steeling himself. This was not how it ended. They could kill him, but he wouldn't give up. . . .

Yet, the pain was deep. Dellenbaugh coughed and a spitwad of blood-tainted saliva shot out, landing on his thigh. His chief of staff was usually correct. Dellenbaugh grinned as he fought off shock. Adrian was right:

There isn't going to be any speech, sir.

51

Dewey stood at the console of the Hinckley Runabout 29. It was white, black, quiet—and fast.

Dewey took the boat up the East River from the south, throttling the boat to its max. He moved back and lifted the engine casing, then disabled a green wire—a circuit he'd been trained in—along the side of the big engine. The wire, he knew, was there to protect the engine, but right now Dewey needed speed. He raised the engine and planed out on the water. As the prop lifted so too did the front of the hull and soon the boat was moving at the height of its maximum speed, barely the prop, barely the hull, everything else suspended in forward motion—and the dial soon read 57 knots. The governor gone, he soon had the boat gliding at an arc up the East River.

He gashed the boat up into the cavern of the East River, smoke across the waterfront, and for the first time Dewey spied the top floors of the UN. Then he looked lower. It was in flames.

He was still far away. Yet he saw the city in ruins, and parts of the UN were on fire. Whole sections had been destroyed.

He tapped his ear twice.

"CENCOM."

"Identify."

"2495–6."

"Go."

"I need to speak with the president," said Dewey.

A pause, then a high-pitched monotone.

"I'm not getting through," said the voice.

Dewey waited and waited as he moved up the East River. As he came closer—within sight line of the smoking explosion at the tunnel near the UN, he spoke.

"Anything?" said Dewey.

"I've run it repeatedly," said the CENCOM operator. "No answer."

52

The perimeter of the UN was highly secure and most of it was inaccessible—high-voltage electronic iron fence stretched around the seventeen-acre complex. The front of the facility faced First Avenue, and this was the only way in quickly. But it was heavily guarded with UN Security forces and, on this day, U.S. Secret Service, FBI, and NYPD.

These gunmen were firing back at Mansour and his soldiers, but with six vans and two buses filled with trained Hezbollah soldiers, the attackers were gaining ground. First Avenue near the UN looked and sounded like a combat zone. Hezbollah was encroaching with each passing minute. The external layer of UN Security had either retreated back toward the tower or had been shot in cold blood.

Still, as Mansour tucked against a sedan on First Avenue, he looked south and saw six or seven dead Iranians.

It would be over soon. The whole thing would be over soon.

He heard sirens—more NYPD was coming.

Mansour ignored the carnage and broken glass and moved toward the UN. He cut across First Avenue, clutching an

AR-15 and gunning toward any movement he saw from the Americans.

Within the piece of land, the footprint of the UN building occupied less than an acre.

Mansour knew that his men needed to get to the tower and control access. That meant controlling the lobby. It was operating leverage; a confined space that, if secured, enabled its possessor to control the tower. Control the lobby and roof, that was what they had to do. It was his soldiers' job to take hold of the lobby. To control the roof, that was why he bought missiles and had men stationed to use them as needed.

Mansour was pinned down behind an SUV on First Avenue, struggling to get closer. He watched, in the distance across the courtyard, as uniformed UN Security, NYPD, and FBI SWAT were pushed backward across the large, open concrete area outside the tower; ineluctably backward, ducking and afraid, spraying bullets at the Iranians, trying to protect themselves in a last-ditch effort.

He saw one of his soldiers breach the outer ring of the courtyard. Several Hezbollah gunmen moved in, but in moments two of them were shot dead, dropped to the hard ground. But the wave of Iranians was winning out and the Americans were dropping quickly. Hezbollah moved in closer. He glanced right. Windows on vehicles were shattered, and there were hundreds of bullet holes in cars. There were dead civilians along the sidewalk on First Avenue. Several of Mansour's men were down, dead, killed—but the UN cordon had been broken.

Now Mansour skulked from behind the SUV. Suddenly, slugs rained down from the UN building. He was at least a thousand feet away, yet the bullets had come close. He tucked back against the SUV just as several bullets ricocheted inches from him.

Mansour had been marked. A sniper inside the UN building had him locked. He wasn't about to let go.

Mansour paused a few moments, on his heels, crouched back against the vehicle.

On the other side of the SUV was a sidewalk, and then a three-foot-high line of pine shrubs, then an iron fence, and beyond was the courtyard in front of the tower he needed to get to.

Mansour stuck his hand out ever so slightly in front of the back bumper. He held it for a few moments, then instinctively yanked it back just as a dull *boom* echoed from the tower and a slug slammed into the bumper where his hand had just been.

He saw red and blue lights north of him, up First Avenue.

A Hezbollah soldier was positioned in that direction. The gunman started hammering bullets at the oncoming NYPD cruiser. The cruiser abruptly swerved and smashed into a parked, or abandoned, car. Mansour lurched through the break in the vehicles and sprinted across the sidewalk, leaping at the fence, hitting the shrubs with his feet and scaling the fence as bullets flew just behind him. Bullets pulsed the concrete just behind him.

A guard booth was on the other side of the fence. It would provide shelter from the sniper. As he got over the fence, he heard another boom in the same instant his knee erupted in blood and pain. He was hit—but he continued moving even as white-hot pain burned through his kneecap.

"Fuck," he muttered as he moved to the small guardhouse, out of the sniper's aim.

He looked down. His right knee was a mess. Blood was all over the place; a patch of his pants was torn. He ripped material aside, exposing the wound. The bullet had only grazed him. He could still function as long as he stemmed the blood and could deal with the pain.

He glanced around the guard station. He gazed across the concrete courtyard before the entrance to the tower, as his gunmen created a shock wave of cover around the outer edges of the facility, where law enforcement was trying to fight them off, pumping slugs back at them, but there were too many Hezbollah.

Mansour's team was hatcheting through whatever security existed at the UN—even though dozens of his most loyal and talented men lay dead on the ground.

He felt cold wetness at his ankle. He'd already processed the pain and was moving it to a box inside his mind, as he'd been taught. But he needed to deal with the blood that was trickling, like a faucet that hadn't been turned fully off, from his knee.

53

Lee Van Allen was broadcasting live. The monitor cut to a wide-angle, grainy video feed showing clouds of smoke, in real time, over part of Manhattan.

A bright red digital strip cut across the bottom of the screen: *SPECIAL REPORT.*

"One," said Wood in Van Allen's ear. "Go, kid."

"This is Lee Van Allen, reporting to you live from CBS headquarters in New York City. It is nine oh nine A.M. and what you are seeing is what appears to be some sort of terrorist attack on New York City. . . ."

Abruptly, the feed cut and displayed a different camera angle, this time from the air.

It was the under-mounted camera on the local CBS affiliate's helicopter, used mainly for traffic reports. The chopper was above the Lower West Side, where tall spires of thick smoke reached into the sky.

"I believe what you're seeing is the Lincoln Tunnel," said Van Allen, her voice wavering as she narrated the stunning scene. "I'm seeing this just as you are. I'm going to do my best not to get emotional but I can't make any promises. It appears that once again New York City is under attack."

As the helicopter cut across the city and climbed, the camera picked up three more towering columns of smoke rising at the boundaries of the city. Van Allen knew immediately what it meant.

"Oh my Lord," she said, even though she was live. "Ladies and gentlemen, this is live footage from above New York City, where it looks like at least four large explosions have taken place, all in the vicinity of the tunnels leading into Manhattan."

As the chopper moved toward the East Side, the UN came into view, in the distance, shrouded by clouds of smoke pouring out of the Queens-Midtown Tunnel, but also from the UN building itself. Part of the front of the building was destroyed—a large hole in the sleek blue glass marred the front, halfway up—then another missile sped from somewhere on the ground up into another part of the building and punched a hole in a different section.

"My God," said Van Allen. "They're attacking the UN where, as I speak, President J. P. Dellenbaugh is scheduled to address the General Assembly. . . ."

54

The president crawled on his back even as the glass stabbed him in the torso. He came to a dead woman and found a cell phone in her hand. He dialed 911.

It rang several times, then an operator came on.

"NYPD Emergency," came a female voice.

Dellenbaugh tried to speak but only coughed.

"Hello, this is NYPD first response, is someone there?"

"Yes," whispered Dellenbaugh. He sounded weak and lost. "I have a piece of glass in my stomach."

"Thank you," said the operator. "I see you're at the UN. We have teams of first responders either there already or on their way."

"I need to speak to someone with medical training," said Dellenbaugh slowly.

"Sir, I'm not sure that's feasible," said the operator. "However, I can send an ambulance and EMTs to your specific location. What floor are you on?"

"Eighteen," said Dellenbaugh. "This is J. P. Dellenbaugh, the president. I need to speak to someone immediately with a medical background."

The operator was silent for a few moments.

"Oh, sir, Mr. President, forgive me. Please hold the line. I'll have someone in a few moments."

Dellenbaugh lay down on his back, propping his head on the leg of the dead woman. Then a new voice came on the line.

"Mr. President, this is Alison Scott, are you there?"

"Yes."

"I'm a trauma surgeon at Mt. Sinai. Where is the glass, Mr. President?" she said.

"My right side," said Dellenbaugh. "Stomach."

"How big?"

"I don't know. A foot. It's thick."

"How much is inside you?" said Scott.

"A few inches."

"That's good. Is your nose or mouth bleeding?" said Dr. Scott.

"I don't know," said Dellenbaugh.

"Put your hand to your nose and your mouth," she ordered. "Tell me if it's bleeding."

"No, it's not," he said.

"That's good. I want you to pull that piece of glass out of your stomach," said the doctor.

"It's too deep," said the president weakly.

"You need to do it," said Scott firmly. "I'm here with you," she added empathetically. "People are coming. I know the FBI or Secret Service will be there soon." Then her tone got harder-edged. "But I need you to pull the glass out right now."

Dellenbaugh was breathing heavily, trying to live through the pain, which was exacerbated by every tiny movement.

"I know you're feeling like you're about to die, but you're not," said Scott. "I need you to pull that glass out, right now. Just yank it out. This isn't over. It's just the beginning, but I need you, we need you, to join the fight."

• • •

Dellenbaugh forced himself to sit up and crab to a wall near the entrance to the suite. He looked down and saw his midsection. It was a riot of blood, soaking wet. A trail of blood was on the floor. He put the cell down and wrapped both hands around the large shard of glass at its tip. Groaning in a low, deep voice, Dellenbaugh pulled for several moments, trying to get the object out, but it was too painful. He gave himself a few seconds as he caught his breath. He was sweating profusely and in agony, though he took the glass again and rocked it back and forth as blood oozed out from the seams around where it was stabbed into him. He pulled as hard as he could and felt the end of the glass slide out, making a terrible sloshing noise. He dropped it on the floor as he tried to catch his breath amid the wracking pain.

He glanced down. The wound was leaking blood.

He picked up the cell.

"Doctor?" he said, coughing.

"Are you okay?" she said.

"No," said Dellenbaugh.

"How bad is it bleeding?" said Scott.

"Bad," said Dellenbaugh.

"That's okay," said Scott. "Now take off your shirt. As much as it hurts, you need to press it against the wound. Hard."

Dellenbaugh tried to unbutton his shirt, but he couldn't. His fingers were numb.

"Push it hard," said the doctor. "As deep as you can."

"I can't get my shirt off. I can't feel anything," coughed Dellenbaugh.

"What floor are you on?"

Dellenbaugh watched as the cell dropped to the floor. He stared at the open wound in his stomach until, at some point, with the doctor's frantic shouting in the background, his eyes shut and he again fell into unconsciousness.

55

Tacoma tapped twice on his ear as he pulled on a pair of running shoes and an orange T-shirt. He moved to a wall of mirrors and put his thumb against a digital reader and the door opened up.

"Tracer code," said Tacoma.

"Identify."

"NOC 887–01."

"Hold."

Behind the doors was a weapons cache. A small closet held an array of weapons: submachine guns, shotguns, automatic rifles, handguns, knives, axes, and machetes.

Another wall was covered in shelves that held various other pieces of equipment and gear, including vests, communications devices, night and thermal optics, passports, cash, sanitized credit cards, and leather satchels full of gold Krugerrands.

Tacoma holstered a P226 beneath his left armpit and another at his waist, in back. He picked up an MP7 and threaded a silencer into the muzzle.

He pulled on optics and then a tactical vest, and stuffed it with mags.

Then he heard a scream—

Through the terrace window.

He crossed the apartment and walked out onto the penthouse slab of granite and steel, an aerie forty-six floors above the city. He put the optics to his eyes and looked down from the terrace. He watched as a woman ran down Fifty-ninth Street. He saw a police cruiser. Then he heard automatic gunfire—loud steel thuds from a high-powered rifle.

Through the optics he saw two gunmen run from the shadows holding AR-15s. They killed the woman, blowing slugs into her body as she ran.

He watched as they started firing at the police cruiser. Then turned and shot at anything in sight—cars and trucks, people on the sidewalk—killing everyone they could.

A gunshot from a car felled one of the gunmen, but then another gunman emerged from somewhere and he pumped bullets into every vehicle he could. Another gunman came from a side street and soon they were spraying bullets across Columbus Circle, at vehicles and storefronts.

Tacoma stepped inside and dropped the MP7 on a chair. He walked to a mirrored bar area. He reached in and found a small screen, and pressed his fingertip against it. A moment later, the floor in the middle of the room started moving, sliding slowly apart, as a set of blue lights suddenly emanated from the space in the floor. A few seconds later, after the floor had opened up, two walls arose from the concealed space beneath the floor.

He heard a voice:

"Rob, it's Bill," said Polk.

"Hey Bill," said Tacoma. "What were the explosions?"

"The tunnels into Manhattan were blown up," said Polk. "The bridges are immobilized. They're cutting off Manhattan."

"Who?" said Tacoma.

"Hezbollah. They activated some kind of operation, like nine/eleven," said Polk. "Cabbies, unemployed, grifters, Uber drivers. They're isolating the president."

The concealed space beneath the floor held a half dozen sniper rifles along with a pair of surface-to-air missiles and a MANPAD.

Tacoma picked up a sniper rifle, a Howa HCR with a twenty-six-inch barrel. He slammed in a mag of 6.5 Creedmoors.

Tacoma heard shouting and gunfire. He went to the terrace and looked at the street below. Enemy gunmen wandered purposefully, looking for people to kill. The air was smoky, and the aroma of explosives had started to waft over the city. Tacoma could smell it. It was a sour, chemical stench he didn't recognize, mixed with smoke and fire.

Tacoma positioned the rifle on the steel railing. He screwed a bipod atop the railing for added precision. He took aim at one of the gunmen. He was walking near the Central Park side of the fountain at Columbus Circle. Tacoma paused an extra moment, then pumped the trigger. The slug hit the terrorist in the side of the head, kicking him sideways as his skull was destroyed, brains and skull dumping red into the fountain.

"Bill, I'm at Columbus Circle and there are hordes of active shooters just walking down the street, killing people."

"I know."

"So what's the plan?" said Tacoma.

"The president is at the United Nations," said Polk. "There is no plan other than try and get him out."

Tacoma swept the rifle and locked into the second Iranian, standing on Fifty-ninth Street. By the time he realized what had happened to his cohort, Tacoma pumped the trigger and sent a bullet at him, striking him in the chest, dropping him to the street in a clump.

He scanned for the third killer, but he was gone. Still, he'd dropped a pair of the motherfuckers.

Tacoma stepped back inside his apartment as he waited for Langley. He went back to the wall of equipment. He pulled on a tan-and-black camo tactical vest then started filling the pockets with magazines. He found a set of optics and pulled them down over his head, around his neck.

He heard more gunfire and sprinted back to the terrace. He saw four men stalking down the street, shooting at cars.

He put down the Howa and picked up the AR-15.

Tacoma set the fire selector to full auto as he stepped to the railing and took aim, then started firing. The gunfire was like an eruption, and the crew of terrorists turned and looked up as Tacoma mowed them down in a fusillade. It was a challenging distance, but he made up for it by firing large amounts of steel, quickly. It was impossible for any of them to return fire. He homed in on one of them, crouching near a curb, pelting the man and spraying red across the street. When the mag clicked empty, Tacoma ejected it, then slammed a new mag in, flipped the fire selector to semimanual, and killed the remaining men with a series of well-placed triple bursts.

"Do you want me to go to the UN?" said Tacoma.

"Yes, start moving over there," said Polk.

56

King stood behind his desk. His office was crowded with people. In addition to Calibrisi and Bruckheimer, Dale Arnold, the secretary of defense; White House national security advisor, Josh Brubaker; FBI director, Dave McNaughton; and several key White House and National Security Council staffers were there. There were at least a dozen individuals.

King had lost contact with the president. His face was pale. He stared down at a triangle-shaped phone console.

Meanwhile, a pair of bright, wide LCD screens covered one of the walls. Each was tied into various law enforcement, military, and intelligence feeds. The right screen was a checkerboard of real-time video from NYPD, including stationary video cameras and body cameras. It was a cross-section of mayhem, and it provided a good proxy for what was happening street-level across Manhattan.

Gunmen moved through New York City. The cameras all showed a similar scene: young Iranian men with rifles and submachine guns, running down Manhattan's sidewalks and streets, shooting whoever and whatever they could, as well as scenes of NYPD engaging in firefights, citizens running for their lives, and traffic jams everywhere.

The left screen showed live video from the air.

King could see what was occurring from behind his desk. The on-the-ground video streams all showed gun battles. The other screen was a macro perspective, and it was shocking because the four explosions—and their smoky, fire-crossed aftermath—could be seen from afar. It was like watching a forest fire. The views were dramatic but antiseptic. Where the four tunnels into Manhattan connected with the island itself, billowing, round clusters of black, orange, red, and gray fire were blossoming into mushroom clouds.

An NSC algorithm meshed the two views, and part of the left LCD displayed Manhattan from above, with the aggregation of on-the-ground active shooters, NYPD, and FBI, with the four bright red circles irradiated in green, emphasizing the heat.

The view essentially incorporated everything that was possible to know, at least visually, in terms of the attack on Manhattan.

Dale Arnold, the secretary of defense, approached King.

"Adrian, this is an attack on the United States by Iran," said Arnold. "We need to fight back."

"Yeah, no shit," said King.

"I'm talking about Pearl Harbor," said Arnold quietly.

King looked at Arnold.

"I know what the fuck you're talking about," said King. "Are you recommending dropping a nuclear bomb on Tehran?"

"Yes," said Arnold, leaning in across King's desk. "That's exactly what I'm saying. If the president is still alive, it might save him."

King stared blankly at Arnold.

"Look, even if I knew the fucking nuclear codes, Dale, which I don't, I have no idea what to do with them," shouted King, gesticulating wildly, "and guess what, *I don't know the fucking nuclear codes!* I'm not authorized, nor are you! Oh, by the way, we don't have a goddam vice president, so if anything happens to President Dellenbaugh, guess what? Then we got some left-wing nutjob from Massachusetts running our country!"

Everyone in the room suddenly looked at King.

He pointed at the screen. *"This is a fucking shit show,"* he said.

"Which is why we need to strike back right now," said Arnold.

"They are literally trying to kill our president, if they haven't already. To not respond will show pathetic weakness."

"Sorry, Mr. Secretary," said King. "But right now our focus is on New York, on the president, on killing the active gunmen, and on rescue efforts for anyone in the tunnels. After we get through this, as far as I'm concerned, we can turn Tehran into a glow-in-the-dark kitty litter box, but right now we need to get President Dellenbaugh out of there."

"Understood," said Arnold.

King hit his phone console.

"Get me Anna Lungren," said King.

A few moments later, the face of Anna Lungren, the NYPD commissioner, appeared on one of the screens. She was standing in some sort of control room filled with dispatchers and walls of LCD screens. It looked chaotic, like a hospital operating room.

"Give me the status, Anna," said King.

"Adrian, we're assessing this at five hundred to six hundred active shooters on the island of Manhattan," said Lungren. "The tunnels are heavily damaged. It will take months to get through the debris. The bridges are intact but absolutely immobile for vehicles. Traffic isn't moving, and people are getting out of their cars and running for New Jersey, Queens, and Brooklyn. You get the picture."

"What about the UN?"

"We're encountering fierce resistance," said Lungren. "They have tiers of gunmen. They're running a geographic matrix. They appear to have taken control of all entrances to the facility. I just read a sheet on my first team that got close. We suffered heavy casualties."

"Hold on for a second, Anna," said King.

"Got it," said the NYPD commissioner.

King looked at Calibrisi, who was studying the screens from one of the wing chairs in front of King's desk, which he'd turned around to face the wall of LCDs. Calibrisi had a disbelieving but calm look on his face. King nodded to Calibrisi. Calibrisi stood up from the chair and followed King into the corner behind his desk, out of earshot.

"What do we do?" said King.

"NYPD needs to focus on the active shooters," said Calibrisi. "If NYPD, or even the FBI, are in charge of saving the president, he'll die. That's just my opinion, Adrian. Let them focus on killing the active shooters."

King walked back to the screen:

"Anna, you need to focus on the active shooters," said King, "and humanitarian shit."

"What are you saying?" said Lungren.

"I'm saying, back the fuck off the UN," said King. "You have five hundred active shooters running around killing people, not to mention a shitload of corpses all over the place, in the tunnels, on the bridges, sidewalks. You have a fucking shit show on your hands. We need to divide and conquer. Let us handle the president. If we can't get him, I'll call you."

"I'm with you," said Lungren, "but I want to be in constant communication."

"Only you," said King. "And if you violate that I will come down hard on you."

"I understand, Adrian," said Lungren.

"Thanks, Commissioner."

King pressed the console, shutting down the conversation. He looked at Calibrisi.

"So how the hell do we get Dellenbaugh?" seethed King.

"I scrambled SEAL Team 4," said Calibrisi. "Two choppers from the *Eisenhower*. They're on the way."

57

Rokan glanced nervously out the window as sirens wailed from NYPD cruisers on the streets below. He saw smoke in the distant sky, but he didn't stand up.

Rokan was seated at a desk in the hotel suite. He studied the screen on the laptop. It displayed a digital pyramid, green digital lines against a black backdrop. The three-dimensional pyramid rotated slowly. Each of the three faces of the geometric structure contained numbers that were constantly changing as they filled in each face of the three individual triangles. The numbers moved quickly up toward the peak of the pyramid, and when they got to the top, suddenly all three triangles were wiped clear—and then the numbers reappeared at the base of the pyramid.

As the digits started scrolling up the faces of the triangle anew, Rokan studied the patterns. He learned to understand the speed of the scroll, and looked for patterns.

He typed a four-digit sequence as the pyramid rotated, and the face of the pyramid flashed yellow and became solid. As the second triangle came into view, with its scrolling numbers, he watched as they filled in the upper part of the triangle—then he saw something and typed, this time six digits. The second triangle went yellow and became solid. By the time the third triangle face rotated, the numbers had scrolled within a few levels of the top of the final triangle.

The pyramid was a digital simulacrum of the Federal Reserve. Rokan had created it so as to simulate the governors' room at the Fed; the room, and more importantly the system, he was about to attempt to break into. It was his best approximation of the sophisticated algorithm by which the U.S., and specifically the four governors of the Fed, managed America's financial reserves. Rokan knew that if Mansour's men could get him inside, that he would then face the hardest challenge. For once inside the governors' room, he would be faced with the complex matrix that the four governors were faced with every day.

Each triangle face of the pyramid represented the holographic chute of digits by which the Fed governors moved money digitally. When he succeeded in turning the screen yellow, it meant that he'd seen the pattern and then been able to insert a "kill" or "self-destruct" code.

He would only need to do it once, but by creating the simulacrum, Rokan had trained his mind to recognize the ever-changing digital algorithm by which the Fed managed the assets of the U.S. government.

His abdomen shot a burst of pain up through his chest and he shut his eyes and tried not to scream or even moan, not even a whisper. He was dying, he knew, but only Mansour knew. Rokan would not show the pain or weakness.

Rokan looked at his watch and stood up, shutting the laptop, grimacing as he held the back of the chair.

Just one more hour, he thought, *just a little while longer.*

He walked to the door and stepped into the hallway, just as a voice came over the corridor alarm system.

"This is an emergency broadcast. Please stay in your rooms."

58

King left the busy room alone and walked through the West Wing, then took the elevator up to the private living quarters of the Dellenbaugh family.

The first lady, Amy Dellenbaugh, was in the kitchen.

"I need to talk to you."

Amy's face furrowed in emotion.

"What is it?"

"New York City was just attacked," said King. "We believe it's Iran. Suicide bombers. They blew up the tunnels into the city. They have active shooters running around."

She stared blankly at King.

"The president is in danger," said King. "I want you to be aware of it."

"What do you mean 'in danger'?"

"They're going after the president," said King. "They're attempting to trap him at the UN. We're extracting him."

"When?"

"As soon as the helicopters get there."

"Why not immediately?" said Amy.

"They're in the air," said King. "Two Black Hawks are in the air, filled with Navy SEALs. We'll remove him from the rooftop. I'll keep you posted, Amy."

59

Four men sat in different parts of the large lobby of the Westin Hotel, which was very busy. A hodgepodge of business travelers and tourists moved briskly about as, outside, chaos descended. Hotel security had closed off the entrance to the hotel and several armed security guards stood near the entrance. They had a difficult task—on the one hand, letting people in to find refuge from the active shooters now moving down Manhattan streets—and on the other, being prepared to shoot any of the terrorists if they attempted to enter the Westin.

The four Iranians in the Westin lobby all knew one another. They'd trained together, first in QUDS, then in North Africa and then in Neyshabur, near the Turkmenistan and Afghanistan border, after being recruited by Hezbollah. Yet the four men didn't acknowledge each other.

Each man was young, early twenties. The oldest was twenty-four years old.

Each man was dressed in casual clothing. No one stood out. Even if they'd been sitting together, they probably wouldn't have raised many eyebrows, even though they all looked vaguely Middle Eastern.

Each man had spent the morning chopping off thumbs and plucking eyeballs from the sockets of the four governors of the Federal Reserve.

Away from the lobby, the elevator doors opened and a dozen people stepped out, including a short, bespectacled man in a gray suit and no tie. He had dark hair, combed neatly to the side. He was thin, even gaunt. He had a mustache. He had droopy eyes, with bags beneath them, though his overall mien was that of a successful businessman or lawyer. Of course, no truly successful businessman or lawyer would stay at the Westin near Grand Central, but that didn't matter, for he was only trying to look anonymous.

The man, Rokan, walked to a chair out of the way. He put a backpack on the floor next to him and opened it. Rokan looked up, making sure no one was about, then eyed one of the men who'd been waiting.

The man approached and reached into his pocket as he came close. He took a plastic ziplock bag and surreptitiously dropped it into the backpack. Rokan handed him a plastic card.

"Eight twelve," said Rokan in a whisper.

Three other Hezbollah operators approached Rokan over the next minute, each placing a plastic bag in the backpack.

Rokan stood without saying anything. He strolled across the lobby with four eyeballs, four thumbs, and an address.

In room 812, the four killers of the Fed governors gathered.

A pair of large duffel bags were on the bed.

In silence, the gunmen took weapons from the duffel bags. It was a mix of guns: three Uzis, an AR-15, a Kalashnikov, a DP-12 twelve-gauge pump-action shotgun, and a bunch of various handguns. The important part of the cache was the ammunition, and each man, after selecting his weapon of choice, found spare magazines and stuffed his pockets as full as he could.

One of the men used the bathroom.

They sat in the room, in silence.

Two of the men, Muhammed and Turan, knew each other like brothers—but they didn't speak. Instead, they waited.

The one who'd used the bathroom spoke:

"We wait a minute," he said, chambering a round. "Turan, you go first. We'll meet up on the other side."

60

Mack Perry, the thirty-one-year-old director of Special Operations Group, was pulling into the outer entrance to CIA Headquarters when his cell phone suddenly shrieked a high-pitched series of repetitive beeps.

He tapped his ear.

"Perry," he said. "I'm just pulling in. I need a breaker at the gate."

"You got it," said a female voice. "Opening in five, four—"

"Thank you," said Perry as he swerved around a corner of the parking lot. He pulled an IV from his forearm, a mobile unit of chemo he'd made the hospital rig up for him.

No one knew yet about Perry's cancer. Today, at least, he wanted to keep it that way.

"Patching you in," said the woman.

Perry heard a few clicks as he veered out of the line of cars.

The gravelly voice of Bill Polk, the head of the National Clandestine Service boomed in his ear.

"Mack, where the hell are you?" said Polk, his boss.

Perry drove a slightly beat-up white Chevy Suburban, and slammed the gas as he moved out of the line of cars and bolted toward a special entrance at the north corner of the gate.

"I'm pulling in. Where are you?"

"Targa," said Polk.

"Be right there."

He spun the wheel and was soon barreling toward a high steel fence, which was slowly opening electronically. He shot through the opening and came into a half-empty basement-level embankment, barely lit.

In Perry's ear:

"What's your MANSET at the UN?" said Polk.

"What happened?" said Perry.

"All four tunnels leading into or out of Manhattan were blown up," said Polk. "Destroyed. We have an extraction team airborne to get Dellenbaugh but what's your MANSET?"

"I have a team on the river," said Perry. "Six frogmen."

Perry parked, opened the door, and threw up. When he finished, he sprinted to the closest door, which was being held open by a man in a suit and no tie.

"Where's the team?" said Polk in Perry's ear.

"Fifty-second Street, under the FDR," said Perry.

"Who's running the go boat?" said Polk.

"Ferrara," said Perry.

Perry charged down two flights of stairs, then went through a steel door into a brightly lit, eerily modern, windowless hallway carpeted in white, silent enough to hear a pin drop. He saw Kaufman—the CIA general counsel—ahead; the fact that he was at the meeting signified everything.

The shit was hitting the fan.

He heard Polk's voice in his ear just as he came to the door to Targa.

"Hold," whispered Polk.

A moment later, Perry's eyes met Polk's through the open

door. Polk nodded. He wanted to tell Perry something before he entered.

"Do not come in yet," said Polk, still whispering.

"Roger."

Again, Polk, barely above a whisper:

"The president's chief of staff, Adrian King, is live-wired watching this," said Polk. "So is the SECDEF. Get Ferrara running right now, *before* you walk in. We've lost contact with the president, and his last known position was the eighteenth floor of the UN."

Perry watched Polk talk into his hand, hiding his words, from fifty feet away.

"Full recon, right?" said Perry.

"Affirmative," said Polk. "Safeties off. Watch your point of attack, and watch your fields of fire."

"Okay, give me a sec."

Perry moved down the hall, past the operations theater.

"CENCOM, cut me in to Ferrara."

"Yes, sir."

He heard a beep.

"Vinny?"

"Yeah, Mack."

"Are you aware of the situation?"

"Affirmative."

"There's an air crew coming in to extract Dellenbaugh but this thing is a shit show," said Perry. "When you see choppers, your team is go, move out. Don't go until you see the choppers. Got it? Get close by and use your 'not nice' side. We got to assume the worst."

"Roger that," said Ferrara. "But just so we're clear, what do you mean by 'worst'?"

"This is Extreme Priority," said Perry. "Assume the helicopter exfiltration doesn't work. You need to get in there and get him out some other way. Take the building and get to eighteen. Start looking for the president there. Enemy is already at the UN."

"Got it," said Ferrara. "I need commo on the air crew."

"CENCOM, live-wire all comms through SIPRNet," said Perry.

"We're in a full-combat situation in Manhattan. Sanitize any actions taken by NCS personnel inside or near Manhattan. This is an open-territory situation and their actions will be deemed necessary on behalf of the U S of A, per Perry as of this event."

"Yes, sir," came a female voice from CENCOM.

61

Both helicopters were similar in their setup: Sikorsky UH-60s off the deck of the USS *Eisenhower*, which was north of the coast of Connecticut.

The choppers swooped in toward the coastline, cutting above the water at a furious pace.

Each chopper was painted in a special paint diffused with microparticles of amber stealth alloy, which made the helicopters blend into the coloring of the sky to anyone looking up, and more importantly, refracted and confused advanced radar systems.

Minelli, in the lead chopper, peeked into the small cockpit of the Black Hawk. Minelli was geared up. Tight-quarters combat, daylight—he wore a camouflage set in white, olive, black, and blue, a tactical vest, and clutched a beefed-out M4.

"What do we got?" he said.

"Six and thirty," said one of the pilots, over comms, without moving.

Minelli tapped his ear.

"CENCOM, this is Lieutenant Colonel Lincoln Minelli, SEAL Team 4."

"Go, Colonel."

"I need access into whoever is running the extraction."

"Hold."

A voice came on. It was Perry.

"Who is this?" said Perry.

"Minelli, lieutenant colonel, U.S. Navy, SEAL Team 4."

"Nice to meet you," said Perry. "I was on Four, too."

"I know."

"Where are you?" said Perry.

"We're a few minutes out," said Minelli. "What are you thinking?"

"I want a lead chopper with green-line backup a hundred feet up, but that's just a suggestion," said Perry. "Remember your combat training; this is a force recon. I didn't fly choppers but I certainly flew *in* my share of choppers. I always think speed and eyes. You do what you need to do."

"You got it."

"You've got a team of UDT coming in by water," said Perry. "Don't shoot 'em."

"Affirmative," said Minelli. "We are on that. Do we know where the president is?"

"We've lost contact with the president. Last communication, he was on floor eighteen. This is hopefully going to be a rooftop extraction," said Perry. "If POTUS isn't there when you get there, you need to enter the building and get down to eighteen."

"Roger that, Mack," said Minelli.

Minelli stepped back into the cabin. He looked out a window and saw the other helicopter cut up, tracking behind, a hundred feet above, moving gradually into a tight attack pattern with the lead chopper. Minelli glanced through the cockpit window and studied the scene—a smoke-filled skyline above iconic skyscrapers. He registered the four smoke stacks above the island of Manhattan as the choppers approached, moving closer. The city seemed infinitely large and the two choppers tiny against the smoky sky.

At least, that's how he hoped their approach would be perceived by anyone on the ground.

Then he saw the tower of blue glass that was the United Nations.

A section of the building itself—several lower floors—was destroyed and on fire.

Minelli turned back in to the cabin. He tapped his comms, tying him into the other commandos as well as everyone on the second chopper, trailing just behind.

"We're getting close," said Minelli, looking at the other Navy SEALs, six in all. "This is a recon of the president of the United States. If he's not on the roof, we will need to deploy and engage. Last comms, he was on eighteen. Watch your fields of fire. We have the lead and will take the roof. Air Two, you approach in an RPO line above the East River and hold until we have POTUS—or something goes wrong, in which case move in. This a binary operation and the exfiltration of the president is the only objective. Pilots should assume enemy engagement. Let's get there fast and hard. Eyes out the windows, everyone's, but especially pilots'."

The pair of Black Hawks moved at the maximum capability of their design—227 mph—across the Atlantic Ocean, just off the coast, each chopper tilting forward slightly, then they split apart above Brooklyn, slashing left and down, right and up, maintaining speed. The lead chopper balanced out at approximately rooftop elevation as the backup chopper soared several hundred feet higher. They both cut south until they were at the confluence of the Hudson and East Rivers. Swerving again, they flew up the East River.

In each Black Hawk cockpit, the pilots wore dark helmets with black visor glass, enabling them to not only fly the helicopters but to also manage the weapons systems bolted to the underbellies of the highly customized choppers. It was also more reliable than looking out through the front windows. The air was a cloud of gray, white, and black smoke and soot. At certain moments, it was impossible to even see the Manhattan skyline. The pilots were going on instruments only.

Minelli leaned in.

"Evasive measures, guys, both choppers," said Minelli. "Jack up your fuckin' radar. This reminds me of getting shot down in Baghdad."

"Me, too," said one of the pilots.

62

Perry entered the mission theater. The amphitheater was dimly lit.

Targa was one of five mission theaters inside the Directorate of Operations. It was an amphitheater of several dozen built-in, theater-like leather chairs ascending away from a large, rectangular LCD sheet, and two data management stations occupied by analysts.

On the screen were several live feeds, spread like tiles across the screen: Two were aerial views of Manhattan, one by satellite, one by drone.

Both showed Manhattan from the sky. Blue sky was visible but not in and around Manhattan, which looked, by satellite, as if it was on fire. Four clusters of smoke and fire lit up the view.

The view from the drone was more intimate, several cameras displaying live feed simultaneously of Manhattan from a few hundred feet in the air, directly above. Yet the views from the drone were even more illustrative as to the situation. The streets were afire in gun battles, and red sparks of gunfire dotted the view.

"Give us POV from both helicopters as well as the boat," said Perry.

The screens in the theater flashed into two live video feeds, one feed from the lead helicopter, the other from the Zodiac CZ7 now hidden beneath FDR Drive.

The CIA theater was displaying live video feeds of all available aspects of the operation.

A deep monotone voice came through the feed, the low sound of engines behind it. It was Ferrara, the captain of the fastboat.

The screen shot large for everyone in Targa, live feeding from Ferrara's helmet.

"Coming in range," said Ferrara.

The view showed the bow of the Zodiac and the water beyond—straight to the destroyed shoreline south of the UN where the Queens-Midtown Tunnel fed into Manhattan. From the boat's vantage point, it was a fiery mess of clouds and flames. The FDR Drive was ripped in seams of tar and steel. Cars were dangling and then falling into the fast-moving river from above.

It was a horrible scene. Several people in the room audibly winced or groaned. It was utter mayhem.

Perry stood in front of the screen, analyzing the view.

"Look right," said Perry. "Give me a slow scan of the waterline."

Ferrara looked to his right, idling the engine, and the view in the theater showed the shore of the East River, a stone-and-concrete structure that was at least twenty feet taller in height than the river. There was no access, but that wasn't what Perry was searching for. He didn't need to tell Ferrara how his men should get up. Perry was looking for hostiles. But he saw nothing.

The boat engines purred. The Zodiac was still beneath the UN Tunnel. Then it emerged into the light just beneath the UN.

"Mack, I'm right below," said Ferrara.

"Air team is inbound," said Perry. "Hold at the embankment point."

"Roger that," said Ferrara.

Perry suddenly felt a wave of nausea coming on from the chemotherapy. He turned and found Polk.

Polk stood and walked to Perry.

"Good presentation," said Polk.

"Thanks," said Perry, "are we missing something?"

"Probably," said Polk.

"Have you run the Tier Ones?" said Perry.

"Yes—Andreas, Tacoma, and Singerman," said Polk.

"Awesome," said Perry, wincing as nausea hit even harder.

Polk took Perry quietly aside and walked with him toward the door into Targa, as if privately discussing some issue involving what was going on.

"When were you going to tell me?" said Polk.

"Tell you what?" said Perry.

"My wife had cancer, Mack," he replied, holding his shoulder and walking with him. "I understand. Let's get to the bathroom."

"I'm fine," said Perry.

Perry walked to the bathroom alone. Once inside, he found the toilet and collapsed to his knees. He vomited profusely for almost a minute. Perry flushed a few times as he spat out. He washed his hands and face, and walked back across the dimly lit hallway. Polk was waiting for him outside the door to the mission theater.

Polk put his arm on Perry's shoulder.

"I'd tell you it gets better, but it doesn't," said Polk, opening the door. "Now let's get Dellenbaugh out of there."

Inside Targa, Perry studied the half-arc of theater seating semi-filled with people, even as he directed the operation. He looked at the screen displaying the view from the undersides of the two helicopters as they flew across the sky toward the UN building in the distance.

Perry looked at another screen. The vantage point went to a Zodiac on the East River. The camera was on the helmet of one of the Navy SEALs tucked beneath the FDR.

Perry stood to the left of the screens, watching along with the others in the mission theater.

On the right screen, the Zodiac suddenly revved forward, out from beneath the overhang of the FDR Drive, beneath the UN.

Meanwhile, on the left screen, the lead Black Hawk flew toward Manhattan, directly into the path of a smoky cloud thundering up from where the tunnel leading into the city had been destroyed.

Sound from the two teams was on low but still discernible, mostly verbal interchange between Minelli and Ferrara.

Perry looked at Calibrisi.

"Any word from the president?" Perry said, barely above a whisper.

"Yes," said Calibrisi. "A trauma surgeon spoke to him on the phone. He was struck by a piece of glass. She said that he either died or became unconscious during the call."

63

Tacoma took an elevator to the second floor of the building. He exited and moved down the hallway until he came to the fire stairs. Before entering, he removed a suppressed SIG Sauer P226 from beneath his armpit. He chambered a round as he lifted the pistol next to his head.

With his free hand, he felt for a knife, sheathed at his torso, an old habit, an insecurity; simply seeing if the blade was still there. Next he reached over his shoulder, making sure the MP7A1 was positioned properly for a quick go.

Tacoma put his hand on the door to the fire stairs. He heard automatic-weapon fire from the lobby—sharp bullet fire—and there were shouts.

He removed his cell and opened an application called Trojan Spirit. It was a proprietary application developed by the Pentagon's DARPA team with interagency involvement that included CIA, NSA, DHS, and State. Its purpose was simple. Trojan Spirit was basically a field-level chat room and messaging system outside the internet and could be purposed on the fly for certain groups, such as, in this case, retired members of the military who had served in Special Forces, and who remained in good standing and thus were provisioned into the application. Trojan Spirit could only be used for "critical communications during threats to U.S. national security."

It was Tacoma's first time ever opening the application. He typed quickly, segmenting an audience of ex-operators confined to New York City. He sent six texts:

TROJAN SPIRIT
FLASH (Y) activation
This is Tacoma ex SEAL 6
HEZBOLLAH @MANHATTAN approx 500+ active shooters
Permission ddcia to take up arms activation extreme priority
Kill as many motherfuckers as u can
** know your fields of fire

Tacoma pocketed the cell and opened the door to the stairwell, training the P226 in a tight arc, finger on the trigger. The stairwell was empty.

Tacoma moved rapidly down the stairs as another round of automatic gunfire could be heard from just below. He came to the ground floor of the Mandarin and saw a door to the lobby. He approached the door warily. Through a small window, he saw a gunman, patrolling just on the other side of the door. The fatal tunnel. Tacoma ducked before the gunman could see him. He glanced one more time, from a sharp angle, and saw corpses strewn about the lobby.

Tacoma cut in the opposite direction, away from the door, and traveled down a maze of corridors until he found another door. Through a small window, he could see into a corridor. He holstered the 226 beneath his armpit and lifted the MP7A1 from over his back. He flipped the fire selector to full auto, then clutched the trigger and opened the door.

He heard more gunfire—the single crack of a pistol. He heard a woman shouting, and more gunfire . . . and he picked up his pace.

Tacoma came into the lobby across from where the gunman was positioned, kitty-corner to a bank of elevators. Pausing for a second as he heard the sound of more gunfire, he reached to his thigh and found a long cylindrical object, a B&T alloy suppressor, and screwed it quickly to the muzzle of the gun, then flipped the fire selector to manual. He moved out in front of the bank of elevators, training the weapon at the lobby as he emerged into the light-filled atrium. He registered blood splashed on walls and bodies across the entrance floor. Then he saw a gunman. He was across the bank of elevators, still guarding the fire door. Tacoma sighted him and pulled the trigger. A bullet spat from the end of the firearm with a metallic *thwack*—ripping the front of the killer's forehead. The man dropped with barely a groan. He heard voices in Persian. He flipped the fire selector to full auto and stepped toward the hotel's vast, light-crossed glass-walled lobby, clutching the trigger but not firing as he entered.

A man at the door . . . someone pivoting . . . bodies, blood.

A young, dark-haired man with a beard turned as Tacoma entered. He had on a white T-shirt and held a Kalashnikov. The gunman swept the gun toward Tacoma. Tacoma's eyes went past the gunman and he saw two others. They were similar-looking—young, dark hair, holding weapons. That was all he had time to understand before his finger instinctively pumped the trigger. The *spit spit spit* of suppressed gunfire was audible, but muted. The ammo burst leveled the man who was about to shoot—then Tacoma turned the submachine gun at the two other terrorists. He fired and slugs ripped sideways across the foreheads of the men, sending dark, misty clouds of blood across the lobby and dropping the men to the marble floor.

Tacoma saw other gunmen outside the building. He counted five men as he walked across the lobby. Out on the street in front of the Mandarin, he saw one of the corpses he'd blown away from his deck. Someone had seen him and they were there to kill him. Tacoma pulled the trigger and a wash of bullets tore through the glass. He clutched the trigger, moving the SMG from left to right, emptying the mag. He dumped the mag and slammed in another.

Tacoma walked outside through a destroyed wall of glass. One of the gunmen was still moving and Tacoma fired a short burst of bullets into his chest, killing him.

64

9:15 A.M.
COLUMBIA UNIVERSITY
116TH STREET AND BROADWAY
NEW YORK CITY

Singerman was almost at Broadway when he heard the crack of gunfire just in front of him. From the pavement, he watched as a man stepped from a car holding a submachine gun—and started firing at people indiscriminately. There were screams and then Singerman saw another gunman emerge behind him.

Singerman dived behind the gates that marked the entrance to Columbia. He waited as the two killers started to move south on Broadway, automatic rifles out.

He watched and began to get up when—through the gates—he saw one of the killers turn.

Singerman recognized the gait. He tucked himself against the bricks.

In his ear, Polk was still there:

"Aaron, where's your weapon?"

Singerman looked at his briefcase. He opened it and ripped out the back, revealing a long, thin, fixed-blade Benchmade combat knife. He got to his feet, crouching.

Automatic-weapon fire erupted just feet away—on the other side of the gate.

As the gunman walked past the gate, Singerman lurched and

slashed the blade into the gunman's stomach, ripping fast sideways, cutting almost back to the man's spine, and the terrorist's stomach and organs spilled to the bricks along with a burst of dark crimson as he let out a horrific scream.

Stepping over the dying terrorist's body, Singerman picked up the gunman's Uzi. He moved to Broadway in a crouch and found the other gunman, across Broadway and a few car lengths down, clutching an AK-47 and looking around. Singerman pumped the trigger, sending bullets in the direction of the unsuspecting terrorist. A line of nickel-sized holes shredded the man across the chest, leaving a miasma of crimson.

Singerman ran down the curved slope from Broadway to Riverside Drive. Halfway down the block, he came to a wide limestone-and-brick townhouse. At an old iron gate, he found a small black digital box, which he put his left index finger against, and the gate unlocked.

"I'm clear," said Singerman.

Singerman went inside and crossed through the grand but empty entrance to the kitchen and went to a door in back, then descended to the basement of the town house. He flipped on the lights. A large gun safe stood alone in the dimly lit basement. It was green and red, and said BROWNING along the side. He opened the heavy door.

"What do you need from me?" said Singerman into his earbud as he put the Uzi down. He picked up an MP7A2 and threaded a silencer into the muzzle, then jammed a tactical vest with mags.

"Get armed up and down to the UN," said Polk. "The president is under attack."

"Roger that, Bill, on my way," said Singerman.

65

Mansour was slumped against the guardhouse, inside the UN complex, but away from the major gun battle, though he was involved. Pinned down.

Mansour was bleeding from his knee. The sniper had moved and reacquired him from inside the UN building. Each time Mansour started to move out from behind the security station, a bullet slammed the ground nearby.

The sniper had him locked in.

On either side of the security station, toward the tower, was open concrete, slightly away from the main battle. But he had no chance to run across it now, not until the sniper ran out of ammo or was dead.

How could he have been so stupid? He was sure that he'd thought of everything, but clearly he hadn't.

Meanwhile, his knee throbbed with pain. His shoe was drenched in blood. It had trickled down his calf and ankle from his knee.

He was going to bandage it, but he was slipping into shock and was in the pre-stages when the pain becomes so overwhelming it makes one dull. It wasn't bleeding obscenely, but it was bleeding badly, and he was losing the energy to bandage it. Mansour knew he had to, but he was too tired. He had to deal with the pain, he knew.

When he felt his eyes become droopy and start to involuntarily shut, he knew he was on the verge of slipping into shock.

He reached to a pocket of his coat and took out a small circular container. He unscrewed the top. Inside was a pile of small white pills. Oxycontin. He took three and swallowed them. Mansour knew he would lose part of his capabilities by taking the pills, yet if he didn't treat the pain he would fall into shock and then he'd be dead, shot by the first NYPD SWAT to come across him, or the sniper.

He felt warmth and a sense of elation, and the pain started to ebb.

Voices across First Avenue, then Mansour saw an FBI man weaving toward him from up First Avenue. The agent was dressed in jeans and a sweatshirt, clutching an MP7. He wore a bulletproof vest, with the letters FBI in yellow. Mansour remained still as the man cut between vehicles, shielding himself. Mansour raised his rifle, moved the fire selector to manual, and fired. The bullet hit the FBI agent in the eye, kicking out the back of his skull and spraying blood and brains across several cars.

Mansour took out his cell phone. He hit a speed dial as he looked up at the glass-and-steel skyscraper across from the UN, on First Avenue. A luxury building filled with foreign diplomats. One of the four Hezbollah missile men was on the roof.

"Commander," said Kouros.

"I need one of your men to do something," said Mansour.

"Yes, Commander."

"There's a sniper at the UN. He has me trapped. I'm behind the guardhouse."

"Facing First Avenue?" said Kouros.

Kouros was on the East River side of the UN.

"What floor?" said Kouros.

"I don't know," said Mansour. "A low floor."

Kouros texted his soldier, a man who was on the roof of a luxury condominium tower across First Avenue from the UN.

> Sniper low floor

>> *Yes I see him third floor*

> Prepare to kill

"My man sees him," said Kouros.

"Can you shoot him?" said Mansour.

"May I be honest?" said Kouros.

"Lies are useless to me," said Mansour.

"It's too far for my soldier's rifle, Commander," said Kouros. "But, sir, he can destroy him with one of the Strelas."

"Do it, brother," said Mansour.

66

Dewey had the boat gunning, throttles wide open, and was moving fast across the open Upper Bay of New York Harbor. Between Governors Island and Brooklyn there was a channel, and Dewey steered the Hinckley into it, even as a procession of sailboats, ferries, motorboats, and even rowing shells moved down the channel and away from Manhattan.

He could see Manhattan to his left, like a monolith behind Governors Island, covered in clouds of smoke, and he was but a small speck in the boat. Nevertheless, he knew the Iranians were likely watching the mouth of the East River. That's what he would do in their position.

It was a race against time. There was no way Hezbollah could keep American forces out for very long—but the Iranians didn't need to keep them out for more than a few hours at most; they only needed to keep them out for as long as it took them to find J. P. Dellenbaugh and kill him.

Dewey kept the Hinckley as close as possible to Brooklyn's shoreline, on his starboard side, to the right. After passing Governors Island, he exited the channel and moved north, along Brooklyn's crowded waterfront, into open water, exposed, though at least a quarter mile from any part of Manhattan, and was soon at the mouth of the East River, cutting between Manhattan and Brooklyn.

The currents were fierce as the river poured into the harbor.

At the mouth of the East River, he could suddenly hear the faintest *rat-a-tat-tat* of automatic-weapon fire coming from somewhere at the southern edge of Manhattan, to his left—Battery Park, Wall Street, or the Seaport. There was no way to tell where the noise was coming from, but it didn't seem as if they were aiming for him. But as he kept going, sporadic gunfire grew louder.

In the distance, spanning the low sky between Brooklyn and Manhattan, was the Brooklyn Bridge. It came into view gradually, but through the mist Dewey could see a small fire at approximately midpoint of the bridge.

Hezbollah had blown up the openings to the four tunnels. They didn't need to destroy the bridges. All they needed to do was tie up traffic. The Iranians were doing it by simply killing motorists. The cars would provide the barrier. It was, tactically, a smart move. The result was chaos. As he moved closer beneath the bridge, Dewey heard screams and shouting, and the sound of gunfire became louder. He registered people running toward Brooklyn, away from Manhattan. Small dots of red, white, orange, and black in the distance.

The sheer scope of the Iranian attack was mind-boggling.

From a purely tactical perspective, it was coordinated, overwhelming, detail-oriented, and above all fast. They had huge operating leverage, meaning that with a relatively small group of soldiers they could inflict a great deal of damage. Four bombers in the tunnels. Active shooters mowing down a thoroughly unprepared citizenry, taking advantage of streets clogged with vehicles whose drivers were now dead or had run. It was a major challenge for law enforcement.

Where the East River met the ocean was a wide spread of water. Getting upstream to the UN wouldn't be a problem. He was a tiny moving part of a larger maelstrom. Any gunmen looking for attacks coming from the river would need to be focused. Moreover, any Hezbollah on the bridges were likely there to settle traffic on the bridge. Dewey guessed that any men looking for people in boats would be set up in a separate location from the frontline shooter, or shooters, on the bridge.

As he came up to the Brooklyn Bridge, Dewey watched a woman running along the bridge, trying to get away, as a pair of Hezbollah gunmen fired submachine guns. Her body was interrupted in a violent thrust—she didn't make it. He eyed the two killers as the boat approached and started to go out of sight, beneath the bridge. He raised the rifle. The closest one, a young man with a beard and mustache, with long, black hair, was too focused on the bridge to look down.

They didn't notice Dewey below.

Dewey knew his responsibility was to get to the UN and yet he couldn't resist. He set the fire selector on the AR-15 to manual. Just as the boat went beneath the outer steel of the bridge, he found the bearded thug in the optic. Dewey pumped the trigger. A slug from the rifle struck the killer square center in the ear, kicking him back—blowing his skull in a wet, red rain across the windshield of an empty SUV just as the Hinckley went beneath the Brooklyn Bridge.

Dewey quickly tied a line to the wheel, keeping the boat straight as it could go and letting it steer itself. As he acclimated to the speed, the shift in the Hinckley, and the movement of the Iranian, he stared up at the bottom of the Brooklyn Bridge.

The other gunman would no doubt see his dead comrade and come to the north side of the bridge to kill him.

Dewey went to the stern of the Hinckley. He crouched and moved the fire selector to semimanual, then targeted the bridge above, adjusting his eyes against the dark of the steel, knowing he would need to fire just as bright light hit after the bridge. He adjusted the optic. It took him several moments staring through the sight, but he locked in on the side of the bridge, tracking it, before even seeing anyone. As the boat moved out from beneath the bridge, Dewey heard gunfire from above as bullets ripped into the aft end of the boat. Dewey saw muzzle flash. He registered a gunman, aiming down and firing. Dewey swept and fired, spraying slugs which struck steel, and then one of the bullets hit the Hezbollah in the forehead. The killer stumbled over the railing of the bridge, twisting in a limp somersault and splashing into the East River less than twenty feet from Dewey's boat, then he was quickly swept away by the fierce current.

Dewey went back to the steering wheel and took control, steering the speeding Hinckley along the opposite side of the East River from Manhattan, close to a wall of steel, brick, pier, and industrial construction along Brooklyn. He cruised beneath the Williamsburg Bridge, purposely not looking over at Manhattan, a horizon of smoke with distinct funnels of darker smoke.

He tapped his earbud. He waited for voice recognition but there was nothing. He tapped it again—but all he heard was a faint metallic beeping noise. He tapped again, knowing full well something was going wrong with his comms.

As he sped up the Queens shoreline, Dewey scanned the area around the UN along the Manhattan shoreline, from south of the UN to the Queensboro Bridge above it. He didn't see anyone or anything suspicious—but it was all suspicious. The waterfront offered a multitude of places where someone could easily hide out.

He registered several gunmen along the UN Plaza that overlooked the river. It was impossible to tell if they could see him. He knew by staying with the shoreline just behind him he would blend in to a certain extent. He was at least two thousand feet away, too far for anything but a skilled marksman and a very well-made long-range rifle. He couldn't assume they didn't see him. In fact, for the purposes of his coming approach, he assumed they did.

He passed a small rock jutting out of the water, then the river split on both sides of Roosevelt Island, just offshore from Manhattan's East Side. He went to the right of the island, still moving the boat along the shoreline.

Roosevelt Island sat between Manhattan and Queens, in the middle of the East River, a quarter mile above the UN.

The city had become more chaotic than before. Sirens and alarms screamed from every imaginable place and people were running, some even leaping into the river itself, believing it offered a better chance for survival. But Dewey saw bodies occasionally float by. The fast-moving, turbulent currents of the river harbored no allies; it was a vicious river with a hard, unpredictable undertow.

Dewey came to a piling at the very southern tip of Roosevelt Island, a wall of steel pilings sticking up and surrounding walls of granite rock. He tied the Hinckley off to an old steel piling support and stepped to the aft of the boat. He found the duffel bag he'd packed on Jenna's boat, from her father's weapons room.

He pulled the fins on his feet as an errant wave splashed against the pilings and drenched him. He didn't seem to notice.

Dewey took an optic and studied the perimeter of the United Nations from the shallows of the water near the island. There was a line of gunmen. He counted six, then saw another. As he suspected, the gunmen were indeed scanning the river in front of the UN, looking for intruders.

The current was running rapid; he guessed it was five knots.

He hated water.

Dewey took a deep breath and dived beneath the surface. He fell into the tumbling current and it took all he had to stay just beneath the water, staring up at daylight from below the surface. He swam until his lungs hurt, then surfaced just barely, as quietly as he could, and only for long enough to exhale and take a breath, then he descended again, even as the current swept him quickly downstream.

He repeated this several times, each time taking a breath only when necessary, praying he wouldn't be seen, for as he got closer, he swam beneath the wall of gunmen looking for anything to shoot.

Beneath the water, he kicked furiously toward shore.

Dewey kicked as hard as he'd ever kicked. He finally reached the bank of the river. He found a jagged edge of mortar jutting out. He pulled himself to it and held on. He coughed out water and caught his breath. He treaded water, against a hard current, but his grip on the slight notch of the wall kept him close as he breathed hard and remembered why he was there.

A pair of black helicopters slashed low overhead. The air riffed with the wind from the rotors. Dewey watched as the two choppers moved toward Manhattan, and then up the river, splitting up at the crest of the city and moving into a vertical attack pattern, toward the United Nations. This was the recon.

Dewey tapped his ear as he studied the flight path. This time, his comms were working.

"I see choppers," said Dewey. "Is that the extraction?"

"Yes," said Calibrisi.

"What about manpower inside the building?" said Dewey.

"The Iranians are close to taking over the lobby or they already have," said the CIA director.

"Who the hell was guarding him?"

"There'll be plenty of time for blame afterward. Right now, we need to get him out," said Calibrisi.

67

Kouros was tucked in between two pallets stacked with bags of cement mix. It was a temporary dock used for maintenance and repair and was fastened to the river bank. The wood was weathered and a small crane sitting on top of the piers was rust-covered. It looked as if no work had taken place for years.

A month before, Kouros had hidden firearms here, including three handguns and an assault rifle. He also left several candy bars on the front seat of the crane. The firearms were expendable. Kouros was trying to figure out if anyone actually used the docks anymore. He knew that if workers were there, it would be a bad location for the surface-to-air missiles. Two days before, he'd come to the docks again, in the middle of the day. It would be much easier to explain the trespassing if he was caught. No one was there when he returned. The firearms were untouched, same too with the candy bars in the cab of the crane.

Now, Kouros was positioned between the crane and the wall of shoreline, tucked in and out of view. Strapped across his shoulder was a missile launcher. He was smoking a cigarette.

Just a few hundred feet downriver, columns of smoke barreled out from the ground just above the waterline.

Kouros heard the helicopters before he could see them. He'd tracked choppers already but these were ones he recognized, Sikorskys, UH-60 or some variation thereof.

He put his eye to an infrared optic and spied the two inbound helicopters. He locked in on the first chopper, knowing that he needed to fire and reload fast. When a green light flashed in his eye, he knew the Strela had acquired the target, and he fired. His shoulder and body kicked backward, and he quickly reloaded, loading another Strela, locking the second chopper in, and he fired again.

Kouros watched as the two Russian-made missiles pirouetted into the smoldering, smoke-crossed sky.

68

Ferrara scanned the smoke-filled sky as the Zodiac moved out from beneath the overhanging FDR, into the lee of the current-swirled river, and the attack boat arced right.

Ferrara was patched in to the overall operation comm channel, and was listening.

"Approaching target landing zone," said the pilot.

"Affirmative," said Perry.

Ferrara heard the sound of the inbound helicopters overhead. He put optics on and turned downstream. He saw no one, but then, when he looked farther ahead, far beyond the UN, he found a body imprint in his digital green, in his optics. Someone at water level, not moving, but definitely alive. A quarter mile below the UN, Ferrara saw the thermal imprint of a man in the shadows. . . .

"Target up to the right," said Ferrara. "He's looking south. Let's get over next to the bank and move in, assume enemy status."

A fierce-sounding noise—a hissing—followed by a boom.

The river's edge brightened.

Where Ferrara had just aimed the attack, everyone on the Zodiac heard, then saw, a surface-to-air missile shoot up into the sky, followed soon after by another missile. Ferrera had a hard time breathing.

"Air One and Two, you have incoming!" yelled Ferrara as he started firing downriver at the terrorist.

69

As Dewey held on to the riverbank, a sudden flash of electric white came from somewhere just down the river. There was a low but loud *boom*, and then a streak of fire. A missile cut into the low sky. Smoke and fire trail dissipated in a gray-white line. The missile had been fired from somewhere just down the river in front of the UN.

He hit his ear twice.

"CENCOM, get them out, it's a trap!" said Dewey.

A few seconds later, a second missile was fired from the same location.

The missiles screeched upward in yellow-orange fire and each one pivoted and swirled as it converged in on the helicopters. The first missile acquired the lead Black Hawk as it tore across the smoky skyline. The missile slammed into the bottom of the chopper, pulverizing it. Steel and bodies dropped down from the sky in flames, a horrible, metal-filled dive to the river.

The second chopper slashed abruptly down and sharp to the right—evasion tactics. The missile was gaining speed, trailing smoke and flames, soaring closer and closer; by this time in its attack sequence, the missile's tracking algorithm was calibrated to potential evasion techniques. The second surface-to-air missile hit the second chopper in the fuselage, a double-shot explosion that erupted in black, gray, green, and red. Steel, glass, and smoldering bodies dropped like proverbial bricks into the swiftly moving East River and disappeared.

Then, a few hundred feet below, Dewey saw a Zodiac emerge from a dark alcove beneath the FDR Drive. Before he could warn them away, another *boom* echoed up the river. Another missile had been fired. It was from the same place. Dewey watched in horror and anger as the missile moved across the surface of the water and slammed into the boat of Navy SEALs, obliterating everything.

Dewey paused a few moments, treading water, looking south toward where the missiles had been launched from. He let go of the granite outcropping. He dived down beneath the cold water and let the current take him in the direction of the missile launcher.

70

The right screen at the front of the operations theater went red and white, a visual alarm, then a computerized voice hit the screen as a small object was locked in on in the middle of the screen.

"Incoming missile," said the male voice calmly. "Identify, Strela nine two approaching at one one five zero feet per second and accelerating. Time of impact, less than five seconds."

The object sharpened—a grayish-green cone at the front of the missile—plumes of heat like orange flower petals around the cone, then the screen shot black.

The left screen, on the SEAL boat, was still active and the view—from Ferrara's helmet—showed the choppers exploding in smoke and fire. Then Ferrara turned downriver and the screen—as with the other screen—flashed red and white, as a missile approached along the top of the water.

"Incoming missile," said the male voice calmly. "Identify, Strela nine two approaching at four four zero miles per hour and accelerating. Time of impact: *immediate*."

Inside the amphitheater, there were moans as the screen went black, then Perry barked into his comms.

"Vinny!" he yelled. *"Minelli!"* even though everyone in the room, including Perry, understood that the frogmen and the men from SEAL Team 4 had just gone down in a pair of choppers and a Zodiac.

71

Adrian King's tie was lowered and the top button of his shirt was unbuttoned. A line of empty water bottles crossed the front of his wide and long desk. The mood was tense. Everyone in the chief of staff's office was stunned.

King looked at the assembled group of about a dozen. He nodded at Calibrisi and Arnold. They came over behind his desk.

"Well, Adrian?" said Arnold.

"You're right. We need to act," said King. "America needs to respond. It needs to happen right now."

There was a long pause.

"Chief?" said King.

"I agree," said Calibrisi. "We're under attack. Suleiman is watching from his little office. They're going after our president; I see no reason why we shouldn't do the same."

"So the question is, what do we do?" said King.

"Let me just reiterate," said Arnold. "Either we're nuking them or we're dropping enough bombs to turn Tehran into a smoking pile of rubble!"

"We're not dropping a nuke on Iran," said Calibrisi. "Only the president has the authority to order a nuclear strike. Not to mention, the people of Iran didn't do this, their leaders did."

"*They're trying to kill our fucking president!*" shouted Arnold.

"So let's kill theirs," said Calibrisi calmly. "Let's light up Suleiman today, right now. I have no problem with that."

"What about chain of command?" said King. "I've read through the laws. I was a federal prosecutor. All I can conclude is that there's no chain of command right now."

"That's right," said Calibrisi. "If the president is dead, it would be Healey, but we don't know if he's dead."

"I'll be damned if we're not going to fight back," said Arnold. "There's no way that's what the framers of our Constitution wanted."

"No, it isn't," agreed King. "At the moment, we *are* the chain of command."

"Even if we aren't, I'm willing to go to jail for doing it," said Arnold.

"Me, too," said King.

Calibrisi looked at Arnold. "This counterstrike is on you. You need to handle it. Right now. I need to focus on Dellenbaugh. That's my only priority."

"I got it," said Arnold.

"We know Suleiman's patterns—we have for years. Suleiman will be in one of four locations," said Calibrisi. "We just need to target all four with overwhelming force."

"Can you make it happen, Dale?" said King to Arnold.

"I'll assemble the Joint Chiefs," said Arnold, standing. "We'll make it happen."

72

Igor stared at a large curvilinear computer screen.

His apartment at the Carlyle was luxurious and had the feeling, usually, of a peaceful aerie high above the Upper East Side of Manhattan. His apartment was austere, with very little furniture. The windows were specialized, wrapped in a thin velum of microcopper membrane. The walls, ceilings, and floors contained custom manufactured insulation and even the electric current in the apartment went through a cipher. All of it was there to prevent electronic eavesdropping.

Igor could hear the roar of multiple sirens from the streets.

The table was long, rectangular, and glass. He had a perfect view of Madison Avenue. In the distance, the sky was hazy and crossed with smoke clouds, like a volcano that's just erupted. It was detritus from the tunnels miles away to the south, spewing heat and ash into the sky. But Igor wasn't looking at the view at this particular moment. Instead, he was focused on the curvilinear computer screen.

The concave LCD was lit up in a maze of photos, live videos, digits, and letters. There were at least twenty separate applications running on Igor's computer. All of it was somehow correlated to the attack on New York City.

Igor was tapped into Langley, Quantico, and NYPD's operating platform through the main trunk, enabling him to see what activity was taking place on the ground and behind the scenes, in real time.

Part of the screen was taken up by a gallery of several dozen individual live video feeds, spread across the screen like a checkerboard, each feed inputted by some sort of surveillance camera, including several attached to the gear of NYPD officers, police cruisers, CCTV surveillance cameras. Igor did not control any of these feeds; he was, in essence, eavesdropping on the real-time efforts of law enforcement.

The individual feeds lurched between different scenes of panicked New Yorkers running through the streets, and gunfights. Several feeds displayed the four tunnels and the shorelines closest to the tunnels, where whole buildings had collapsed and fires were spreading out.

Another section showed feeds from the air—drones, helicopters, and satellites—each a different vantage point of the chaos. Smoke and fire from above. A macro view of Manhattan in disarray and chaos.

Other than when Igor typed, the only noise was the diffuse sound of sirens and gunfire from the streets.

A section of the wide curvilinear screen was taken up by scrolling lines of green letters and numbers moving rapidly down. Igor had opened up a host of diagnostic applications he was now using to attempt to understand what was going on, and what was going to happen next, based on various metadata and electronic signals intelligence, or SIGINT. He was provisioned inside the NSA's ThinThread network, poring through the original signals data from the Berlin initiation point several hours before. Taking the ThinThread discovery, Igor had isolated a string of individuated metadata—basically a marker code—and run it against a proprietary algorithm he himself had written. He had determined that the long string of random letters and numbers were from a SIM card issued by MTN Irancell, the state-owned cellular provider in Iran. He couldn't determine who made the call, only that the card used was a one-month tourist SIM card, purchased at Tehran's Imam Khomeini International Airport three days ago. By rank-stacking the SIM card's issue number, sandwiching it between the card bought before and the one bought after, Igor had been able to pinpoint the card's time of purchase within eight minutes of when it was bought. From there, it was a matter of simply pushing all purchase data from the airport MTN Irancell store against all flights that left Tehran after that, focusing, obviously, on that day and moving outward.

That's what one of his screens was now doing, trying to find correlations.

But as Igor waited for the results of his analysis as to the origination of the call, a different part of the wide computer screen abruptly froze. This was a screen he hadn't even really been using, other than as a catalog of sorts for the various programs he had running on other screens.

The screen flashed a neon red icon in the upper right corner. Across the frozen section of screen, the word NOCOS appeared in white caps.

"Enter on four one," said Igor with his thick Russian accent, speaking to the computer as he watched the icon—after recognizing his voice—burst into a live video feed.

He was looking straight ahead, through a camera on an individual, a chest-mounted wireless camera. It was body camera footage from someone in law enforcement. It was a recording only hours old. The officer was lifting the limp head of a dead man, a body slumped over in a car, a riot of blood, a hole in the neck, and, on his face, a missing eyeball, a horrible-looking empty hole, surrounded by blood and recently mauled tissue.

Igor spoke:

"Program."

"Everest," came a robotic, synthetic female voice.

Everest was a facial recognition platform.

From the dead man's right eye—the remaining eye still in the socket—a digital balloon interrupted the screen.

A bright white digital box. The file photo of a man.

TOP SECRET
-NOSEC—NOSEC—NOSEC—NOSEC—NOSEC—NOSEC—NOSEC-
ALPINA 42.6
IDENTITY:

LAWRENCE, PHILLIP
GOVERNOR adjutant 14
U.S FEDERAL RESERVE

Igor spoke:
"Why am I looking at this?"
The computer:
"Einstein 3, high-value incident," said the voice.

Einstein 3 was an NSA algorithm that filtered secure government gateways for metadata, including the most mundane internet traffic, always focused in on government officials, even at a local level. Igor had customized it so that it was always on but only made its presence known when it found something.

The screen showed the dead man, Lawrence, in a photo from a few years before. He was one of four individuals: three men and one woman.

The screen popped up a document.

_____THE UNITED STATES FEDERAL RESERVE
CHARTER AMENDMENT TO UNITED STATES TREASURY c.67T
ACTION 290-B
FEDWIRE
TC CODE: 1000000000-1
DECEMBER 5, 1998
_____4
EXECUTIVE SUMMARY:

-Action 290-B establishes a central and secure digital framework for the management of all transactions by and between the U.S. Federal Reserve and any governmental or non-governmental entities.

-Action 290-B establishes a U.S. Treasury enterprise composed of four (4) individuals whose responsibility—as a necessarily combined redundant entity—is to effectively manage all debits and credits of the Federal Reserve whose transactional value are more than one billion dollars.

-THE FEDERAL RESERVE WILL CHARGE SUCH INDIVIDU-
ALS, HEREINAFTER REFERRED TO AS GOVERNORS, TO MAN-
AGE ALL MOVEMENT OF FEDERAL RESERVE ASSETS AND
SHALL BE INDEMNIFIED HEREBY FROM SUCH ACTIONS, PER
ACTION 290-B

Igor realized that the man who'd been murdered was one of the individuals who managed the Federal Reserve.

As Igor read on, his mouth went agape, and he felt his heart palpitating. The dead man, Lawrence, had been flagged on a remote NSA algorithm. Lawrence and three other individuals were in charge of something even he barely understood, Fedwire. They controlled, day in and day out, approximately $5 trillion of sovereign American wealth—the entire liquidity of the United States Federal Reserve and thus the United States of America.

The ebb and flow of money.

Igor believed he knew everything, and yet, in a fraction of a moment, he realized he didn't know anything.

He typed furiously, attacking levels of information deep inside government servers, using the NSA root to find another level of information. It was a Level 3 file, so secret that it was locked inside a cryptographic fortress, layered with various encryption keys, but Igor quickly bored into the kernel of highly secure data in which the identities of the four governors was displayed with photos and links to their backgrounds:

FENNER, DAVID [670–3 T.9]
JAKLITSCH, ADAM [411–1 Q.4]
LAWRENCE, PHILLIP [700–3 V.0]
WINIKOFF, KARA [329–0 Z.1]

When the screen froze again, a cold chill washed over him. Another algorithm appeared on the screen. A small red circle started flashing.

The algorithm was cued off the profile Igor was now pushing against every available database he could find. It was metadata, a cell call to 911, only just live. In this case a woman, her eyeball missing.

She was already known to Igor, for she was on the LCD next to Lawrence.

Kara Winikoff.

He ran all four names against the data cipher that had flagged Winikoff. The results came back almost immediately. All four were dead.

_____FENNER, DAVID [670–3 T.9]
—deceased—
Per NYPD Brooklyn 17 06:15 AM EST

_____JAKLITSCH, ADAM [411–1 Q.4]
—deceased—
Per NYPD Manhattan 71 06:45 AM EST

_____LAWRENCE, PHILLIP [700–3 V.0]
—deceased—
Per PD Mt Kisco NY 06:57 AM EST

_____WINIKOFF, KARA [329–0 Z.1]
—deceased—
Per NYPD Manhattan 44 07:20 AM EST

Igor scanned the reports. Three of them were shot in the chest, Lawrence got it in the neck, all at close range, all inside vehicles.

Each of them had had one of their eyeballs cut out. Each of them was missing a thumb, freshly hacked off. It was a tightly choreographed operation.

Igor cut out of the live feed as Everest scrolled.

_____ All four governors will work at the same time and will coordinate schedules accordingly without exception.

_____ All four must be present for any movement of liquidity.

_____ Place of work should be secure and anonymous.

_____ Latest technology should always be employed to not only move assets but to gain entrance.

_____ Governors shall be selected on the basis of intellectual capability.

_____ A council will be formed of private sector leaders whose role will be the selection of said governors.

_____ The council and governors will remain anonymous and their activities secret under threat of sedition.

Igor picked up his cell and dialed.

"I'm busy," said Polk.

"It's important."

"New York is under siege," said Polk. "The president is trapped. Unless it's more important than that, I don't have the time."

"It's more important," said Igor.

"I'm listening," said Polk.

"Everything is a distraction," said Igor. "It is far more serious and complicated, Bill."

"How?"

Igor spoke Russian:

"Delo v den'gakh. Eto vsegda o den'gakh."

It's about the money. It's always about the money.

"Skazhi chto ty imeyesh' v vidu," said Polk.

Say what you mean.

"They're hacking into the Federal Reserve," said Igor. "The president is a subterfuge. The room where it's all managed must be in Manhattan."

"There's no way," said Polk.

"What do you know about the governors of the Fed?" said Igor in a sharp voice, communicating the urgency of the question. "Fedwire?"

There was a pause.

"I'm not allowed to discuss that," said Polk.

"All four were killed this morning," said Igor, interrupting. "Four governors, four different locations. They each got shot and each one of them is missing a thumb and an eyeball."

Polk was silent for several seconds.

"This is turning into a really shitty day," said Polk.

"The eyes and prints allow them into the room," Igor said. "It's an iris-based provisioning structure backed up by prints. All four individuals need to be there simultaneously in order to enter. Or at least their thumbs and eyes."

"Entry protocols," said Polk. "I'm hooking us into someone who knows about the Fed, especially the systems you're talking about. In the meantime, try and get a handle on the entry architecture. CEN-COM, establish Igor, Singerman, and me over JWICS."

"Yes, sir."

73

Singerman left his town house and cut down to Riverside Drive. Cars, SUVs, minivans, delivery trucks, motorcycles, and throngs of people just walking or running, were moving north toward Harlem and, presumably, out of Manhattan—or at least away from the chaos that enveloped Midtown and below. Traffic was at a standstill. Singerman approached a black Suburban, stuck in the line of traffic. He approached a male driver and got his attention.

"I need to borrow your vehicle," said Singerman, weapon at his side, though clutched in his hand. "It'll be replaced."

The man waved him away, yelling at him from behind the glass.

Singerman raised a submachine gun and aimed it at the driver.

"Get out," said Singerman.

The driver flipped the middle finger. Singerman fired. The bullet shattered the driver's side window as it cut in front of the driver then exited through the passenger window, shattering it also.

The driver raised his hands and opened the door.

Singerman carjacked the Suburban and slammed the gas, maneuvering over a low concrete divider and roughing it over thick shrubbery in the middle of Riverside between south and north.

Singerman executed a U-turn on Riverside Drive. He swerved into the southbound lanes and gunned it.

Above Riverside Drive, and indeed the upper part of the island of Manhattan, the sky was blue. But clouds of smoke pirouetted into the sky in the distance.

He was at 115th Street and he hit the gas hard. The southbound lanes were mostly clear. Some people, not content to wait in the northbound lanes of Riverside, were driving north in the southbound lanes, and Singerman had to dodge and weave to avoid the oncoming vehicles, though he pounded the gas pedal hard and was accelerating. By the time he reached Ninety-sixth Street, it was barely possible to get by. The road was a logjam as people abandoned their vehicles, or else remained in them trying to push around the vehicles that had already been abandoned. He started using the sidewalks and was not afraid to push aside vehicles by ramming them at the front or back bumper. By Eightieth Street, he was feathering the pedal, moving through whatever small chutes existed in the roadway, sometimes playing chicken with a northbound vehicle. At some point, he started bouncing against oncoming vehicles on the sidewalk, trying to get out of the city. It was chaos, and when he saw a wall of stopped cars above Seventy-second Street, Singerman pounded the gas and cut right, plowing the Suburban to a pedestrian running path that led down into Riverside Park.

Singerman banked right off a brick column with a brass plaque at the top of the stairs and accelerated down a flight of concrete steps, slamming hard at the base of the stairs into tar as sparks shot out and metal scraped. When he grounded out, he slammed the gas and was soon moving fast through the pedestrian park. He kept his foot on the pedal, hard to the floor, honking when necessary to scare people away before he ran them over.

He heard a beep in his ear and reached up.

"CENCOM, identify."

"NOC 3390 AB2," said Singerman.

After a few low beeps:

"Aaron, you have Bill and one more person."

"Aaron, it's Bill," said Polk. "You also have Igor, who is a DCIA NO/SEC. Where are you?"

"Riverside Park," said Singerman as he cut back and forth between pedestrians.

"Hi, Aaron, my name is Igor," came a deep, crisp voice with a sharp Russian accent. "Bill said you have some knowledge of the United States Federal Reserve?"

74

Dewey saw where the missiles had come from. He drifted down the river, pulled along by the current, at times violent enough to heave him down beneath the surface. He kicked his way so that he was in a direct path toward the dock. At the bank of the river he reached up and felt a wall of granite blocks. He continued to be swept by the current but let his hand feel along the wall of granite. It was slippery, covered in years of algae, oily spillage, and other sorts of dirt and grime. He found a small divot—a missing corner of a rock above his head—and he held on and kicked off his fins. He pulled up on the small, slippery inch of rock and hoisted himself up, above water, then let the water pour off him and his weapons. Dewey's foot found an edge and he started scrambling, grasping for pieces of granite, his feet reaching desperately for small edges, and he slinked up the wall of stone and came to the esplanade. Then a surge of river hit him and he was back in the furious current, tossed into the river which swirled him a sudden five feet away from the bank.

He caught his breath and resurfaced. The river appeared to be calm, yet beneath it was constantly churning and hauling Dewey down.

He let himself drift—he didn't feel like fighting the river anymore—and the current carried him closer and closer to the tower of smoke still pouring from the end of the Queens-Midtown Tunnel where the explosion had occurred. He saw the dock. It was a maintenance dock. It was stacked with machinery, a crane, and piles of cement bags. A temporary dock, clinging by a chain to the shore.

As Dewey drifted closer, he registered movement. Halfway down the dock. It was a man looking up the river in his direction. Dewey watched as he abruptly placed the rifle down and picked up a shoulder-fired missile. Dewey realized he was the one who had shot down the American helicopters on the way in to save the president.

Dewey took a deep breath and went below the water, submerging a few feet and swimming hard. He let the river take his body in a drift, then swam up when he saw the dark outline of the dock above. Quietly, he grabbed the underside of it with one hand. He moved carefully to the back of the dock, until he was at a thin gap between the dock and the bank.

He surfaced and took a noiseless breath as he glanced down the length of the dock. It was crowded with pallets of stone, bags of cement, stacks of buckets, tools covered by tarps, and a mobile crane. His clothing blended into the background, and he wasn't moving, like a rattlesnake hidden in tall grass. The terrorist, now clutching an AR-15, was approximately three-quarters of the way down the dock.

In the distance, on the streets just above the river, gunfire was rampant. Sharp staccato fusillades of submachine guns interwoven with pounding single blasts from automatic rifles. There were screams, sirens, and the air, even down on the water, smelled like gunpowder.

Dewey went back underwater. He moved along the back of the dock, holding himself below the water. He looked up through the water and tracked the dark edge of the pier against the sky. Holding his breath, Dewey reached to his ankle and removed a knife from a sheath strapped to his leg. It was a steel combat blade: SOG SEAL

Pup. It was nine inches long. The blade was black and double serrated. He put the hilt of the knife in his mouth and bit down, clutching it between his teeth, as the fast-moving water coursed against him, and his lungs started to burn. He paused below the water until he felt he couldn't hold his breath any longer, then emerged and climbed silently onto the dock, behind the Iranian, lifting himself up with his hands then stepping onto the wooden platform, blade between his teeth just as the Iranian sensed or heard him. The Iranian pivoted—AR-15 in his clutch—and swept the muzzle toward Dewey. As a drumming of bullets cracked the air, Dewey lurched and slashed the blade down at the killer, slamming the knife into his chest. He ripped it beneath the terrorist's armpit in a violent hacking cut, gashing through clothing, skin, muscle, and bone. His cries of agony were muted by the surrounding din. Dewey buried the knife deep inside the terrorist's chest, from the side, then, just as quickly, wrenched it back out, yanking up and letting the upper serrated teeth of the SEAL Pup gore through yet more of the man's insides. Without taking his eyes off him, Dewey dunked the bloody blade in the river to wash it off, then resheathed it.

He stared down at the young Iranian who was bleeding out. Dewey took the AR-15 from the terrorist's hands. He inspected it as the man made a few last flails, hitting at Dewey's legs. Dewey ignored the dying man and reached down, removing two mags from his vest. He aimed the rifle at the Iranian's skull, but then put it slightly to the side and fired, testing the firearm. The Iranian jerked to the side, even though Dewey hadn't shot him. A dime-sized hole tore into the wood of the dock. Dewey ran his hands over the weapon and then clutched it in his right hand.

Dewey finally focused in on the bleeding-out Hezbollah on the dock. Dewey looked down into his eyes. The man fought to keep his eyes open, looking up at Dewey as dark, almost black maroon blood chugged from his nostrils, mouth, and ears, like a faucet.

"I'm sorry this didn't work out," said Dewey to the terrorist. "I'm afraid I'm going to have to ask you to leave."

Dewey put his foot beneath his torso and kicked forward, tossing the bleeding terrorist into the river. He watched as he drifted away in the fierce current, at first trying to swim, then rolling and sinking beneath the black water.

"Don't forget to write!" Dewey yelled.

75

The man leaned over the edge of the building. He was across First Avenue from the UN building. He trained the optical on the American gunman down below.

The building he was on had ninety floors. Firing a missile down at the sniper who was targeting Mansour would not be easy. He knew the missiles were not designed for the type of firing sequence he would be putting it through. He saw the sniper on the third floor of the UN building. He focused in. The gunman was scanning the area between the tower and First Avenue with his eyes but had the rifle aimed at the guardhouse, where Mansour was hidden.

Smoke from the Queens-Midtown Tunnel just to the south swirled like fog across the streets and buildings across a concrete canyon that separated the UN building from the plain of skyscrapers on the west side of First Avenue. First Avenue was a parking lot of abandoned vehicles, windshields blown out, and bodies littering the street and sidewalks.

He locked the sight into the American sniper, paused, then pressed the trigger. There was a loud *smack* then a high whistle noise as the Strela shot from the launcher. The man watched through the hazy trail of the missile's flight. He saw the sniper suddenly turn and look up in his direction. The American had recognized the shrill cry of the incoming missile, though it was too late.

The missile slammed directly into the tower, a little high, through a window on the fourth floor, but it was less than ten feet above where the gunman was and it didn't matter. There was a loud explosion and glass for several floors above rained down as the third and fourth floors along the northwest corner of the tower were eviscerated.

76

Mansour heard the telltale snap of the missile launcher, then the low whistle. His eyes caught the smoke trail from the roof of the building across First Avenue from the UN. He watched as the missile slammed into the low part of the Secretariat Building, followed by the explosion, which blew out everything in and around where the sniper had been. The ground vibrated beneath him.

The sniper was gone. The hit had been almost direct.

Mansour moved.

He saw several of his men in the distance, shooting their way into the lobby. He watched as one of them dropped, struck in the chest from inside the lobby, a nest of security, trying to hold the lobby.

Mansour pumped bullets at where he guessed the nest of gunmen was retreating back into the lobby and trying to hold it, shooting back at his men, encroaching foot by foot, numbers on their side.

Mansour fired at the lobby, emptying the mag, switched out mags, then started to move along the fringes of the courtyard, weaving toward the UN building.

He watched from the distance as one of his men stalked from the opposite side of the lobby, entering the atrium, now littered in broken glass and dead bodies. Mansour recognized the gunman, and he felt a surge of pride. Most of the large windows were either cracked or destroyed. He watched as the soldier made a quick dash to a concrete pillar, then cut silently around the pillar toward the interior of the tower, where the concentration of American security was trying to hold out access to the elevators and stairs.

Mansour sprinted across the open courtyard toward the tower, exposed to the gunmen in the lobby. He could hear the staccato fire of his gunmen, overwhelming the cluster of last-line defense from UN Security, FBI, and Secret Service. He leapt through a shattered opening in the lobby glass, ninety degrees from his men, but directly across from the area of the lobby where the few remaining Americans were hiding. They were trying to stay down and take shots at the flank of Hezbollah at the far side of the lobby. Mansour stepped over a body and targeted the rifle at the group. He pumped the trigger, holding it back as bullets hailed in a furious spray across the open atrium of the tower lobby.

77

"What do you need?" said Singerman, tapping his earbud as he drove south, weaving in and out of the crowd of panicked pedestrians.

"They're going after the Federal Reserve," said Igor. "This morning, all four governors were murdered. The killers removed an eye and thumb from each one. Bill said you have some knowledge of the Fed."

"Give me a sec," said Singerman as he came toward the end of Riverside Park near Seventy-second Street. He charged the Suburban up a set of stairs and barreled out onto a crowded street, littered with cars not moving. He went right down along Riverside Boulevard, staying along the Hudson River, driving up onto the sidewalk and hitting the gas.

Singerman tapped his ear.

"Are you sure they have the fingers and eyes?" said Singerman as he weaved south on the sidewalk, barely avoiding people running to the north.

"Yes," said Igor.

"That's not good," said Singerman. "They're going after Fedwire."

"What's the exposure?" said Polk.

"Exposure is down to hard assets," said Singerman. "Cash and gold."

"Is there any way for me to provision inside the cordon and create redundancy?" said Igor.

"It's a single-point-of-entry protocol system behind an iodine sheet field," said Singerman. "It's a single-track system and all data is outward facing. You need to be in the room itself."

"What happens then?" said Igor.

"It's a Risch algorithm," said Singerman. "It's complicated."

"Risch is about antiderivatives?" said Igor. "I thought it wasn't possible to build Risch and make it manageable? Too much computing power required over limited time."

"You're right, but it is possible, I did it with my professor," said Singerman. "The problem is that was ten years ago. Someone this sophisticated will undoubtedly introduce some sort of higher-order pattern-unification algorithm to break away at it. Once inside the room, an experienced hacker will code a path into the core of the Risch. It will only require a matter of time to get to the metadata. Minutes, not hours."

"Divert to the Fed, Aaron," said Polk.

78

Dewey was dripping wet. His clothing—a canvas vest over a long-sleeved polo and khakis—clung to his body.

He took the terrorist's AR-15 and put it down on the wood of the dock. He took a snub-nosed oblate spheroid silencer from his khaki pocket, a custom-made multi-caliber silencer. He screwed it into the muzzle of the rifle and walked down the maintenance pier with his finger on the trigger, staring up at clouds of smoke, hearing intermittent gunshots. He found a set of makeshift temporary stairs up to the street and started climbing.

The river was approximately one floor below the FDR Drive and the streets that ran beneath the UN complex. The UN was one floor above the roadway.

Dewey arrived at street level and looked at the mess of cars and trucks scattered in the roadway. Traffic was stopped though a few cars were still trying to burrow through lines of abandoned vehicles. He saw movement in many vehicles, people hiding out and hoping that by remaining there they would be safe. It wasn't a bad instinct. By now, the pandemonium across Manhattan was established. Whoever had done this knew how to create a distraction.

Dewey put the weapon across his chest and climbed onto a concrete embankment along the highway. He moved to a column at the corner of the FDR Drive, a wide piece of steel rebar helping to hold up the level above, where the UN esplanade—a massive concrete visitors' park—spread out, and where the entrance to the UN building was.

Dewey felt the column and grabbed at an edge with both hands, finding a line of leverage. He jumped and, holding the steel and pressing his feet against it below, he scaled the column quickly, moving up until he could grab the lower edge of the concrete above, then lifting himself up onto the esplanade.

It was the large area behind the UN building, away from First Avenue, bordering the river. A secure area, gated in, largely empty, supposedly guarded, but now Hezbollah had killed whatever UN Security and Secret Service was supposed to be there and there was an abandoned feeling to the concrete patch.

Dewey ducked behind a bench and then looked through slats at the tower in the distance, where Dellenbaugh was. He listened and watched. Anyone looking in his direction would see only a shadow. He lifted the AR-15 and positioned the barrel on top of the bench, remaining crouched. He scanned from the outer edge of the periphery. He saw one man directly to his left, fifty or sixty feet away, and he acquired him. When he was about to shoot, he saw movement. Through the optic, he found another man at the far end of the esplanade.

Dewey paused.

The man near him was standing against a concrete wall, guarding a pathway leading to the UN building. He held a submachine gun and was looking around. Next to him, on the ground, was a MANPAD, a firing kit, with a missile.

Dewey studied the gunman at the far border of the esplanade through the optic and focused tightly in. He moved the fire selector to semi and pumped the trigger. Three bullets spat from the rifle in a brief hail of lead. The man was kicked to the ground in a crimson burst, his groan loud and awful.

The gunman to Dewey's left registered the shots and swept his rifle toward Dewey, pounding rounds across the pavement, but Dewey fired before the gunman caught up to him. Dewey's bullets were on target, and a lake of red burst across the young Iranian's stomach. The killer was kicked back off his feet as the slugs slammed him broadside, dropping the thug in a pool of blood.

Just as the man fell, Dewey turned and scanned, making sure there were no others. He walked to where the dead Iranian lay, coming on him with the alloy tip of the silencer zeroed in on the dying man's skull. The killer was paralyzed in agony. Blood coursed from his chest and torso. He looked up at Dewey with gray eyes. Dewey pulled the trigger and ripped bullets across his neck, then turned and started charging for the tower.

79

Tacoma was on foot, running south on Eighth Avenue. He weaved his way down from Columbus Circle toward the UN. The traffic on Eighth Avenue was still moving in places but would not be for long. Sirens from police cars and ambulances were in the dozens, along with sporadic gunfire. He cut over on a parking lot–like West Forty-ninth Street, stalking at the corner, looking out for any of the Iranian active shooters running rampant.

Tacoma had on stretch khakis, running shoes, and a long-sleeved navy blue T-shirt with a Tampa Bay Lightning logo on the chest. He gripped a suppressed submachine gun—MP7A1—and wore a tactical backpack over his already stuffed weapons vest that held extra magazines. Beneath his right armpit was a customized holster that held a suppressed P226. Like most operators, he also had several combat blades sheathed in key places across his person. Tacoma had seen combat in urban settings on several occasions. Moving quickly—and in large chunks when you have open theater—was important. So was killing.

He heard a noise just behind him, then saw a man on a motorcycle moving along the sidewalk down Eighth. Tacoma tucked against the egress of a restaurant, watching the man. Perhaps he was just a citizen trying to get away? But then he saw the man raise a pistol and fire at a car, followed by a scream.

Tacoma sighted him and pumped the trigger. The bullet *thwacked* from the MP7 and hit the motorcycle rider in the head. He crashed, slamming into the wall of a building across the street. Tacoma kept moving east across the city.

The streets were shut down, and a canopy of silt and smoke was in the sky, a layer of black above Lexington Avenue and in the air above, cantilevered between skyscrapers. Cars had long ago been abandoned as people ran for cover.

The sidewalks and streets were almost empty, but some people were still trying to run away. Screams, sirens, and the *rat-a-tat-tat* of gunfire filled the air.

People ran to whichever building was nearest and attempted to enter, seeking shelter and safety. Still others ran down sidewalks, as if there were a destination.

Bodies littered the ground. An old woman carrying a Bergdorf Goodman bag had been shot in the back in cold blood. One of the shooters had already come through, killing everything in his sight.

Tacoma stalked down Lexington, clutching the MP7, flash suppressor screwed into the muzzle of the gun. An extended magazine sticking down. He hugged the buildings on the left side of Lexington.

A tall black-haired man came into Tacoma's line of sight, emerging from a building several blocks away, down Lexington, holding an AR-15. The man pumped the trigger as he ran, and he'd had it set to full auto. A sound of screams and pandemonium echoed back up the avenue. Bullets spat from the rifle and several people were abruptly shot in cold blood as they sought to flee the chaos.

The sky overhead was smoky and gray. A vague smell of burning chemicals was everywhere.

Tacoma moved down along the left-hand side of the avenue, running in the lee of the buildings, knowing his movement would blend into a continuum in the peripheral vision of the killer. Tacoma was sprinting hard; in stride he let go of the MP7's strap, letting it settle behind his back, as he pulled a suppressed P226 from beneath his armpit.

On the other side of the avenue, the killer was walking calmly down the sidewalk shooting people.

Tacoma was across the block, running and yet skulking, in the shadows, out of view.

This man was irrelevant. He needed to get across town to the UN.

It's on the way, he told himself, as he cut right.

He came closer to the tall man, watching at all times over his shoulder as he came within a half block of the Hezbollah.

Tacoma broke right—toward the avenue, running across several lanes of cars, all abandoned, weaving in and out, as quietly as he could. He raised the P226 as he came onto the sidewalk. For the first time, the killer turned and saw him, and Tacoma by now was at a full-on sprint. Tacoma trained the pistol on the gunman, even as the killer swiveled and sighted Tacoma, triggering early; the harsh *thwack thwack thwack* of automatic rifle cracked and echoed against the skyscrapers.

As the killer came closer to acquiring Tacoma, Tacoma pumped the trigger. The bullet hit the gunman in the stomach. Tacoma fired again, hitting the gunman's leg at the knee, dropping him to the street in a world of pain.

Tacoma pulled the AR-15 from the gunman's hands as the Iranian moaned in agony. Blood pooled almost immediately on the sidewalk beneath the man. Tacoma stepped over him, training the P226 down at his eyes.

"Iran?" said Tacoma inquisitively.

The Iranian clutched at his knee as blood oozed out. He didn't respond.

Tacoma placed the tip of the suppressor against the Iranian's eye and pushed hard, into the socket. As he held him tight beneath the suppressor, Tacoma knelt and reached down toward the killer's arm. He grabbed the man's collar at the shoulder and yanked, ripping material at the seam. He could now see the man's shoulder blade. Tacoma saw a small tattoo, a blue lightning bolt.

Tacoma stood.

"Hezbollah," he said, nodding.

He met eyes with the gunman, then Tacoma pumped the trigger, blowing a large section of his head onto the sidewalk.

80

Rokan exited the Westin through a revolving door that fed into a crowded, chaotic, even violent sidewalk on Forty-second Street.

Smoke filled the sky and people were running and they didn't give a shit about who they ran over.

Traffic was still moving, though it was every man for himself, and he saw a minivan hurdle the sidewalk as it attempted to move west on Forty-second.

There were police sirens wailing in every direction.

But there were no active shooters. His path to the Fed would hopefully be clear. For even though he was on their side, any embedded Iranian shooter would have no way of knowing Rokan from anyone else. As such, Mansour had forbidden any actions on Forty-second Street.

He fell in with a stream of people moving toward the west, away from the UN. They all seemed to realize that the area to the east—behind them, where the UN was located—was radioactive. Smoke and dust were everywhere.

Rokan had never been deployed into a live operating situation. He was a technologist, a computer wizard of the highest caliber. But if he expected to feel fear, Rokan found himself in a state of giddiness, even delirium. Rokan's father had been one of Iran's highest-ranking nuclear scientists until the morning he and Rokan's mother were blown up by a limpet bomb attached to his father's car by Americans. As Rokan jogged west on the sidewalk, he pushed people aside, ignoring screams, and remembered his father and mother. He was receiving his second Ph.D. at the time, at Carnegie-Mellon in Pittsburgh. He dropped out the day his parents were murdered and went back to Tehran, applying for transfer and being accepted to the Iranian military's war college, the Supreme National Defense University, where he graduated number one in the advanced cyber training platform, a multidisciplinary doctorate considered the hardest and most prestigious degree at the university.

Rokan's life was altered the day his parents died, altered with but one purpose: to avenge their deaths. But until this moment, as he jogged down the sidewalk amid pandemonium, he'd always understood his hatred for the U.S. in a way that was intellectual. Now, for the first time, he could *feel* it. It was the danger of the mission, certainly, but more so it was a feeling of exhilaration as he risked his life to avenge the death of his parents.

At Sixth Avenue, Rokan went right, moving along the west side of the street. Sixth Avenue was gridlocked. Screams echoed down the avenue and there was intermittent gunfire just a few blocks ahead.

Rokan charged between cars stopped in traffic, running north.

He came to a skyscraper, an older building of dark blue glass and limestone that arose in an austere rectangle, forty-five stories into the sky.

1135 Sixth Avenue.

Rokan paused as he reached the entrance. The sidewalk was crowded, as was the entrance. He stepped toward the street, where a line of black sedans was queued up. There were armed security men inside the lobby, guarding the entrance. Rokan walked to the door and waved at one of the guards.

The guard held a submachine gun, which he kept trained on Rokan. Behind the guard, the lobby was mostly empty, though a few people ran for the elevators.

"I work here," said Rokan. "They're killing people! *Please, I just want to go to my office.*"

"Of course, sir," said the guard, lowering his weapon. "I just need to see some ID."

"Yes, please hold on," said Rokan. "Thank you."

Rokan reached into his backpack as if retrieving his wallet. He removed an Uzi Pro 9x19 and started pumping the trigger as he whipped it around at the security guard. A dull, staccato drum of metallic *thwap thwap thwap thwap* echoed in the stone atrium as bullets splattered in a diagonal line up the guard's chest. Rokan kept firing as he stepped inside the lobby, shooting down half a dozen people, as bullets from a handgun shattered glass just behind him. Rokan registered the source—a second guard behind the security desk—and whaled on him with the Uzi, spraying slugs in a furious collage in and around the man, hitting him in the head.

He went behind the security desk and pressed a series of buttons beneath it and there was a hydraulic noise as a steel wall descended inside the glass lobby, along the outer-facing glass, shutting off access in or out of the building.

Rokan had never liked the violence or killing. Though he was trained thoroughly in all manner of firearms and explosives, self-defense, and cold weapons, including years spent learning face-to-face combat, though he knew how to do it all, and do it well, this was not a source of pride. Rather, he found numbers, and their correlation to the real world via computers, to be the world in which he excelled. As he looked down at one of the dead security men, his chest and face already layered in congealing blood, he paused. What he did with numbers was far more cruel than what he had just done to the security officer. Yet the sight of the dead man made him sick to his stomach.

"I'm sorry," said Rokan, kneeling and touching the man's hand.

On his way to the elevators, he saw a woman he'd already shot, trying to crawl through her own blood. He lifted the firearm, pumped the trigger, and sent a few bullets into her head.

He reached the dead security guard and removed an access card from his pocket.

There was no doubt the Federal Reserve did not allow security personnel onto its floor. Rokan knew the card wouldn't get him provisioned to twenty-five. Not yet, anyway. He held the barcode up to his phone and scanned it. The program scanned the barcode and then went into the underlying layer of XML, rewriting it so as to allow entrance to the floor Rokan wanted to go to. After a few moments, the screen lit up with a self-generated barcode provisioning Rokan. He stepped into the elevator and placed the phone in front of a scanner. The doors closed and the elevator cab ascended. When it stopped, he stepped off. The number "25" was on the brass jamb of the elevator, though the floor itself was sterile and strangely lit with bright chemical lights in white along with diffuse orange and light blue.

Rokan moved to his left, down a corridor without doors, walking in the direction of the light. A low humming noise grew louder as he walked toward the source of the light. When, finally, he came around the corner, he took in a sight he'd only just imagined. It was the entrance to the governors' room. The room was across a thin hallway and in between was a mesmerizing wall of digital orange, white, and light blue.

It was the American government's last line of defense—an iodine sheet field, a wall of energy with unbelievable heat and power. Rokan had studied the general concept of sheet fields and understood the basic idea: a controlled plane of energy created by computing power connected to it. The Americans had built a way of managing its money and, with the iodine sheet field, used the electrical heat of the metadata to create an impenetrable fortress.

There was no way in but with the irises and thumbprints of the four governors, and all four of them at once.

Directly before the thin corridor to the governors' room there were four waist-high lecterns, atop of which were digital screens, where the governors were provisioned in by eye and thumb scanners. Beyond was a corridor that led to the governors' room. The passageway was bright and glowing. An incessant, audible buzz permeated the air, like a bug trap.

Rokan walked slowly toward the four screens. He took a pen from his pocket and threw it at the sheet field. As it crossed the threshold into the delta of light, the pen disappeared in a millisecond of orange and a faint sizzle.

Rokan took off his jacket and hurled it at the passageway and watched as it disappeared in a crooked wisp of blue. There was not even a hint of smoke, and only the faintest noise.

Rokan put his backpack on the floor. He knelt down and removed the four small ziplock bags and held them up in front of him. He felt sick from the sight of the eyeballs and fingers, most of all from the blood. He stood up and went to the scanners.

81

Dewey ran for the UN building. He heard a scream to his right, followed by the metallic *rat-a-tat-tat* of a submachine gun. He turned and saw a woman in a business suit running toward the river. His eyes went to a lone gunman. He watched the killer shoot her from behind, spraying the woman with bullets from an Uzi. She kicked sideways, down to the concrete, falling into the path of her own blood.

Dewey took a knee, targeting the gunman as he searched for others to kill. Dewey marked him in the crosshairs of the optic, waited a second, then pumped the trigger. A low twangy *thud* was the only sound. In the same instant, the bullet hit the man in the neck. The Iranian dropped as a hole gashed straight through his neck, and soon he was gushing blood as he toppled to the concrete in agony.

Dewey continued along the hedge until he was directly left of the UN, across a few hundred feet of concrete, brick, and various greenery and statues.

The sound of gunfire was constant now. He stopped and listened, and tried to watch. He had to discern what was happening. The noise was emanating mostly from the tower. The Iranians were in the process of creating—or already had created—a security cordon. It was clear they'd taken the lobby. They were now enforcing the perimeter as police and other law enforcement agents attempted to get into the UN from First Avenue, a battle of commitment and attrition. It was a fusillade in both directions.

Beyond the tower, Dewey could see a car speeding away from the area around the UN complex. Down a one-way street, then onto the sidewalk, scrambling to get away. Some unlucky individual, maybe a tourist, who had stumbled onto the scene.

Smoke and fire were in the mist. Panic and fear had overtaken the city. Sidewalks going away from the UN that Dewey could see showed people running from the gunfire around the UN. Sirens pealed from emergency vehicles, lampposts, and buildings.

It was the worst mayhem he'd ever seen.

Irregular war. Guerrilla war. Close-quarters combat.

What he always remembered:

Avoid direct confrontation.

Dewey had just killed part of the cordon and now he needed to move.

There is only the time between when you create the opening in the perimeter and they realize.

He looked at his watch. *9:33.* He had to attack now, there was no time anymore.

He saw movement at the outer edge of the tower. Another gunman. The man had seen Dewey. He hadn't moved quickly enough. The man ducked behind a bench and started firing at Dewey with a high-powered rifle. The second or third bullet clanged against the rifle, kicking it in the barrel, barely missing Dewey's hand.

As multiple rifles turned in Dewey's direction and fired, he knew he was outnumbered. Bullets ricocheted near him as he turned around and sprinted back along the boxwood hedge. With his left hand he took the AR-15 and pumped the trigger, shooting back in the general direction of the tower, creating cover for himself as he ran toward the river and the stairs he'd come up from. He cut in a zigzag pattern as they fired and he fired blindly back, then he came to the East River. He leapt up to a concrete embankment and jumped, kicking his feet as bullets shredded the air near him. He vaulted into open air above the river, trying to get to water, then in front of him and below he saw the top of the mobile crane. He felt the air and suddenly slammed into the crane neck halfway down, his hands catching steel just as bullets pulsed the neck of the crane a foot above. Dewey slid down the crane, slipping out of range, even as gunmen ran closer and fired at the crane, hemming him in. From the crane, he didn't go all the way down to the dock but rather stopped halfway down the crane, as bullets pounded the steel just above him. Dewey leapt to the FDR Drive, beneath the esplanade, and sprinted for his life down the tunnel. The FDR was smoke clogged, crowded with empty cars, not moving, many still running, and sirens roared. The entrance to the Queens-Midtown Tunnel was just below and foul-smelling smoke and ash spiraled up across the air nearby. Dewey sprinted between the lanes of cars and trucks, running to the north along the jammed highway beneath the esplanade.

When he came to the overhang at the north side of the tunnel he leapt onto a concrete barrier, then jumped up to a rusty steel fence that guarded the northern edge of the UN property. He clawed up to the top of the fence and climbed over, dropping to the ground in a restricted work area bordered by trees, where containers were stored along with a backhoe and various landscaping equipment. He maneuvered through the trees toward the esplanade. There, he spied three gunmen looking for him around where he'd jumped.

He was at least five hundred feet from the three men. Balancing the barrel of the rifle on a branch, he trained in on the closest terrorist and yanked hard on the trigger, ripping bullets across the distance. One by one, the men were hit by bullets. Each dropped to the ground.

A spike of adrenaline radiated up from the base of his spine like fire. He counted five bodies of Hezbollah scattered on the esplanade, dead. He had killed them all. He knew there were more, but it was a start.

Dewey was inside the Hezbollah cordon. The perimeter was now fragmented. He'd penetrated the cordon for the second time. This time, he couldn't lose strategic advantage. He sprinted to the UN building but at the opposite side of the tower from where he'd begun—at the north. The crack of automatic gunfire from out in front of the building grew louder. It was almost constant, emanating from in front of the UN.

The terrorists had had strategic advantage after securing the lobby of the tower but now there was a break in the line, a break they weren't even aware of.

Irregular warfare.

Hezbollah would leave the bodies of their own. QUDS battle theater strategies and systems were built to suffer casualties and keep fighting. Another layer existed, and then another, until you got to the layer that was in charge.

Dewey was within striking distance of the Hezbollah front edge. But he needed to act before some other level of the cordon chased him back to the water, or killed him.

Dewey moved to the tower. The front and back of the rectangular skyscraper were all glass—but the north- and south-facing parts of the rectangle, the thinner walls, were windowless.

The walls were just limestone.

Dewey ran to the north wall, then went to the First Avenue corner. He looked around the corner, assessing the area in front of the tower. A gun battle was taking place between the tower and First Avenue, between Hezbollah inside the tower and law enforcement. It was loud, and the sound of weapon fire in both directions was fierce.

It was a tightly planned, highly coordinated operation. As long as they held a layer between them and the president, that was all that mattered. Soon, they would give up the lobby. Their goal was to kill Dellenbaugh and they were all willing to die doing it.

It wasn't guerrilla war. It was a suicide bomb.

A weapons vest made of worn canvas covered Dewey's torso and chest. Three extended magazines for the MP7 were belted at each side of his lower torso. Beneath his armpit was a holstered Colt M1911 A1 .45 caliber semiautomatic pistol, suppressed, chambered, safety off. Mags for the .45 lined the upper part of the vest. His shirt and khakis were still damp from the swim. He breathed heavily in and out, trying to think.

He put the AR-15 down on the ground and unscrewed the suppressor. He pulled the MP7A1 from over his back.

The Iranian attack was perfectly planned and well executed. But the best operations were always vulnerable to something more powerful than perfection. The proverbial fly in the ointment. A lone operator. It was the one thing no mission could rule out, as hard as it might try.

Glancing low around the corner of the tower, Dewey saw a man just a few feet to his left, guarding the front of the tower. He was oblivious to Dewey's presence, yet Dewey held off, even as he slowly pivoted the end of the suppressor toward the young Iranian. The killer had long hair, a mustache, and was dressed in jeans and a tan short-sleeved shirt. In his hands was an Uzi Pro SB. Dewey put his finger to the fire selector on the MP7A1 and moved it to manual. Dewey stepped out beyond the corner of the tower. The terrorist turned, searching. Just as his eyes met Dewey's, the killer saw the glossy black rim of the suppressor, now aimed at his head. Before he could say anything, or even move, Dewey pumped the trigger on the MP7A1. A slug whacked the man in the forehead. As he fell Dewey slid the fire selector to full auto, and took a few steps in front of the tower and fired—spraying bullets into the lobby, then stepping back, using the corner of the building as a shield. He repeated the move three times—a quick spray of bullets, then retreat. On the fourth try, a gunman emerged from the tower. The Iranian fired—Dewey ducked, pivoted, and pumped the ceramic trigger. He hit the terrorist with the first hail of bullets, a concentric circle across the man's torso, killing him in a tornado of slugs.

Suddenly, Dewey's thigh was slammed by a bullet from several floors above. He was thrown down and sideways and blood spilled from his leg. Dewey crawled back to the corner. He looked up at the face of the tower, trying to stay out of the way but still trying to find the gunman. As he cursed at the slug in his thigh, he saw movement. A small piece of black steel—muzzle—then the gunman leaned out, holding a rifle in his right arm as, behind him, another arm clutched the man's belt, holding him so that he could lean out and target Dewey again.

Dewey pulsed the trigger on full auto. Bullets washed up in the direction of the terrorist. He heard a shout; he lost sight of the gunmen even as he held the trigger hard, pumping slugs. He threw everything he could up at them, until he heard a yelp and saw a small burst of red, then he heard a horrible scream that echoed down through the smoke-crossed air. Both men tumbled forward from the open window, somersaulting to the concrete and landing next to each other just a dozen feet away.

He looked at his thigh. He knew the bullet was lodged in there. It hadn't gone straight on through, but it hadn't broken his femur and though it hurt, Dewey tried to compartmentalize it, put it in a box.

Pain was Dewey's strength. He understood how to endure pain.

Dewey took the blade from his ankle and cut away the material of his pants near his thigh. He stuck the end of the knife into the red spigot of blood, hitting steel. Dewey put a finger into the opening of the wound, as horrible electric pain shot from his leg. He pulled the bullet from his thigh as blood gushed down his knee and calf and shoe. He cut the arm of his shirt at the shoulder and tied it across the wound, then he moved.

82

Singerman sped the Suburban down Twelfth Avenue. Polk had ordered him to divert to the Federal Reserve, as fast as possible.

The area looked like a wasteland, streets clogged with cars that had either been abandoned or contained people who'd already been shot and killed. At the sight of a park at Fifty-fourth Street, Singerman decided to abandon the Suburban. He ducked onto Fifty-fourth, where there was another standstill wall of cars. He drove to the sidewalk and stopped, preparing to climb out. Then he heard automatic gunfire, a staccato *rat-a-tat-tat* from nearby. He remained still inside the vehicle, slowly raising the MP7A2. He scanned and found a gunman walking alone in the park. He was short and wore jeans and a dark hoodie. He had a short tan submachine gun Singerman recognized immediately: Uzi Flattop X95-S with a built-in suppressor. He pumped slugs when he saw someone hiding in the park, or running. He came to Fifty-fourth Street just a hundred feet away, pumping bullets into car windows, then aiming up at buildings, randomly selecting a building and firing, then turning in an unpredictable arc and shooting something again, then changing out mags.

Singerman climbed out of the Suburban, ducking prone to the pavement, invisible to the dark-haired gunman. Singerman squared the butt of the MP7 on the bumper, aimed, and pumped the trigger. The bullet missed and the gunman turned, looking for the source of the gunfire. Singerman flipped the fire selector to full auto and fired again. Bullets ripped into the shooter's shoulder, dropping him.

Singerman moved in the direction of the man he'd just shot, knowing he wasn't dead yet. He came upon him as the gunman sat up, blood coursing from his shoulder. As the killer reached for his Uzi, Singerman fired again. A handful of bullets hit the gunman's forehead, splattering his skull and everything above his neck across the sidewalk.

Singerman went to the dead Iranian and lifted his Uzi, and then looked at the dead man. Singerman knelt and put the Uzi down next to the killer's head. He unbuckled an ammo belt from the terrorist, stacked with spare magazines, and wrapped it around his own waist, tightening it. He lifted the Uzi and moved, hiding in an alcove in the lee of an office building. Beneath the alcove, he strapped the MP7A2 across his back and inspected the Uzi.

He heard gunfire coming closer and two men came into view. Both men were clutching rifles and—as with the last man—shooting anything that moved, and a lot of stuff that didn't. The sidewalk was still, littered already with bodies of the ones who hadn't managed to get away. Singerman acquired a firing line and clutched back on the Uzi trigger. A metallic fusillade rang out above the din. He hit both men in a line of slugs across the midsection of their bodies. Blood sprayed behind them onto vehicles and the street. Singerman watched them drop awkwardly to the pavement.

Now on foot, he moved in the direction of the skyscraper that housed the governors' room. It wasn't a sexy building or even that remarkable. They'd created a corporation called Interchem to house the system, buying the building, renting out unused floors so as to create the illusion that nothing important occurred there. Singerman had spent so much time there he knew every inch.

. . .

The economies of the world lived and grew upon a digital framework, a series of debits and credits, protected by technological encryption, redundancy, an agreed-upon set of rules that the world's treasuries adhered to, or else faced a blighted existence outside the financial and economic mainframe. The mainframe was the U.S. Federal Reserve. It was the bulwark of the world economy.

Singerman, as a doctoral student at Wharton, had designed it all. Though his professor had helped him, the technological framework for the Federal Reserve had been his idea. It was his Ph.D. dissertation. He'd come up with an architectural construct designed to achieve certain ends based on an algorithm that, if harnessed properly, offered *galactic* scalability and numerical outcome perfection. His professor had seen the implications immediately. It was a way to harness energy based on an inherently large path of defined numerical outcomes. But to run it required a massive amount of energy in a highly defined, extensible, and scalable footprint. In other words, actually using the algorithm to, for example, guide a set of financial transactions, required massive amounts of energy confined within a finite space. Thus, as part of the algorithm Singerman designed, a heuristic link was made to a wall of pure energy they called an iodine sheet field. Because it was fueled with the radioactive output of the algorithm itself, it created, in essence, a self-fueled machine faster and more powerful, per square inch, than any computer in the world, by a factor of one trillion times. There were more powerful computers, but powering them required massive server farms spanning football fields and caverns in Iceland.

When he was recruited to implement the design for the Fed, Singerman had designed entry protocols and basic functionality dependent on human interaction. Singerman, even then, feared that removing the human in the day-to-day management of the Fed grid, while theoretically possible, would lead to unforeseen consequences.

His design: a parabolic DNA-based security corridor—in essence a room—whose door could open only if four individuals pressed a thumb on a reader and looked into an ocular scanner at the same time. While it sounded simple, Singerman had calculated the odds and it was basically impossible to hack into because of the human layer. It was game theory, extrapolated into a physical design so as to prevent penetration. Singerman hadn't been worried about someone breaking in. The design was based on his fear of AI. He inserted a human alloy between the hacker and the Risch algorithm.

Blocks from the Federal Reserve, he heard a beep in his ear. Singerman tapped it.

"Aaron, it's Igor. Are you close?"

83

9:37 A.M.
LOBBY
UNITED NATIONS SECRETARIAT BUILDING
FIRST AVENUE AND FORTY-SECOND STREET
NEW YORK CITY

Gunfire continued, though now it was the Iranians who controlled the lobby of the UN building.

Mansour whistled, holding up two fingers. His men stopped firing, though bullets continued to rain in from outside.

Blood and bodies were scattered everywhere in the light-filled vestibule. An eruption of violence.

Mansour counted out men and saw that he had nine soldiers still alive. He spoke in Persian.

The lobby is ours. Four men at the windows, now! Now is when we build strategic advantage!

Mansour nodded at one of the men, a tall bald man named Sayyari. They crossed the lobby, stepping over dead men.

Gunfire continued as the four soldiers pumped slugs back out at American law enforcement disaggregated across the open area between the lobby and First Avenue.

His four men—using the building itself as protection—were holding back an army of NYPD and FBI SWAT.

Despite the bullets now pilfering in from First Avenue, Mansour walked with Sayyari to the front line of men. He got close enough so that he could give them one final command.

He again spoke in Persian.

"You four stay here, in the lobby," said Mansour. "Brothers, we need just a little more time. Hold them off." He looked at Sayyari and two other men. "You lead. Come in from above. If they're still working, take the elevators to twenty. Guard the nearest stairwell and the elevator banks on twenty and nineteen. You," said Mansour, pointing at Sayyari, "if you get there before us, kill him."

Mansour pointed at the remaining two gunmen and said, "You're with me." He started walking to the stairs, then turned.

"Shoot everything you see," said Mansour. "Take no prisoners."

84

Mike Murphy was on his stomach, tucked behind a large display case designed for tourists, in the lobby of the UN building. The front of the structure showed a pictorial history of the UN. Behind the case was empty space, out of sight. That's where Murphy was hidden.

He was hiding for his life.

When the first Hezbollah gunmen encroached upon the tower, Murphy had, in point of fact, been looking at the display case. After Dellenbaugh arrived and went up to the office of the UN Secretary General, Murphy decided to hang back and kill time. He was looking forward to watching Dellenbaugh give his speech, watching him excoriate the UN for being utterly worthless. He'd been looking at the photos when everything went haywire, and he'd ducked behind the display case. Now, that display case was the only reason he was alive.

Murphy watched in absolute shock, consternation, and horror as a gun battle took place to his right, across the lobby. He'd watched as men were shot and killed. In front of him bodies of both sides were scattered.

The lobby itself was a mess. There was broken glass all over the place. He peeked around the end of the display and saw carnage. Several large windows were shattered. Bodies were strewn across the lobby, corpses. But now a group of terrorists patrolled the lobby.

Murphy tucked back in and stayed motionless. He'd been that way since the gunfight between Secret Service and whoever was out there moved inside the tower. He pulled a phone out of his pocket. He looked again, and counted three gunmen, then saw a fourth . . . and then another. He didn't actually know how many there were, but they were now in control.

Murphy scrolled through his contacts, then hit a button. After a few seconds, it rang.

"Yes?" said Amy Dellenbaugh. She answered immediately and her voice was emotional. She had a heightened, concerned demeanor in her voice.

"Amy, its Mike," Murphy whispered as—in the background—he heard voices.

"Where are you?" said Amy.

Murphy heard a voice nearby; one of the gunmen was just on the other side of the display case.

"Hold on," said Murphy in a whisper.

Murphy listened as the young Hezbollah spoke Persian in a quiet tone. He wished he could understand. He heard shooting at the far side of the lobby and peeked around the display case, watching one of them run.

"I'm at the UN. I need your help," said Murphy, in a hushed voice.

"Oh my God."

"Please can you get Adrian King to call me?" breathed Murphy. "Or anyone."

"Yes," said Amy. "Yes, right now, of course I will."

85

Dellenbaugh was awakened by gunfire nearby. Then he heard a shout. His first thought was that it didn't sound like law enforcement.

He opened his eyes, looking around at the destruction, then remembering. He turned his head and could see the open wall where glass had been, where the missile had come through. Sirens and gunfire echoed in the distance, but faintly, and the decimated floor seemed surreal. The ceiling was gone in one large section, and desks from above, and people, had fallen through. There were dozens of corpses. It was impossible to recognize anyone. He glanced down and looked at his wound. It was still bleeding but not as badly. He reached out and touched it, sending a stabbing thrust through his stomach and he closed his eyes as the pain swept over him again.

He wanted to call Amy. She probably thought he was dead. Yet he knew all that would do was expend energy he needed to survive.

Again, he heard automatic-weapon fire. It wasn't from outside. It was in the tower somewhere below. He felt more lucid. The pain was acute—but maybe it was waking him up. Dellenbaugh was still leaning on a woman's leg and he turned to look at her. Her skull was crushed and he couldn't recognize her. He reached out his hand and touched her bloody hand, the woman whose leg he'd been resting on, whose cell he'd borrowed. Dellenbaugh remembered the doctor's words. He swallowed the pain and unbuttoned his shirt. Once it was off, he held it and tried to breathe deep and stop the pain. The shirt was wet from sweat and stained from blood. He tied it around his torso and yanked, tightening it against the wound.

He heard screams, then more gunshots—fierce bursts of rifle fire. This time it was closer.

Dellenbaugh lifted his head up from the woman's leg and tried to stand, but he didn't have the strength. His legs felt brittle and weak. He started crawling on his side, using his hands to pull himself along. He came to a dead agent and pushed him over, searching. Beneath the man's arm was a holster.

Dellenbaugh removed the pistol and got down onto his stomach next to the dead agent, holding the gun in his hand aimed back at the entrance to the suite, tucking it against his leg, pretending to be dead. A young gunman entered the suite, clenching a submachine gun. A second terrorist entered just after him.

Dellenbaugh watched from the corner of his eye, pretending to be dead.

The two gunmen walked into the suite. They spoke back and forth in Persian. They assayed the carnage, but were searching for signs of life—for Dellenbaugh.

He watched as one of the men looked at the trail of blood, still wet, across the floor, that led to him.

As the man turned, Dellenbaugh fired. His bullet hit the gunman in the leg, dropping him. Dellenbaugh moved his arm and aimed at the second man, then fired. The bullet struck him in the mouth, shattering his head. Dellenbaugh aimed the gun back at the first gunman and fired several times into his torso and chest, killing him.

86

Dale Arnold flew by helicopter from the South Lawn of the White House to the Pentagon and was soon jogging to his office, passing through several outer rooms filled with both uniformed and civilian staffers and into the secretary of defense's massive office. The room was brightly lit, had coffered ceilings, and mint-hued, light green wallpaper, along with two large seating areas. His desk was in the middle of the spacious room.

Jessica Park, Arnold's chief of staff, followed him in.

Already seated were the eight members of the Joint Chiefs of Staff—the chairman and vice chairman, along with the service chiefs of the Army, Marine Corps, Navy, Air Force, Space Force, and National Guard. A few key Pentagon staffers were also present.

"Let's hear it," said Arnold. "What do we got?"

"Well, Dale, I think there's a divergence of opinion here," said the chairman of the Joint Chiefs of Staff, General Gus Mailer. "Three of us think we should drop a tactical nuke on Tehran. The other five believe we should drop two."

Arnold grabbed a cup of coffee from his desk and walked to the seating area. Other than Arnold and Park everyone was in military uniform.

"Not going to happen," said Arnold, taking a seat.

The eight members of the Joint Chiefs traded glances.

Admiral Bill Pollard, the Navy chief, spoke:

"They're midstream on a deep penetration of America," said Pollard. "We need to stop them in their tracks."

"We're going to make it hurt a lot more than a nuke would," said Arnold. "A surgical removal of the man who ordered this. What do we have nearby, Bill?"

"The *Nimitz* Carrier Strike Group is in the Gulf of Oman. That includes the *Nimitz* itself, the guided-missile cruiser *Princeton*, and three *Burke*-class destroyers, along with nine fighter squadrons," said Pollard, highlighting the ships on the map. "That's approximately two hundred and twenty Tomahawks, give or take."

"Deployment and time to target?" said Arnold.

"About an hour."

"And what are the targets?" asked General Mailer.

"Four possible targets," said Arnold, standing up and walking to the door. "Suleiman's residence, his office, his country house, and the mosque where he worships. Make it happen, immediately. Consider this my final sign-off, General Mailer, you have command."

87

9:42 A.M.
LOBBY
UNITED NATIONS SECRETARIAT BUILDING
FIRST AVENUE AND FORTY-SECOND STREET
NEW YORK CITY

Mike Murphy's cell came to life.

KING A

"Mike?" said King. "Where are you?"

"At the UN."

"For fuck's sake," said King.

"I'm in the lobby. There are bodies everywhere. I'm hiding. They don't know I'm here," said Murphy, "and I want to try and save him."

There was a long pause.

"There's an attack going on and they're isolating the president," said Murphy.

"No shit," said King.

"They have it blocked off," said Murphy. "I'm behind their lines. Just tell me what to do."

King was silent for several moments.

"Mike, I want you to just stay put," said King. "Let law enforcement do their job."

"Goddam it! They're trying to kill the president!" said Murphy in a shouted whisper.

"Do you have a gun?" said King.

"A gun?" said Murphy incredulously. "No, I don't have a fucking gun. I'm a goddam political consultant."

"Exactly," said King evenly.

"Fine, I'll go up there myself," said Murphy sarcastically. "Thanks for the help, asshole."

"Chill out," said King. "I'm trying to save your life."

"I'd rather die than just watch," said Murphy.

"Look, we're trying to get inside the building," said King. "If you run up there on your own without a weapon, you're useless. You *will* die. But we're trying to get in. I'll make sure they know you're there. Stay put, Rambo."

88

Mansour and two other gunmen took the remaining working elevator to seventeen and got off. They found the fire stairs and charged up one flight to eighteen. Mansour opened the door and entered a hallway behind the elevator banks. Then he cut left, immediately feeling wind whipping through broken windows.

Mansour clutched a PS90 as he came around the corner. The entrance was gone—destroyed—and the rest was a chaotic mess of corpses, bent metal, pieces of what had been furniture, and above all, blood and glass everywhere. The wind whipped through the open wall. Outside, sirens and gunfire sounded from different directions below.

He knew it had all come down to this, and he realized the American president was dead. He had to be. Mansour would be satisfied if Dellenbaugh was dead. It would signify a successful operation. But a pang of loss ran through him. Mansour had wanted to be the one to put a bullet in the president.

"Colonel," said a voice.

Mansour turned, searching.

The voice was weak: "Here."

Mansour's eyes went to a blood-soaked body he hadn't noticed. It was Sayyari. He lay on his back next to another corpse, behind a broken desk. Mansour stepped closer. Part of Sayyari's chin was missing.

Mansour came to Sayyari and knelt. He examined the wound.

"Who did this?" said Mansour.

"He's right over there," whispered Sayyari as blood chugged from his chin and mouth. "The president. He has a gun."

Mansour put his hand to Sayyari's eyes and closed his eyelids.

He looked at the two other Hezbollah.

"Find the American president," said Mansour. "He's here."

89

Tacoma jogged down Lexington Avenue, weaving his way toward the UN. The street was largely deserted—the people all inside buildings, or dead on the street, or in cars. It appeared like a combat zone, wrecked by prior violence.

There was no way for NYPD to get close with a vehicle due to the cars and trucks clogging the streets. It was mayhem yet largely empty of people. The active shooters had already passed through this block and it looked like the coast was clear. He ducked in front of a shot-out Italian restaurant, littered with customers and employees someone had gunned down in cold blood.

Through the sirens, Tacoma heard footsteps. He saw a man walking slowly down the middle of the street, weaving in between abandoned vehicles. He held a submachine gun. He was short, with long black curly hair, a beard and mustache, and olive-colored skin. Tacoma held still in the shadows and waited for him to pass by.

Hezbollah.

Tacoma wiped his mouth and raised the rifle, feeling a warm sensation, the anticipation as he tracked the killer walking confidently down the street. There was disdain in the gunman's confident swagger, as if he'd already won, already humiliated America. He walked like a victor.

Tacoma watched as the gunman continued to skulk down between the cars. He slid the fire selector to manual. As the gunman reached the next cross street, Tacoma inched from the alcove, acquired him, then yanked back on the trigger. The bullet bucked out of the gun—making a sheer metallic *thwack*—and thumped into the back of the gunman's head, misting a cloud of brains, skull, and blood into the air behind him. The killer dropped with an animal yelp and that was all. He spiraled in a twisted morass to the street.

Tacoma kept moving down Lexington, along the sidewalk, in the shadows of the east side of the avenue's skyscrapers. Soon, he was in a fast-paced run, galloping down Lexington in a hard sprint.

Tacoma caught the movement, to his right: a flash of steel. A gunman emerged at the corner.

The gunman marked Tacoma and fired.

Tacoma dived down to the sidewalk just as bullets ricocheted in the granite of the building behind him. He swept the MP7 and fired. A suppressed bullet caught the side of the gunman's head. He fell to the street as Tacoma started running again.

90

Dellenbaugh crabbed across the destroyed floor to the shattered window at the front of the tower. He sat back against a desk that was still there. He held the handgun he'd taken from the dead Secret Service agent. He felt overwhelming pain. He looked down; the bandage wrapped around his stomach was already soaked. He looked at the front of his pants and there was a large patch of wet red, blood that had already seeped from the wound and was now drenching him.

Dellenbaugh knew what it meant. Something was still embedded inside his body. He leaned back and could feel an odd, sharp, deep sensation of horrible pain. When he leaned forward he felt it less, but it was there.

Just above his head was a bent steel structural rod. He was seated at an angle of advantage and would see anyone enter. He knew they were coming. He would shoot them from where he was. Yet, the overwhelming sense of pain and torpor ripped at him from the inside, like a knife stabbing at his spine.

At the same time, he felt a sense of calm coming on. He knew it was shock from the pain. He couldn't allow it to take him over, to envelop him in its painless cloud. If he went into shock, he would shut down.

Dellenbaugh reached his hand to the bandage and pushed the wet bottom of it up. He stuck his index finger into the wound, where the glass had penetrated, feeling amid a gelatinous surface as another part of him registered the entry of the foreign objects, the fingers from his own hand. Each fragment of an inch created pain he'd never imagined could exist. Tears of sheer pain, and the fight against it, streaked from Dellenbaugh's eyes as his index and middle fingers found the source of the agony. It was a thick piece of glass, the size of a quarter. As shock reared its head again, and burning, razor pain hit him, he pulled the shard of glass from his stomach and put it on the ground, his fingers soaked in crimson, just as movement came from across the suite.

He looked at the small object, and, like removing a splinter, on some level felt relief—a lessening of the pain.

Dellenbaugh raised the gun just as a man entered the suite. He aimed the gun, though his arm was wobbly. When the gun fell from his hand all he could do was watch as the killer approached.

91

9:45 A.M.
UNITED STATES FEDERAL RESERVE
1135 SIXTH AVENUE
NEW YORK CITY

Rokan was in the governors' room, staring at the four identical lecterns in a row. Each one stood waist high. On top of thin stainless steel poles sat four digital screens.

Rokan started at the first lectern. He opened a ziplock bag. He removed the wet, slimy eyeball. It was coated in blood and several stringy veins dangled down from it. He placed it on the screen with the front of the eye staring down into the screen. Next, he took out the thumb from the bag and put the print against the screen.

Suddenly, the iodine sheet field displayed a name in black letters across the electric energy field.

SECURE95: 094612 FENNERD

Rokan worked quickly. He repeated what he'd done and soon had the eyes and fingers on each screen, cataloguing his progress by virtue of the appearance of the names of the governors.

SECURE44: 094636 WINIKOFFH
SECURE19: 094702 LAWRENCEP

There were now three bands of writing across the sheet field. He placed the fourth set of objects on the last screen. After he adjusted the eyeball several times, the sheet field lit up with a fourth name:

SECURE62: 094752 JAHLITSCHA

A computerized male voice spoke from somewhere:
"Access one minute."
Then the field of energy abruptly disappeared. He had one minute to get inside.

Rokan put each eyeball and finger back into a separate bag, starting with the last one. He would need them to get out.

"Forty-five seconds," came a spine-chilling voice.

He bagged up the first three sets of eyeballs and thumbs.

"Thirty seconds."

He had plenty of time, though he fumbled a bit. As he stepped to the last screen, he felt his foot on top of something and felt an unnatural burst, as if he'd stepped on a balloon and it popped. His eyes shot to the last screen and saw only a thumb. Rokan didn't need to look down to know what had happened. The eye had somehow rolled off the screen. Rokan had just stepped on it. Lifting his shoe, he saw only a pile of messy veins, blood, and white sludge. He'd just inadvertently ruined one of the eyeballs he needed to ultimately get out of the room.

"Fifteen seconds."

Rokan stared at the destroyed mash of eyeball, not bothering to try to pick it up. As much as he had already accepted the fact he would die today, the realization was sudden and brutal. Once inside, he could never leave.

If there was another way in, he would be found, alive or dead. From here on in, it was a suicide mission. He had so wanted to grow old and someday do nothing but read and garden. . . .

"Ten seconds, nine, eight . . ."

Rokan stepped past the lecterns and ran as the seconds counted down.

"Five, four, three . . ."

Rokan walked past the lecterns and down the thin corridor. He entered the room he'd only imagined as, behind him, he heard the voltage of the wall reignite and slash back across the entrance to the room.

92

Dewey entered the lobby in silence. He slammed in a fresh mag as he surveyed the scene.

The lobby of the tower was cavernous, several stories high, and it was scattered with bodies.

Alarms—mounted at various points inside the lobby—screeched high-decibel warning sounds, and lights flashed bright red and white.

The dead were the people who'd been inside when the terrorists first entered: diplomats, security people, staff members, journalists, and others. There were at least a dozen sprawled in blood on the ground . . . a killing field. There were also SWAT and other law enforcement dead on the ground.

He crouched, out of sight.

There was shouting and more gunfire as SWAT from the FBI and NYPD engaged the Iranians from First Avenue.

Dewey had killed several men. Still, he wondered, how many were there? How the hell were they still fighting?

From the back of the lobby, he studied the front of the tower. Along First Avenue, he could see a pair of yellow school buses. This was how Hezbollah had penetrated the facility, arriving on school buses, packing soldiers in, then, upon arrival, using the fact that security would let their guard down for a few moments, expecting a school bus filled with children.

He saw several ambulances, with red lights flashing, and too many police cars to count—and yet, they all seemed pinned down by whatever Iranians had taken control of the entrance to the UN. Now, he was behind them. He stayed behind a pillar, out of the way of incoming fire.

He heard a beep in his ear. It was Calibrisi.

"You have a friendly to your left," said Calibrisi. "Don't shoot him. His name is Mike Murphy. He's the president's political guy. Give him a gun if you can use him, otherwise it's cut off, we'll get him later."

Dewey tapped off.

93

Rokan stepped into the central governors' room. His eyes saw the wall he'd read about in Winikoff's journal, which they'd hacked into. Her words, however, didn't do it justice. It was astonishing.

It is a cylindrical tower of data, bright letters and numbers in yellow, red, green, and white, moving up the center column of data, which is sheer. It is three feet in diameter. It runs from below and then disappears above. It is not connected to the internet but rather is run through a series of high-density cable networks that span the globe, all controlled by the United States. We do not control the cables and infrastructure. Rather, we control what moves along them. It is the real-time interrelationship between the Federal Reserve and other entities, including banks, foreign countries, and even the U.S. government itself. We are the gatekeepers, though we do not pass judgment, we simply move the money. The colors indicate time to the event, that is, the movement of the money. Red means within one minute, green two, and so on. In this room, in that column of light, we four alone manage approximately five trillion dollars. It is a mesmerizing sight and I found myself, for the first month or two, staring at it.

It looks like a bouquet of lights, constantly moving, but eventually I learned to see past that and do my job.

Rokan's mouth went ajar as he stared at the column. He removed his jacket and tie as he sat down behind a wide curvilinear keyboard, his eyes at all times on the center of the room.

He knew he had several hours of work in front of him. To get here was one thing—but the greater challenge was still ahead. He needed to learn how to enter the chessboard—and then destroy it.

94

On King's office walls, bright LCD screens showed four separate feeds. One played Fox News, another BBC, then NBC, and ABC—all networks featuring wall-to-wall coverage of the attack on Manhattan.

Today's date had the inauspicious luck, for the Iranian attackers, of being October 11th. All four networks ran tickers across the bottom of the screen. They were calling it "10/11."

The volume was turned down. The screens were filled with live views of Manhattan from helicopters, an island shrouded in smoke. All of the networks intercut the view from above with street-level video—much of it sourced from social media—of dead bodies and people being shot.

Video also showed the harrowing moments just as two American Sikorsky helicopters were shot down over the East River. Still other video, taken from news helicopters and from buildings nearby, showed the damage and continuing chaos around the four separate tunnels.

The mood in King's office was tense. Everyone was waiting for Bill Polk, the deputy CIA director, to arrive via video conference. He asked Calibrisi to assemble the interagency leadership now attempting to manage the different aspects of the attack and America's response.

One particular scene had gone viral across the globe. An ABC reporter was attempting to try to do his feed from near the Lincoln Tunnel on the West Side. The video was interrupted by the reporter's chest being hit by a slug, kicked out in a graphic picture of gory violence, then the video went dark, followed, presumably, by the killing of the cameraman. All networks across the globe were replaying the awful footage.

Meanwhile, King continued to pace back and forth behind his desk.

He could see the screens from the distance, but he paced nevertheless, separated from the group. He was in front of the floor-to-ceiling windows that looked out on the South Lawn.

In King's office were King; CIA chief, Hector Calibrisi; Secretary of State Bailey Miller; Secretary of Defense Dale Arnold; Treasury Secretary Michelle Goncalves; Josh Brubaker, the White House national security advisor; Mark Hastings, chief justice of the Supreme Court; and John Schmidt, the White House communications director. A White House Communications Office engineer sat on a chair near the door to King's office, managing the video feeds.

King looked at her and nodded.

Two of the news screens went dark. Then they cut internal feeds from CENCOM. Richard Baum, chairman of the Federal Reserve, came on the screen from a private airplane flying to Washington, D.C., from San Francisco. He was in a khaki shirt, arms crossed, seated in a white captain's chair on the jet. Another screen flashed bright and showed Bill Polk, head of the National Clandestine Service, standing inside a mission theater at Langley.

King stepped around the desk and looked at Polk, on the screen.

"Well, Bill?" said King.

Polk, a bald man with round tortoiseshell eyeglasses and dressed in a coat and tie, nodded at King.

"The following information cannot be discussed outside of the individuals in this meeting," said Polk. "I need you to all understand that we are now operating on American soil. We have three assets inside Manhattan. I'm not going to answer questions about what they're doing. Three non-official covers. All three men have in-theater command control and are exonerated in any actions they may take. Based on what we're seeing, we could be in a circumstance in which our agents are the last line of defense."

"Who is it, Bill?" said King.

"Dewey Andreas, Aaron Singerman, and Rob Tacoma," said Polk. "All three were in the vicinity of Manhattan and have been brought in and are operational."

"Can we take a step back," said Bailey Miller, the secretary of state. "What are we talking about here?"

"We have a three-tier attack going on," said Polk calmly. "Streets, president, Fed. We're behind, unprepared, and potentially in a situation where the president ends up dead and the nation's wealth has been erased." Polk paused. "Cut off Manhattan, kill the president, wipe out the Fed. That's the operation. They're creating an island."

One of the screens flashed into four photographs, four head shots of individuals with their names:

DAVID FENNER | ADAM JAKLITSCH
PHILLIP LAWRENCE | KARA WINIKOFF

"There are the four governors of the United States Federal Reserve," Polk continued. "Kara Winikoff, Adam Jaklitsch, Phil Lawrence, David Fenner. These four individuals manage the Fed's money, and thus America's money; about five trillion dollars. Alone, each individual is powerless. Together, they're the most powerful people on earth after the president. Each died this morning in cold blood; each was missing a thumb and an eyeball." Polk paused. "The attack on J. P. Dellenbaugh was a red herring. This is about destroying America. Wiping out the Fed, wiping out anything not in cash or gold."

There was a long silence.

"There have to be redundancies in the Fed data," said Brubaker. "Backups. Richard?"

When apprised of the situation, Baum, the chairman of the Fed, for whom the four governors technically worked, put his hand to the bridge of his nose, holding back emotion.

"Richard, we need to understand the significance of what they're after," said King, pointing at Baum.

"Anything not cash or gold will be worth its intrinsic value, and the data will be worthless," said Baum, staring back at King. "We're talking about five trillion dollars. If they liquidate the Federal Reserve, the actions of the active shooters will look like child's play. Even assassinating Dellenbaugh won't matter. *There will be no access to capital.* Banks will triage and deny people their money. There will be no way to pay for anything, money will become a weapon."

"There have to be redundancies that record the transactions," said King. "Backup systems?"

"This *is* the backup system," said Baum. "Understand—if they wipe out the data at the Federal Reserve, that money is simply gone. You'll have riots in every city in America and that's just the beginning. My guess is other world capitals and cities will also descend into chaos. We are the prime provider of liquidity to half the countries in the world. America will be vulnerable to military attack, and you might not even have a president."

"To repeat, the system *is* the redundancy," said Goncalves, the Treasury secretary. "The activity in that room *is* the central bank. It's the backbone not only for the U.S. but it also undergirds banking systems, balance sheets, and foreign governments. We are the backup system."

"How can someone just go in there and wipe out trillions of dollars?" said Brubaker.

"The security is designed to prevent it," said Baum. "Nobody could've envisioned the kind of actions taken this morning. The crimes, the planning, and the brutality. But yes, theoretically it's possible to do it. It's happening."

There was a long pause.

"Well, that's just fucking great," said King, shaking his head. "What the hell are we going to do about it?"

"We need to start thinking about the possibility that they succeed," said Miller, the secretary of state.

"What does that mean?" said King.

"If they kill Dellenbaugh and wipe out the Fed, life still goes on," said Miller. "At the end of the day, we're still the United States of America, we're still a country, and we're still the leaders of this country. We need to start running contingencies."

"Bailey's right," said Arnold, the secretary of defense. "Military response, Congress, and dealing with the humanitarian consequences, the tunnels, the dead, the families. We need to know what we're going to do."

"Right now, we need to get to the president first and stop whatever is happening at the Fed second," said King. "Failure is not an option. We can worry about all that shit if it happens, but it ain't happened yet."

95

Murphy felt his phone vibrate. He looked at the screen.

NO CALLER ID

Murphy tapped the phone.
"Yeah?" said Murphy.
"Mike?" came a deep voice.
"Yes."
"To your right," said Dewey.
"Who am I talking to?" said Murphy.
Murphy felt like he was going to have a heart attack.
Suddenly the door opened and a male figure stepped into the lobby from a remote doorway. He was rough-looking, his right leg was red with blood, and he held a submachine gun. He was wearing a canvas vest over a striped polo shirt that looked dirty, wet, and ripped in several places. He had messed-up brown hair. But he looked American. Murphy, who was still slouched on the floor behind the display case, suddenly stopped hyperventilating and sat up.
Dewey stepped into the lobby at Murphy's right, eyed Murphy,

knelt, removed a pistol from beneath his armpit, placed it on the marble floor, then slid it across the floor to Murphy, who picked it up.

"Did you see anyone go for the elevators?" said Dewey.

"Yes," said Murphy.

"How long?"

"Two, three minutes," said Murphy. "I heard an elevator bell."

"So Mike, I need you to listen to me," said Dewey.

"I'm listening," said Murphy.

"I'm going to clear out the lobby," Dewey said. "Dellenbaugh is on eighteen and as far as we know, he's alive. We have a few minutes at most. Go find an elevator in the back of the building. Floor eighteen. That's where he is."

"What do you want *me* to do?" said Murphy incredulously.

"Wait for me to clear out the lobby, then go," said Dewey. "Eighteen. Until I clear the lobby, stay out of my way."

"I mean when I get to eighteen? What if I'm the only one who gets there?" said Murphy.

"Then try and save him," said Dewey. "They're terrorists. Shoot as many as you can. Don't waste bullets. Also, don't shoot me."

"Then what happens?" said Murphy.

"What do you mean 'then what happens'?" said Dewey, speaking into his earbud and casting a glance at Murphy.

"What happens after that?" said Murphy nervously.

"*How the fuck should I know?* I'll take you to Disneyland, how's that?" said Dewey, tapping off.

96

Singerman jogged down along sidewalks, cutting in a zigzag pattern, moving closer to the Interchem building.

The sound of automatic gunfire emanated from every direction, echoing inside the abandoned concrete corridors of skyscrapers and automobiles, and bodies on the ground.

At Seventh Avenue, he came to a marble-and-steel office tower and moved around the corner. He caught sight of a pair of enemy shooters immediately. They were emerging from an office building across the street, after a shooting spree inside. Each man clutched a rifle and was firing at anything moving. They pumped slugs up at windows in whatever building they happened to be in front of, shooting out glass everywhere.

Singerman knelt and fired—he sprayed the pair of terrorists in a burst of bullets from the SMG, dropping them to the sidewalk. He ran several blocks down Seventh. He was getting closer.

Ducked behind a hot dog cart, he heard a siren nearby. A police cruiser suddenly swerved around the corner. He knelt with the Uzi next to him. Singerman's eyes caught the muzzle flash from the second floor of an office building as glass shattered in the same set of moments the police car was pounded with slugs, causing it to swerve and smash into the curb. The gunman continued firing from the building.

Singerman waited a minute then ran across the street, behind the cruiser, to the far corner of the block. He sprinted along the block—always with a hand on the building, hugging it in order to stay out of the assassin's range.

He moved back toward the building where the sniper was holed up. He went through a revolving glass door and crossed a lobby scattered in blood and corpses. He took a stairwell and leapt three steps at a time, in silence, came to the door to the second floor, and paused. Singerman moved the door latch. He took several moments, each hundredth of an inch a particular moment to focus on, in utter silence. Inside, after shutting the door behind him, he sneaked along a dark corridor of offices. He heard the sound of gunfire. He opened a door and light streamed in through office windows, outlining the sniper, holding a rifle. He was a bearded man, in his twenties, and Singerman pumped the trigger, spitting two bullets into the man's chest.

Singerman took the gunman's firearm and saw the Iranian move, ever so slightly, still alive and trying to fight back. Singerman pumped the trigger. The bullet slammed the struggling Iranian in the neck, and it silenced him for good.

He glanced out the shattered window. Streets and sidewalks below contained a combination of dead bodies and abandoned cars. A man came jogging down the block, followed by another man. They had on street clothes: jeans, dark T-shirts, and running shoes. Each man clutched a submachine gun. They were looking for people to kill, and they held up on the sidewalk just below the window. He framed one of them through the broken glass and pumped the trigger. As a bullet struck the terrorist in the mouth, Singerman fired again, pounding the second man in the forehead.

He went back down to the lobby and—after inspecting the street in front from behind the window, and seeing no one—went back outside through the revolving door. He saw the dead Hezbollah he'd just killed. They were lying next to one another in contorted piles atop a growing red flood.

Singerman ran along the side of the buildings, cutting toward Sixth Avenue and the Fed. When he saw the Interchem building, he tapped his ear.

"Igor, it's Singerman," he said. "I'm at the building. I'll call you when I'm on the floor of the room."

As Singerman crossed the final street before the entrance, he heard gunfire just as he felt a bolt of white-hot pain in his back. He was sent forward and down, a pained grunt coming from him. He knew he'd been shot in the back. On the ground, he saw blood above his navel.

"Fuck," he moaned, trying to move his legs.

He saw the man who'd shot him, behind a car. From the ground, Singerman pulled out a handgun. As acute pain stabbed all over his body, he raised his P226 and fired at the terrorist, missing with several shots, then hitting the man in the torso, dropping him.

"Fuck," he said again, looking at the Interchem building. He knew he was in deep trouble. He couldn't walk. Looking down, he saw blood spilling from his chest. He reached to his mouth, and his fingers came back bloodstained. Singerman understood he'd be dead soon. The destruction of the Fed was now inevitable.

97

Dewey leveled the MP7A1 in a strike position and switched the fire selector to manual—single shot.

There were four Iranian gunmen—Hezbollah—facing the front of the building, holding the lobby against the waves of law enforcement trying to breach the terrorists' cordon. Each one of the four had to know that they would die. Yet they'd already accepted that, and today was about going out fighting against an enemy they'd been taught to hate. That knowledge somehow gave them strength. They were firing rounds back out through the front of the lobby toward First Avenue, holding back law enforcement as the kill team moved up to Dellenbaugh.

Dewey gave Murphy a stern look, as if to remind him to not do anything, not even move. Above all else, he didn't want Murphy to fuck it up somehow.

Dewey paced slowly into the atrium, tucking behind walls and columns, not to hide but rather so as to not get hit by incoming fire from SWAT. The environment was too loud for the gunmen to hear him; their attention was not on a penetration behind them.

Dewey skulked until he was at the nexus of the lobby, near the elevators, behind the four gunmen who were approximately a hundred feet away. The gunmen were focused on what was happening on the outside, and assumed the lobby was secure behind them. The lobby was so vast that they didn't notice him.

Dewey pumped the first slug into the back of the head of the terrorist to his right. A gunman at the left swung his AR-15 as he shouted. From across the atrium, Dewey registered the gunman's movement and pumped the trigger on the submachine gun. A short burst of suppressed slugs hammered into the gunman's upper chest and neck. A third gunman turned. The Hezbollah fired blindly, spraying bullets. Dewey ducked and pumped the trigger on the SMG. He heard bullets whistle over his head as the man shot at him then was caught by Dewey's gun—kicked violently backward, off his feet, tumbling down onto the marble floor. The fourth man—looking behind him to see what had just happened—was abruptly struck in the head by a high-caliber bullet fired from across the street.

98

Admiral Dave Morris stood on the bridge of the USS *Princeton*. The guided-missile cruiser was pointed directly at a spread of land at least two hundred miles in the distance, an invisible point of land, but which was there.

"Firing sequences," said Morris to one of his aides. "Lock and hold."

Flouting Navy regulations, Morris had longish black hair, interspersed with silvery gray, and a thick beard and mustache, also scattered with gray. At six-foot-seven, Morris towered above everyone else on the bridge of the *Princeton*.

The bridge was the ship's radar and war room. Morris had the con. He was widely considered one of America's greatest naval tacticians. He'd fought unpublicized battles on water for nearly four decades now, unseen skirmishes never reported, and had nearly died in the Straits of Gibraltar, after a vicious but victorious exchange with Vladimir Putin's navy.

He heard the high digital tone of the systems finally aligning.

"V5 weapon control system targeted and launch ready, sir."

"Fire on three, two, one," said Morris, "fire."

The air was abruptly, and violently, rocked by loud explosions.

Four Tomahawk missiles blasted one by one into the air, ripping into the sky above the ship. Each missile weighed almost two tons and cost around $1.5 million. Today, the Tomahawks would pay a surprise visit to the Republic of Iran, a six-million-dollar present from the United States to the country's leader, Ali Suleiman.

Morris glanced through the window and looked around the bridge.

"Let's raise security levels across the board," said Morris. "I want battle stations. Please ask the *Nimitz* to send out a group protocol immediately."

99

Igor sat upright, in front of a wide arc of computer screens. They spread in a curvilinear concave on top of a glass desk held up by brass stanchions.

Igor was sliding and pivoting on an Eames office chair on wheels—high-back, stainless steel, and clad in bright lime green leather—skating along the mahogany floor in front of the array of computer screens. The screens were filled with various activity. Igor was shirtless. A can of Dr Pepper was next to an elongated, unusual-looking red keyboard with white letters and numbers. Behind the Dr Pepper can were half a dozen others, all empty.

Through the windows, the faint roar of sirens and occasional screams could be heard from the streets below.

Igor, for a computer hacker, was in good shape. He wasn't brawny, but rather sculpted, thin, and tan. He had earbuds in both ears. Usually he would've been listening to music. But right now he was tied into a central communications tree at the highest levels of the U.S. government.

Igor's fingers moved intuitively across the keyboard, while his eyes swiveling back and forth between the two large screens, which were each cut into quadrants. Igor kept his eyes on eight different sections, watching everything as his fingers played the keyboard like a concert pianist.

The information on the screens was mostly streams of code, either white, green, yellow, or red against black, or black on white. This was the Fed. One section displayed a complex blueprint that he manipulated with the keyboard. It was a layout of a project in a Parametric Technologies digital CAD drawing. It was the architectural blueprints of the building that housed Fedwire, that part of the Fed that controlled all U.S. liquidity.

The second section of the screen was an algorithm written to determine the Federal Reserve's security access to the room that housed the Risch algorithm that controlled the Federal Reserve, and thus the wealth and liquidity of the United States of America. He searched for vulnerabilities. Singerman had told him there was a security weakness in the entrance hardware. The entrance itself was some sort of electronic "sliding door" at the end of a fifty-foot corridor. To enter the governors' room, one had to walk through the tunnel, which meant one had to turn off the electronic sliding door.

At the beginning of the tunnel were four screens. These were the screens the four governors of the Fed looked into, and pressed their thumbs down upon, in order to get into the tunnel. Igor obviously understood. This was why the governors had all been murdered.

One of the screens flashed green. It was providing him with signals metadata from the entrance corridor:

PEC: SCAN A-3
Ft. 50.0 Ht. 14.4 Temp. 4098.7 F

"*Iisus*," said Igor aloud. "*Chetyre tysyachi gradusov. Eto goryacho.*"

Jesus. Four thousand degrees. That's hot.

Igor ran the readings against a database he kept in a folder on his main platform, a folder composed of advanced weapons systems, beyond guns and ammunition, beyond chemical agents. All those were in a different folder. This one contained experimental weapons

349

programs in the U.S., at the Pentagon and CIA, as well as what he'd been able to hack out of Russia, China, Saudi Arabia, Germany, Israel, and other countries, along with the private sector, companies like General Dynamics, Boeing, Airbus, Halliburton, Raytheon, and several others. The cutting edge of defense systems. It was a compendium of advanced, technology-based systems, still secret, still in their infancy.

He doubted the readings would find a match. Yet, after half a minute, a quadrant in the lower portion of one of the screens flashed bright red:

Dassault Systems
Lyon, FR
ETY: FOR/Svi
Testing: UNIT 4672–87
Summary: *Iodine sheet field*
Certainty: *96.4%*

Igor continued reading about the defense system that was guarding the Fed.

Dassault's Iodine Sheet Field ("ISF") is a SIGINT binary, iodine-based heat defense system capable of being confined within a geometric walled parallel. ISF has been shown to turn on and off with thermal and/or chemical residue at 00.0013548 tHs per programmed grid pattern. It is the closest any government or company has gotten to a so-called force field, capable of being turned on and off, and heat and/or chemical protocols are untraceable immediately. The Dassault System ISF effectively vaporizes anything in its field of range, including human beings but more importantly any weapons and weapons systems, including bullets in flight and MANPADs. ISF is as of yet unknown to China or Russia. It was implemented by the U.S. Treasury Department at a cost of $16.4 billion. The location of the implementation is unknown, but it is most likely an end-of-days protective mechanism guarding the central trunk of the U.S. Treasury and the U.S.

Back on the first screen, Igor watched as new electronic signals emanated for the first time in hours from the Federal Reserve. But it was not benign. This was primary SIGINT moving down through the trunk of the steel box housing the Fed. He knew what it meant. Someone was inside the Fed, and whoever it was was typing.

He started to worry. He realized he needed Singerman's help. There was no way to hack the Risch algorithm from the outside. The only way was for someone who knew how to get in to do so. Singerman had to get in and stop whoever it was.

Igor tapped his ear twice.

"Aaron, it's Igor," said Igor.

He heard nothing and waited, watching as signals activity from the Fed picked up.

"Aaron?" Igor repeated, but there was no reply.

100

Adrian King's office was large—though somewhat thin and rectangular—but it had amazing views of the South Lawn and more important was next door to the Oval Office. The far end of the office, behind King's desk, was all French doors and windows, and led out to a granite terrace that ran around part of the West Wing. Often Dellenbaugh or King would simply step out onto the terrace and walk to the other man's office.

The rest of the office had furniture on one side—an extra-long red leather sofa, a few club chairs, a long glass coffee table—and the walls above featured a tightly packed set of paintings and framed photographs. The opposite side of the office contained bookshelves. The shelves slid aside when a button was pressed, revealing a massive LCD screen that could be used to watch TV or engage in meetings with world leaders.

Right now, there were approximately a dozen people in King's office. The screen was currently divided up into smaller screens showing various newscasts, the volume muted. Suddenly, the entire screen went white. A man appeared, wearing a mic and sitting in front of a computer console.

"CENCOM," the operator said, interrupting everything in King's office—and taking over the volume on the screen. The young man stared into the screen and found King. "Adrian, this is Emergency Priority under section Indigo and overrides all tertiary activities."

King's office went quiet.

The screen shot dark, then, a few moments later, lit up, divided in half. On one side was a young black woman named Patricia Johnson, an NSA cryptologist who ran all NSA financial gathering, analysis, and synthesis. Johnson oversaw the NSA's capability set in terms of data-level financial information, managing hundreds of analysts and adversarial operations employees who tracked financial activity, in all formats, across the globe and provided the government with essential information on enemies and hostile regimes. In addition she helped enforce such things as sanctions—in the darkest parts of the web—and protected the United States through a massively datacentric framework based on the agency's ability to parse trillions of individual electronic transactions executed each day by people and entities across the world. She also controlled offense and ran an interagency team of hackers who were capable of inflicting great damage on America's adversaries, and spent most of their time doing it.

Johnson was in what looked like a NASA control room, filled with people at workstations, beneath a massive wall of screens.

King looked at Calibrisi, both of them understanding that if Patricia Johnson was segued in, it meant this was about the Fed. Calibrisi hit his cell, and the other half of the screen went from black to a live feed of a man in a red, blue, and yellow flannel shirt sitting at a keyboard, typing. His hair was unbrushed and shimmered—though it was blond, dark streaks were around the fringes and bangs, caused by perspiration.

"Pat," said King, looking at Johnson. "What's going on?"

"They've accessed the governors' room," said Johnson. "According to signals coming off the event, they are now inside the room and I assume cutting through whatever code the system algorithm is written in."

"Do we have the capability to know how long it will take?" said Calibrisi.

"No," said Johnson. "But it's a heuristic algorithm."

"Meaning what?" said Calibrisi.

"In terms of breaking the algorithm, each step is dependent on the last step," said Johnson. "That's a good thing because it takes sequencing and time. Still, assume they'll introduce an attack algorithm. It will run something back against the sequence and eventually, just by sheer volume, break it all down. It will take time, but not much."

"How long?" said King. "Are we talking hours or minutes?"

"Minutes," said Johnson. "Single-digit minutes. Just look."

Johnson stepped away from the frame and pointed at a large LCD at the front of the room. It showed a series of lines that cut from left to right. They were red lines across a white digital background.

"What is it?" said King.

"That's the measurement of the hacker's progress," said Johnson. "Each line represents a cluster of time-based degradation of the core algorithm. Notice how the lines are drawing closer each capture. The hacker inside the room is getting closer and closer to the core code. When the lines cross, it means they have administrative power over the algorithm that runs the Fed. They can simply start erasing the Fed's reserves until it's gone."

IOI

Igor tried to reach Singerman at least a dozen times, but he didn't answer.

He stared at a rectangle on the screen, thinking . . . hoping. What it showed was the Risch algorithm. There was no way to access it. So, instead, Igor stared at the rising columns of random numbers. It was the last few yards of protection via code, written by Singerman and America's best computer scientists. He hoped that whatever secrets it was built on would hold. It was the proverbial last line of defense from anarchy.

Igor suddenly understood something that perhaps only he and the Iranian now inside the Fed understood. That he, Igor, was now powerless, and that he'd lost. The Fed itself—the internal room where the governors controlled all of America's wealth—was now under enemy control, and it was only a matter of time until they wiped out the entire financial underpinnings of not only America, but the civilized world.

Hezbollah had sent a hacker of the highest order—and whoever it was was now sitting inside the governors' room, provisioned inside, typing away, introducing attack algorithms designed to exploit vulnerabilities. That was the SIGINT he could see on a separate screen. It was only a matter of time before he found the entrance to the core code base.

Trying to hack into the Fed was futile. To access the true capital of the Federal Reserve—the daily volumetric inflows and outflows—one needed to be inside the room. It was a closed-loop system up and until it intersected with the grid somewhere on an outgoing path. It was a bubble. One needed to be inside the room. That realization was the genius of the Fed system—but now it represented its downfall.

Igor shut his eyes. He shook his head. Igor understood at some moment that there would be no way he could stop him, that the Iranian hacker was inside the central core of the American financial system.

He tapped his ear. He tried Singerman one more time.

102

Singerman crawled from the middle of the sidewalk to a store-front, beneath an awning. He could no longer feel his legs. He knew he was dying. Behind him, a trail of wet blood shimmered. He dragged himself with his hands and arms. Singerman tried to remember where he was but he was so tired. . . .

He looked down at his blood-soaked legs and stomach. He wanted to do more, but what more could he do? He let his head start to wobble into sleep. But then he remembered the training. He took the Uzi and aimed it at his foot. He couldn't feel his feet anymore. He fired at his foot—smashing a bullet into his toes. A piercing ripple of electric pain shot through him. But he was awake now.

Singerman heard his earbud. He tapped it.

"Yeah," said Singerman.

"Aaron, it's Igor," came a Russian voice. "Are you there?"

"No," said Singerman. "No, Igor, I'm sorry, I'm not."

"What happened?"

"I got shot."

"Oh, Christ, I'm sorry," said Igor.

"Where are you?" said Singerman.

"At the iodine sheet field," said Igor. "Someone is inside the governors' room. I've got Fedwire up and down. I can see what he's doing in real time but he can't be stopped unless someone takes over the keyboard. The security membrane is not penetrable, unless you have the eye scans and thumbs. It's hard-wired. Is there a back door?"

Singerman coughed blood as he struggled to listen, and to register the voice. It was a Russian voice, he thought as he drifted further into shock. He was now in a cloud and felt himself somehow rising up and starting to float away, in harmony, drifting into whatever oblivion lay next—and then he fired again, spraying bullets into his other foot. This time he barely felt it, though it was enough to cause him to groan.

"Yes, I put it there myself," said Singerman. "You can turn off the sheet field for approximately two and a half seconds."

"How?" said Igor.

"There's a trigger in the reboot in the power source," said Singerman. "It will only work once. It tells the reboot to pause for two point five seconds."

Singerman coughed violently as blackness descended, and nothing could prevent the inevitable conclusion of his life that was coming. He was dying this time. He couldn't even lift the Uzi to shoot at his legs. Maybe he was already dead. . . .

He suddenly remembered designing the system, under the tutelage of his mentor, Professor Richards, at Yale. It was when he started working for the agency.

"JACK314," said Singerman.

"What?" said Igor.

"JACK314," said Singerman, fighting just to speak. "Do you have it?" he said.

"Yes, I wrote it down. What is it?"

"It's a crypto code to shut down Fedwire," said Singerman. "It will stop anything the hacker has done. It has to be all caps, Igor."

"Got it. Where are you?" said Igor. "I'll send someone, an ambulance."

"It's too late," said Singerman. Then he whispered his last words: "I'm sorry I couldn't get there, Igor."

103

Dewey pressed "20" and the elevator doors shut as the cab started climbing.

He removed a combat knife, a fixed-blade SEAL Pup, from a sheath at his calf and pried the electrical control panel ajar, bending the corner back. With both hands, he yanked back on the panel and ripped it off the wall, exposing the internal workings of the elevator. He found the wires to the bell and lights, took the blade, and severed them. Immediately, darkness cloaked the elevator.

Dewey crouched in the corner, putting the hilt of the knife between his teeth. His eyes acclimated and he saw a thin seam of light between the two elevator doors as it went higher. He targeted the MP7A1 at the seam of light. Dewey found—in his mind—a shooting seam between the elevator doors, and waited. A square opening no bigger than a deck of cards. He targeted the silencer into the mental aperture, completely still. The elevator came to a stop and the doors opened and he prepared to fire.

Nothing happened for several moments. He stared from the back corner of the elevator and listened in silence. He heard alarms in the distance, on other floors, but nothing on this floor, it was a ghost town. After several silent moments, the doors slid shut. The elevator remained sitting there, and Dewey acclimated to his shooting point by the trails of light around the edges of the elevator cab, cast through seams around the now closed doors. He waited a half minute, and still the doors remained shut.

He listened, feeling each passing second like a belt whipping across his back. He could hear nothing. Inside the dark cab, only the occasional creak of a cable somewhere spoiled the silence.

In the background was the incessant wail of emergency alarms inside the building.

Then the doors opened.

Dewey pressed his finger harder against the trigger, though he didn't fire. There was nothing there, just an empty corridor. After several seconds, the doors shut. He remained fixated on the doors.

Dewey had killed the man who built QUDS, Abu Paria, in a Macau casino. He'd almost died that night in a casino restroom. He'd seen firsthand the savages QUDS made. They had no regard for human life. Yet Dewey learned that night in Macau that he was more of an animal than even Paria.

A few moments later the elevator doors opened and a man stepped quietly into the hallway outside it. He had on a black ski mask and was dressed in a gray sweatshirt and jeans, clutching a PS90. Dewey pumped the trigger, catching the gunman with a bullet to his forehead, then fired a second time, a staccato *thump*. The second bullet pounded a hole in the man's chest, kicking him sideways—two fast shots that dropped the gunman with a dull grunt, in a contorted pile on the hallway floor.

Dewey stepped over the dead Iranian into the hallway, SMG clutched in his hands and blade between his teeth.

There were no lights on, but ambient light cast a yellow hue to the silent corridor. He paused and skulked to his right, looking for stairs. As he came to the corner of the elevator bank, he paused and listened. He waited a dozen seconds then rounded the corner, led by the suppressor at the end of the MP7. A red light with the word EXIT shone a few feet away.

Dewey slung the SMG across his back and, with his right hand, took a suppressed Colt M1911A1 semiautomatic .45 caliber pistol from beneath his left armpit. He took the knife from his teeth into his left hand. He entered the stairwell in silence.

The stairs were flashing between utter darkness and bright momentary bursts of red from battery-powered emergency beacons every few seconds.

He moved down the stairs, hugging the back wall and crouching as he descended toward the eighteenth floor. He heard a noise—just the faintest movement of a shoe scratching concrete. There was someone on the stairs below.

Dewey got down on his stomach. He started crawling down the stairs, like an alligator, at the edge of the back wall, trying not to make a noise. Dewey was tilted down the stairs on all fours, his feet up behind him, his hands on the concrete aimed down the stairs, in each hand a weapon. With each step down, he came closer and closer to eighteen. When he turned a corner on his stomach, he saw, in the flashing red light, a shadow. Dewey crawled down the next set of stairs, just before the turn. He let his hands go and his body suddenly started sliding down the stairs. As he passed the corner of the stairwell—sliding painfully—Dewey saw the gunman in the flashing red light. He was looking up the stairwell for him. Dewey pumped the trigger, hitting him in the temple and dropping him.

Gunfire erupted from just below.

Dewey got to his feet and lurched to the outer wall as bullets pelted the ceiling and wall just above him. Dewey holstered the Colt and put the knife in a pocket. He took the MP7 from over his back and found the trigger for the M203, an attachment under the barrel that fired antipersonnel rounds. He pumped the trigger and sent a grenade down at the gunman. The blast was loud and shook the stairs. The grenade hit way past the gunman but the force of the explosion kicked him awkwardly forward, blown out by the grenade. The weight of his momentum carried him over the railing and he tumbled over it and dropped into the chasm, screaming, his skull clanging several times along the sides of the stairwell as he plunged to his death.

He set the fire selector to full auto as he entered the eighteenth floor. He moved quietly down the corridor. There were dozens of people scattered dead on the ground, blood spilled out in maroon pools. Desks were turned over. Shattered glass was everywhere.

Wind pulsed in from a blown-out window.

This was where the missile attack had taken place.

There were bodies everywhere. The killing was fresh. Holes in walls, broken, turned-over furniture, missing limbs, tons of glass, and the remnant smell from the explosion.

As he scanned the large suite for Dellenbaugh, he sensed movement and turned.

104

Mansour followed a trail of fresh blood from near where Sayyari had been shot. Whoever had shot this man was still alive.

At the same time, he scanned the bomb-scarred floor for J. P. Dellenbaugh. Many people were missing limbs, several were unrecognizable due to blunt trauma in and around their heads. It was like a plane crash.

He and the other two men searched, with Mansour leading a path out across the destroyed office space, stepping over furniture and bodies. Following the trickle of crimson.

Mansour found Dellenbaugh against the wall, facing out near the broken windows. He was clutching a gun, but he was weak and nearly unconscious. He saw Mansour and tried to move the weapon but could not.

Mansour's men pulled the American president down the hall and into an empty office suite, part of the floor that hadn't been destroyed.

They sat Dellenbaugh in an office chair and flex-cuffed his arms behind his back, so that he couldn't fall over. One of the men stepped back and started to frame the scene in his phone, preparing to video the fallen president. He hit the flashlight on the cell and suddenly the bleeding president was illuminated in bright light.

The second man removed an object from his shoulder pack. It was a folded-up black flag with the Hezbollah white crest in the middle. He hung it over a painting on the wall behind the president.

Mansour approached the president. In broken English, he said, "If you say you are the Great Satan, I will spare your life."

Dellenbaugh's eyes were glassy and weaving around as he attempted to stay alive. He looked at Mansour.

"Fuck you," he coughed, spitting a mouthful of blood at Mansour.

Mansour raised his submachine gun and brought it to within an inch of Dellenbaugh's bloodshot eye. Then he remembered: the moment was coming. The message would be captured on video and sent to TASS, CGTN, CNN, DNC, Al Jazeera, and *The New York Times*, and then every other news outlet in the world, those first outlets being the first to see the video because they would quickly seek to exploit the killing of Dellenbaugh for their own ends.

Mansour would ultimately be the one who killed Dellenbaugh.

He couldn't believe how everything had gone according to plan.

Mansour lowered the PS90 as one of the others prepared to film the assassination of the president. Mansour pulled on a black balaclava and removed a knife from a sheath at his waist. He stepped behind Dellenbaugh. He put the sharp edge of the KA-BAR against Dellenbaugh's neck.

"Go," said the man filming on his phone.

As he was about to slash the president's neck, Mansour heard gunfire from just down the hallway. He sheathed the blade and charged through the empty office and into the hallway with the submachine gun out in front of him and his finger on the trigger.

As he came around a corner, he saw a figure. He was too far away for an easy shot but he set the gun to full auto. A man was walking across the silent floor of dead bodies and broken glass, clutching a submachine gun. Mansour recognized him.

After everything, after the failure in Georgetown, he couldn't believe how easy it would be to kill this man. It felt almost anticlimactic—though now that he thought about it, that was how he felt about the entire day. It had been hard, and yet so easy. Dewey Andreas.

Mansour stepped forward into Andreas's blind spot as Andreas searched for Dellenbaugh. Then the American turned.

By the time Dewey noticed him, Mansour was less than ten feet away and Dewey's MP7 was aimed in the wrong direction and both men knew it.

Andreas's eyes met Mansour's as Mansour marked him in the crosshairs of the SMG. Dewey remained still.

"Where is he?" said Dewey.

Mansour was quiet as he trained the gun on Dewey. As he held Dewey tight in the aim of the PS90, Mansour nodded toward the hallway.

"If you put your gun down onto the floor, I will take you to him," said Mansour.

"Why not just kill me?" said Dewey, still clutching the MP7.

"Because I want you to see him die," said Mansour.

105

Igor looked at his watch, a gold Rolex Daytona with a bright green bezel. He calculated the time it would take him to get to 1135 Sixth Avenue, the Interchem building.

He had a gun in his closet, but he'd never used it and didn't know if it even worked, or if he would be able to find bullets. Not to mention how he would get there.

Igor wanted to do more. He felt helpless.

He cut out of one of the screens and found a GPS tracking tool, remembering that in addition to Singerman, both Dewey and Tacoma were in New York.

A map shot wide on the screen and two flashing green circles showed where they were. Dewey was at the UN—but Tacoma was on Forty-fourth Street, moving in the direction of the UN.

Igor tapped his ear.

"CENCOM," came a female voice.

"I need to be patched in to Rob Tacoma."

"Identify."

"I don't have an identification. He is a NOC and I need to speak to him."

"Why?"

"To prevent a catastrophe."

106

Slowly, Dewey put the submachine gun down on the floor.

"Now the pistol," said Mansour. "Slowly."

Dewey began to lift the .45 from beneath his armpit as Mansour took a step back, creating an impossible angle for Dewey. Mansour kept his finger hard on the trigger of the SMG. Slowly, Dewey placed the Colt M1911A1 on the ground.

"Hands over your head," said Mansour. "Lock fingers."

Dewey did as he was told.

"Now start walking," said Mansour, nodding down the hall.

With Mansour a few feet behind him, Dewey went down the hallway, took a left down another hallway, and entered a quiet suite of offices. In one of the offices, someone was holding a phone and taking video. For the first time, Dewey saw Dellenbaugh, tied up to a chair, blood trickling from his nose and mouth, his eyes closed and his head tilting listlessly to the side.

"Wake him up," said Mansour to the other Iranian.

He slapped Dellenbaugh across the face. Dellenbaugh's head shot sideways, like a broken toy. The man slapped him again, harder this time, hard enough to draw blood from Dellenbaugh's lip.

Dellenbaugh looked up, semi-lucid.

"Dewey."

The president was barely conscious. His stomach was bleeding badly. He coughed, and watched Dewey with blank eyes.

"Go," said Mansour, aiming the gun at Dewey. "Sit down on the ground next to him."

107

Tacoma's earbud chimed and he tapped his ear.

"Rob, this is CENCOM, I have 'Igor' for you," said the operator.

"Put him through," said Tacoma, holding up on Forty-fourth Street.

There were a few beeps, then Igor came on the line:

"Rob," said Igor in his thick Russian voice. "I don't have time to explain. I need you to go to a building on Sixth Avenue."

"What's the address?" said Tacoma.

"1135 Sixth Avenue," said Igor, "between Forty-third and Forty-fourth."

Tacoma turned and ran back west on Forty-fourth Street and cut down at Sixth Avenue. He saw the skyscraper. Though simple in its appearance, its black steel rectangular structure loomed—walls of reflective blue glass hovering above the street below.

"Why?" said Tacoma.

"That's the location of the Federal Reserve," said Igor. "They're inside and are attempting to wipe out the Fed."

Tacoma crossed and came at the entrance from the side of the building. He held a suppressed AR-15. He paused at the corner of the building and glanced inside the lobby. There wasn't any movement. He made out three or four bodies on the floor of the lobby. The lobby area was hard to delineate through a window. It was filled with walls of interior windows and mirrors, intended to obfuscate the view from outside.

He watched for almost a minute and saw no movement.

"Where am I going?" said Tacoma.

"Floor twenty-five," said Igor.

A shadow crossed in a reflection somewhere on the far side of the lobby. He moved the fire selector on the AR-15 to full auto.

Tacoma walked stiffly down the street as if just a lost pedestrian. At the entrance to the building, he came to a set of double doors. He pulled back on the left door with his left hand as his right arm swung the AR-15 into the door opening. But there was no one.

He found a dead security guard and took his ID. He went to the elevators and inserted the ID into a slot, then hit "25." The doors shut. Tacoma changed out mags on the rifle, then removed his P226 from the holster at his waist. He ejected the mag on the P226 and slammed a fresh one in, yanking back, loading the chamber. He holstered it just as the doors opened on the twenty-fifth floor.

It was a strange setting, austere, lit in an iridescent warm white glow, the strangest, eeriest thing he'd ever seen. In one direction was a wall. In the other direction was a field of light. He stepped closer. Behind the wall of light was a windowless tunnel. The tunnel was bathed in a strobe-like yellow light. At the end of the tunnel, fifty feet away, he could see a room. Though somewhat obscured by the field of light, he could see a man seated at a table.

Four waist-high digital screens stood at the opening to the tunnel. Tacoma began his sprint into the tunnel, eyeing the door at the end of the corridor.

"STOP! *For the love of God, stop!*"

He heard Igor's voice just as he started into the tunnel, then pulled up. As Tacoma got close, the tunnel light gradually brightened, with blue fluorescent spotlights illuminating the inside of the fifty-foot-long tunnel from a hundred different pinpoints. Another series of light streams shot out in follicles of orange, brightening the space even more. The two sprays of color streams, one orange, the other blue, glowed in a precise pattern across the tunnel, interwoven, like a hand intersecting with another hand, the fingers intertwined.

Tacoma stopped at the last moment, finding one of the screens with his free arm to keep him from going forward.

"What the hell is it?" said Tacoma.

"A security perimeter," said Igor. "You touch it and you're dead. This is America's last defense. It is virtually impenetrable, unless you have the thumbprints and the eyeballs of the four governors."

"Well, Igor, I don't have them," said Tacoma.

He turned to move back away from the tunnel but unintentionally swept the suppressor of the rifle and the barrel out into the tunnel entrance. The metal and steel were suddenly incinerated, just inches from where Tacoma stood, with barely a noise.

"Jesus," said Tacoma. "What is it?" he asked Igor.

"It's called an iodine sheet field," said Igor.

"A what?" said Tacoma.

"A force field," said Igor. "Four thousand degrees. You shouldn't try and go across. It's hot enough to incinerate a missile. Imagine going to the sun for a few seconds."

Tacoma gulped.

"Got it," Tacoma said.

Tacoma looked at the ruined weapon. He hurled it into the tunnel, where it made just a brief burst of orange crackling light and disappeared.

"Wow," said Tacoma, eyeing the iridescent corridor. "So, any thoughts?"

"Yes," said Igor. "How fast are you, Rob?"

108

Dewey sat down next to Dellenbaugh, looking him in the eyes. Dellenbaugh looked as if he was about to die. He was fighting just to hang on. Dewey spied the black-and-white Hezbollah flag on the wall behind them. It would be the backdrop for their video. Hezbollah would kill Dellenbaugh and Dewey and show it to the world.

Dewey sat down on the carpet. The floor was bloodstained from Dellenbaugh's seeping wound. He crossed his legs at the same time removing a blade from his left ankle, in line, in silence, and quickly tucking it in his right hand back up against his wrist and forearm, blade out. He felt the teeth of the upper serrated edge of the knife against his skin.

He looked up at Dellenbaugh, whose head was askew and limp. His eyes were open. He was flex-cuffed to a chair so that even if he wanted to fall over he couldn't. His head was tilted atop his right shoulder and away from Dewey. He wanted to make eye contact to try to tell Dellenbaugh to hold on, but it wasn't possible.

In front of them were two men, each holding a gun aimed at

Dewey. The closer one also held a cell phone. He put on the light, getting ready to video the killings.

"You are about to be famous," said the gunman in back.

"Is that a threat?" said Dewey.

The gunman said nothing, then started laughing.

"That was funny," he said. "It took me a while."

"Abu Paria would've laughed too," said Dewey. "Unfortunately he's dead."

The gunman's grin went cold. He took a few steps forward and put the muzzle of the PS90 in front of Dewey's head.

The other Hezbollah seethed: "Zakaria! This is going to be live! Don't kill him yet!"

Dewey looked up at the muzzle of the submachine gun.

"Looks like you're a pretty good aim, Zakaria," said Dewey.

"Shut the fuck up," said Mansour, aiming the gun at Dewey.

"I bet you can't hit me, Zakaria," said Dewey.

Mansour looked down at Dewey. Dewey had a shit-eating grin, taunting him.

"I'll tell you what, if you hit me, you win," said Dewey. "If you miss, you can try again. Winner take all."

Mansour inadvertently laughed again.

Buying time.

Mansour realized it and stepped back.

"Get the camera ready," said Mansour in sharp Persian to the other man as he stared at Dewey.

Ten minutes before, Dewey didn't think he would live to see even this moment in time. When he encountered the terrorist for the first time, Dewey saw in the man what he'd seen in Abu Paria. He knew that the man was QUDS, that he knew who Dewey was, wanted to kill him, and could kill him. That he was an experienced operator, highly trained, and most important that any unnatural action would result in a slug to Dewey's skull.

He never questioned his instincts, but as he saw the camera light come on, as he found the man who'd taken him, standing a few feet back, with a PS90 aimed at Dellenbaugh, he wondered if perhaps he should've taken the chance? He would've died out there, he knew, but maybe that would be better than what they were about to do? He would've died trying to fight.

Still, he felt the knife handle in his hands. Dewey watched as the man with the phone framed the picture of Dellenbaugh and him in front of the Hezbollah flag.

Then the Iranian with the phone nodded.

"You're live," he said.

"Today, we have found guilty enemies of mankind," said Mansour in heavily accented English. He stepped into the frame of the video, his face covered in a black balaclava. "Today, we declare guilty two Americans, guilty of crimes against the Republic of Iran and the world."

Mansour aimed the gun at Dellenbaugh. Dewey averted his eyes, then heard the gunshot . . . followed by a horrendous, guttural cry. . . .

Dewey looked up as Mansour's face contorted and he clutched at his neck.

A black hole at the larynx spilled blood and he fell forward, tumbling down onto the floor.

Dewey looked to the doorway and saw Murphy. He was standing in the doorway, long blond hair, glasses, two hands on the gun he'd just fired, visibly shaking.

The other terrorist was stunned, motionless, watching Mansour clutching at his throat as he bled out. Before he could react, Dewey lurched across the short distance separating himself and Dellenbaugh from the cameraman. He thrust the blade as he dived at him, stabbing it into the man's chest, then pulled it back out. The man's eyes rolled back up into his head and he dropped dead on the carpet.

Mansour was on his back, writhing in pain, drowning in the blood now choking his airways.

Dewey stood up, sheathing the knife. He picked up Mansour's submachine gun.

He looked at the Iranian as he inspected the PS90.

"Nice gun," said Dewey. "Do you mind if I borrow it?"

Mansour had his hands against the bullet hole in his throat, trying to stop the bleeding. He squirmed. Dewey shot him in the shoulder. He moaned as he was slammed sideways by the slug.

"Wow," said Dewey. "It's really easy to use. Does it come in any other colors?"

"We'll get you," Mansour coughed.

Dewey aimed the gun at Mansour's head. Dewey's face became stone, his eyes a shade of hard blue. He waited for the Iranian to look up one last time.

"No matter who you send, we will beat you," said Dewey.

He pumped the trigger. The bullet hit Mansour's right eye. The back of his skull was blown across the ground beneath him.

Dewey picked up the cell phones of both terrorists, pocketing them. He looked at Dellenbaugh. The president was alive, but he needed serious medical attention. He needed a trauma surgeon and he needed him now.

He tapped his ear. There was no response.

He looked at Murphy, who was still standing in the doorway, frozen, holding his gun.

"Lower the gun, Mike," said Dewey. "Bring me your cell."

109

Jenna paced back and forth inside her father's office at the stern of the *Dorset*.

She'd been monitoring the effort to rescue President Dellenbaugh but her data feed was abruptly shut off. Her computer screen went bright green and a black rectangular digital box appeared. White lettering crossed the black rectangle:

INDIGO STATUS : ACCESS DENIED

She'd been shut off from the feed, some sort of elevated security classification she didn't even know existed. Britain had a similar access level, called Claremont, to which she'd been privy. It was a communications platform at the highest echelon of government, induced at times of crisis—not simply war or a terrorist attack, more like apocalypse.

Bottom line, though, she was cut off.

She considered calling Calibrisi or Polk, but didn't want to bother them if something worse was indeed happening, which it evidently was.

Jenna stood up and walked to a window. It showed the smoky skyline and she felt her very heart ache as she watched. It didn't matter that it was not her home country. Instead, it was just a feeling of sadness, wondering why, in a world so filled with beauty and joy, such pain and suffering could exist at the same time. This day would change everything. She was surprised at how much love she had for her new country. Jenna had thought she would spend a year or two in the U.S. and then return to London. Now she didn't want to leave. As much as she fought against it, she could only think of Dewey as she stared out the window.

When her cell beeped, she picked it up immediately.

"Hi," said Dewey.

"Where are you?" said Jenna.

"In the tower. I have him but he's almost flatline," said Dewey. "I need a helicopter."

"We just happen to have one right here. I'll be right there," said Jenna. "How long until you're on the roof?"

"Five minutes," said Dewey.

Jenna went to the deck and found her father.

"I need the helicopter, Dad," said Jenna.

Farragut stared at her for several moments.

"I read Barnes's dossier," said Jenna. "He was a pilot in 902 Expeditionary Air Wing for five years. It will be up to him, of course."

"I don't care about the helicopter, but I do care about you, and I care about Barnes," said Farragut. "I'm worried about you, sweetheart."

"I know, Daddy. I'll be okay," she said. "This is my country now and I intend to help."

Jenna tapped her ear.

"CENCOM, this is Jenna Hartford. I've heard from Dewey Andreas—he has the president. He's alive but badly injured. I'm retrieving them in five minutes, by air. I need directions to a hospital with a helipad, and a trauma team on standby."

110

Tacoma waited outside the elevators, leaning against the wall. He stared at the four screens and the tunnel. The wall of light, the iodine sheet field, hummed.

After several minutes, silence in which Tacoma listened as Igor typed, Igor finally stopped typing and spoke.

"Rob, I can create a window for you to get through the sheet field," said Igor. "It's fifty feet. How fast can you run fifty feet?"

It took him a little over ten seconds to run the hundred-yard dash. During a race, the runner goes different speeds at different parts of the hundred yards. A good runner was fastest in the last section.

"I need four seconds. I might be able to do it in four," said Tacoma, standing before the elevator banks.

Igor was silent for a few moments.

"Unfortunately, I believe I can only get you two point six or seven seconds, Rob," said Igor in a soft Russian accent.

Tacoma stared blankly at the tunnel in the distance.

"Not even three?"

"No," said Igor. "It's two point six, maybe seven. If you can't do it, don't try."

In his head, Tacoma counted out the distance between the wall at the far end of the elevator banks and the tunnel. He guessed it was approximately twice the distance. A hundred feet.

He understood he would have two and a half seconds to run through the tunnel, and that's if he and Igor timed it perfectly. He wasn't sure he'd ever run fifty feet that fast.

If any part of the sheet field came into contact with him, he understood the result: he would be burned alive. He would disintegrate like a matchstick tossed into an inferno.

He walked to his right, away from the tunnel, to the end of the hallway. Tacoma estimated the distance from the wall to the beginning of the sheet field. He guessed it was a hundred and twenty feet.

He had to hit the apex of his human capability at one hundred feet and accelerate. He had to hit the screens and be still accelerating when he reached the iodine sheet field. He had to run as fast as he'd ever run, and if Igor somehow fucked up and couldn't turn off the sheet field he would die.

"Let's do it," said Tacoma. "I'll start running from the elevators."

"How long until you reach the sheet field?" said Igor. "I need to know precisely how long."

"Exactly four seconds," said Tacoma.

Tacoma walked to the back wall. He paced out the path all the way back to the screens, examining the carpet, looking for any ridges or anything else that might trip him up.

"On your go," said Igor.

"Okay. Give me a minute."

Tacoma removed his loafers, socks, pants, and shirt, dropping them in a pile on the ground. He had on a pair of red-and-gray close-fitting athletic boxers and he kept them on. The only other thing Tacoma had on was a silver necklace with a cross. He kept hold of his P226. He unscrewed the suppressor and tossed it on top of his shirt, then swung it slowly up and down, thinking about how to run with it.

Tacoma bobbed up and down on the balls of his feet, pistol in his hand. He passed it to his left, then back to his right as he jumped up and down, twisting his head, breathing quickly, getting his heart rate up, kicking his legs out. He looked like a prizefighter before a fight, raring to go, though then he took his warm-up further. He swung his arms left right and right left, then slashed a 270-degree kick to the air, pivoting in the air as his foot struck an imaginary object, eight feet above the ground.

"I'm almost ready," said Tacoma, huffing and puffing. He held the gun in one hand, and put his right hand against the wall as he squatted into a starting position.

"You sure?" said Igor.

"Yeah," said Tacoma.

"On my go," said Igor. "I'll count down and shut it off at exactly four seconds after I say the word 'go.' So you know, and this is not the countdown, that means five, four, three, two, one, go. At 'go' you start running. Not before, not after."

"Got it," said Rob.

"Here comes the countdown, Rob. Good luck."

There was a long silence. Then, Igor spoke:

"On my mark," said Igor. "*Five, four, three, two, one—*"

Tacoma kicked off the wall before Igor said the word "go."

His first step hit the floor just as the word came out.

He started into a hard sprint, pistol in his hand in stride as his arms stroked furiously through the air. His legs reached for the right balance of distance and torque, and, as he approached the security screens he felt his head adjust slightly backward, as if watching as his body performed.

He was moving fast as he passed between two of the screens. He hit the tunnel at precisely 3.9 seconds after the word "go," and fortunately Igor had anticipated it.

Tacoma entered the tunnel galloping as he kicked into the most important piece of the run. The tunnel abruptly shot dark. Tacoma hadn't thought about the fact that the lights would go out, but he found a distant light above the far door and he pushed even harder, knowing that any loss of even a fraction of a second would kill him. He accelerated a second after he passed the screens, pushing himself as hard as he could, finding a pattern between his legs and his arms that meshed together in a continuum. He felt sharp pain in his feet, abdomen, and lungs, but he also felt the warmth of the pursuit.

Tacoma closed out the last few feet and charged across the end of the tunnel, arms pumping, not thinking about stopping, just as the corridor shot bright yellow right behind him, in a laser-like tapestry of blue and orange light.

There were no windows. A column of numbers streamed up in dazzling colors at the center of the room. It looked like nothing he'd ever seen before. A round chute of vivid digits scrolling up, ascending in a tunnel fueled from within by light, a grid that climbed into the ceiling and disappeared. He searched for the hacker, but the table was empty. Tacoma turned just as a man—hidden at the entrance—swung at him, striking Tacoma in the stomach, following with a knee to Tacoma's chin, then pivoting in a roundhouse 270-degree kick that met Tacoma's mouth with brutal force.

As Tacoma fell, he fired. The sound of unmuted gunfire was followed by a dank thud as the bullet ripped a hole in the terrorist's shoulder, but the man charged at Tacoma and dived to his arm, wresting the pistol from Tacoma. The hacker stood up, despite the blood coursing down his shoulder, and stepped back, giving himself room in case Tacoma went after him again. He stood at the entrance to the room. He aimed the P226 at Tacoma.

Tacoma stared into the muzzle of the pistol, then looked past the gunman, his eyes widening, as if he saw something or someone just behind the Iranian. The hacker turned and as he did his arm and part of his face were suddenly incinerated by the iodine sheet field. He dropped to the floor and blood and pieces of his internal organs spilled out.

Tacoma stood, rubbing his jaw, and kicked the dead terrorist into the sheet field. He sat down at the keyboard. He tapped his ear.

"Igor, I'm here," said Tacoma, looking down at the keyboard, and then the lights in front of him.

"Where are you?" said Igor.

"I'm in front of a keyboard," said Tacoma. "What's next? Is it like a video game?"

"Whatever you do, *don't fuck with the keyboard!*" shouted Igor. "I want you to type the following, all caps."

"Go ahead." said Tacoma.

"JACK314," said Igor.

Tacoma typed in the letters and numbers.

"Okay," said Tacoma.

"Hit Enter," said Igor.

Tacoma hit Enter. In front of him, the chute of light disappeared.

"Okay, now what?" said Tacoma.

"*Now what?*" yelled Igor. "Now you're a fucking hero. You just saved the Fed. No, you just saved the world!"

Tacoma turned, looking down the hallway at the iodine sheet field that surrounded him.

"That's great," said Tacoma. "One question. How do I get out of here?"

III

Dr. Hiroo Takayama was in the finishing stages of a six-hour cardiac operation, carefully sewing an almost invisible plastic ring to the mitral valve of someone's heart.

A female voice came over the operating room speaker.

"Dr. Takayama," the voice said. "The president of the United States is being flown to the hospital. He's in critical condition. Are you close?"

"Yes," said Takayama. "What happened?"

"A terrorist attack," she said.

"How bad?" said Takayama, continuing to work.

"Assume an ISS of seventy-five," said the woman, "and please prepare for emergency surgery."

There was one other surgeon in the OR, along with two anesthesiologists and a half dozen nurses.

The procedure was being filmed. Takayama's surgical techniques were studied by surgeons across the world, regardless of language or nationality.

Takayama finished the weaving of the area beneath the man's mitral valve, then nodded at the other surgeon as he cut from the operating theater, disrobing as he moved. Beneath his purple surgical garments, Takayama wore a pair of worn jeans, a T-shirt, and running shoes. He was soon sprinting to the elevator. He took it two floors down and ran to his office. He opened a filing cabinet and removed a small steel suitcase, then ran.

Takayama took the elevator to the roof. There, he opened the steel case. Inside was a form-fitting protective cushion. There were three things inside, nesting in the foam. One was a tall vial filled with a hazy yellowish fluid. There was a syringe. There was a black rectangular box, made of lead.

The vial contained pure adrenaline which Takayama had purchased himself from a cattle farm in Matsuzaka, Japan, extracted from the adrenal glands of bulls. Takayama worked routinely with synthetic adrenaline but the manufactured version, epinephrine, was different from the real thing.

He threaded the syringe and opened the tiny cork on the top of the vial, filling the syringe so that it was ready to be injected. He replaced the cork in the vial and set both vial and syringe back into the steel case next to the lead box, shut it, then stood next to the helipad, waiting.

For the first time, Takayama looked at the sky in the distance. His mouth opened, though he was speechless. A pair of nurses appeared and came to Takayama's side, followed by a team rolling a bed.

Takayama pointed at a man near the door.

"Please get a second team up here immediately," said Takayama. "Also, page Dr. Argenziano and Dr. Lee. Make sure the theater OR is ready."

112

Dewey looked at Murphy, who'd lowered the pistol and was staring in disbelief at the two dead Iranians, as well as Dellenbaugh.

"Let's get out of here," said Dewey.

He pulled his SEAL Pup from the sheath at his ankle and cut the flex-cuffs holding the president's wrists together. Dewey looked at the president's wound. It was just above his navel. He didn't pull material back or attempt to inspect it. There wasn't time for that. It was obviously a mess and Dellenbaugh was bleeding out. A large oval of dark red shimmered in wetness. He scanned below. Dellenbaugh's legs were both wet with blood.

A large pool had spread across the carpeted floor beneath the chair.

But waiting for first aid—or for that matter administering it—was not feasible.

"This is going to hurt," said Dewey to an unconscious Dellenbaugh.

Dewey reached down, wrapped his arms around Dellenbaugh's waist, and lifted him up, throwing him over his shoulder, a fireman's carry. Dellenbaugh was heavy, and Dewey grunted as he hoisted all two hundred and twenty pounds of him. He positioned him on his right shoulder and moved. Dellenbaugh groaned in agony as his wound pressed against Dewey's shoulder.

"I'm the one doing all the work," said Dewey.

Dewey moved, the president on his shoulder, and Murphy followed. When they got to the elevators, Dewey said to Murphy, "Do you mind picking up those guns over there?"

Murphy walked to an MP7 and a suppressed Colt M1911A1.

Dewey took the MP7 into his right hand, his finger moving to the steel trigger.

He carried the president to the elevator, but before going through the door, looked around one last time for any more Hezbollah gunmen. With Dellenbaugh on his shoulder, he went onto the elevator, along with Murphy.

113

Sayyari awoke in pain, knowing he'd been shot. He was awakened by shouting from Mansour. Sayyari stood up and put his hand against the wall, going toward the noise.

He came to the suite entrance and saw the American president strapped to a chair, and next to him Andreas, on the ground. Before he went in, Sayyari looked through a seam in the doorframe. Sayyari made out Mansour clutching a submachine gun aimed at Dellenbaugh.

Suddenly, a blast of unmuted gunfire rattled the room. Sayyari looked right. A man was standing in the doorway, holding a pistol. His eyes traced the direction of his aim and saw Mansour on the floor, hit in the neck. Then Andreas stabbed the other soldier.

Sayyari felt for a weapon but he didn't have one on him.

His brothers were on the floor, one shot dead, one stabbed to death, and Andreas was lifting Dellenbaugh onto his shoulder.

Sayyari let Dewey retrieve the president, remaining ducked behind the door. He was too weak to try to take Andreas by force. There was nothing he could do.

Andreas was extracting the American president. The video of an

American president being beheaded on live television was now no longer a possibility. Even killing him was now gone . . . or was it?

He waited and followed Andreas, the gunman who killed Mansour, and Dellenbaugh, staying out of sight. After the elevator doors shut, he watched where they were going. The lights climbed. Andreas was taking the president to the roof.

The entire world would be watching.

It wasn't the original plan—but it was perhaps even better. What the entire world would be watching would not be Dellenbaugh's beheading. Instead, the President of the United States would be shot from the sky. His rescue would be interrupted in the cruelest of ways.

Sayyari gathered his strength and pulled himself to his feet. He went back and found his rifle. He made his way back to the elevator and pressed "39." When he reached the roof, he stayed tucked into the side of the elevator, his finger on the Door Open button. When he heard no one, he skulked silently out of the elevator and took a knee behind a partial wall, out of sight, watching. He could see Andreas and Dellenbaugh at the edge of the helipad as wind buffeted the air. The distinct electric rotor slash of an approaching helicopter was unmistakable. He saw a sleek black helicopter weaving up through smoke and dust, within a steel-and-glass canyon, in between buildings.

The helicopter came in for a fast landing. Andreas carried the president the last few steps and a blond woman emerged and opened a door to the cabin. He watched as Andreas loaded the president into the helicopter. The female climbed back in just as the rotors on the chopper began to churn furiously. Sayyari checked his optics and placed his finger against the trigger, wondering why they were paused. Then the other American emerged from a door to his left and started running to the waiting helicopter. It was the man who'd killed Mansour.

Sayyari aimed at the running figure, fired, missed, then fired again, this time ripping a bullet into his chest. Sayyari turned back to the chopper, but it lifted quickly up and gashed right and down, out of range.

114

Dewey leaned into the cockpit.

"Get back to the tower," said Dewey. "Come up from the west, give me a firing line."

Barnes nodded in response.

The chopper sliced right and did a daring rotation around the tower a few floors below the roof, then tore skyward.

Dewey lifted his MP7A1 and trained it out an open window.

As the chopper crested the plane of the roof, the killer came into view. Dewey pumped the trigger, missing wildly, kicked by the furious wind and motion of the helicopter. He fired again, slamming a slug into the gunman's forehead. He tumbled to the concrete next to Murphy.

Murphy was lying on the concrete next to the helipad. His chest was ruined in crimson.

Dewey glanced at Dellenbaugh, who was unconscious, then his eyes met Jenna's. She stared blankly back at him.

After the chopper set down, Dewey climbed out and lifted Murphy up onto his shoulder and carried him to the waiting helicopter.

Both Dellenbaugh and Murphy were unconscious and bleeding badly.

Dewey said nothing. He just breathed rapidly, trying to catch his breath.

Without moving her eyes away from Dewey's, Jenna tapped her ear and spoke:

"CENCOM, we have the president and one more. Both gravely injured and unresponsive, one definitely cardiac," she said. "We need two trauma teams at the nearest location you have."

"Understood. Tell your pilot to go to Columbia-Presbyterian at 168th Street. Two trauma teams will be waiting on the helipad," said the voice. "Where are the injuries?"

"One is a deep puncture wound in the abdomen," said Jenna. "The other's a gunshot wound to the chest, looks like the heart."

115

Ali Suleiman was dining alone in his small apartment inside the Presidential Palace when he heard yelling from outside the door, followed by footsteps. Suleiman got to his feet as the footsteps grew louder. There were several people running down the corridor, and he recognized Marwan, his chief of security, yelling over and over in Persian:

"Open the door! Open the door!"

One of the armed soldiers posted outside the door opened the entrance to Suleiman's apartment and Marwan sprinted inside, looking desperately for Suleiman.

"IRGCAF near Jiroft detected at least four inbound missiles, sir. These are American Tomahawks, coming from a ship in the Gulf of Oman," said Marwan. "We must get to the underground bunker immediately, Your Excellency."

"What about our air defenses?" said Suleiman, an angry look on his face. "Do we not have the ability to shoot them down?"

"These are not drones," said Marwan. "The missiles have evaded three separate Sevom Khordad TELAR units including one south of Kavir Park. One of them is within minutes of Tehran, Imam. Please, sir."

"And do you know it is coming for me?" said Sulieman as he extended his arm and allowed Marwan to lead him to the door.

"No, sir, we do not know that, but your protection is our most sacred priority," said Marwan.

Marwan and several more soldiers surrounded Suleiman at the entrance and walked briskly down the high-ceilinged hallway as, suddenly, air-defense sirens pealed from outside the palace. At the end of the hallway they went right, where two men in dark suits, clutching submachine guns, held open the door to an elevator.

"Hurry, Your Excellency, please hurry," beseeched one of the gunmen.

Suleiman had just stepped into the elevator when a spine-chilling whine broke through everything else. It cut through the sirens, the thick walls of the palace, the urgent cries from his protectors. It was a deep, loud sonic *whiss*—the telltale audible of an inbound missile—growing louder and closer with each passing moment.

One of the men inserted a key and pressed a button for a secure part of the palace several floors belowground. The elevator doors moved shut. As the elevator started to descend, the incoming missile could still be heard. Suddenly, there was a massive explosion, a thunderous vibration, so loud it sounded as if it had struck just feet away. The elevator went dark, rocking and bouncing from side to side as it continued to go lower. After a few moments, emergency lights came on and Suleiman looked around at the men with him. The faintest hint of a smile came to Suleiman's face and he found Marwan.

"You saved my life, Marwan," said Suleiman humbly. "You all did. How can I ever thank you enough—"

But Suleiman's words were abruptly cut off by the sharp *twang* of the elevator cable snapping. They all heard it in the same moment, then they could feel it. It was the horrible feeling of falling, the feeling of dropping with no brake or parachute to stop. Several of the men, including Suleiman, screamed as the elevator cab dropped ten stories in an uncontrolled race to the ground, smashing into a concrete pad. Every occupant of the elevator was crushed in a pulp of clothing, weapons, body parts, and bones.

116

The helicopter carrying Dellenbaugh slashed down toward the helipad atop Columbia-Presbyterian Hospital in Manhattan.

The helicopter was met by a large rolling bed and a team of nurses, surgeons, and, in the backdrop, security. An Asian man with black hair stepped forward, carrying a metal briefcase.

Dewey climbed from the chopper as it touched down and grabbed the president, lifting him up and carrying him to the bed, where he set him down. The man with the briefcase looked quickly at Dellenbaugh, saying nothing, then the team whisked him inside the hospital.

Dewey turned and went to the open door of the helicopter. He lifted Murphy up from the floor of the chopper as another team came running across the helipad with a bed. He put Murphy on it as the Asian took a quick glimpse at Murphy. His face was emotionless. With his free hand, the man grabbed Murphy's shirt at the neck and ripped violently, exposing the wound.

"I'll handle both men," he said to a nurse. "Same room," he added. He nodded at Murphy. "Irrigate the wound, debride it, get a full spectrum of antibiotics moving through him."

He looked at Dewey.

"Who are you?" said Takayama.

"No one."

"Hi, no one. I'm Dr. Hiroo Takayama," he said. "Are you my main contact as it relates to the president?"

"No," said Dewey. "Actually, I guess until someone gets here, yes."

"I'll try and keep you posted."

Takayama walked to the door through which Dellenbaugh and Murphy had just entered, catching up with the team taking Murphy inside.

Takayama stepped into the operating room just behind the teams carrying the president and Murphy. He waited, arms crossed, as they hooked Dellenbaugh up to life monitors, then Murphy. Murphy was still alive, but a dull monotone beeping noise repeated in concert with the green digital flatline on the other monitor. Technically, Dellenbaugh was dead.

"Timing now," said Takayama in a Japanese accent. "Thirty-second intervals."

"I have that," said one of the nurses. "Starting now, Doctor."

Takayama looked right. An ER trauma nurse was already holding a tray of scalpels. He grabbed a long, slightly curved scalpel from the tray, and cut fast and hard with the thin blade down Dellenbaugh's right side, slashing away like gutting a fish. There was nothing kind about this cut. When he'd serrated a foot-long section of Dellenbaugh's torso, he handed the scalpel back to the nurse.

"Optics," said Takayama and, already anticipating the possibility, a nurse moved a set of optics to Takayama. She strapped them on Takayama from behind as, with his bare hands, Takayama dug down into the folds and veins of Dellenbaugh's stomach, pushing slowly by organs.

"Thirty seconds," said the nurse.

"Move in, twelve by six," said Takayama.

Suddenly, his view of the area that he was examining inside Dellenbaugh's gut was magnified.

"Right three, less one," said Takayama.

"One minute," said the nurse.

He examined the area, but saw nothing. Takayama focused in on an area near the pancreas, studying it.

"One minute thirty seconds," the nurse repeated.

Though Murphy's monitor made a steady beeping noise, the horrible-sounding flatline of J. P. Dellenbaugh's life monitor was the only thing Takayama could hear.

"In sixty-six, right four, in twelve, left one," said Takayama.

The view was magnified by thousands, and then Takayama found a small shard of glass, stabbed into the pancreas, invisible to the human eye.

"I need five-and-a-half-inch tissue forceps, and bring the briefcase over here and hand me the syringe," said Takayama.

"Two minutes," said the nurse.

He was handed a specialized set of surgical forceps. Takayama quickly shimmied the razor-thin shard of glass from Dellenbaugh's pancreas. He set it on the tray and dropped the forceps next to it. A nurse opened the briefcase and held it out for Takayama.

"Open the box," he said.

Another nurse reached for a thin rectangular box, made of lead. She opened it. Inside was a misshapen silvery-black object that looked like a piece of graphite. It was several inches long and shiny.

But it wasn't graphite. In fact, the thin piece of rock was plutonium.

Takayama had the nurses irrigate the opening of the wound over and over. He quickly sewed up the torn area around the wound.

"Two and a half minutes."

With his own hand, Takayama picked up the shard of plutonium, leaned down, and held it near the wound.

One of the other surgeons in the OR was shaking his head as Dellenbaugh's life monitor continued to show a flat green line and sound a single-note monotone beep.

"At three minutes it's too late, Hiroo," said the surgeon.

Takayama held the plutonium near where he'd retrieved the piece of glass.

"Three minutes," said the nurse.

There was no movement or activity.

"Hiroo," the surgeon said again.

"Three and a half minutes," said the nurse.

Gently, Takayama removed the fragment of plutonium and placed it in the lead case. He nodded to the woman holding the box, telling her she could shut it.

Takayama took not one but two suture needles and—as every eye in the room watched—sewed up both sides at the same time with each hand, in a weave of suture, almost too fast to see, tying the suture off seamlessly, as he reached to his right.

"You've killed him," said the same doctor.

Takayama didn't acknowledge him.

"Paddles," said Takayama.

Takayama walked to the defibrillator machine.

"Four minutes, Doctor."

He looked at the settings on the defibrillator. It was set for a 150-joule charge. Takayama, with bloody hands, spun the dials around as high as they would go, amperage, torque, frequency. He put it up to 360 joules, the max it would go. Takayama walked back to Dellenbaugh as he waited for the monotone telling him they were charged. When the incessant beep hit, Takayama leaned down and looked closely at the president.

"For God's sake," said the surgeon.

Then the nurse: "Four and a half minutes, Doctor."

He reached out his hands and the nurse handed him the paddles. Still, Takayama waited. Then he placed the paddles down on Dellenbaugh's chest and hit the chargers. A fierce shock slammed through Dellenbaugh's limp body, bouncing him. There was no response.

Takayama hit him again.

Still, nothing.

"You waited too long," said the surgeon.

"You're relieved," said Takayama to the surgeon. He glanced to a man at the door. "Get him out of here."

Takayama hit him one more time; the life monitor started making noises and showing a pulse and heart activity.

Takayama looked at one of the nurses.

397

"Let's get something down his throat so he can breathe," said Takayama, turning to the second surgical table, where Murphy lay unconscious and bleeding.

Murphy's heart monitor was still producing blips, indicating life.

Takayama took a clamp and spread the wound out. He dug in with forceps and pulled out a long, misshapen piece of steel, the bullet, then looked at one of the nurses.

"Where's anesthesia?" said Takayama.

"Right here," said a doctor to Takayama's left.

"We need to get him on a heart-lung," said Takayama. "I want to go in through the femoral and I'll cut in through the sternum."

"Ten-four," said the anesthesiologist.

Takayama turned to Dellenbaugh. He'd been intubated and was breathing, and alive.

He turned back to Murphy as a team cut into his femoral artery, at his groin, and inserted a device. A long, rectangular, futuristic-looking machine was rolled into the room. Takayama watched as they began the process of rerouting Murphy's heart and lung functions through the heart-lung machine, then stilled Murphy's heart chemically. He had several minutes before he could operate. He stepped out into the hallway. It was hushed. Takayama looked around and found the man who'd accompanied both the president and the second injured man to the hospital.

"The president is alive and should make it," said Takayama to Dewey. "Who's the other guy?"

"His name is Mike Murphy," said Dewey.

"His heart got nicked," said Takayama. "I'm going to try and repair it but he already had a coronary." Takayama looked at Dewey's thigh. He stepped forward and ripped Dewey's pants where the wound had occurred. Beneath was a mess of blood, still oozing. Takayama looked at one of the attending medics. "Get this guy sewn up," he ordered, pointing at Dewey. "Make sure there's nothing in there."

Takayama turned and went back into the OR. He made eye contact with a surgeon hovering over Dellenbaugh.

"Please move him into ICU," said Takayama. "Run cloxacillin and sulbactam, along with painkillers."

Takayama focused in on Murphy. He took something that looked like a regular drill—a sternum saw—and began sawing into Murphy's chest plate.

"Please, I need a twelve and mosquitos," he said as he cut down and across, as another surgeon and a nurse inserted retractors and gave Takayama room to work.

A nurse handed him a curved scalpel and forceps.

He took the tiny curved blade and cut into Murphy's heart. "Could I also get a drink of water," said Takayama as he went to work. "This is going to take a while."

117

Columbia-Presbyterian Hospital was the center of the world's attention, even as FBI, NYPD, and various military assets killed off the final vestiges of the attack on New York City. No one had truly started thinking about what was next, though all knew that what faced the United States—and in particular New York City—was a decade-long recovery. It was estimated that the body count was higher than even 9/11, and approached five thousand. It would take weeks for even basic cleanup and to put out the last of the fires spreading from the tunnels.

But the eyes of the world were on Columbia-Presbyterian, where the president of the United States lay in ICU. The country, the world, even America's enemies, waited with bated breath to see if J. P. Dellenbaugh would live.

A secondary story did manage to take the media's attention away from the hospital every few minutes. Iran's Presidential Palace had been hit with a direct strike by a missile. Though unconfirmed by the Iran government, reports were that Ali Suleiman, Iran's leader, was dead. The Pentagon had not commented.

Columbia-Presbyterian Hospital was shut off to the public. Outside, behind a rope line thick with armed soldiers and SWAT, a cabal of reporters and media, cameras and vehicles, from every network in the world, gathered and delivered the news back home, and yet there was no news. For hours, not a word had been released by the White House or by Columbia-Presbyterian.

As the BBC put it:

DELLENBAUGH FIGHTING FOR HIS LIFE

The truth was, however, Dellenbaugh was in ICU and breathing on his own. Though still unconscious, he would, it seemed, survive. Rather, it was Mike Murphy who was hanging by a thread.

After Murphy's main life functions were rerouted through a heart-lung machine, Takayama operated on Murphy's damaged heart. Surgery lasted several hours. Finally, Takayama looked up.

"Let's get him off the heart-lung," said Takayama as he prepared to stitch up the opening in Murphy's sternum. "It's repaired."

The team went to work taking Murphy off the heart-lung machine. Slowly, they transitioned the body's heart and lungs off the machine as Murphy's heart started pumping again. A steady beat chimed on one of the monitors as the screen displayed a serial line of jagged but steady beats.

118

Dewey stepped out of a black sedan and was surrounded by U.S. Navy SEALs, who pushed through the throng of reporters and were let through by a heavily weaponized member of the Secret Service.

Dewey entered the atrium of the hospital and was led down a hallway where a woman in a business suit met him and nodded.

"Mr. Andreas?"

"Yes," said Dewey.

"Please follow me," she said.

They stepped into an elevator. The young woman pressed a button and he looked straight ahead.

"Are they alive?" Dewey said.

She paused.

"Yes," she said. "My understanding is that they're both okay. President Dellenbaugh asked for you."

When the elevator doors opened, they stepped out into a brightly lit, austere hallway. Straight ahead was a large, walled-off square space where the doctors, nurses, and other medical professionals managed the activities on the floor. To the right was a large waiting area. It wasn't crowded, but there were at least two dozen people.

Dewey saw Amy Dellenbaugh, sitting on a couch in between her two daughters.

The air had a fluorescent quality to it, a stillness as if history or time itself had stood still.

Dewey felt a hand on his shoulder and turned. It was Adrian King, the White House chief of staff. King looked up at Dewey, saying nothing. He stared into Dewey's eyes.

"He almost died," said King. His voice held no emotion or sadness, just a hint of anger. "That he didn't is thanks to you."

King waved Dewey into Dellenbaugh's heavily guarded hospital room. The president's head was bandaged in white. He was attached to several IVs and various life monitors. Both eyes were black and blue.

As Dewey approached, Dellenbaugh held out his hand. Dewey took his hand and held it. He felt a faint squeeze and looked down into Dellenbaugh's eyes. Dellenbaugh smiled. He mouthed the words "thank you."

Dewey held Dellenbaugh's hand until he fell back asleep. Dewey went back out through the door to the ICU. The nurse who'd led him inside was standing there.

"Where's Mike Murphy?" he said.

She nodded at the door next to Dellenbaugh's.

Dewey pushed the big steel door aside and stepped into the room. Murphy was out like a light, and attached to at least twice the number of IVs and life-monitor devices as the president.

The monitors beeped in a steady pattern.

Dewey stepped to Murphy. His arms were tucked beneath blankets. Dewey reached out and put the palm of his hand against Murphy's neck. He moved his fingers together, gently, pinching the skin at his neck, but ever so slightly.

"Hang in there," said Dewey. He leaned closer, even though Murphy was completely unconscious, and spoke softly into his ear. "Mike, it's Dewey. You did it. You saved the president and the country. Looks like I really am going to have to take you to Disneyland, you son of a bitch."

119

Tacoma sat in a chair inside the governors' room, waiting. It had been more than twelve hours since he entered the room and still the iodine sheet field purred with a low electric hum. He could see down the corridor, where the white energy field continued to guard the room and prevent his exit.

Tacoma had taken a nap on the floor. He'd done 1,450 push-ups. He'd taken a second nap.

He heard a beep in his ear.

After a few clicks, Igor's voice came on.

"Hi, Rob," he said. "How's your 'staycation' going?"

"I'd like to get out of here," said Tacoma. "Can you at least turn it off for a few seconds so I can try and run back out?"

"The problem is, Robert," said Igor, "the system has an AI component and is self-learning. The two-and-a-half-second flaw no longer exists. I'm trying to figure out another way."

"There has to be an on-off switch somewhere," said Tacoma.

"There isn't," said Igor. "Yes, it can be turned off. It can be turned off forever or for an hour, but only with the four governors. They designed it a certain way for security purposes. NSA, Langley, and the company that built it, Dassault, are all working on it. The idea was to create a truly secure system and they succeeded. It's a fortress."

"What about just, I don't know, cutting off the electricity supply?"

"Of course we've thought of that," said Igor. "The electricity is self-generated. We've even considered bringing a crane in and ripping out the floor above you. Remove the roof perhaps. The problem is, what if the sheet field, not being constrained, fries everything, including you? As my father used to say, before you pull the trigger make sure the gun isn't aimed at your own head."

As the hours dragged on, Tacoma had spoken to Calibrisi and Katie, but when he was attempting to reach Igor at around midnight his earbud stopped functioning.

The temperature inside the governors' room had increased. At first he thought it was his mind playing tricks on him. But after a few hours, it was unmistakable.

It was getting hotter. He could feel it. He wasn't going crazy.

By 3 A.M., he was drenched in sweat. He estimated the temperature to be in the nineties.

Tacoma walked to the restroom. As he splashed his face, he stared in the mirror, then looked down at the drain. What if Igor and all those other brains were just making this more complicated than it was? The water had to come from somewhere and it had to drain somewhere.

Tacoma lifted the ceramic lid on the back of the toilet and hammered it against the wall. It barely made an indent. He kept pounding the heavy commode top against the wall, as hard as he could, slamming it over and over, breaking through a stainless steel surface until he was at concrete. He kept at it, his face and body dripping in perspiration.

After almost an hour, a chunk of concrete broke from the wall and fell, crackling as it was immolated by the sheet field just beyond.

He kept at it until he had exposed the area just behind the wall. It was a chasm, filled with white and blue light. He leaned closer. He smashed the lid through the opening, inching it through a hole in the wall. At some point, the end of the ceramic lid abruptly disappeared in tiny crackling flashes of orange and red, smoked by the sheet field.

Tacoma pulled the ceramic back out and smashed as furiously as he could, hammering into the concrete until the hole was big enough.

He climbed out through the opening in the wall, carefully, staying tight to the wall even as the white, blue, and orange sheet field hovered just inches away. He gripped a piece of steel at the bottom edge of the floor. He held on to the concrete and dangled, then stared down. He saw a wide pipe stemming out from the bathroom floor. He swung and leapt, grabbing the pipe. Tacoma shimmied down the pipe as the iodine sheet field hummed just inches away.

Tacoma knew that where the pipe met the energy field below would present either an opportunity—or else he would have to climb back up to the suite of rooms.

He descended quickly and in silence. He paused and looked up. The floor where the Fed was was basically a box, suspended on steel girders and cables, surrounded by the iodine sheet field. He came to the bottom of the field of energy. There was a break in the white field of light near the plumbing. But it was barely larger than the pipe itself—a circular hole in the sheet field through which the pipe could pass, and enough space around it to not melt the pipe itself. He inched closer. He estimated that there was about a foot of free space in a circumference around the pipe. If any part of him entered the light it would simply burn away in milliseconds and would either kill him or disfigure him forever.

He wrapped his arms and legs around the pipe and pressed his face as hard as he could against the steel. Slowly, and with his eyes shut, he inched below, allowing himself to slide bit by bit down the pipe. He could feel warmth as his feet entered the opening and then along his legs and torso. The electric hum grew louder and his closed eyes were suddenly hit by brightness, and he couldn't help himself. He opened his eyes and stared into the light. It was like a line, several inches wide, of pure white energy. He shut them again and kept moving down, until he knew he was below the sheet field, and even then he kept inching down until his feet hit an object. It was the top of a floor. He climbed onto a dusty slab of concrete, crossed by steel girders, and looked up at the box of white light.

He sat down and breathed in and out, staring up. He sat still for several minutes. Then he stood. He searched the unlit space and found the elevator shaft and the doors where the elevator had once let out. He pried it open and saw he was on an abandoned floor, covered in dust and empty. He found the fire stairs and descended to the lobby below.

120

OVAL OFFICE
THE WHITE HOUSE
WASHINGTON, D.C.
ONE WEEK LATER

John Schmidt stepped into the White House briefing room for the first time in a week. It was packed with reporters. While the White House had given daily statements as to the president's health, recovery efforts in New York, and responses to the new Iranian regime put in place following Ali Suleiman's death, Schmidt and the White House had yet to step out in front of a hungry corps of White House reporters from across the world.

The subject of reelection was almost an afterthought. The election was in sixteen days. Dellenbaugh was projected to win all fifty states in a landslide.

Schmidt had let his brown and gray hair grow out a bit and he had a rough-looking beard and mustache.

"Welcome back, John," said one reporter.

Schmidt nodded. "Thanks, Fred. How y'all doing?"

A low murmur of responses came from a few of the reporters, but most said nothing.

"It's good to see you all. I have nothing further to add to this morning's statement," said Schmidt. "So without further ado, can I take some questions?"

"How is the president?" said Carol Watkins from *The Wall Street Journal*.

"President Dellenbaugh is on the mend," said Schmidt. "He's doing fine. When he gets mad and tries to chase me around the West Wing, he can't catch me yet, but he's getting closer, if that's any indication."

The room erupted in laughter.

"When is he expected to name a nominee to be his vice president?" said Archie Perry, from AP.

"Good question," said Schmidt. He pointed at another reporter as people laughed again.

He pointed at a female reporter, Irina Kastenn from CNN.

"John, I'm sure you saw the report in the *Financial Times* yesterday detailing issues involving the Federal Reserve?" said Kastenn.

"Yes," said Schmidt.

"The report indicates that there have been widespread outages in terms of the Fed's interactions with various counterparties, including the U.S. government itself, but also the IMF and several large American banks," said Kastenn. "Has something happened in terms of the Fed's capabilities? Its technology? And was this in any way related to the attack on New York City?"

"The Fed continues to be the main supplier of liquidity not only in the U.S. but in the free world," said Schmidt. "Next?" he said, pointing at a reporter from the *New York Post*, Miranda Devine.

"I'd like to ask about Iran," said Devine in a distinct Australian accent.

Schmidt looked nonplussed and waited in silence for her to finish her question.

"Is the White House considering further military action against Iran?" she said.

"Nothing is off the table," said Schmidt.

"According to *Jane's*, America has three nuclear submarines in striking range of Iran," said Devine.

"Actually four," said Schmidt.

"Does this mean the U.S. is considering a nuclear strike?" said Devine.

Schmidt looked at a piece of paper on the podium.

"So far, five thousand, two hundred and eighty-nine Americans were killed in New York City by Hezbollah terrorists trained, sponsored, armed, and ordered to be sent by the mullahs who run Iran," said Schmidt. "In addition, there have been, to date, approximately forty-five thousand hospitalizations." Schmidt paused. "Nothing is on or off the table and it is the policy of this administration, and President J. P. Dellenbaugh, that we do not discuss specific possible military actions before those actions are taken. Thank you."

As reporters yelled more questions, shouting Schmidt's name, he stepped down off the podium and walked to his right, exiting through the door that led toward the Oval Office.

Schmidt stepped into the Oval Office, glancing about. The group inside was small. CIA Director Hector Calibrisi; National Security Advisor Josh Brubaker; Secretary of Defense Dale Arnold; Secretary of State Bailey Miller; Cory Tilley, the chief speechwriter; and the White House military aide, Dan Guerney, a U.S. Navy captain and former F/A-18 pilot.

No one was talking, nor was anyone looking at a cell phone, document, or anything else. It was a somber mood, created by the mere fact of Guerney's presence along with his sidekick, a slightly worn, large steel briefcase, a Zero Halliburton, chained to his wrist. It held the codes to America's nuclear weapons arsenal. This was the so-called "football."

The door to the Oval Office opened and President J. P. Dellenbaugh entered. He walked slowly, limping. Beneath his eye was a dark bandage. His other eye was blackish purple.

Everyone stood.

Dellenbaugh normally would have said something, a wry remark such as, "Hey, guys, what have you been up to?" but the president was in an altogether different place. He'd seen the edge of the abyss. He looked angry. His brown hair was combed neatly back, parted in the middle. Dellenbaugh looked battered and bruised, bloodied, yet somehow tougher and stronger because of it.

"Good morning, everyone," said the president. He sat down behind the desk. "Nice job, John, I watched it from upstairs."

"Thank you, sir," said Schmidt.

"Where's the statement, Cory?" said Dellenbaugh.

"Here, sir," said Tilley, standing and walking to Dellenbaugh. He handed him a sheet of paper.

Dellenbaugh read it aloud:

"A week ago, the Republic of Iran declared war on the United States, invading our shores, killing innocent people, destroying vital infrastructure, and spreading their own uniquely hateful brand of terror. Today, the United States of America has responded. A few minutes ago, I authorized the launch of three nuclear missiles on the Republic of Iran. The United States wishes war with no one. If we are attacked, however, we will respond in kind, and if we are attacked the way we were in New York, we will respond with unprecedented and overwhelming force."

Dellenbaugh finished, wincing a tiny bit at some spike of pain in his body, then ran his hand back through his hair, swallowing the pain as he looked at the American people, and the world's inhabitants.

"Excellent," said Dellenbaugh. "Let's call a press conference for an hour from now and I'll authorize the nuclear strike."

He looked around the room. Everyone was silent.

"Where's Adrian?" said Dellenbaugh, suddenly realizing that King wasn't present.

"He's in his office," said Calibrisi, standing up. "I'll get him."

Dellenbaugh, grimacing, stood up.

"No, Hector, I got it," said Dellenbaugh.

The president limped to a door that opened into a private hallway connecting the chief of staff's office to the Oval Office. When he arrived at King's door, he knocked.

"Yeah," said King.

Dellenbaugh opened the door. He stepped inside King's office and shut the door. He sat down on King's sofa. King was behind his desk. He nodded at Dellenbaugh and smiled.

"Hi, Mr. President," said King. "How you feeling?"

Dellenbaugh ignored him. Finally, after King said nothing, Dellenbaugh leaned forward.

"So I take it you don't think this is a good idea?" said Dellenbaugh.

King walked around from his desk and handed Dellenbaugh an envelope.

"What is it?" said Dellenbaugh.

"My resignation," said King. "If you're going to hit Iran with a nuclear strike, I can't stick around."

"Adrian, you're the biggest hawk in this entire administration," said Dellenbaugh in disbelief.

"Yeah, no shit, but dropping nukes is just a bad fucking idea, with all due respect, sir," said King.

"They killed five thousand innocent people!" shouted Dellenbaugh. "They killed children, parents, brothers, and sisters!"

"And if you go ahead with this, we'll kill at least a million innocent Iranians," said King. "*A million!* Those sick bastards in Hezbollah should be wired up by their nutsacks as far as I'm concerned, but you know as well as I do most Iranians had *nothing* to do with it. We can kill as many of the bad guys as you want, but I'm not in for turning Tehran into a glass parking lot. Harry Truman was stopping a war. This would start one. This is about revenge. You know it and I know it. I've got kids, you've got kids."

Dellenbaugh nodded, deep in thought. He reclined, wincing, and stared at the wall of bookshelves. Neither said a word for at least a minute.

"You're right," whispered Dellenbaugh. "This isn't who we are."

He reached out and took the envelope from King. He didn't open it.

"What was I thinking?" said Dellenbaugh.

"You were angry, just like I am," said King.

"Adrian, you've been my chief of staff for a long time now," said Dellenbaugh. "Normally, I wouldn't accept your resignation. But I'm going to."

King nodded.

"But only on one condition," said Dellenbaugh.

"And what is that, Mr. President?" said King.

"Will you serve as my next vice president of the United States of America?" said Dellenbaugh.

King looked shocked. Slowly, he reached his hand up and rubbed the bridge of his nose.

President Dellenbaugh stood up slowly. He extended his hand. King walked toward him and put his hand into Dellenbaugh's, and they shook hands.

"I'd be honored, sir," said King.

Epilogue

It was a remote island, that was for sure. A place of stunning beauty near Bora Bora, owned by a client of Katie Foxx and Rob Tacoma and their private security firm, RISCON. Katie had asked the client—a forty-one-year-old Silicon Valley billionaire—if she could borrow the island for a few months, with the understanding that he would tell no one.

It was a private island with a full staff and various luxury amenities.

After the events of 10/11, Calibrisi, Polk, Dellenbaugh, Katie, Tacoma, and Jenna all wanted to hide Dewey, even if he didn't care or seem to notice. That was the real reason they were on the island. For a few weeks or months on a remote island near Bora Bora, he would disappear.

Katie, Tacoma, Dewey—and Jenna—off the grid by design.

Hammocks on trees, surfboards, kayaks, chaise lounges, several swimming pools, a tennis court, a beach that circumscribed the entire island in dusty, soft white sand. The beach had overhanging palm trees, the water was a spectacular shade of light blue, and they spent hours sitting on the beach. At night, they enjoyed huge meals prepared by staff.

After two weeks on the island, Dewey was, as usual, lying out on a small wooden dock that was moored a few hundred feet from the shoreline. He'd brought, also as usual, a cooler stuffed with cold beer.

Jenna went for a slow barefoot run around the island with Katie. When they passed by where Dewey was, she slowed up.

"I'll meet you back," said Jenna.

Jenna dived and swam out to the dock. She climbed up onto the dock, dripping wet. Dewey was lying on his back. He wore a blue bathing suit with white stripes down the sides. A small bandage was still wrapped around his thigh. Next to his head by his left ear was a half-full bottle of beer.

Jenna walked to Dewey and stood over him, dripping water on him. After a few moments, he noticed. He turned his head and looked at Jenna, dark sunglasses still on. He smiled. He didn't get up or even raise his head.

Jenna took off her bikini top.

Dewey reached up and lowered his sunglasses slightly, looking at her over the top of the frames.

"I was wondering when you'd get here," said Dewey.

ACKNOWLEDGMENTS

Thank you to everyone who encouraged and assisted me during the writing of *The Island*.

Let me begin with my readers, both new and those who've been there from the beginning. I'm so fortunate to have you all out there behind me. Thank you for your support and friendship, as well as for your impeccable taste in literature. I know this was a tough year for everyone. I hope *The Island* meets your expectations and finds you curled up in a hammock somewhere or on a big beach towel.

To my agent and friend Nicole James at James Literary Agency, you're the best.

To everyone at St. Martin's Press and Macmillan Audio, whose patience and support are exceeded only by their charm and good looks. Thank you all, and particularly Sally Richardson, Jen Enderlin, Andy Martin, George Witte, Martin Quinn, Paul Hochman, Rafal Gibek, Christina MacDonald, Rob Grom, Alice Pfeifer, Hector DeJean, Robert Allen, Mary Beth Roche, Guy Oldfield, and Ari Fliakos. Most of all, thank you to Keith Kahla.

A note of appreciation to Adrian King, Tad Goltra, Jon Ziefert, Rorke Denver, Tolu Edun, Mark James, Chris George, and Emily Robertson. Your friendship has been especially critical this past year.

Finally, to Shannon, Charlie, Teddy, Oscar, and Esmé, I love you all. While I wouldn't necessarily want to go through what we went through this past year all over again, I have to admit that lockdown was a lot of fun with you guys. Kind of a cross between a slumber party and *Huis Clos* by Jean-Paul Sartre. We always found a way to laugh, to break bread together, to make the best of it. Here's to the future.